Hayner Public Library Di
W9-DGB-810
8

RECEIVED
JAN 12 2006
BY:
MAIN

BRONZE

Other books by Kit Reed

Novels:
Thinner Than Thou
@expectations
Captain Grownup
Fort Privilege
Catholic Girls
J. Eden
Little Sisters of the Apocalypse
Magic Time

Collections:
Dogs of Truth
Seven for the Apocalypse
Weird Women, Wired Women

Kit Reed

Night Shade Books
San Francisco & Portland

Jacket layout by Claudia Noble
Interior layout and design by Jeremy Lassen

First Edition

ISBN
1-597800-08-2 (Hardcover)
1-597800-09-0 (Limited Edition)

Night Shade Books
http://www.nightshadebooks.com

Stealth dedication
for d., purveyor
of the Jujyfruit cake

surprise
—Shelley Hyde

Before

I'm so ashamed. It's all he can think of as he flees the Wayward plantation; scrambling down the back road out of Wayward, Jimmy Daley may be scared—no, terrified—but before anything, he is ashamed.

Laid out by a Carolina gentleman in richer, far less fearsome times, the front road into the Benedict compound at Wayward is overgrown but orderly. A double avenue of trees lines the approach to the antebellum house with its formal gardens and outbuildings. Come in by the front way and Wayward is picture-perfect Old South, with banks of blossoming azaleas and oleanders, carefully placed pecan trees and liveoaks festooned with Spanish moss. The Benedict foundry is not visible from here, nor is the boathouse perched on the edge of the marsh. Certain portions of the compound are closed. You will come and go by the front gate and never guess the truth.

Like their best work, the nature of the Benedict heritage is carefully hidden. What meets the eye is beautifully maintained, precisely groomed. Everything is quiet, orderly, expected. Nice.

But there is another way out.

The few who know the back road are afraid to take it. The escape route is notoriously unsafe—twin grooves in slippery Carolina mud. It begins deep in the woods behind the Benedict house. Pebbled walks taper to nothing and artful planting gives way to weeds. Cutting through thick growth to the water's edge, the track gives onto an eroding causeway over the marsh. The causeway is so narrow and treacherous that any sane person would take the long way around to avoid it.

Old Beaufort Benedict made the last generation of slaves dredge him a causeway out of the muddy bottom of the Inland Waterway long before the War Between the States. They paved it with oyster shells so he could leave Wayward for the mainland unseen. It was built so long ago that if they knew, the town has forgotten. Whether that particular Benedict was hiding something criminal or trying to forge one more link in the underground railroad, nobody can say, but the ruined back road is treacherous. It's been abandoned for years.

Halfway to the mainland, a decaying wooden central span bridges the channel, and on the far bank the land is so bleak that it's hard to know why anybody would want to go there. The decaying causeway is overgrown in some places and in others it's disintegrated into mud with planks thrown across the shifting surface. There's no telling what's underneath. Once you are on the causeway, there's no getting off. On either side the salt marsh gives way to something that is neither land nor water, and in the channel under the center span whirlpools wait like hungry mouths.

At any moment the planks can shift and leave the traveler mired.

Once your car clears the Benedict property there is no turning, and if it breaks down there's noplace to go. The terrain is treacherous; in some parts of the marsh birds roost and insects burrow in the mud; in others the bottom is liquid, waiting to devour you. A man can drop out of sight here before he knows what has hold of him; he can drown before he has time to scream.

What things lie buried in the gluey bottom stay there forever: leached bones of slaves who died building the causeway, old enemies of the early Benedicts perhaps. Family treasures thrown into the swamp to preserve them from the invading Union soldiers. For centuries the marsh has claimed whatever it wants: here a flawed bronze angel with an arm sheared off, surrounded by imperfect submerged cupids—and there, just off the point on the mainland, marched into the sawgrass by an ignorant drill sergeant, the skeletons of an entire platoon of lost Marines. There may be others deep in the muddy marsh that borders the Inland Waterway: the bodies of Charlestonians long ago reported missing, corpses begging to be exhumed.

Waiting somewhere in the mud there is a beautiful woman with her mouth frozen open in a perpetual scream.

It isn't safe.

But here is Jimmy Daley, struggling through the mud and undergrowth to the causeway. It's his last hope. Clearing the woods, he throws himself onto the oyster shells. Hitching along on his elbows, he advances slowly, dragging the rest of his body behind. The ruined would-be sculptor with the beautiful blue eye can't hope to make it to the other side. Not the way he is. He can't even hope to outstrip his terror, but he has to try. Sobbing, Jimmy goes along on bloody hands and elbows, trailing shattered legs and broken feet.

At Parsons, where he was an art student bent on being a sculptor, handsome, tow-headed Jimmy was a happy guy, affable, a little shy. His careless grin told people he had plenty to say even though, like most artists, he couldn't necessarily find the words. Deep, right? People liked Jimmy on sight. How did he stray so far from home, and how did he get so...

I'm so ashamed.

The grin is long gone. It was scraped off his face in a series of gouges that took one of those nice blue eyes; his mother would be *so... Oh, Jimmy,* she would wail, *Jimmy Daley. What happened to you?* Only a mother would recognize him now. He is wrecked, body and soul. It's a wonder he can keep going. In fact, he's made it this far only because it serves somebody's purposes.

At the top of the cavernous house behind him something stirs: the figure in the window observes the little progress on the causeway. Waits.

What does Jimmy hope for, dragging himself along, inching through mud up to his elbows in some places and in others hauling over jagged shells that bite his raw hands? Does he really think he can make it across, or does he hope some rescuer will hear his sobs and scoop him up in a boat? Maybe he's pretending he can make it to the far highway where RVs and eighteen-wheelers go barreling north, and one of them will see him and...

He has to hope for something. If he can just make it to the highway, maybe he can haul himself up like a flag on a scrub pine, waving like a distress signal. Or else he'll hang there just like a real person, hitching a ride. *Oh hi. Going to town?*

One look and they'll know. They'll never guess why, but a blind fool will know at once that Jimmy Daley is afraid and, worse, that he is soiled and ashamed. So very ashamed.

Never mind. He has to go!

He fixes on the narrow track in front of him. One yard more, one yard more, how many yards will it take to get across? He doesn't know. All he knows is that he can't go on the way he is, he has to go. All he can hear is his own breath sawing in his throat. Behind him all of Wayward looms: land, trees, elegant house sprawling on a slight rise, doomed inhabitants caught in a dark globe of family obsession, terrible and huge.

Who they are, the Benedicts—no, *what* they are doing—explodes in Jimmy's consciousness. In a flash he comprehends Ava Benedict, his beautiful, cold mentor and her real intentions; Ava and her students, the work, the unknowable *other*—everything at Wayward driven by the same inexorable force.

Something darker than fear drives Jimmy Daley now.

In the house behind him, the abiding spirit waits. Does Jimmy know he's being watched? Is he really trying to escape or is he only trying to get Ava's attention? When he shakes his bloody fist at the house is that real defiance, or does he expect Ava to see and come after him? God help him, he couldn't help what he did, he loved her. He did. Damaged as he is, ruined forever by his time at Wayward and bent on escape, Jimmy Daley may want something else. Maybe he really does wish Ava would come. Unless he wants her people to overtake him and finish him.

Anything to keep him from feeling this way.

From being what he is.

I'm so ashamed.

What's Jimmy Daley running away from? What's he really hoping for? In the deep, grieving part of him, Jimmy needs to be caught and punished.

Not for what he's done. For what he has become.

Before he left Parsons for Wayward, Jimmy was different. Talented. Borderline charming. Happy. A nice, ordinary guy.

All that has burned away. The only thing left of him is shame.

After Ava demolished him, he crawled under the potting shed. He hid until he was strong enough to flee. No matter how far he goes, he'll never outrun the shame. Filth mats Jimmy's hair and filth clings and drips from all his orifices; even now he can't remember what he did or agreed to do or what he let happen to himself that was so wrong, exactly, or why or how he got the way he is, but in the lexicon of shame what Jimmy Daley does next is the ultimate verb.

The quality of the air has changed. He hears the rumble of a car in low, a cautious driver creeping along. For a second Jimmy mistakes the source. *Ava,* he thinks, gulping greedily; *she's coming for me.*

He turns back toward Wayward with the desperate, guttural roar that some men make at climax.

Behind him, the road is deserted. Jimmy fishtails in the mud, confused. This car is coming from the mainland. No! Some outsider who knows nothing of Wayward is heading his way. *They'll see me! How can they possibly understand?* He can forget the Benedicts. They aren't coming for him, even with one eye destroyed, Jimmy can see that the Benedicts don't care.

The car is almost on him. In another minute the driver will see him for what he is. What he has become.

Oh, my God.

The driver is a girl. One look at Jimmy and she'll retch and turn away. He is repulsive. Even if she let him into the car, even if he got away... How can he explain what he has become? How can he admit what he's been up to here at Wayward. How can he go on living in the filthy wreckage of his body? This ruined face?

How can he live with the shame?

Can't let her see me, he thinks, and this is the end of Jimmy Daley. Even if he gets out, he won't escape. He could spend the next hundred years trying to find his way home to who he used to be and never get that person back. He sobs. *Not the way I am.*

Something inside him breaks in two.

Tears stream from Jimmy's good eye and the blind one, stinging his torn flesh; *God, if only.* But there's nothing left of the looks or the intelligence or the talent, the grin that won him so many friends. He is no longer who he was.

As the car approaches Jimmy rolls into the sawgrass, dragging himself through the mud. He's been warned about the quicksand underlying the marsh, riptides in the channel. He welcomes it. Sobbing, he lunges for oblivion. Sawgrass whips his face but he drags himself along, toward the deep place where the swamp will swallow him... *She's coming, she'll see me, can't let her, I have to get away!*

Yes!

Raising his arms like a descending angel, the ruined artist loses himself in the muck with the silent grace of a swimmer on a hot day, slipping into a cool pond.

One

Something writhing across the road...

Squinting, Jude tried to make it out. At this distance it was no more than a grey blur in the road ahead, a shadow that disappeared when the car yawed and she blinked. —What?

It could be nothing.

It could be something.

It could be anything.

Person, water snake, she wasn't sure; out in the unfamiliar Carolina countryside like this, on a narrow causeway over marsh and wide water, you imagined things. It was strange territory, ragged and wild. The road seemed to sit on top of glittering green water. It was like being on a stage set in a floating opera. On the shore Jude's destination waited like the set for Act Two—an elaborate frame house sprawling under great, artificial-looking trees.

Careful, she told herself. *This is the South. A strange country. Anything could happen here*. Flying in last night was like coming into Oz. Landing in Charleston in the middle of the night, Jude Atkins and the other passengers had to come down a ladder and walk in to the terminal from the runway. After Boston on a crisp day in autumn, it was like walking into a warm bath. The light in the sky was different, the silhouetted trees were different, everybody *sounded* different. Jude's baggage, including all her funky jewelry samples, was adrift in the Washington-Baltimore Airport, where it failed to change planes with her. Her Charleston hotel had never heard of her and in the early dawn outside, a gat-toothed, grinning street kid in a tattersall vest handed her a spray of azaleas ripped off some bush and played the harmonica until she gave him money to stop.

On the way down here from Charleston she veered around a pack of dogs like carnival midgets boiling out of a blazing car—crazy, she told herself, edgy and shaken; maybe it was only a TV shoot. Just as she left the interstate she caught a flash—bears, or was it two enormously fat people dancing underneath the bearded trees. What if they weren't dancing?

Should I stop? Could I help?

She was going too fast to make it out. What could she have done to help anyway? Would they thank her, Oh thank God you've come, or would they separate and pound her to bits? It was all too new for her to know. The deep South went by too fast and in the context of the unnervingly usual—superhighway, generic exit signs, flashy markers on stilts broadcasting nearby malls—what you thought you saw didn't necessarily make sense.

So maybe she really did see something strange hitching across the narrow causeway like an enormous rodent or a leper fleeing so she wouldn't have to see his face.

Judith, stop!

So OK, she'd been awake for two days straight. That kind of thing makes people weird. Jude woke up in Boston before dawn yesterday, she'd been running hard on no sleep. She packed, finished up at work, got to the airport three hours ahead of flight time. By the time she finally found a hotel room in Charleston it was five a.m. and she was too wired to sleep. She ended up drinking too much coffee in the hotel dining room, after which she set out on her fool's errands in a rented car. What was she doing driving into Wayward anyway? What was she doing in South Carolina three days before Peter expected her anyway?

He promised to meet her at the airport in Charleston on Friday after work. He wanted to take her to his apartment to see his paintings. Then they were going out to this wonderful restaurant on the Battery. But Jude couldn't help herself. She'd given in to this subversive impulse to catch Peter Benedict in his native habitat. She had to see him before he saw her coming. As though then she'd know what he was really like. Crazy, but she had to see what Peter was like when he didn't know he was being watched. A woman who's crazy enough to fall in love with a guy she met online needs to compensate by doing something sane. She had to find out who was behind the emails and the letters, the voice she fell in love with over dozens of late-night phone conversations.

There was that one rushed meeting in Boston; he was there between planes and he came out through Security to meet her in a Starbucks: public place, coffee, plenty of people around in case he turned out to be weird, but there was nothing weird about Peter Benedict. Tall. Sandy hair. Sweet looking, she thought. As he headed back through security she heard herself saying, "If only you could stay!"

"I can't." He took her hands; the line moved forward. As her fingers slipped out of his he said, "If only you could come!"

Now here she was. Not spying, exactly. Jude let herself fall in love too fast last time, and Phil hurt her badly on his way out. This time she wanted to be sure.

So she drank too much coffee in the sunny dining room of her Charleston hotel this morning, and went to the Front Street address just before nine. She wanted to catch Peter coming out on his way to work. She needed to see him before he saw her. Follow long enough to catch him in an unguarded moment. Study him and decide. Was he really as nice as he seemed in their rushed ten minutes or was it an act he used with all the girls he met? What was he like when he wasn't trying to impress? If anything went wrong—and Jude had no idea what she meant by *anything*—she could write this off as a bad deal and walk away. He'd never know. By the time he came to the airport on Friday night for their long-awaited, carefully scheduled meeting, she'd be gone. All those emails and all those letters—all those phone calls and one brief meeting. *I'm in love. Am I in love?* Jude thought so, but she was afraid.

When you've been hurt as badly as Jude Atkins, you go forward, but you go forward with great care.

As expected, she found Peter's name on the mailbox next to the right number on the street where she'd sent him so many letters. It was the last thing that unfolded as expected that day.

First, the place wasn't at all what Peter led her to expect. The snapshot he sent put him in front of a pair of gracious-looking long windows on the porch of a beautiful house. His mailbox was bolted to the frame of a narrow, mean-looking door in a wall that showed nothing to the street. If the inside looked like the outside, Peter Benedict lived in a dump. What's more, even though Jude waited until midmorning, he showed no signs of coming out. Exhausted, anxious and impatient, she got out of the car and went up to the door. It opened as she was deciding whether to knock.

"Can I help you?"

Caught. "Ah. I. Not really, I think."

In the flowered dress and the straw hat, the old lady looked like a fugitive from *Gone With the Wind*. "May I ask who you're here to see?"

"I was just going." Jude blushed. *Why am I falling all over my feet?*

She fixed Jude with a military glare. "Why, whoever you are, I've been watching your car. There must be some reason you are parked outside my gate."

"I'm—ah, a friend of Peter Benedict's? From up north?"

"Oh you poor thing. Come in!"

In the South, Jude had read somewhere, appearances are deceptive. At the old lady's back wild roses tumbled around wooden columns and twined around the railings of the double row of porches that ran across the front of the magnificent old house. Forget the run-down external wall, it was a little like Tara here inside the gate. For whatever reasons, the old lady could not stop blinking.

Jude said, "He does live here, right?"

"He does and he doesn't," the old lady said.

"Um, is this the right place?"

"It is and it isn't," she said. "Oh, don't fret! Off course he lives here but at the moment, I'm sorry, he's gone."

"Oh, no!" Jude sagged.

"Honey, it isn't the end of the world. I know he'll be sorry he missed you but he was—called home unexpectedly? His mama, well, something came up and I'm afraid there's no telling when he's comin' back."

Exhausted, Jude heard herself losing it. "But I came all this way!"

"You poor thing, all this way and our Peter isn't even here." The old lady patted her arm. "He's gone down to see to the family, at Wayward? Family is so important to Southerners, and Peter's family, well, you must know all about his family, everybody does."

"I'm sorry, I don't..."

"Sure you know, everybody knows about the..." The old lady broke off, patting her flowered front. "When Peter goes, there's no telling when he'll be back, oh, but you're the little girl I've heard so much about, oh dear, are you all right? I'm Violet Poulnot, Peter's landlady, do let me give you some iced tea."

"No thank you, I have to..." She didn't know what she had to do.

"Come on, you look like you could use a little perking up..."

At Violet's back there was a gracious courtyard and above it long porches sprawled, *this is more like it*; the house was set at right angles to the street so the only thing outsiders would see was a blank wall and that mean-looking gate—deceptive, Jude thought, like everything else down here. One more reason to study Peter from a distance. See how he acted in his native habitat. "You don't know a man until you know his family," Violet said.

"Oh yes, family really is important," she echoed, looking at Violet over the sprig of mint in her glass.

"In these circles, family is everything."

"Well I'd love to meet Peter's," Jude said.

"They aren't real social."

"Since Peter and I..." She flashed the ring Peter had sent her with the plane ticket—an aquamarine set in silver filigree. "If I just knew where they lived..."

"Why, I don't know if the Benedicts... It isn't that easy. More tea?"

"After all, we are engaged."

"Oooooh, that's wonderful!" Violet closed knobby fingers on Jude's hand. "You know, he was so miserable after..."

"Ma'am?" *What? After what?*

"To tell you the truth, I was worried about the boy, but now..." The old lady beamed. "Now you're here."

"And he's gone!"

"Oh, honey, don't look so sad, Wayward isn't the end of the world, you know. It's only a little bit south of Beaufort, why if you wanted to go down there, it would only take you half a day..."

"I don't suppose you have a map?"

Violet's parting words taunted her now. "Why, everybody knows where Wayward is."

Why didn't I insist? As it was Jude said politely, "If I had a map..."

"Wayward, oh, Wayward isn't on any map. But don't worry, the Benedicts are famous. Let me call Peter and tell him you're on your way."

"No, please. I want it to be a surprise."

"Isn't that sweet. Honey, if you lose track along the way, all you have to do is ask. Everybody knows."

Indeed.

The minute Jude left the interstate, she made a series of wrong turns. In spite of all her stops for directions at trashy gas stations and country stores, every road dwindled from cement to asphalt to oystershell to sandy twin tracks. ("Ma'am, didn't you see the sign?" "What sign?") The last set of directions led her into a *cul de sac* she thought marked terminal lostness until she ran into a hick kid working on a jacked-up Corvette in a roadside clearing and stopped to ask one more time.

He had a Mr. Goodwrench T-shirt and silvered jeans that matched the eyes he turned on her; they were like windows in his head, so clear you could see right through to the Carolina sky. "Wayward?"

"Wayward."

"Everybody knows how to get to Wayward," he said.

"Except me. I'm, ah. From out of state?"

"Up north, you mean." The grin made it clear that nobody else would be stupid enough to take the back road to Wayward, only an outsider would end up here.

"So. If you could just tell me..."

"Ma'am, it's right over there." He waved at a spot where the trees thinned out. "Across the water, over there on the point?"

She shook her head in frustration. "You mean I need a boat."

"Not really."

"Then what?"

The kid said reluctantly, "There is a kind of road. But I wouldn't be using it if I were you because it idn't safe."

"You mean it's impassable, or what?"

"No Ma'am."

She tried not to sound irritated. "Then what's the big problem?"

"I just wouldn't be going in on the Benedicts by the back way, you know?" He studied Jude, the subcompact rental car; maybe he saw her head rattling with exhaustion and her whitening fingers clamped on the steering wheel because he relented. "Look, Ma'am, you don't need to take the causeway. You can make it to Wayward easy on the state road. It's a straight shot from town."

"Town?"

"Yes Ma'am," he said helpfully. "Just go back the way you came and you'll hit town in a couple of hours. An hour more and you're at the Wayward front gate."

"Hours!"

"You might could get there by boat if you could rent one, but." He gestured toward the spot where the trees thinned out; twin ruts led to the water. "Nobody uses the causeway, Ma'am."

"But it's so close!"

"Look, the front gate idn't that far. It's only three hours. If you start now." After a pause, he said, "Besides."

"Oh, *please*."

"The Benedicts have a nice guy that takes your name and unlocks the gate for you."

"Unlocks!"

"You know how they are about tourists," he said ominously. "They're expecting you, right?"

"Not exactly."

"Then lady, you don't want to go."

She'd seen this in movies: visions of angry rustics running out of the house with shotguns and hounds to chase intruders over the dismal swamps. Jude said carefully, "Is there something going on that I ought to know about?"

"What?" The kid took her meaning. Too quickly he said, "Oh no, no ma'am."

"I mean, ah. You know." This was awkward but Jude tagged it and filed it under *preliminary investigation,* which meant she was able to ask flat out: "About the Benedicts? That people aren't supposed to know?"

He didn't exactly answer. "I think they want tourists to be satisfied with the museum in town."

"Museum!"

"All them statues, you know."

"I'm sorry, I don't. I just came looking for my friend."

"You're *friends* with them?" His expression slid from: *uh-oh* to *oh wow* to: *amazing;* it couldn't settle.

"Yes. No." This was embarrassing. "Well, sort of."

He stepped back. "Well if you know them, and all..."

"I know Peter," she said. This both was and wasn't true.

"Then I guess it's OK. Look, that track puts you on the causeway, or what's left of it. That out there is Wayward, way out at the other end?"

Jude was afraid the last thing the kid said to her came straight out of some movie; as the Carolina kid watched her drive through the trees and onto the causeway, she thought she heard him calling after her with an it's-your-funeral wave: "But I wouldn't be going there if I was you."

She didn't know how hard it was going to be.

So, fine, she told herself, *you're seeing things. It's only hysteria or fatigue or both. Unless.* Squinting, she stared at the road, trying to see what had crossed her path and where it had gone. Whatever it was, it had disappeared. This was not going well. Her car was locked into twin ruts like a plastic toy in a roadracing set. If the road crumbled or gave way, then rental car and all, Jude Atkins could drop out of sight. Like that.

So it was her fault, she supposed, for charging in here on her own. But Jude ran her life in a series of checks and balances, and in the cold light of reason, the foolhardy, loving, needy Judith who had logged onto an Internet dating service in a crazy attempt to get over Phil, the injured Jude who had found Peter and fallen in love with him sight unseen, was superseded by bright, tough Jude Atkins, who'd been hurt once, and vowed never again. She would do anything to keep from getting hurt again.

She'd even sneak into Wayward by the back way and catch Peter where he lived. Then she could make up her mind about him. She might even do it without his knowing, and if that was spying? Fine. She would be gone before he even knew.

Jude told herself this side trip to the Carolinas was only a pretext for walking out of her old life. She couldn't keep running around Boston hoping Phil would change his mind and take her back. With or without Peter, she had to forget Phil and move on. If this with Peter didn't work out she had plans to keep going South to Savannah or Jacksonville, where there were plenty of boutiques that could use jewelry like hers. She'd sold out her half of the business to her partner and walked away with enough money to buy in someplace new. Forget two-timing Phil Forrest, and if he didn't measure up, forget Peter Benedict. With or without him, Jude was going to start a brand new life in the heart of the American South.

She had to do something to get past handsome, unfaithful Phil Forrest, whom she'd loved almost half her life.

Phil was her last mistake. He had to be. Brooding, she drove on without seeing. If there was anything unusual struggling across the road ahead, disappearing into the water, Jude wouldn't know. If there was an agonized cry, she would not hear. By the time she passed the spot, Jimmy Daley had disappeared into the water without leaving so much as a ring of ripples or a trace of froth to mark the place.

Then something caught her eye. Unnatural. Out of place here. Shapes protruded from the water like... What? With a start, Jude recognized them before she even knew how she knew.

Lord, those could be...

She saw a series of jagged edges sticking up out of the water, delicate shapes like the spires of a submerged city just clearing the surface in a formation that suggested something huge and unexpected below.

Those look like...

The little convoy of shapes emerged further as Jude came closer and the tide dropped, tips of whatever lay mired in the swampy waters just off Wayward. At first she thought it was a cluster of mangrove stumps jutting, but slimy and overgrown as they were, they looked like something else. She was almost close enough to see.

Oh lord, they are!

Statues. Bronzes, shrouded in slime.

It was creepy at first, frightening and glorious to know what these things were, sticking out of the water like broken branches: here a hand rising in the sweep of a graceful arm, there a wingtip, there a horse's hoof, and although the water was murky and the objects buried in mud, she could imagine the rest, flawed goddesses, broken angels, all mired so deep that no collector would ever be able to find the right equipment to dig them out. "Good lord." Why hadn't she known? She felt head-bashingly stupid. The public monuments. The dazzling bas reliefs. The family of sculptors. The fame. Everybody knows the Benedicts. I'm sorry, I don't. "Oh. Oh! *Those* Benedicts."

This must be where they bury their mistakes.

Two

Private: Keep Out.

Jude was in bad enough shape, sleep deprived and disrupted by what she had just seen—the garden of drowned sculpture, the *thing* plunging into the marsh. The sign stopped her cold. Here she was, looking less than fresh in the gold earrings and embroidered shirt she had put on this morning for—OK, for Peter, in hopes they'd be together.

Now this stands between them. The buildings of the world-famous studio at Wayward, looking exactly the way they did in all the art history books.

Peter Benedict told her he was from South Carolina. Why couldn't she add two and two?

Oh. Those Benedicts.

The man she thought she was in love with—just a painter, Peter said, you know, an ordinary guy—wasn't ordinary after all. He came from all this. No wonder he wanted to meet her at the airport. No wonder he said he was from Charleston, was he afraid she loved him for his money? For whatever reasons, he didn't want her to know. By that time Jude was so nearly in love with Peter Benedict that she forgot to ask questions.

Now the submerged shapes—broken hands, flawed profiles and the cracked wings of lost angels—reproached her. *Don't you know how famous our makers are?* In the shallows the Benedicts' cast-off bronzes reached out like living people, lifting their arms like the damned, begging to be rescued. Shimmering under water, the rejected sculptures gestured as if in warning—or regret, whether for her sake or their own she could not say.

Not good enough for the Benedicts.

Wait a minute. Doubt rolled into her like a cannonball. *Am I?*

Jude was barraged by images—stills from books she'd looked at as a child. The Benedicts. She should have known! Most Americans may not be able to name the makers but everybody recognizes the nymphs and angels wrought by generations of Benedicts, their brave Civil War heroes on stupendous horses, their ferocious, God-struck monumental bronzes, and on public buildings, bodies fluid as pure thought chasing themselves along a bas relief. Every schoolchild knows the name. Americans see their work in parks and in museums. Titans live here. The Benedict name has become legend, and now?

Peter.

Jude was startled by a thudding in her ears: the sound of her own blood. In all those letters and phone calls about life and love and Charleston, Peter never told her who he really was: rather, what he belonged to, and now look.

Private: Keep Out.

The woods between here and the big house were forbidding. So was the barbed wire embedded in the muddy bank. This was the Benedict compound. Secret. Closed. Remote. Everything about their arrangements shouted, *Keep Out.*

Would she wreck things with Peter by blundering in?

Too late to turn back. When she put the car in reverse and touched the gas experimentally the wheels spun and sizzled. Her cheap rental was stuck in the mud.

Groaning, she got out. Mud slimed her ankles and oozed into her shoes. Could she wash off the mud and pretend she'd come in by the front gate? She didn't know. She had to try. She stepped off the causeway onto the point, following what remained of the road. She should have been afraid but this was too weird to be real. The woods emptied her onto the grounds behind the great house.

It looked deserted. There was nobody moving on the grounds that she could see, nobody going in and out of the various outbuildings; there were no boats moored off the point and no cars or trucks parked under the trees or in the driveway. Where was everybody?

She might have been poised on the gangplank of a ghost ship.

Yet everything spoke of the Benedicts. It was amazing: flawless, carefully tended grass; banks of azaleas, oleanders, dense beds of flowers she could not name. Ancient trees overshadowed the antebellum house, drawing her eyes along and up, through veils of Spanish moss to the rooftree; the place was so big that she found it hard to make out the design. It crouched like an enormous animal with a hundred eyes and a thousand moving parts. At the top there was a little cupola with a widow's walk. Just below the third floor the roof extended to cover a second-floor veranda—a long gallery, the kind of place a prosperous family would gather on summer nights in the old days, to look out at sunset over the water and dream.

Did the Benedicts have Security? For all she knew they did. For all she knew, Security had orders to fire on intruders.

She was too excited to care. Through the woods she thought she saw... A double stairway led out of French doors on the first floor, curving down to ground level, and the curve took her eyes down and out to the woods beyond the house, where something extraordinary loomed.

Through moss-shrouded trees and snaking undergrowth she caught sunlight glinting off gold: a massive shape obscured by a high oleander hedge.

What. *What?*

Excitement dried her mouth out and made her hands jitter at her sides.

What she thought she saw. That she remembered without knowing what it was or why.

Whatever it was, it was huge.

Jude did not so much see as *know* the shape. She knew it by heart. Every school kid knew the outlines of this monument although until today, nobody but the Benedicts knew where it was. Looming, veiled by oleanders but terrifyingly familiar, their greatest work waited for her.

The Benedicts' missing masterpiece.

She was trespassing. There might be guards. She needed to go. She couldn't go until she saw. She had to be sure!

Jude's favorite picture from childhood was of Beauchamp Benedict's famous *God and His Creation*. Its disappearance was a great mystery, right up there with the unsolved mystery of the *Marie Celeste.* How did this monumental bronze designed for the grounds of the National Cathedral go missing just as the Benedict family locked the gates at Wayward and withdrew from the world?

Nobody knew.

One day it was on a flatcar, outside Washington. The next morning it was gone.

The Benedicts cut themselves off from society the day the news got out. No police, no interviews, please. No visitors. No reporters and no more art historians.

You will state your business by mail.

From then on the sculptors worked alone. Benedicts might go out into the world to get their educations but they returned to secluded Wayward to do their work. The bronzes went out on flatcars, but nobody came in. Although scholars speculated and journalists pried, nobody knew why. An early tragedy turned them away from the world, some people said. Others believed they'd locked themselves away because they were afraid of kidnapping or extortion, and others said they were afraid of terrorists. Or of having their work cheapened, or commercialized. Unless the reclusive Benedicts were hiding something: the secret to their success. The work was brilliant. The process was a mystery. An early Benedict had strangled a would-be journalist who popped up in his studio with a camera, and honoring his passion for privacy, the local coroner declared an accidental death.

Before he died in the late nineteenth century, old Beauchamp Benedict issued a caution: *Let this be read into the history books. The work stands alone. We are invisible.*

Assistants traveled with the Benedict bronzes and oversaw the installations. Sitters for the portrait busts were photographed and videotaped and then cast in plaster by apprentices in spite of which the images the Benedicts sent back were brilliant, real enough to speak, so passionately wrought that it was as if they were living things. Benedicts grew up in the family compound and after they finished school they returned to the studios and stayed. This was their sacred charge. They disappeared into their lifework so completely that no Benedict bronze was signed with a first name, only the hammered artists' chop. Twin Bs back to back identified the maker: another Benedict. Variant styles indicated which work was old Beauchamp Benedict's because he was after all the first, and which was done by his son Bernard and which by his daughter Benta, but when it came down to Barton's generation or Benton's, there was no saying which of the bronzes might have been done by his brothers and which by his sons. If you wanted to thank a Benedict for a piece of work or praise or even make payment there was a law firm in New York that took care of all communications.

And she had blundered in after Peter, who had made such a big thing of being an ordinary guy.

The online description that attracted Jude to Peter in the first place read: *Let's say goodbye to the past.* After Phil Forrest broke her heart, she was more than ready to forget. *Cut loose with me*, Peter wrote on the web for all to see. *Love free form in art, plenty of color in vivid splashes, love life and freedom, love to travel.*

Great writing, great looking picture, you bet.

In the chat room where they first met to talk online Peter flirted like a kid. They hung online for hours every night. He wrote joyful emails and sweet, goofy letters with beautiful drawings dropped into the text like gifts. On the phone he was immediate and delightful, and in their rushed encounter at the airport coffee shop he was so happy and excited that they both laughed. The Peter Benedict Jude knew was an artist without a care. He was all that and she loved him and behind the laughter, there was this. Her wonderful, unconventional guy bore the weight and responsibility of the Benedict legacy. He carried it like a stone that he couldn't use and couldn't put down because it was his sacred charge.

The Benedict legacy.

This gave her the dry swallows. What if he was in there right now, doing important, secret family things?

Back out, Jude. Leave. If you can't get your car out of the mud, walk away. Hitchhike back to Charleston. When Peter comes to meet you on Friday, pretend you don't know.

If she left now she could take a cab to the Charleston airport Friday; she could dance into the terminal as if she'd just gotten off the plane. When Peter finally told her who he really was—if he told her—she'd act surprised. If she left now, Peter would never know she knew.

But she was *this close* to *God and His Creation*. She had to see!

She'd had fair warning: that sign, the ruined sculptures, buried deep. *Maybe that's what they do to people too.* Jude felt like a vandal skipping into the Louvre after hours; she was excited and guilty, giddy as a naked stripper in church.

In fact it was a little *like* church: the hush surrounding the old house with its trees shrouded in Spanish moss. The gravel walks leading around and away from the house were laid out like paths in a convent garden, marked by mossy plinths with what looked like bronze busts of the great and the near-great stationed at each turning, heroes and geniuses given perpetual life by generations of Benedicts and forgotten here, hidden but strongly present.

And there was this massive shape, or manifestation, rising behind the oleander hedge.

How could she leave without seeing it?

At Jude's back all the windows seemed to bulge a little in the slanting light of late afternoon, as if the house was letting out a tremendous groan.

Somewhere deep inside the building, something stirred.

Somebody cried, *Oh, please don't!*

Jude didn't hear. She was drawn to the tremendous bronze behind the hedge. Looking around for dogs, watchmen, any threat, she edged along in the shelter of the azaleas. One bad sign and she could run for the woods. If she could—just—see it from here! But the hedge did its work. The object behind it was nothing more than an outline. Jude kept to the shadows for as long as she could, but to proceed, she had to show herself.

Only half aware of what she was doing, she approached. She was still too far from the house to hear the rattle of quick footsteps on the second-floor veranda, or the thud as somebody larger and slower crossed the porch in pursuit; entranced, she didn't hear the rumble of voices in the ground-floor room under the double staircase, a discussion or dispute that went on and on.

Leaving the cover of the bushes, Jude took a deep breath and launched herself, crossing walks and tiptoeing through beds in the cut flower garden until she reached the protective hedge. She pressed herself into the bushes, trying to see through.

The thing seemed to grow out of the earth. When she saw it, Jude lost track of who she was and where she was and what she'd thought she might be afraid of. For the moment there was just Judith Atkins, who had come too far to turn back, and the object she'd risked discovery to see, foolish Jude Atkins overwhelmed, mesmerized by Beauchamp Benedict's legendary masterpiece.

God and His Creation. Here.

It was more powerful than she'd dreamed.

As a small child Jude loved the image in Daddy's picture book; she thumbed the book to death because she loved happening on it all over again, a panoramic photograph of Beauchamp Benedict's famous missing bronze, *God and His Creation*. It was the first strong memory of her conscious life.

Even diffused by the fretwork of leaves and blossoms, it was arresting.

She had to see it clear.

As she looked for an opening in the hedge something inside the great house sighed. In one of the outbuildings a phone began to ring. Drawn by the monument, Jude hunched her shoulders and, flinching at the noise, crunched through the hedge.

Emerging, she held her breath, looking to the right, the left, everywhere but at the tremendous form that dominated the space. There was nobody in sight. The phone had stopped ringing. The place was as silent as the tomb after the Mummy has departed, or the cabin of the abandoned *Marie Celeste.*

When she was sure she was alone, Jude stood back and looked up.

It was everything she wanted it to be.

Massed bronze figures strained, no, flowed upward from the granite base, following the brilliant nymph with wings on her heels straining at the vanguard, flanked by two archangels surrounded by women and men as glorious as angels, followed by angels without equal with massed cherubs coming along behind, all their bodies twined, wings and shoulders and straining arms and legs, until there was no separating any from any other, or each from each, rushing forms caught in motion as if enchanted in midflight, all urgency and strength and grace, the lot of them surging along flanked by coursing dolphins and lions, leaving a wake of beautifully wrought bronze foam.

Everything at the base rushed forward but it also moved upward, taking the eye to the figures of the four evangelists being borne along as they in turn raised the cornucopia from which the figure of God emerged far above the striving bodies, forever close but just beyond their grasp. The figure was huge, gorgeous and ferocious, with blazing eyes and jaws glaring wide enough to devour the earth: Beauchamp Benedict's famous figure of God the Creator, with all creation around Him, swarming up...

Jude thought, *But I thought it was at the...* No. That was part of the wonder and the mystery. The National Cathedral, near the dawn of the twentieth century, a Gothic monument to worship rising on St. Alban's Hill in Washington, with the Benedict masterpiece on a flatcar outside of Union Station, destined for the entrance to the cathedral grounds. Thousands flocked to see it before... One night it disappeared. *God and His Creation* gone, as if it had never been wrought.

Now it was here.

But why, and how?

"It's OK now." She was startled by the sound of her own voice. "OK. Right, Jude, you've seen it. Now you can go."

As it turned out, she could not. Sometime in the suspended moment she had spent circling *God and His Creation,* a craggy, bearded figure in overalls had lurched out of one of the outbuildings, crossing the grounds and entering the enclosure through a gate in the hedge.

He was at her elbow before she knew. "Ma'am."

"What!" She did not scream.

"You can't be here, Ma'am." Distressed, the ungainly workman swayed like a tall building in a wind.

For one crazy moment Jude thought he was going to fall on her. Part of her went scrambling for a solution, what did mad scientist's assistants look like in all those monster movies. What did the monster look like? He loomed with a concentrated look. What did you say to a, what was he, watchman, monster, what... But before Jude could form a complete thought the gardener or guard if that's what he was took her by the shoulders and turned her around and without explanation, started her on a forced march.

"Let go!"

"You have to leave now." Rounding the hedge, he turned her at a sharp right angle and began propelling her along the diagonal path toward the woods. "Thorne got your car out of the mud."

"Who?"

"You don't need to know. It's out front."

"He couldn't, it was too..."

"In the driveway. Now, march."

When she tried to jerk free he tightened his grip. Dirty hands, she noted. Gardener? "Stop that. Ow!"

"I'm sorry, Ma'am, you don't belong here." It was not a monster's voice.

She tried, *"Let go and I'll leave."*

He pushed her along. "No you won't."

"I, ah, know the people here?"

It was as if she hadn't spoken.

"Really. I was invited." There was no pretending she'd never seen Wayward now. "I'm a friend of Peter's. Peter Benedict's?" Even though Jude dug in her heels to slow their progress the gardener or whatever he was moved her along doggedly. Nothing she said or did slowed him down.

"There," he said, opening the car door and propelling her around it so he could line her up with the driver's seat. He turned her so they were facing and pushed her down.

All her breath came out at once.

"I'm sorry, Ma'am. But there. OK?" His hands were nicked and grey and there were black rings under the fingernails; she noted hysterically that he'd lost most of the little finger on his right hand. Released, she saw two things: first, that this was no movie monster, but a perfectly ordinary-looking young guy with a young guy's expression, not menacing, only intent on his job today, which appeared to be new to him. The hands didn't get like that from farm work or digging shallow graves; that was sculptor's clay under the nails and smeared on the front of his overalls, the nicks were from accidents with the tools and except for the maimed finger, they were like the hands of a dozen people she had known at school.

"You're a sculptor!"

Found out, he flushed. "Not right now."

"Oh look, I went to RISD, I..."

Fixed on some imperative she had no way of recognizing, he was too distracted to respond. "Right now, I have to do this?"

She squinted into his face. "Are you a..." Benedict? Assistant? Security? What?

He didn't let her finish. Instead he slammed the car door on her. "Right now I'm in charge of getting you out of here."

He couldn't know that Jude was stalling, spinning this out because at his back she saw somebody emerging from the woods, a lanky man who closed the distance between them with familiar grace. "Peter, thank heaven!"

His face was going through so many changes that there was no telling what he was thinking. "Jude!"

"You're just in time!" Was he glad to see her? She wasn't sure.

"What are you doing here?"

"Oh, Peter, I..." Everything in her rushed out and in the next second she was ashamed. Caught. In the act. And here, where she had no business being. She didn't know what to do with her face, or with the would-be bouncer in the baggy overalls, who was still trying to fold her back into the car. Dizzied by the possibilities, she rushed on as if she and Peter had run into each other at a party, saying brightly, "What are you doing here?"

Peter looked not so much angry as upset. "Jude, how did you..."

She wanted to burble on, pretending they'd accidentally run into each other here at Wayward, but this was no accidental meeting. His expression made clear that she was in the wrong place at the wrong time. "Oh Peter I'm so sorry," she wailed.

"I'm on top of this, Mr. Benedict." The young man in the overalls seized her elbow in an attempt to do his job. His fingers dug into her arm so sharply that she yipped.

Peter snapped, "Don't!"

"But Mr. Benedict."

"Jude, how could you."

To her complete surprise, she blurted, "Oh Peter, it was a mistake!"

"Sorry about this, Mr. Benedict. Another minute and she's out of here."

"It's OK, Jake. I'll take care of this."

"No, really, Mr. Benedict." Jake was still trying to jam her into the car. "Color her gone."

And if Jude had been in any doubt about Peter's place in the dynasty, he settled several questions at once. A little silence fell in which Peter Benedict, whom she barely knew but, at some deeply personal level, *knew,* turned into somebody else. His face hardened in a glare of command; he seemed to get not so much taller as *bigger,* as finely wrought as any figure sculpted by the Benedicts: driven by dynasty, surrounded and enforced by the generations that had gone before. He could have been a landowner dismissing a servant. Or an angry God. "I *said,* let her go."

As Jake backed off, Peter turned to Jude and his face softened in the grin she knew. "Pay no attention to that man behind the mirror." In an instant he changed back into her Peter, the one she'd talked to through long nights and written to over all these months, and loved on sight.

Jake slouched away with his hands in his pockets and every line in his body slanted in reproach.

When Jude was sure he was gone, she spoke. "What *was* that?"

"Sorry," Peter said. "The mother's students have to..."

"Students!"

"...protect the family," he finished uncomfortably. "There's a lot of pressure here."

He looked so miserable that she rushed into an apology. "I'm so sorry, Peter, this is my fault, for barging in. Really. I'll just go."

"I thought you were flying into Charleston," he said unhappily. "I was going to meet you at the airport and show you the town. Dinner, nice places, whatever... You know. We were going to get to know each other before..."

"Before you broke the news?"

He bit his lip like an embarrassed little boy. "Pretty much."

"Don't worry. It's fine." *If I love you, I love you regardless,* she thought but did not say. "If we're going to..." She could not say what she really wanted to say; *If we're going to be together...*" Instead she started over. "I just wanted to..." She knew better than to say *observe you in your native habitat.* She thought a minute. "Meet you at home."

He said bitterly, "This isn't home."

"But you..."

He grimaced.

"Peter, this is your *family.*"

"In a lot of ways, no." For whatever reasons Peter kept shifting his eyes from Jude's face to the woods to the ridgepole of the house, alert to what might be approaching or who might be close enough to overhear.

"Is something the matter?"

"Not exactly."

"Like, are we being watched?"

His expression wouldn't stay put. "Look, this is kind of a complicated time for us."

"You and me?"

"The Benedicts." Then unexpectedly his whole body stiffened and he stood with his head lifted, as if listening to a sound she could not hear. He turned, studying the house. Without explanation, he turned and bundled her into her car. "I think it would be a good idea for us to get you away from here."

Before she could protest, Peter Benedict accomplished what poor Jake had not been able to manage in three passes. He had her behind the wheel. "It's OK," he said, "I just want the two of us to start over where I can do it right, OK? This is a bad place for us right now." He was half ordering, half begging. Meet me in Charleston."

"But how..."

"Please," he said urgently. "You have to hurry. Look, Jude, just do this. For me, OK?"

He didn't leave her room to refuse.

"I'll be along before you know it." He leaned in the window. "I'll be back in Charleston in time for dinner, OK?"

She slipped the car into gear. "I wish you'd come!"

"I can't." Peter walked along beside the car as she backed slowly and followed him along to the drive that led to the main gate. At the last minute he leaned in, muttering, "Main dining room, Fort Sumter Hotel. Eight o'clock."

Then, as if speaking for an unseen audience, Peter raised his voice and went on in a stagey tone that would carry his words wherever he wanted it to take them: "Sorry you got such bum directions, lady. The road to Parris Island is over there. Yes Ma'am, somebody definitely told you wrong."

Jude stifled the questions struggling to surface. Fatigue and frustration bubbled up and she cried, "Why didn't you tell me who you were?"

At first she thought she only imagined the expression of pain on Peter's face but his tone underscored it: Peter Benedict, too young—too nice!—to have to carry all this history, saying like a kid at a birthday party, "Because I was afraid you wouldn't come!"

Three

He had given up his true vocation to elude them; he had moved many times.

He had even changed his name.

Although he was sent to Italy to study with the Italian branch of the Benedict family, Beau Benedict wanted more than anything to free himself from the Benedict legacy. He renamed himself Bertolo because, he told Aunt Flavia and Uncle Giorgio, it made him feel more like he belonged to them. Once it became clear that whether or not he kept the name his father gave him, all the same things were expected, Bertolo Benedict ran away. He disappeared one night, dropping out of the Benedict legend, he thought, as surely as he dropped out of his parents' lives. He left the Italian Benedicts' villa with little money and few clothes. He was fourteen. Tiptoeing through the moonlit atrium, he gave a little sob of grief for what he was leaving behind, for he had to leave everything: his aunt Flavia, who was an Agnielli and not a Benedict; the graceful villa with its painted walls and marble courtyard, with no hope of returning. In his grief and haste he even forgot his sculptor's tools, but never mind. Determined to elude the family destiny, he would turn away from clay and bronze.

His father's cry of rage could be heard from the Via Appia all the way to Wayward, South Carolina. Imagining that kidnappers had snatched his most gifted son, Benton Benedict pleaded for the boy's safe return on global TV. He offered a reward in the low seven figures, no questions asked. Bertolo's older brothers went looking for him. How could they know he'd changed his name? Their brother had gone to ground in a Franciscan monastery. He'd shaved his thick, bright hair into a tonsure and put on the brown robes of a Franciscan monk. He entered under a new name. Except when he was in chapel, where monks bared their heads before the Sacrament, Bertolo Baachi hid the distinctive Benedict profile under the monk's hood of heavy brown sack cloth.

Working in the rustic gardens in the daytime and by night painting a mural on the terra-cotta wall behind the altar in the humble chapel, the gaunt Bertolo grew to manhood in the monastery. Going along under the grape arbors with his head bent under the hood and his restless sculptor's hands folded like any other monk, he could pretend that he was no different from the rest. But his talent haunted him; he painted *trompe l'oeil* archangels along the cloister walls and began the fabled Communion of Saints on a stucco wall in the refectory, adding cherubim and seraphim, thrones and dominions, detailing and embellishing until his spiritual director told him that he was wasting time on their poor walls, that God expected him to use his talents in the world.

It was hard for Bertolo to say goodbye and thank you to the monks, who had taken him in without hesitation and asked no questions, but he had to begin his new life. The day he left, they wept. If the monks heard from Bertolo now it was in the form of handsome donations delivered anonymously, via money order from a post office in Maestre, where Bertolo Baachi, *ne* Beauchamp Benedict IV, had spent an anxious few months as a bricklayer before he opened his first little studio and began earning enough to start repaying their kindness.

Because he would do anything to thwart destiny, Bertolo never worked in bronze. He worked in marble and granite. He opened his next studio in Venice, where he could hear the gloriously pure and beautifully hollow bells ringing out over the water without any of the sinister and secret associations that poisoned his heart at Wayward when he was a boy. He could disappear in Venice, where so many people crammed the streets and bridges that it would be hard to say who had gone into or come out of which villa, and even if you could identify one man with one house—say, the pale green palazzo overlooking one of the lesser canals—you would have no way of finding out who he was, or what he did. To frustrate his pursuers further, Bertolo confined the work he sold to replacement parts for ornamental sculpture in the city's deteriorating buildings. The work he did for himself, Bertolo kept to himself, a platoon of stone gladiators and archangels that filled one end of his long studio like old friends; a bevy of reclining nudes in pink marble gathered like women waiting to be loved. Because he was afraid to reveal himself, Bertolo's marble beauties were the only women in his life. Sometimes he dreamed about sculpting a woman in clay, of casting her in bronze, and in his dreams the bronzes came to life. He woke tear-drenched and shaking, whether with loss or fear he could not say.

He was safer in the territory of stone gladiators and emerging angels. Bertolo's work in marble and stone might not have the light and grace of Benedict bronzes, but it was his and his only: pure and strong, lovely and clean.

He owed nothing to his family because he took nothing from them, and if it was lonely here and Bertolo was sometimes starved, not for recognition but *kinship,* then that was his problem, even as this solitary work had been his choice. It was his offering to the Almighty—recompense for the family's terrible uses, thanks for his freedom here. At night when his work was finished, he got on his knees and thanked God.

Therefore he was both distressed and frightened when he came back to his studio after installing a stone gargoyle in an unseen spot in the interior of San Toma to find the door to his villa standing open—not by much, a half-inch, perhaps, but open nonetheless, where he was sure he'd left it locked. His first instinct should have been to turn and walk away from his studio, from Venice, from this life; if he left now he would be free to start again in some new country, but it had been so long and Bertolo felt so secure in his deception that he shook his head in annoyance at the apparent carelessness of Lupa, who cleaned for him, and pushed the door open and went in.

There was no sign of incursion in the front hall, nor was there anybody in the brocaded parlor on the left or in the sparely furnished vestibule on the right, where Bertolo did business with the Venicians who came to beg him for his services. He went on through to his studio, the long room that ran the width of the villa and contained the company of angels he had created in marble and stone. Sunlight shone in the wide windows and light played on the ceiling in watery reflections from the canal outside.

He had ripped out the walls of three salons to make this work space and when he closed the door behind him Bertolo felt serene and happy as he was nowhere else. This was his place; here he was alone and safe, surrounded by a family of his own making. He could speak to his angels and gladiators, run a wistful hand along the flank of one of his nudes.

Then the shrouded figure in the shadowed corner among his half-finished stone gladiators and unborn marble angels shifted slightly and he jumped. It spoke in the cadence of the twenty-first century.

"OK, Beau, that's enough."

His brother's voice knifed through him and Bertolo flinched. "Don't call me that!"

"Nice to see you, Beau."

"Whoever you are, go away!"

"Do you want time to pack or shall we just take off?" The interloper approached him, shedding one of Bertolo's dropcloths as he came. They could have been cast from the same mold: same profile, same self-assured tilt to the head that came with the entitlement of generations. Bertolo's brother was no avenging spirit; he was just William, a lithe, youthful-looking man in chinos and a polo shirt—he could have been any American, dropping by after a day's sightseeing on the Grand Canal.

"Will!"

"Yeah, it's me."

"But I thought..."

"Thought you were well hidden? Sure. We may be dumb but we're not stupid," his oldest brother said.

"Then why did you..."

"Once we had you located, Dad said lay back, you'd keep."

"Oh, God!"

"It isn't *that* bad, Beau."

"Oh yes it is."

"Shh. There wasn't any point in dragging you home until we needed you," Will said matter-of-factly. He was looking at his watch. "We've had your number for years."

"Years! How?"

"The monastery. That painting in the chapel. Did you really think you had anybody fooled?"

"The monks were so good to me—I—wanted to do something for them," Bertolo said brokenly. "They—told you where I was?"

Will shook his head. "No. The head monk was just so proud of you. A blind monkey could see who the artist was. Those checks you sent? Our people can find anybody when there's a bank involved."

"Then why didn't you..."

"Why should we? You weren't going anywhere."

Bertolo said brokenly, "And all this time..."

After all these years Bertolo's brother still knew how to get to him; he was not taunting, exactly, but his tone was wise and snide. "All this time you thought you were safe."

"Oh, God."

William's voice dropped. "You're never safe."

"I never wanted this!"

Will said quietly, "But you're one of us."

Backing into a table, Bertolo wheeled on his brother, brandishing a maul. "You can't make me come with you."

"Put it down, Beau," his brother said in a weary, patient tone. "Nothing you do is going to make any difference."

"I could kill you." He couldn't, but he kept his arm raised.

"No you couldn't."

He had never been able to fool William but Bertolo said, "Oh yes I could."

"Time's up, kid, come on. I've got a motorboat waiting on the Rialto."

"You expect me to come home with you."

"More," William said, as if he could lift his brother with his voice. "To Wayward."

"Wayward!" Bertolo groaned. "I won't."

"Oh yes you will."

"Tell them I died."

"But you haven't," William said. "Listen, everybody's coming."

He picked up the nearest weapon. "Everybody but me."

"The Paul Benedicts are coming, from the United Kingdom, and the Lafe Benedicts, from Hokkaido."

The maul was heavy; at some level Bertolo missed his family; he'd missed Will, and in spite of everything he was glad to see him. His voice was leaden but he tried anyway. "And the family from Rome."

"Not Aunt Flavia."

"Poor Annabella," Will said. "But of course you don't know; Flavia died."

"Except Flavia." Bertolo shuddered with grief. "And me."

His brother advanced on him, unswerving. "The whole family, Beau. You too."

"You don't need me."

Will threw him a look that made him drop the maul. "They want everybody, Beau."

"They'll never miss me."

"Sure they won't. Fourth-generation namesake like you?"

"Oh please."

"This is necessary. Let's go."

"Oh please. Oh, God! Is there anything I can *give* you?"

Will said gently, "Come on. My boat is waiting."

Bertolo shook his head. "I can't. I won't."

"Oh yes you will." His brother's low voice carried the weight of generations—everything that had been given, everything that was expected. "Come on, Beauchamp," he said. "It's time."

Weeping, Bertolo looked at Will through a rack of fingers, which he dragged down his face without even feeling the gouges the nails made in his cheeks. "God. God."

"What's the matter, Beau?"

He could not stop weeping. "Oh, please."

With a delicacy that touched Bertolo even as he resisted, Will pulled his brother's hands down so he could look into his face. What he saw made him say kindly, "Look, Beau, if you want a couple of minutes I can wait out front."

"Please."

"Five minutes, OK?"

Sobbing, he nodded.

"And you won't make me come back in and get you, OK?"

It would only take five minutes, Bertolo thought. He nodded again and when Will lingered in the doorway he managed to choke out the words. "OK."

With a deceptive little wave of the fingers Bertolo watched his brother go out and when Will turned once more with a dawning worried frown, Bertolo managed a wavery grin.

And in the five minutes which his sympathetic brother would let stretch into six because it had been such a long time since Will Benedict had seen poor Beau, and because Will understood as well as anybody how hard this was for him; in that five, almost six minutes that fell between the call to Wayward and the expected departure, Bertolo Baachi, who had been born Beauchamp Benedict IV, the fourth-generation namesake of their maker, Bertolo Baachi, who hated the family imperative so much that he'd do anything to keep from answering the call; the agonized, grief-stricken Bertolo wrestled one of his unfinished stone angels onto a dolly and trundled it through the double windows onto the terrace at the back of the studio, where he set it down on the very edge of the worn marble lip. And as his sympathetic older brother, who was trying to be understanding but had already begun looking at his watch, called, "Beau. Beauchamp. Beauchamp Benedict," Bertolo Baachi who in this lifetime would never again be called Benedict, or anything else for that matter, walked into the enfolding wings of his partially realized creation and lashed himself to its chest. Then for good measure he locked his arms around it in a death grip and lunged hard; for a minute the thing tottered and then, master and creation, art and artist, toppled into the canal.

Four

Waiting at a window table in the dining room of the Fort Sumter Hotel, Jude tapped the lamp with its rosy little shade, trying hard to keep from swiveling from window to double doors, window to double doors, watching for him. She sat there long after the other diners left. She sat there after the other tables were cleared and set for the next day's meals, long past the time when she should have paid for the endless glasses of Perrier she'd ordered when she still expected Peter to walk in the door, and the desperation Baked Alaska she'd ordered when she understood he wasn't coming. She knew she should go, but she couldn't quite give up. She had put on clingy red silk for him tonight; she was brilliant in the best piece of jewelry she'd ever made, a glittering spray of golden wire that swept up from one ear to plant stars and planets in her dark hair; for a woman tottering through her second day without sleep, she looked fine. Who wouldn't wait, just in case?

The dining room was empty. It was OK, the maitre d' said she was welcome to stay through the after-theater supper hour; it may have been the golden stars and planets twinkling in her hair or it may have been the fact that she was, so clearly, a woman in distress—which is what she was, because one more time, Jude Atkins had been stupid in love.

Her problem was, she always wanted to believe. Phil went to graduate school in art history. He preached about high art and Jude believed. She believed he loved her, too. She designed and made jewelry just to please him. She put her heart into it because she wanted to make him proud. Phil glanced at her best pieces with that snotty art-historian superiority. "That's very nice." Her heart broke when he paused, adding, "For what it is."

When they split up, Phil said, "You'll always be my best friend but the signals I was sending were not the signals you were receiving."

This was her very first and only love talking to her, Phil Forrest who grew up with perfect parents in an overdecorated house in suburban West Hartford while she and her mom scraped by in the inner city, sweet perfidious Phil

Forrest, whom she had been in love with since she got bussed into his school in the seventh grade. They were *this close* to getting married, she thought, but she was wrong. She found out the day he left for some conference of art historians in Miami Beach. Certain things she found in his suitcase. *Oh Phil, how could you?* She wouldn't name them, but she knew. They played their last scene with Jude's wet hair dripping on her funky T-shirt, fresh from the shower, and Phil standing there with his idiotic briefcase, looking more or less bulletproof in his professorial tweeds.

"You said you would love me forever."

"What was I, fifteen years old?" This is how he destroyed her. "I've grown, and you..."

"Phil, please don't."

Impervious, he finished "...you haven't."

She sobbed, "I still love you."

"Of course." Phil's heavy sigh was the worst thing. "We were just together for too long."

"Wait," Jude said, and she would never forgive herself for being right. "Who is she?"

Surprise, Phil answered, just like that! "One of the Lowells, from Boston." *More appropriate.* Right, his parents never did approve of her. And then, implied: *smarter than you. Better educated than you.* He actually blushed. "She's getting her PhD in Art History."

"Like you. Oh, Phil!"

"I was going to tell you, but the time was never right." She was grateful to him for exiting on a note that made her angry enough to survive. "All things considered, it's really just as well."

Now there she was by a window in Charleston, South Carolina, all dressed up and hopeful in spite of herself. Asking for it.

When she began this Jude actually thought she could try out a new man and get away with it. Ironic, right? She picked him off a web page. Downloaded the video and watched it a dozen times before she poured out her heart in an email.

He mailed her right back: *It was funny about that ad. I got three hundred emails from the dating service. But only one I liked was yours.*

She let him wait a day before answering. *Gee, all I did was tell the truth about myself. I thought if you liked the digis of my jewelry, you'd probably like me.*

Peter's next mail took her breath away. *Your work is wonderful! It's new, that's what I like about it. I love people like you,* he wrote. *You're making art* now *instead of dragging centuries of past history.*

Angry at Phil, the overbearing art historian, she wrote back. *The past is over. Everything that really matters is in the future, right?*

All this, before they ever talked online. Before the first phone call. Before they actually met.

It was wonderful. Peter sent pictures: himself in a sunny studio standing in front of an easel rich with color. Even reduced to wallet size he was good-looking; he had an ease, or grace that she loved. Unlike Phil Forrest, whose smile congealed into a superior, king-of-the-world sneer while they were still in college, Peter faced the camera with a crooked, self-deprecating grin.

Peter wrote, *You wouldn't know it to look at me buried down here in the deep South with my so-so job and my great studio in historic Charleston, but I'm dying to bust out.*

She wrote, *Me too, We both want revolution.* Take that, Phil Forrest. *Me too.* Then because it was important to be honest, she wrote, *Just so you know, I don't come from money.*

Seconds later he mailed back: *Do you think I care? I just want to be me, with nothing but the money I make and the socks I stand up in, with no demands and nobody to think about but the woman I love. What do you think, Jude? Is that too much to ask?*

Wonderful!

She told herself if it didn't work she could still back out without getting hurt. She planned to move slowly this time, keep him at a distance. Advance in stages, and only when she was sure. It might have worked, too, if they'd stuck to online communications, phone calls, the letters, but Peter couldn't leave it at that. He flew into Logan and they talked for ten minutes, and that first meeting clinched it. It was only ten minutes over a cup of coffee but at the end Peter reached across the table and took both her hands. "I don't know, Jude, I feel like I know you better than anybody I've grown up with."

Scarred by her experience with Phil's family, Jude drew back. They were kind enough, but the way you would be kind to a fresh-air-fund kid bussed in for a summer weekend.

"What's the matter?"

"What about your family?"

He gave her an odd look. "What about them?"

"You, bringing in some woman you don't even know."

"They don't matter," he said. "You're the only one who matters here."

"Oh Peter." It sounded *right*. Somebody who had no past and wanted no present except Jude and Peter, Peter and Jude.

What did they promise each other then?

"We'll just be us," he said. "You and me."

"Against the world."

Then he surprised her. He said, "Against the past. Oh, Jude. Come be with me in Charleston. Please."

Who wouldn't close up her apartment and follow him here?

Well, here she was.

And if he didn't come?

Jude, get hold of yourself. Your real prize is getting away from Boston and all that misery with Phil.

No matter what happened with Peter, she was free. From here she could take her jewelry anywhere—Savannah, Jacksonville, Atlanta or even Memphis, anyplace that would get her away from Boston winters and the winter in Phil Forrest's heart.

If Peter didn't show up, she had probably brought it on herself. She never should have blundered into Wayward that way.

If she wasn't good enough for Phil Forrest's parents, how could she measure up to the world-famous family of sculptors?

Why didn't he tell her, was he ashamed? *Oh,* she thought. *Those Benedicts.*

And I thought Phil's parents were a hard number, she thought. How could she possibly fit into that venerable establishment?

Still, Peter promised to meet her here tonight no matter what, and the foolish, stubborn part of her that was already in love with him kept her in place.

Blundering in unannounced, Jude had happened onto something she didn't understand. Peter was one of *those* Benedicts, sure, but with a difference. Dealing with clumsy Jake, Peter spoke like the master of the house, but there was something else at work in him. He rushed her off the place not because he was ashamed of her, Jude thought, but because he was not comfortable there. A shadow flew across the back of her mind. *Unless he was afraid for me.* Afraid? Afraid of what? At the time she thought he was more embarrassed than surprised by her finding him at Wayward like that. Apologetic, as if he needed to separate himself from the grand house, the grounds, the heritage so he could be declared not guilty. What was he shrugging off then, the family history? Their fame? Their way of life? She didn't know.

When he put her in the car and said goodbye his eyes were warm and brimming with—what?

She had to find out. She would wait until he came.

After all, he promised.

OK, she told herself at nine, he isn't coming.

OK, she told herself at ten. Of course he isn't coming. One look at me in that place and he knew I didn't belong.

Time to give up, pack it in, turn in my team jersey.

Another woman would go running home to Mom. For Jude, this was out of the question. Around the time she and Phil ended it, her Mom recovered from losing her dad—good lord, all those years in the cramped apartment with the dinky job and the cheap wardrobe Reba Atkins had been *mourning*. Mom woke up one day and decided to get better, went to makeup class, went back to school. She'd married a nice guy and was living in a sleek condo in Palm Springs.

Jude couldn't even go back to her apartment—she'd sublet it to two randy graduate students who promised never, ever to give parties; she'd moved all her things into storage and their lease wouldn't be up until the end of the year.

She could go back to her hotel and leave no forwarding address, but she couldn't live there forever, at least not on what little money she'd brought with her.

Besides, he had promised he would come.

He had...

"Jude, oh, Judith! I was afraid you'd be gone."

"Oh!" She'd been waiting for him for so long that she'd almost forgotten his name. "Peter?"

"You waited!"

She met him with a wry grin. "All this time."

He looked stricken. "All this time." Standing by the table, he swayed with fatigue: Peter Benedict, dressed for town in a light khaki suit but with his collar jerked open as if the tie had been ripped out, and with smudges on the elbows and a rumpled expression that made her want to ask if he was all right.

All she could find to say was, "Oh, Peter."

He looked so distressed that she couldn't even be mad at him. "Jude. Oh look, I'm so sorry."

"What's happened to you?"

"It's not important." His tone told her it was.

Her hands flew up; she wanted to pat him all over: there there, there there. "Is there anything I can do?"

"Just be here," he said and if she had been in any doubt about coming to South Carolina—about any of this—his look made her glad she'd come, and even gladder that she'd hung in here in this deserted dining room, waiting for Peter Benedict on the strength of his promise that he'd be here which, after all these uncertain hours, he was.

The *maitre d'* was heading their way; for a second Jude thought he might be about to reproach Peter for being out of uniform—no tie—but instead he was beaming, bringing a silver cooler of champagne. He murmured, "You should have told me you were waiting for Mr. Benedict, Ms..."

"Atkins."

"Everything's fine, Claude, thank you for taking such good care of her." As she watched Peter's head lifted and his shoulders squared. Like lightning, he changed from ordinary guy to *somebody*. He seemed to sit taller. He could have been a planter, state senator, governor, anything. Even in the rumpled khakis he had an elegantce, an air of ease and entitlement.

"Thank *you,* Mr. Benedict. If there's anything more you need..."

"We have everything we need, and thank you, but the lady and I don't want to keep you overtime. If you'll put the champagne on my bill..."

"Oh no sir." Like a magician, he pulled a towel out of nowhere and wrapped the Veuve Cliquot. He handed it to Peter with a flourish and produced a pair of champagne flutes. "Compliments of the house."

They sat on the seawall on the Battery with the champagne between them, drinking Veuve Cliquot and looking out at the harbor. Jude had a thousand questions but by this time she was spun out too thin to ask them. Part of her didn't really want to know; the part of her that thought it saw something wriggling in the road at Wayward kept raising them, question after unformed question, but the part that wanted to be in love without complications took precedence and smashed them flat. It seemed important not to say too much.

Peter kept murmuring: "so glad," "so good, so right for you to *be* here," squeezing her elbow, "I'm just so *glad*."

Jude heard herself saying how happy she was and because she was so happy and a little drunk, she couldn't help but ask whether she'd ruined everything by turning up the way she did: "It's OK, you can tell me the truth."

She pressed him in part because she already knew how he would answer: "*No* you haven't ruined anything." Then, as they emptied their glasses and threw them into the water she thought she heard him say under his breath, "You've helped a lot," but by that time she was so giddy with exhaustion and too much champagne to know.

"What, Peter? What did you say?"

He growled, "You're dead on your feet."

"Maybe I am." She leaned into his shoulder and closed her eyes, trusting him to take care of her.

Which he did, checking her bag for the name of her hotel and giving an address to the cab driver. The cab took them, not to Peter's place, but back to her hotel. He saw her in and turned back the bed and set her down and patted her in place right before he gave her a kiss on the forehead and in spite of the fact that she was raising her arms to him, murmuring sleepy promises, turned out the lights and left.

Five

"Now Wataru, you will notice I have greased your face thoroughly, and wrapped your hair so nothing will catch in the mask once it is applied. Casting from life is a very difficult process, much more delicate than casting from a mold, and I only want to do this once. You understand that before I go to America, I must send your likeness along ahead. The family needs to know it will fit into the Benedict group effort."

The old sculptor's student was as loyal as he was humble. "But *sensei,* what if I am not good enough?"

Benta Benedict smiled, and her apprentice saw how beautiful she must once have been. "Of course you are good enough, Wataru. We are good enough. Now we must finish the work, so we can prove it."

As she spoke the old woman moved gracefully across her studio, plucking the single flower from the exquisitely spare arrangement on the low teakwood bench. "Here, Wataru, while I'm mixing the plaster you can focus on this. It will help your concentration." Smoothing the linen she had draped over the young man's shoulders, she gave him a rose to hold.

"And whatever you do, don't move. We don't want to run the risk of spoiling this negative of your beautiful face. They are expecting it. It leaves Hokkaido tonight, and we must go tomorrow."

The young man in the rolling chair did not move, but his eyes followed her.

"All the Benedicts are called home for this reunion, and by a nephew I've never met. Unless we are called by his wife. I'm not certain." Her voice lightened momentarily. "I haven't been back in fifty years." Then it dropped like a block of granite. "Since..." she said, and did not finish.

Benta was tall, apparently undiminished by her years. Unlike most women her age, whose spines had compressed and whose backs were bent from bearing children and supporting their tremendous expectations, she stood straight in the simple linen kimono, with thick white hair skewered in a knot at the base of her skull. Although Wataru had spent all his life in Hokkaido and could not know it, the pure lines of Benta's profile echoed and anticipated every generation of Benedicts.

"That's good. Be still. Keep your mind on the rose. As soon as the plaster reaches the right consistency, we'll begin."

In a minute it would close down on him: weight and heat and darkness—the mask. Twisting the rose, the beautiful young man winced as his thumb connected with a thorn. "But Benta-san."

"Shh, Wataru, this won't take long."

"Benta-san, I am yours to propose and dispose of, but you know I am no model. I was hired to work with the lost wax."

"And you've been happy here?"

"I would do anything for you."

"Then be quiet and let me do this."

"Why can you not simply make one of your beautiful clay heads, and take a cast from that?"

"Because there isn't time. Besides, this—*this* is something special. Something different. We are rushing to the gathering. I will send this ahead, and we—we will go when we are ready, my dear. Every Benedict will contribute to this monumental piece my nephew's wife has planned. It is designed to embrace all the peoples of the world—pink, black, red, yellow, brown. She says it will be a master work, every part of it must be beautiful, perfect. That's why I chose you. Now take these."

"But Benta-san..."

"Straws, put them in your nostrils so you can breathe."

"You never said I had to..."

"It's nothing, so shh." In spite of her age Benta's voice was clear, hypnotic as she talked on, gentling her student. "Remember you are descended from a samurai and the samurai undergo great trials without twitching a hair and without once saying what they feel. Imagine you are a Kabuki dancer putting on the lion mask."

"But the dancers are allowed to move."

"Put yourself inside the work, like the Bunraku."

"The Bunraku are allowed to move."

"Be still, Wataru. Be grateful; in a way, you are being given the opportunity to behold what you become. And it will be beautiful."

"But Benta-san..."

"And others will behold you and be glad." She backed off, sighting along a sculptor's tool; where most people were asymmetrical, the halves of his face were perfect. "Don't worry, you are my best student and I would never do anything to hurt you." Waiting for the plaster to reach the right consistency, Benta looked around the room. Like the lines of the old lady's body in her simple costume, her surroundings were uncluttered and serenely beautiful: a few perfect objects artfully arranged in two rooms composed of sliding *shoji* screens. Her studio was defined by a pebbled garden in which her best pieces stood—a far cry from the generous working spaces at Wayward, but Benta ran away from all that at nineteen. She'd landed in bustling Hokkaido, where expenses were high and space was at a premium.

"Some people feel intense claustrophobia when the plaster goes on over their eyes, but you are strong and I know you'll be fine." Her voice was low and beautiful, in keeping with her rooms.

"Now Wataru, I don't want you to worry. I have put an extra coat of Vaseline on the eyelashes and the eyebrows; there's nothing more painful than losing a hair or two when the mask comes off. And believe me, there's nothing more terrible for the mask maker than hurting someone. Unless it's discovering that you've lifted some skin, but that only happens when the artist is careless in lifting the mask. Hold still! I'd rather die than hurt you." Absorbed, she would not hear her voice drop to a worried mutter. "If I have to, I..." She broke off and started over on a brighter note. "My goodness, it's been ages since I cast anything this size."

Although Benta was an integral part of the Benedict enterprise; although like theirs her best pieces soared, the work of a lifetime occupied very little space. Maquettes of Benta's portrait busts and her elaborate sculptural groupings stood on a long table in the studio and in the white pebble garden. Her portraits were superb. Sculptural groupings seethed with energy but even the most ambitious pieces, which looked huge when divorced from their surroundings, were executed in miniature.

Like the late Bertolo/Beau Benedict, Benta had found her own way to dance ahead of fate.

She tested the plaster; it was ready. "I've done everything to make you comfortable. Now all you have to do is hold the thought and be still."

Rolling Wataru's chair closer to the workbench, she rattled on to quiet him. It was rather like a dentist's chair; she pushed a lever and tilted him back.

"Ai!"

"Shsh. Don't be afraid."

"*Sensei.*"

"Shh. Remember the beach."

At the touch of her hands on his temples, he relaxed. The exercise she had given him would remove him from discomfort and put him at rest on a sunny strand.

Benta used words to soothe as she prepared him. "The inconvenience is only temporary and you have such fine features that I can assure you, the results will be beautiful. And I can promise you, your likeness will be integrated into a major master work; it will be photographed for catalogs and reproduced in every book about the great sculpture of the world. Scholars who know excellence will know your face. Everyone will know it by heart."

He could feel her hands tracing his cheekbones.

"And while they are busy with your likeness, my darling, you and I have other things to do. Do you have the straws in place now? Let me seal the edges with a little extra Vaseline. Are you comfortable? Good. Now stay calm while I begin with the plaster; it will be warm, but don't panic. We don't want to take the others a contorted face."

"I do not like this," the young man said while he still could.

"Only because it is new to you," she said, working quickly, "and it's new to me. Indeed this is the first time in years that I've worked to lifesize. But the family..." She paused a half beat too long before completing the thought. "The family has its expectations. Be sure to keep your eyes closed, I'm going to begin with the forehead and work down."

Under the white linen dropcloth, Wataru said in a small voice, "Benta-san, I feel trapped."

"Shh, Wataru. Be still. I'm about to put the first layer over your mouth."

"M. MM!"

"Shh, Wataru. We are at a delicate juncture here." Stirring the plaster mixture, she crooned to quiet him.

"Now, do not be alarmed if you feel a little claustrophobic and be prepared, after a moment or two there will be a sensation of heat, but if you put your mind in a cool place you'll hardly know it's happening. Use the technique I taught you and call up the beach; imagine the heat is the sun on your face and when I remove the mask you'll feel fresh breezes and sweet summer rain. Won't you, Wataru?"

He hummed, "Mmm. Mmmm." Helpless under her hands.

She stroked his arm until he stopped trembling. "Have I ever hurt you? I promise, nothing bad will happen to you. If at any time you are uncomfortable or want to be released just press my hand and even though it ruins the mask, I'll free you at once."

He made what may have been a grateful grunt.

"I know the whole process is a little frightening but believe me, I will be gentle and it will be over in a few minutes. Rest, go back inside your head and lie down and relax and it will end before you know it. That's good. Be still, and while we are waiting I will tell you the story of the very beginning of this great work we are committing: the legend of Beauchamp Benedict."

Wataru took it surprisingly well. Like all good models, he did not speak; he couldn't. In fact he could not move until Benta had satisfied herself that the plaster had completely hardened and she could lift the mask. Once she finished patting the last bit in place and smoothing it with her fingertips, she covered it with a cloth woven from single strands fresh from a silkworm cocoon. Then, murmuring quietly to make him know they were in touch, she washed her hands and put a CD on the player; Scarlatti, as good an aid to meditation as any amount of traditional music on the *shakahachi:* pressed, she'd have to admit the reedy tones got on her nerves.

"Do not let the feeling of closeness upset you and do not think about the heat, my dear," she said as a precautionary measure although now that he was immured, Wataru sat in a stoic stillness she had to admire. "Understand, it seems longer than it really is."

He tried not to sigh.

"Like life, which is unbearably short," she said.

"Unlike art, which is perpetual."

Her breath caught. "If you can find your way into it." Benta said, "You already know it isn't easy. For most, it is impossible.

"It takes sacrifice."

She looked into the middle distance for a long time. Then she began. "When you have studied with me for a few years longer you will be a very great artist, Wataru, because by then you'll know everything I have to teach you. You might as well know that from the beginning, you must be willing to give everything to your art. Like the first Beauchamp Benedict, who sold everything he had to travel to Europe to learn the lost wax process."

She sighed. "He went back to South Carolina and discovered knowledge is never enough."

By this time Wataru was in the zone. Did he hear? Did he not? "Even he didn't know how long it would be or how hard it would be or how much it would take. To make his work endure..."

At last she finished. "Or how great the sacrifice." He would not hear her add, "Or the sin."

Benta patted the silk over the plaster, which was hard now but still hot; she checked the nose opening to make certain his breath was pushing still the silk in and out, in and out. "You are a brave artist, Wataru."

Did he moan?

Assured that everything was going well, she went on. "Remember, Beauchamp took the hard way, working on his own in the Carolinas in the terrible times after the Civil War, when the Benedicts lost everything. The South suffered worlds during the Reconstruction. You probably don't know what reconstruction is. Well maybe first I'd better explain..."

Quiet, gentle, gracious Benta Benedict, sculptor and mentor, considered her work as she murmured on, and if she knew the old story too well to hear what she was saying, her subject was too deep in his own discomfort to attend to it. On her advice, Wataru had gone back inside his head where it was safe, where he was deeply engrossed in the beautiful beach Benta had taught him to create through meditation. Arranging himself on the sand, he could lie here and listen to the waves. The heat! *Just sun on my face,* he told himself, *and in a few minutes the breeze will come and then the rain, soft summer rain...*

"Understand," she said, or Wataru thought she'd said, "like you, Beauchamp had to begin with sacrifice, and the work, oh, God, the work was brilliant. But, the cost! You have no idea. It demanded something... Grave. Too grave." Her voice dropped. "Terrible. It had to stop!"

There was a long silence.

Benta choked and started over. "The family did what it had to, to end the suffering, but you can't outrun the legacy and now..."

But Wataru was lost to the beach and sunlight glittering on bright water, the dazzling expanse of sand.

Groaning, Benta finished, "Now this woman Ava has brought it all back. God, Wataru, she's called us back, and I am afraid. For us. For all of us. Wataru?" She shook him gently. "Are you all right?"

He did not speak.

"Wataru!"

But Wataru did not hear. He was drifting, warm and safe, inside his reverie. What finally brought him back was a gentle rapping on the cast—his master teacher, Benta Benedict, knocking at the doors to his soul. He jerked to attention. In another minute she would lift the mold; because she was his *sensei* and he trusted her, he knew it would be a slow, gentle lifting, a careful breaking of the seal so that the air could separate the plaster from the sensitive surface of his heavily greased face. For Benta-san was an artist; not for her the ripping off in haste; she would remove the mask as she did everything, with great delicacy. He could hardly wait to feel the breeze, the rain.

Startled by the sudden light he stretched his neck and whipped his head around like a new chick, blink-blinking. What? What was it? What had she just told him, that was so remarkable?

"So that's the whole story," she said.

"But *sensei,* wait!"

"That's all for now, Wataru. Oh look at this, how beautiful!" She was staring into the negative space of the plaster of Paris mask.

"Something you were about to tell me, Benta-san."

"Oh," she said.

Troubled, he stirred. "That you *did* tell me."

"Did not tell you. The rest."

"Something." Disoriented, blinking, he tried to bring it back. "Awa?"

"Ava."

"Something..." he could not stop blinking... "remains to be seen? Some... secret."

"I can't tell you." Her face closed. "Not now. Not until I have figured out what to do."

Instead she offered him the mask. She held it up for him to see and Wataru was silenced by its beauty; it was like staring into his own dead face.

And when she had thanked Wataru and gently cleaned his face and watched the color return to it; when she had wiped the last traces of plaster dust from his hairline and thanked him again and sent him away, Benta Benedict ran out of strength suddenly and without realizing how drained she was she sank into the rolling chair and did her best to lose herself, staring into the mask. When she rose again she seemed diminished, as if all seventy-some years had landed on her shoulders at once.

"Ava." She heard her own voice in the empty rooms: "What do you expect?" The next sentence came up from somewhere so deep that it frightened her. "What do you want from us?"

Six

"I took this place because I had to get out of the family," Peter said. "See, things were going in a bad direction."

Jude said, "What do you mean, a bad direction?"

"I'm sorry, I can't tell you. When I left for college, I knew things were bad. When I came back it was getting worse." His voice was ragged, disturbing. He turned to her with an expression she would come to recognize: mingled pride and pain. She couldn't know whether it was the separation that hurt so much or something else that tore into him like a knife in the ribcage and made him grimace in pain. It was about the family, that she knew.

"You don't have to go back."

"I don't know," he said. "I don't know!"

Being one of them, she thought, *that's what hurts*. What terrible power did the Benedict family have over him? How could they skewer a grown man like this, and pull him down in midflight and make him come back?

He said abruptly, "I ran away to save my life."

Jude thought about her own mother, the dinky apartment above Jigger's Package Store, the air thick with unspoken laments. She said quietly, "I know the feeling. Sometimes I think family is destiny, but maybe not. We're both here."

They were standing at one end of Peter's studio, a long, sun-shot room with French doors opening out on the second-floor veranda of Violet Poulnot's house. Even though they were only a block off the Battery in busy downtown Charleston, lush trees nodded in the walled courtyard. Walled as they were, built end-to so they could keep their secrets, old Charleston houses looked like nothing from the street, but the interiors! She could have been at Tara or Belle Reve.

When Jude first came for Peter this morning Violet sprang out of the gate before she could ring. The old lady's genteel murmur did nothing to conceal her naked curiosity. "Why, Miss..."

"Atkins."

"Miss Atkins. What are you doing here?

"I'm here to see Peter Benedict?"

"Well today, at least he's here. Come in. You know he doesn't see just anybody." Violet said, ushering her into the hidden garden. Perhaps thinking to buy secrets with confidences, she whispered portentously, "Especially after poor Gara... Well, you know."

"Who?" Jude turned sharply. "Who?"

Before Violet could answer, Peter thudded down the porch steps in sneakers, cutting her off. "Thank you, Violet. Violet, I said *thank you,*" he repeated until she capitulated and with a loaded, saccharine smile, backed off.

"Be good," Violet said from the door to her own heavily curtained, cluttered apartment. "Have fun."

"Old Charleston family," Peter said apologetically. "Very old family," he added, louder, for Violet. Grinning, he waited until he was certain the old lady had latched her door and just in case he added, "*Very* old family. Been here as long as the Calhouns and Archambaults. And us."

"What was she saying about..."

"My great-greats were a major link in the underground railroad. One thing to be proud of, I guess."

"...Gara." Temporarily marooned at the bottom of the stairs, she replayed the old lady's heavily weighted, "after poor Gara." What *was* that? "Who..."

"Welcome to the South," Peter said drily, and because she still hadn't moved he said, "Come see my place!"

"...was Gara?"

"Southern gossip," he said, and did not answer. "You'll get used to it." Then he took Jude's hand with such assurance that his touch made her gasp, and pulled her up the stairs.

The veranda was lined with a series of floor-to-ceiling French windows that gave on to a long, spare room. There was a door at the far end of the long porch but with a careless grin, Peter pulled her in through an open window. "This is it."

She saw white walls, the honeyed sheen of bare floors, sunlight crashing in, but before all this she saw the profusion of bright color at the far end of the room, oversized canvases massed like ships waiting to move out. His paintings. "It's wonderful."

"At least it's mine."

The paintings were like a living presence in the room. Delighted, she whirled. "You did all these?"

"Yes Ma'am."

"Your work," she said slowly. They were huge, glorious, as real as family. "Oh Peter, they look just like you."

"Uh."

She saw doubts racing across his face at tremendous speeds: did she like the work? Did she not? "I love it!" She went on without understanding exactly what she meant, only that it was true. "They're you!"

"Yes but no," he said finally. It was all he could manage because there were no words for what Peter Benedict was trying to express.

Except for the drafting table and the lacquered cabinet at the far end of the room, the paintings were all there was. It was as if this entire space had been arranged to serve them—light, white walls, pale hardwood floor, all. In this bright place the paintings exploded in slashes of color—gaudy, seductive, wild.

Jude could not stop looking at them even after Peter turned away, trying to show her the rest. "There's a bedroom and a kitchen in the ell, it's kind of a dump but my heart is in here."

She nodded, transfixed. She was studying the paintings.

Perhaps embarrassed by her concentration, Peter tugged her hand. "Hey, this is my great-grandfather's Chinese cabinet," he was saying. "Jude?"

"They're amazing," she said.

"Great-grandfather on my mother's side. They were all sea-captains. Generations of them. Family business," he finished with a shrug.

The silence that followed caught her attention. She repeated, "Family business?"

Satisfied that she was listening, Peter said, "That's family business on my grandmother's side. The Pattersons." When he went on it was with great care. "I guess when things run in families..."

"Like talent."

His face darkened. "...you end up with family businesses."

He was so uncomfortable that Jude said foolishly, "There's no law that says everybody has to go into the family business."

He went on as if he hadn't heard. "You know, all those sea captains? The Patterson family business went belly up when my grandmother's brother got blown up in the second world war. His way of breaking the sequence, I guess."

"But your grandmother was a Patterson. She had children."

He shook his head. "No. When she got married she became a Benedict. The Benedicts swallow up everything they touch."

"That's scary."

"It's the way it is. Everything serves the family."

Jude said quickly, "Not you, Peter. Those paintings. You're different."

He flashed her that look—pride and pain, combined with something she could not identify. "When I was three years old Dad gave me clay to play with, but he made me play by his rules. By the time I was five he had me studying animal shapes in a corner of his studio: he made me draw the skulls before I started my armature and draw the heads before I began putting on the clay and if it wasn't right she came in and slashed it to pieces with one of his tools."

"She?"

"The mother."

"But you were five years old!"

"To Ava I was just another Benedict."

"Who?"

Peter's voice dropped and his face changed. "The mother."

"Your mother! Oh, that poor little kid!"

"I bugged out, anything to be different from the Benedicts," he said miserably. "Now they want me to come back and do..."

"Do what?"

Peter didn't say what, exactly; he never said what; instead he looked into his hands for a long minute and then he looked up. "It's OK, Jude. Really. I'm fighting it."

"Whatever it is," Jude began and gulped hard because Peter had put something in the room—a threat he would not describe and she couldn't identify. She slapped top of the Chinese chest so hard that all the drawers rattled. "You're too good for it."

He shook his head. "Not to them. To them, I'm just part of the machinery."

"No. You have these—*brilliant* paintings."

"Yeah well," Peter said. "The parents would say they're only paintings. So would my brothers. For them the only real life is in the bronze."

"That's terrible," Jude said. "You know better, you're a painter."

"I'm a Benedict."

"Family isn't destiny."

"They think it is." There it was again: that confusion of love and anguish that tore her in two. "One way or another, we all try to break out."

"Well they're wrong," Jude said without knowing where this was coming from or what led her to make assumptions. "We'll fight them."

Peter looked up, grinning. "Hey, with you here, maybe I can make the break."

Then he pulled her into the kitchen and sat her down to coffee and corn muffins planted on his doorstep this morning by Violet Poulnot, who had just called to remind him they were here.

Jude laughed. "She doesn't leave you alone, does she?"

"It's OK," he said in a light voice. "You can bet your life the mother never baked."

The mother? He could have been talking about a dish or a chair—or a national monument. "The mother. You mean your mother?"

"Ava. She makes us call her Ava so nobody will look at us and know how old she is. The brothers and I call her the mother. Ava Benedict," he said, with overtones Jude was too surprised to interpret. "A.k.a. the mother. She's in all the art books, along with the most important Benedicts. She has work in a lot of women's colleges; she specializes in portrait busts of women."

Jude had learned a few things from years with Phil and his art history books. "Not that many women make it as sculptors."

"The mother will do anything to get what she wants."

Jude shuddered. "She's a Benedict."

"Not really. But she is. Before Ava, Benedict wives only stood by and had the kids." The old pride, pain—why couldn't he pin it down—crossed Peter's face, "Then my dad broke the mold. He married one of his students. Ava had the kids all right, but she was ambitious. She took Esther Manifort out of the kitchen to watch us, Esther's ancestors were slaves to my ancestors and I love her more than my family. She was my real mom. All Ava cares about is her work."

"She didn't love you?"

"Oh, she loves us all right," he said with the ease of somebody who'd gotten used to it. "She just doesn't like us very much."

"That's terrible."

"Not really. Kids are only kids; her life is in the bronze. A lot of people say Ava's work is better than our dad's, but that talk doesn't go outside Wayward..." He corrected. "Didn't until now."

"It's OK," Jude said without explaining.

His look told her she didn't need to. "I know it is."

They sat in the sunlight, mumbling through buttered cornbread and grinning foolishly until Jude murmured, "Really nice of old Violet."

Out of nowhere, Peter said, "I guess she saw this coming."

Jude's head came up. "What?"

"Violet? She wanted us to know she was glad."

"No," Jude said like a schoolteacher taking a pupil over the jumps. "I mean the part about how she saw this coming."

His eyes were as clear as the day. "Me. Finding someone. After everything."

It was getting hard to swallow. Jude said, "After Gara?"

"After..." He gnawed his cheek. "Look, I don't know if I can do this now." That smile. "I. Violet thinks it's time I got over Gara."

"Oh, Gara." Certainly. Right. Jude's mind was not on what they were saying now; it was on Arlene Lorimer from home, a studio potter and her partner in the shop, pragmatic, good lady with clay on her hands who saw clearly and tried to make her look ahead.

Look out, Arlene warned when she came into the shop to clear out her stuff. *You don't know this guy.*

I do, I met him and he's wonderful. He's an artist, Arlene. Perfect.

Nobody's perfect, Jude.

I don't mean perfect, she said urgently; she wanted this to work! *I mean perfect for me.*

Arlene shrugged. *Whatever. Perfect for you, everything's perfect, fine fine and then you get to know the guy and you find out, you know?*

Find out?

Find out there's S.W.E.

And Jude, who just wanted to get packed and be out of here got hung up on the initials; she leaned over the counter and grabbed Arlene's wrists. *What do you mean, S.W.E.?*

You know, Some Weird Element. Listen, Arlene warned, *it's the law of averages. Guys who are perfect, there's gotta be something wrong.*

"Jude?" Peter's voice brought her back. "Jude?"

With an effort, she shook off her doubts. Because she thought she loved him, she forced herself to say, "Question."

He caught her tone and said almost formally, "Yes?"

In the next second Jude made the mistake of looking into his eyes and almost didn't ask him at all. But this was Jude Atkins, nobody's fool, survivor of Phil Forrest and therefore twice shy. This was Judith Marsden Atkins, who did not suffer fools. Swallowing hard, she set the words out between them one at a time. "Is there something going on that I ought to know about?"

Every line in his body sagged. He sighed. "You mean that."

"Whatever it is." She took his hands.

"I was hoping this could wait," Peter said heavily. "You won't hate me if I tell you, right?"

"If we're going to amount to anything, I have to know."

"OK." He tightened his fingers on hers. Like a good soldier biting the bullet, he began. "OK, Gara. This time last year, I was getting married. Or I thought I was."

Don't tell me he's another Phil. "You should have told me!"

"I wanted to, but I was trying so hard to move on. Like getting out of Wayward. It's all part of the same thing."

"Gara was at Wayward?"

"Nothing I wanted," he barked. "That's where we ended up in spite of me." He gripped her hands like a castaway clinging to a raft. "It's where everything ends up no matter what I try. Don't pull away, Jude. Listen. You and I are different."

Later she would remember thinking: *Maybe family really is destiny,* but she said what he wanted to hear. "Yes. We are."

"She was a set designer from Savannah when I met her, black hair, fair skin, beautiful, like a Snow White doll, but she had fire. You've never seen anybody like—I'm sorry, Jude." He wasn't even aware that his grip had loosened while he was talking. Now he let her go.

Jude was acutely aware of her average coloring, her OK looks; she made a wry face. "Don't mind me."

"No. You don't understand. Her looks aren't important. It's just part of the picture is all. Gara was from one of those old Savannah families? Like the Calhouns or the Poulnots..."

"Or the Benedicts."

He shrugged. "Or the Benedicts. She came up here from Sea Island to work at the Dock Street Theater, she might still be there if it wasn't for me. Hell, we might still be together if I hadn't taken her home to the folks. I met her at a party and it was like, instant. I thought we were going to be perfect together for life."

"Maybe nobody's perfect," Jude said. She trailed Arlene's warning across his path to see whether he'd pick up on it. "You know. S.W.E."

But Peter was fixed on the past. "So. Ah. Gara. We were in love and I tried to warn her off it, but she had expectations and wouldn't quit. It's all very Southern, OK? She said, 'If you really loved me, you'd let me meet your family.' And I would tell her, 'This isn't any ordinary family.' Then she'd cry. 'What's the matter, Peter, are you ashamed of me?' I knew it was a mistake, but what could I do?"

He was quiet for a long time. "So I took her to Wayward. And once I took her home to meet the family, it turned out she was in love with the family, as in, she knew exactly who the Benedicts were. When we went down to the studio to meet Ava, she got all gushy, like, 'So this is where you work.' The mother never likes anything I do, she hated everybody I brought home but this time...

"Ava looked up from the clay she was sculpting and, what, saw something special in Gara's face? Adoration? Something about the modeling of her head? Whatever it was, Ava approved. 'It is,' she said. 'Come in,' and Gara, you'd think she'd handed her the moon. It was just all wrong. I don't know, I'm looking at Gara and I'm thinking, hey wait. Is it me you're in love with, or the famous Benedicts?"

It took him a long time to go on. "It was the fame. That's what Gara moved to Charleston to find and fall in love with, when all the time I thought it was me."

He should be angry, Jude thought, *he should be pounding on the table,* but he sighed heavily. That was all.

"Our first Saturday at Wayward I come down to breakfast and Esther's the only one left in the house. She says, 'You know that nice girl you brought home, well she's down to your father's studio.' They didn't come out until Sunday afternoon and when they did, Gara had made this amazing clay sculpture: my father's hand, like life. She was good, Gara," he said bitterly. "She was going to be the best."

It was another long minute before he went on.

"So all the time the mother was telling me, 'A good choice for once, Peter. Especially since your brothers have failed us here.'"

"Your brothers?"

"That's another story, Jude. Ava says, 'This is perfect for the family,' and I turn on her, like, 'Don't condescend to me, Ava,' and the bitch is sweeter to me than she's been since I was four years old and broke my leg. She didn't apologize, she just smiled and gave me this hug, kind of like, 'There there.'"

"Are you OK?"

His breath came rattling out of him. "I'm so dumb I thought OK, at least Ava will let me keep this one..."

(*Wait a minute,* Jude thought. *Wait.*)

"...I thought this won't be so bad, the parents will have Gara but I'll have her too. When Gara quit her job and moved to Wayward to study with my dad I thought..." Peter had to struggle to get it out. "No. I didn't think. Ava thought. The mother told me Gara fit the template, so we had her blessing. We could get married and perpetuate the Benedicts. We would just go on and on being Benedicts, and I was so crazy in love with her that I thought OK fine...

"But it wasn't fine," he said. "It was never fine."

"Peter..." Jude wanted to make it better but he cut her off.

"Don't. I would take a sleigh-ride to hell if I could come back Peter Smith or Peter Jones, anybody but Peter Benedict. I want to get out of here and never look back."

In a flash Jude saw the central figure in Beauchamp Benedict's masterpiece: lighted from within. Then Peter sagged and the life went out of him.

"So. Ah. It's over."

"Oh, Peter. What happened to you?"

"Nothing. It's done." He shook his head like a survivor staggering out of a train wreck.

Jude touched his hand with one finger and held it there until he came back. Gently, she asked, "Who broke it off?"

"I guess you'd have to say Gara did. I got up one morning and she was gone."

This seemed like too much; it seemed like not enough; she wanted to grab Peter by the shoulders and shake out the rest: what happened before Gara left him for good, what they said to each other, whether she left a note. She needed to know what happened afterward, did Peter rage or go looking, did he call the police? More than anything she wanted to know if he still loved Gara, but before she could organize her thoughts a door crashed open. Peter got up. For the moment Jude stayed at the table, held in place by, she supposed it was tact. She heard him talking to somebody whose high little voice would not be squelched—it sounded like—like a kid, and once she was certain it wasn't Violet coming to ask what were her intentions, or, worse yet, the celebrated Ava Benedict, out to extinguish the latest threat to the family name, she got up and went into the studio to find out what was going on.

Peter stood in the doorway, waving his arms like a basketball guard, fending off a fat little boy who was struggling to get in.

"Let me in goddammit, let me in."

"Language, Edgar! I'm busy right now."

"Come on, Petesy, I know she's in there."

"It's no big deal Eddy, OK?"

"Pe-terr...."

"Come on Ed."

"Hey lady, I know you're there."

"There isn't any—"

"I just want to *see* her."

"No."

"I only want to say hello."

"And run right straight home and report to the mother. Or is Ava out there in the car?"

"I'm all alone. Now let me in."

"No way, you'll just go back and blab."

"Hell no I won't go back and I won't tell nothing to nobody," the child said angrily. "I'm running away."

Peter's voice sank. "Oh Eds, you can't."

"I'm coming to live with you."

"You can't."

"I'll pay. I'll get a job."

"What can you do, you're in sixth grade!"

"I don't care, I hate her and I'm never going back there." The boy's voice hit a new high. "Ava wants me to..." He groped for the words. "Oh shit. They want me to..." he choked. "I'm supposed to... Oh shit oh never mind..." Looking like a killer bee in his yellow and brown striped T-shirt, the child buried his head in Peter's midsection and started thwapping with his fists.

From the kitchen it had sounded like a pitched battle, but Jude saw that they were both pulling punches, grappling like bunkmates at summer camp, and because the child's voice went up a notch with every syllable and she had to do something, she interrupted in a bright, loud voice. "Hey, is there a problem?"

"Yes," Peter said.

"No," the child shouted. "No problem. I'm running away."

"No he isn't."

"I'm out of there. I'm gone for good."

Peter's face stretched eight different ways; he looked at Jude over the boy's head. "He thinks."

"Not thinks," he howled. "I know. I'm never going back."

"Shhshh Eds, shh shh. Be cool and we'll call Daddy."

"Noooooo."

"Hey, shh, be cool," Peter said desperately. "Listen, guy, I have to tell him where you are."

"They'll come up here and get me," Edgar growled. "They'll make me go back."

"No. I don't think so. I don't *know,* I just... I just don't want Dad to worry," Peter said.

"Fuck you, I'm never going back," the furious child shouted and in seconds he slid from bluster into tears that made him even madder because he couldn't stop. "That's never, OK. Never."

"Oh Peter, isn't there something you can..."

Peter hugged the child so he wouldn't see. Over his head he was mouthing, "I don't know."

Without knowing why it mattered so much Jude said, "You have to do *something.*"

"Sh-sh, Eds, just Shh, OK?" Thumping him on the back, Peter said with his chin in the boy's bristly hair, "I'm sorry, but there are things I can't explain right now." Then he turned him around, hanging on so they made a little unit and said, "So, Ed. This is my friend Jude Atkins. Jude, this is my baby brother Edgar Benedict."

Seven

The sprawling house was quiet for once. Nelly, Petra, Grant and Jake were through policing the kitchen and had gone off to the student spaces on the far side of the garden. Ava's students. Benton Benedict resented them, but they were useful. The resident Benedicts had been working in their studios deep in the woods ever since the first breakfast sitting was cleared—all but Benton, who lingered here. Late-morning light slanted into the dining room, with its oval rosewood table and intricately hand-painted French wallpaper installed by the first of the Benedicts shortly after the Civil War. Patterned with palms and vines, the wallpaper landscape had been there for so long that the owner of the house no longer saw it, or tried to fathom the design, in which elusive figures darted in and out of a Rousseauvian jungle in some pink prehistoric dawn. Right now the head of the house sat musing over a cold *croissant* with the morning sunlight silvering the long, straight hair that fell in a shelf over his forehead. Even though Benton Benedict was still safely within the parameters of middle age, even though he was strong and trim, his hair had gone white and his hands turned transparent, like the hands of a much older man. Behind him, the tall, elegant black woman in a starched blue shift that was not quite a uniform, dusted object on the sideboard, rearranging the candelabra and running a soft cloth over the tiny bust of the legendary Beauchamp Benedict, a tribute wrought in silver by his first-born son. She and Benton were both at home here and they shared the room in the accustomed silence of old friends. Until she spoke. It was like a firecracker going off in a church. "Mr. Benedict, don't make that child come back here."

Benedict turned so they were facing and said painfully, "You know I have to. And please don't call me Mr. Benedict."

"You know I have to," Esther said. Generations of her family had worked here; old patterns died hard.

"No you don't."

"We all do things we don't want to, Mr. Benedict." She waited until he shifted as if to dodge what was coming. When it was clear he was uneasy, she went on. "Like dragging that poor child back home against his will."

"He doesn't know what he wants, Esther."

"You're sure?"

He did not answer. "Besides, Ava is worried about him."

Her contempt cut to the bone. "Sure she is."

"Anything could happen to him."

"He's gone to his big brother, Mr. Benedict."

Benton's tone roughened. "Peter."

"He was your favorite."

"That was before he walked out on us."

"Don't blame Peter," she said. "He couldn't stay, not after what happened."

Anxiety moved across Benton's face like a sheet of summer rain. "We don't know what happened."

"He lost his girlfriend, Mr. Benedict. He's grieving."

When he spoke again it was with resolution. "He could have stayed. We're all Benedicts."

She muttered, "All but Miss Ava."

"Watch it!"

"Mr. Benton, I helped Mama bring you up and I can say what I want to you. I hate to say this, Mr. Benton, but you married trash."

"Esther, that's enough!"

"God knows I tried to warn you when you fetched her, I..."

He cut her off. "If you expect to stay with this family, you have to respect every member of this family."

Esther whipped her dustrag at the table, grumbling, "I'd go in a second if it wasn't for you. I would have gone with Peter if I hadn't..."

"Peter."

"He was pretty broken up about what happened to that girl."

Benton snapped, "We don't know what happened to that girl."

"We can guess."

"Esther, that's enough."

"Peter thinks..."

"Who knows what Peter thinks. Who knows what he's telling Edgar right now?"

"Nothing. The truth."

"He doesn't even know the truth," Benton cried, but Esther was dusting the little silver bust of his great-grandfather with such concentration that he began casting around for the right thing to say to get her to look at him. "Now I love Peter as much as you do, Esther," he wheedled, "but gone is gone and we can't lose Edgar too. He's the baby, he may even be the best and... oh please look at me. Listen, he's only eleven but he's got more talent than all of us put together and we have such great plans for him. Esther?" The maid stood at the sideboard with her back to him, relentlessly moving small objects around on the oiled surface, setting them down in a series of angry clicks.

Benton tried, "You understand, this is a very important time for us."

Nothing.

"The anniversary." When she still didn't speak and wouldn't turn and look at him he said, "This is all Peter's fault."

This got her, all right. Esther wheeled, brandishing the silver bust. "You watch what you say about Peter, you hear?"

"It's his fault for running away from home. It's his fault Edgar's gone."

"That isn't you talking, Mr. Benton," she said, shaming him. "That's Miz Ava. That isn't even you going up to Charleston to drag him back, it's somebody that looks like you, hung up on what that woman wants from you. Or you from her."

"But he's our *baby*."

She slammed the bust down so hard everything on the sideboard jumped. "Well he's my baby too."

"And he needs us. Especially you, he knows who loves him."

"If you really love those children, you'll let them stay in Charleston, where they're safe."

He choked. "I can't."

But Esther would not let up. "It's on you, Mr. Benedict."

"God knows I'm sorry."

"Then let those poor children be."

"I can't."

"Then it's on your soul."

Benton's face went through several changes as he cast around for a way to explain and ended by falling back on the inescapable. "It's part of the pattern," he said unhappily.

"You know you don't want it, Mr. Benedict."

"It doesn't matter what I want." He looked at her mournfully. "If you just wouldn't call me Mr. Benedict."

"I have to. It's part of the pattern," Esther said.

"Sometimes I hate the pattern."

"Then do something about it!"

Benton's voice was heavy with finality. "I can't."

Her silence was like a door slammed in his face.

"Essie?"

It filled the room.

When she didn't even rise to the old name, Benton Benedict addressed her correctly. "Esther? Ms. Manifort?"

She gave back nothing.

Because he couldn't stand her silence, he rose and moved this way, then that, trying to get her to look at him, but the black woman eluded him with easy grace, and because she wouldn't look at him but would not leave the room, either, he persisted.

"Oh Esther, please."

She busied herself dusting the table Ava's students had already wiped clean.

"Look," he said finally, because he'd say anything to keep her from shutting him out. "Edgar's just a child. He's too young to know what's good for him. I promise, he can go back to Charleston and visit Peter lots of times, but it will have to be after the..." he reconsidered what he was about to say. Instead he promised, "we'll let him go as soon as school's out. OK?"

She snorted.

"If you want to, you can even go with him."

The glare Esther turned on him made him ashamed.

Benton heard himself going on foolishly, "Don't you see, it's only the *timing* that's causing the problem. I mean, right now we have this... It's just... Listen," he said, "Ava just wants him here for the anniversary. It's important when we get to the piece."

"What piece?"

Standing there with the morning sunlight silvering his hair, Benton Benedict looked like the head of a great family, but his tone suggested otherwise. "Nothing," he said hurriedly. "I mean, nothing important." Damn the woman, she would not let him avoid her eyes. She was like an unwanted conscience, tracking him down.

She said, "If it's not important, how come you're chewing your mouth raw like that?"

"OK, OK. It's more than a reunion." Benton brightened because it sounded right. "We want all our children here."

"Peter too?"

"Oh, if only Peter would..." There were too many thoughts rushing in to sort them out. He was wistful and apprehensive all at once.

"Sure."

"If he'd only stay, everything would be perfect."

"Sure." Still pretending the students hadn't cleared breakfast properly, Esther made one more sweep of the table, giving Benedict that harsh, proud look he knew better than he knew himself. "Oh, sure it would."

"My brothers are coming," he said like a lawyer making an opening plea. "Bert from Paris and Beau all the way from Venice, and Bernard from the United Kingdom, you remember Bernard."

She managed not to say *I never liked Bernard.*

"Also Aunt Benta, from Hokkaido, with her son by Muio Kobyashi.

Everybody's coming this time, especially because it's Edgar's turn."

Was he saying what he believed or what he had been told to say?

"This is really Edgar's thing, you see. So naturally we want him home in time for the final preparations."

Esther drew herself up like a tribal princess. "Explain 'ready.'"

"His own little figure, ready to incorporate in the piece."

"The piece?"

"The hundredth anniversary, Esther. This is very important. Ava and I are launching a major piece." He thought carefully, laying out a formula she would accept. "All the Benedicts have been working, each of us in our own place on our own figure but it's all part of a whole. It's so big that we have to do our parts without knowing what the whole is going to look like until the end. We work along not knowing, but in the faith..."

"You're not sure, are you, Mr. Benedict?"

"Don't call me that."

Esther's voice softened. "Ben."

His eyes, so light they were almost transparent, blazed with hope. "Oh, but when it comes together..." He was so driven now, running along so fast trying to convince her, that his breath eluded him. When he could, he finished, "It will be magnificent. The greatest ever."

"Greater than that —thing out back?"

"Oh God, I hope so," he said. "But we have to be ready. Have to get the work ready, and my boy. Get new clothes for him, a haircut. Fresh tools. Everything you need before a big party. That's all it is, it's just a party." Benton said too eagerly, "It's fine. Really. But we need Eds."

Oh, she was so careful, asking, "What do you need him for?"

"I can't tell you. It's secret."

"What kind of secret?"

"Ava's."

"Ava's."

He amended. "It's a... It's a family secret."

"Your family," Esther said fiercely. "That God. Damned. Family," she said at last, making a long pause between each word. "Can you look me in the eye and promise me nothing bad is going to happen?"

"Of course nothing bad is... Oh *please* don't look at me that way, I don't want anything to... I..."

But Esther bore down on him. "It's about the family secret, isn't it? Come on, Benny, what family secret?"

Benton jumped at the sound of his old nickname. Esther hadn't used it in years. Distraught, he retreated into silence to look for the right words. When he came back out he said helplessly, "I'm sorry. There are some family secrets I don't know."

And out of the same silence, Esther came up with a different set of words altogether. She laid them out so deliberately that Benton would have no doubt that she meant precisely what she said. "If anything happens to that child, I am going to murder you."

"Esther!"

"Do you hear me?"

"I love him, Essie. You know I would never... Oh Essie, I thought we were still friends." He raised his voice in entreaty. "Oh Essie. Dearest."

She seemed to get even taller. "Everybody calls me Esther, Mr. Benedict."

There was a slight but palpable change in the air in the room. It was as if all breezes had stopped, letting all the dust of the past settle here, in the present. He said:

"You were Essie when we were both young."

When she lifted her head like that it was clear that Esther was still the same person, but her cold tone made it equally clear that everything else had changed. "That was before."

"We used to do play together," he said.

"We did more than that."

"We did."

Her face was still, beautiful. A flawless mask. "That was before."

"We were in love."

"You were too young to know any better. And me not that much older." She sighed.

He cried, "Essie, I loved you."

"Two dumb kids."

"You loved me."

"Now we're all grown up," she said.

His voice shook. "I still love you."

"Don't."

"We were going to run away."

"You thought so but I knew better," she said.

"We should have gone."

"Well, we didn't." Slipping into a stock character she had used against him before, she got the needle in. "Yo' family pattern."

It was his turn to say, "Don't."

"Your ancestors used to own my ancestors."

"I loved you, Essie. I did."

"Well, not enough."

"I did so *want* it," he cried.

"Well, you didn't manage it," Esther said with an ease that suggested she had come to terms with this long, long ago. She said lightly, "You know. Family expectations."

"God, I was so helpless." His voice was thick with regret. "Everything they piled on me. The legacy."

"This is the South, Benny. The studios are here."

"Damn the studios."

"I wish you meant that but you don't," she said. "You've only ever been a Benedict."

"We should have kept on running north and found somebody to marry us that night. We should have headed for New Hampshire, the Klondike, anything to get away from them."

"We never would have made it," she said. "No matter how early we started, or how far we went."

He dug his fingers into his hair and dragged them back, exposing the missing ear. "I wanted to die."

"I've let that one go by, Mr. Benedict, and I think you better had too."

"You deserve so much better."

"It's healthier."

"I don't know why you stayed with us."

There was another long, uncomfortable pause. When Esther finally spoke she drove the breath right out of him. "If I can't have your children, I can at least see they're taken care of," she said.

Benton groaned.

"That woman may serve the family ambitions, but she's not fit to take care of your children."

"Oh please."

"I know her, Mr. Benedict. I was going to leave here after that wedding, I had a scholarship to Morehouse, not bad for a black woman back then..."

"You never told me."

She said simply, "It wouldn't have made any difference."

"Oh God, I did love you."

She didn't choose to hear. Esther was like an engine rolling over a familiar track. "But I saw that redhead redneck woman moving in on you and I knew I had to stay to protect you, and when your folks got killed, I knew I had to stay for sure. Then when she started having your babies, bam bam bam, I saw how she did with them..."

"Did she ever..."

"Oh, she never hurt them, Mr. Benedict. She just ignored them to death." Esther turned to face him; they were almost of a height and anybody coming into the room at that moment could have seen immediately who was the stronger. "You know you can die of love. Like a plant nobody waters."

"You don't have to tell me that, Essie." He advanced with his arms wide and his whole heart in his face. "Oh Essie..."

She did not reproach him; she didn't strike out. She quite simply drew back. "Mr. Benedict, please."

"All right. I won't," he said, beaten. "Esther," he said.

Eight

Who was this Gara Sullivan, who chose petal pink walls for her living room and installed white shutters and chose white carpeting? Who was the woman who had strung a Land's End hammock instead of a living room sofa and put white Breuer chairs around her glass-and-chrome dining table, perfect, like a set design for a chic urban comedy with an upbeat ending that would send everybody home happy. What kind of woman would lavish so much love and attention on her apartment, spare no expense to get exactly what she wanted, and then walk away?

The next question stuck in Jude's throat like a bent pin.

Who in her right mind would walk away from Peter Benedict?

The photo on the side table by the door, the snapshots of the two of them tucked in the mirror above the dresser suggested that at the beginning, at least, Gara had really been in love. Not his fault she cared more about her career than she did this beautiful man. And if Gara Sullivan really was gone for good, and Peter really was over it; if he was finished with her, why did he keep this perfect apartment, like a shrine?

What happened to her anyway?

There were no clues, only intimations. On Gara's shelves, the renderings she'd done for Dock Street Theater productions were sidelined to make space for new works in clay. Abandoned stage sets in miniature collected cobwebs on the bottom shelf. There was a design marked *Six Characters in Search of an Author*—a stark cyclorama with elongated, skeletal trees rising around a graveyard and at the center, a well; she'd made a beautiful Catfish Row for a production of *Porgy and Bess,* but at some point Gara Sullivan's interests changed. The last stage set was unfinished. For whatever reasons, she'd moved on to model a grotto with a blue gel set in the top so the whole thing glowed with an uncanny light. In its belly stood a disturbing miniature: arms, legs entwined bodies rising up in a sculptural explosion that replicated *God and His Creation,* Beauchamp Benedict's final masterpiece; it was beautiful, accurate and unnerving, as though a powerful force had overtaken the maker's soul.

The drafting table was covered with Gara's last efforts—pencil sketches for portrait busts, bas reliefs, monuments, with notes scrawled across them in a bold new hand: cursive capitals in ink. NEEDS WORK, OR: LET'S CAST THIS ONE.

So Gara wanted to be a sculptor. Did she come to Charleston and romance Peter just to get to the Benedicts? What if she didn't love Peter, what if she seduced him to unlock the gates to his parents' studios?

All her life Jude Atkins had been cursed by a logical self that never accepted a story at face value. Like a terrier flushing rats out of a barn, she followed with questions. She couldn't stop herself. Tracing somebody's story, trying to make it make sense, she had too often—right, with Phil!—discovered to their mutual humiliation that she'd caught that person in a lie. But Peter wasn't lying, she was sure of it. She just wasn't sure he knew what was really going on.

In the enchanted second before Edgar burst in and interrupted, Peter almost told her what happened to Gara—she thought. She didn't know, any more than she knew whether beautiful Gara loved Peter as much as he loved her.

He'd kept this apartment—not a shrine, exactly, but with everything as Gara left it. The magazines were current and fresh flowers stood in a vase on the windowsill. Gara's coats still hung in the hall closet. Jude half-expected to go in the kitchen and find pots bubbling as if she had just stepped out, or wander into the bedroom and see the imprint of Gara's head, a long black hair on the pillow signifying that the absence was temporary, she'd be right back. What would she do if she found Jude here?

Peter said he was over her, but Jude wasn't so sure. It was as if he thought keeping everything just as Gara had it would bring her back.

Maybe it would. Who runs away without taking her clothes, or at least tucking in her jewelry (the diamond he gave her—the thought made Jude's breath catch in her chest); who leaves forever without posting a forwarding address, or sending for her things?

There was a bigger question. How could Gara walk out at the exact moment when she got everything she wanted? That gorgeous man, a place among the Benedicts, a bench in their world-famous studios. If she worked with the Benedicts, if she married one and her work went out marked with the Benedict chop, it would fetch thousands. Her pieces would find their way into galleries and museums. It would make her famous. Who would walk out on that?

There were gaps in the sequence, disturbing missing links.

Alone in the pretty apartment, Jude prowled uneasily, half expecting to discover a farewell note that had been overlooked or to find the answers scribbled in the back of Gara's week-at-a-glance calendar, or locked in her diary, but there was nothing.

She was uncomfortable, just being here.

It was nice of Peter to give her the place; it had seemed like a good idea at the time. He and Edgar were tugging back and forth over whether Edgar could stay in Charleston. Embarrassed, she wanted to leave them alone to duke it out.

"I have to go."

"Don't," Peter said. "Wait."

"Just let me crash in the studio," Edgar begged. "I won't take up much room."

Peter turned back to his little brother. "What about school?"

"I don't need to go to school, OK? I brought my toothbrush. I'll even floss."

"You have to go to school," Peter said. "It's part of the deal."

Edgar pounced. "Does that mean I can stay?"

"What's Dad going to think?"

Feisty Edgar: "What do you care what Dad thinks?"

"I'd like not to care." Peter considered. He seemed to be looking at something they could not see. He sighed. "But I do."

"I can sleep in your back bedroom?"

"Maybe you ought to ask Jude here."

Startled, Jude said, "Me?"

"You're important here too."

Oh-Peter-this-is-so-sudden: no crazier than her coming down here on impulse, but too much, too soon. Jude said quickly, "I can't stay here."

"Come on, Pete." Edgar said, wheedling. "We can sleep on the sofas."

"Not on my watch you don't." Peter took Jude's hands. "You need a real place to stay."

Grimacing, Jude freed herself. It seemed important to remind him where they were right now. "If I stay."

He amended. "If."

Peter's eyes were so bright that she had to look away. Jude spoke cautiously, like a doctor. "That's what I'm here to find out." *Whether I want this.* "I need some time."

"Oh come on, Peter, please?" The kid grabbed his big brother's arms, hanging like a little weight. "Pe-terrr..."

She saw Peter was mulling it—whether he could rearrange things to make a place for the kid, whether he could take good care of him—whether it was the right thing to do or all wrong, and all the time Edgar was swinging, working on him.

"You said you'd help if I ever needed it, Pete, you know you did. You know, when you ran out on us?"

"I didn't run out, Eds, I had to save myself."

"But what about me?"

"I'm a grownup. You..." He shook his head. "I'm not so sure."

"Shit, Peter!"

"Ava would freak if she heard you say shit." This was serious, whatever was going on between them; there was no place in their negotiations for Jude in spite of Peter's hasty assumption that they were together here.

She cleared her throat with a furry little sound. "How about I come back later?"

Which is when Peter gave her Gara's key. "What's this?"

"You might as well use her apartment." He grinned. "I can't have you staying in a hotel. Hang on and I'll show you the way. Really. It isn't far."

Jude could see that he wanted to put Edgar's problems aside for a while. Maybe he wanted a minute or two alone with her—she could use it, but Edgar was bobbing up and down at the end of his brother's arm like a bobble head toy, baring his teeth in an urgent scowl. The little boy was so desperate that she had to say no thanks Peter, you have this to do. Just when she most wanted to be alone with him, Jude had to smile and shake her head, saying, "I'll find it, thanks."

Edgar's grin was worth it all. She hardly knew the kid, but they were bonded. They exchanged looks: Friends for life, right? Right. Friends for life.

At the door Peter said, "You sure you can find it? Are you sure you don't want me to come?"

"No. Really. I'll be fine. See you at supper." She grinned at the boy. "You too, Eds."

Edgar gave her the thumbs-up sign.

"OK, Eds," Peter was saying as she left. There was an edge of fatigue to his voice. "I'll see what I can do."

Good. She'd come down to Charleston to meet a man she thought was as free as she was, but no matter. Sure Edgar was going to be in the way, but she couldn't help pulling for the poor little kid. If she and Peter had to go out somewhere to be together, fine.

She hugged them both and went back to the hotel to put her things into the rented car. She left her stuff in the car outside the U-shaped stucco building where Gara used to live. In the courtyard, a Venus spouted water into a mossy halfshell. The apartment was daunting. Perfect. Spotless. Redolent of her.

Now that she'd looked around, she was reluctant to move in. Unlike the hotel room, this place was so clearly Gara's that Jude had no right being here. Instead of going back to the car for her things, she kept opening doors cautiously, shrinking in automatic apology when she bumped into anything, lifting ornaments and putting them back just *so,* as if she expected the true proprietor to come in at any moment and demand an explanation.

Atkins, this is stupid. I know, I know, but. Ah. *But.*

There were Gara's things: the glass ornaments on the window ledges, the Lucite-framed snapshots of her and Peter in the early days, before she slouched off to one of the Benedict studios and lost herself in the family art. She had Snow White's coloring—dark hair, fair skin, eyes that looked violet; photographed in front of Wayward, she fitted against Peter like part of the same sculptural piece. She had a beautiful body—statuesque, wildly graceful. Yeah, right, Jude thought sadly. And he tells me he's all over her. How likely is that? What on earth does he want with ordinary me? Even graced with golden stars and planets, Jude was just an ordinary, nice-looking person. Compared to Gara, she was nothing. Oh, Jude.

Depressed, she went back to the car. When she unlocked her car, she stopped, fixed on the arrangement she had left: two cartons, duffel bag on top. It looked the same. She checked; her key was still in the door on the driver's side and the lock on the passenger's side was undisturbed. The windows were as she'd left them, closed tight. Then why was her scalp itching and why did she have such a hard time flipping the driver's seat forward so she could reach into the back to collect her things?

Nothing had been touched so far as she could see, and nothing had changed. Except for the fact that air in the car was heavy with perfume.

Somebody was here.

She had to shower and change into her best blue string sweater before she felt strong enough to think about it. She was nowhere near ready to deal with the question of who—or what—had been rummaging in her car. It took half a pot of Gara's black tea over ice to get her back into the car. She got herself moving by thinking ahead to dinner in some waterfront restaurant, lobster or blue crab, maybe champagne, with a sip for Edgar. The incursion left her too jittery and disrupted to think past dinner, or imagine what she and Peter might have to say to each other after Edgar went to bed.

At this point it seemed better to think about the child.

Having Edgar in Peter's apartment would complicate things, but it would keep her from going too fast or assuming too much, the way she had with Phil. It would definitely keep her from doing anything dumb. She liked the thorny little kid and besides, she told herself, you can learn a lot about a new man by seeing him with his family.

She stopped at a K-Mart and bought a plastic do-it-yourself monster model for the kid, a flying dragon of the menacing gryphon type with a wing span from here to *here*. If Edgar couldn't put it together by himself, she would help. Although he'd have to start school Monday at the latest, she'd convince Peter to give him tomorrow off so he could sleep in. Running away, telling his family and making it stick must have been hard on him. He deserved a little fun. Tomorrow she and Edgar could stay up all night if he wanted, gluing sequin scales on the creature's back.

"What a beautiful blue," Peter said. He was in jeans tonight; his shirt picked up the green flecks in his eyes; he was bigger than she remembered and fresh from the shower. "You look wonderful."

"So do you."

He gave her a hug. "Come on in."

"I brought Edgar a present."

He coughed and let her go. "I'll see that he gets it."

"You mean he isn't here?"

He wouldn't meet her eyes. He said, "They just left."

"Oh, Peter, what *happened?*"

He didn't answer, exactly. "Dad, I could have handled. With Dad, I could have worked it out. At least I could have told him no and made it stick, but at the last minute something changed..."

"Are you OK?"

He nodded. "What happened was..."

She could see he was not OK. "Are you sure?"

"No I'm not sure. You're never sure with Ava."

"Your mother."

"Edgar's too. That's the whole problem. She knows how to squeeze you out and crumple you up like a tube of paint." Peter looked shaky and exhausted. What had Ava said to him, to flatten him? What had she done? The life drained out of Peter's voice but he was determined to finish, laying it out step by step. "What happened was, after you left my dad called. With Ava, I would have lied, but this was dad and he was so worried that I had to tell him it was OK, Eds was here with me. Ten minutes later he called back. He had orders to come up here and get him, did I mind. I thought, OK, him, I can deal with, so I told him to come ahead. I should have lied, I should have hidden Edgar, I should have..."

"Peter, don't."

"I thought all I had to do was get him here." He looked up. "See, I can talk

Dad out of anything. I knew I could get him to say I could keep Edgar until summer, and if we managed that, I could make them let him come back here to school in the fall." Then he said inexplicably, "There's no reason for Eds to have to go through what I went through."

Her head lifted. "Peter?"

But he wasn't ready for questions; it was all he could manage just to go on. "It's crazy, now that I've left the family for good, I get, ah—homesick for him? Dad was part of the problem but he was never the real problem. So now that we were into it I was kind of, looking forward to seeing him?"

"Oh, Peter." She put a hand on his arm.

He gave her a grateful look. "So instead of taking off with Eds or at least hiding him, I stayed put. We both stayed. Waiting for it. Like two sitting ducks." He went on unhappily. "We waited all afternoon."

"Before *who* got here?"

He let it all out in a long sigh. "It wasn't Dad at all. The mother came."

"And she dragged him away."

"Not exactly." Peter didn't explain; he just went on. "So it was my fault, really. Dad, I could show reason. But Ava gets what Ava wants. No. She knows how to get what she wants and make you think you want it too."

The light changed. Outside, the sun had dropped out of sight.

"By the time she finished with us... Ava has this, this... I don't know how to explain it; she can make you believe anything."

"And she made you give him up?"

Agonized, Peter shouted, "What makes you think I'd ever give him up?"

"Don't look at me that way Peter, he's gone."

"Yuh. They just left." He choked it out, one word at a time. "He. God. Damn. Decided to go back."

"Poor kid!"

"I know."

"But he said he'd rather die."

"You don't understand. By the time Ava finished with him, he was dying to go."

"That's crazy!"

"She's his mother," he said miserably, "He's only a little kid."

"You should have stopped him. You should have stopped her."

At great cost Peter admitted, "She's my mother too."

"Listen." Jude was rummaging for something—anything—she could say to make him feel better, "It isn't forever."

"What Ava wants, Ava keeps," Peter said.

"Oh Peter, don't look like that. Maybe we can catch them." Foolishly, Jude rushed on in an attempt to make everything all right, "Break some speed limits and cut them off."

"We can't."

"Why not? My car's outside. Let's go!"

"There's nothing we can do."

"Peter, we have to try."

The next thing he said astonished her. "It isn't safe."

"She can't be that bad."

"I haven't told you everything. She brought Thorne."

"Thorne! Who the hell is Thorne?"

"Believe me," he said heavily, "you don't want to know."

Nine

"Now Keesha, I am going to lift the mask." Where his sons had cast the faces of a pair of yobs from the local pub to send along with him, Bernard Benedict was working with a beautiful Jamaican art student whom he had met in the British Museum. Whom he had fallen in love with, and whom he was telling the old story while she lay quietly waiting for the plaster to dry. "What the books don't tell you and the family does not much mention is that after he finished his master work, our great-grandfather went mad."

Absorbed as he was, ruddy, rotund Bernard with the pudgy arms and the soft baker's hands lifted the plaster so gently that his subject blinked like Sleeping Beauty waked by the prince. "It was a disturbing business," he said. "But great art is disturbing. This is what makes it great."

Pulling the straws out of her nostrils and wiping her face on the cloth Bernard had draped over her like a careful dentist, Keesha said, "I'm glad that's over."

His voice changed. "It's only the beginning. If they're pleased with your likeness, you'll be a part of the Benedict grouping, *The Miracle of Creation.* How could they not like you? You have a brilliant head." When he showed her the mask she hardly looked at it; she knew he was right. "I did warn you—it's the Carolinas. Things are better than they used to be, but blacks don't always have an easy time."

"It couldn't be any worse than Brixton," she said.

"I know you can handle it." His mind was running ahead to Wayward; he was looking forward to seeing his Aunt Benta, to finding out exactly what was going on at Wayward, and, all right, to learning how to put the family secret to his own uses, but that beautiful, greedy, clever woman his brother married both drew and frightened him. She could tear your throat out with her bare teeth and hand it to you and make you thank her as you bled to death. Bernard was glad he was going home protected by this strong, glorious woman who loved him... at least he thought she did. "You can handle anything."

Keesha nodded. "And afterward I can study at the Chicago Art Institute."

"Unless you want to study with the American Benedicts," he said. "Some great artists have come out of the studios at Wayward." Bernard fell silent until he was certain he had her full attention and began carefully. "If you're willing to do what's expected." Frowning, he finished, "Whatever that is."

The woman laughed and threw back her head, proud as a tribal queen. "You get me invited and we'll see."

"I have to have you," he said. "You and nobody else."

Her smile made him smile.

She's tough, he thought. That's good. But when he spoke again he addressed something completely different. "I hope you don't mind flying at night. Ava wants us there tomorrow."

"His wife?"

"I'm afraid she makes all the decisions now," Bernard said.

"Hold still." With strong hands, she pushed her model back into the chair. "Jake, I need you to hold still."

He loved her, he was afraid of her, he wanted to bolt because he was terrified.

"Quiet, and I mean it. *Hold still.*"

He would stay in place because he loved her. He wouldn't bolt because he wanted her love. Besides, she'd strapped him into the chair.

"If you'd shaved properly this wouldn't be such a mess."

He submitted because she'd made him a promise he could not reject.

"Stop that. Listen. I'm only going to do this once." Irritated, she did not mention the fact that as she slapped the plaster on she could see the hair at Jake's temples protruding in a ring around his bathing cap; no matter how gently she pulled it off it would make him scream. She covered it with plaster anyway.

"You told me you were going to use Jimmy Daley."

She snapped, "Well, Jimmy Daley's gone!"

"He was my friend. Where did he go?"

"I'm the wrong person to ask, now hold still."

But the question nagged; he had to ask, "What do you suppose happened?"

"Wherever he is, I'm sure he's fine."

Plaster obscured everything. *I can't see.* "Please Ava, I get scared in tight places."

"Shut up, I'm going to cover your mouth."

I'm scared of the dark.

"Be quiet and let's get this over with."

When you talk like that I'm afraid you don't like me.

The student's voice went on and on somewhere deep in his throat.

This stuff is getting in my nose.

"What do I have to do to get you hold still?"

I can hardly breathe.

"Be still and afterward..."

She touched him *there.*

"We'll have some good times."

One big hand came out from under the dropcloth and reached for hers. *Don't leave me alone.*

"Go-ood times." Absently, she withdrew her hand, noting that the stunted little finger on her right hand matched his. "If we don't have them now, we'll have them soon."

He tried to hold the tail of her smock. *This is awful. Don't leave me alone in here like this.*

She let his hand graze her flank, rubbed against his palm, and then stepped away. "Be good and I'll tell you a story," she said.

When Ava went on it was in a different tone, feline and seductive. "I told you then and I'm telling you again now, we need a head like yours to create the proper balance in this piece. Poor Benton and my boys and his weakling brothers all hit the high spots when they're going for models, and we have to counteract their sentimentality. You understand, Jake—all that prettiness, when what this arrangement needs is strength."

Hot.

"Strength."

Hot in here.

"The kind of strength old Beauchamp had."

Jake's hands contracted on the arms of the old dentist's chair. *Burning hot.*

Her voice rose. "That I have."

Burning to death. He threw his weight against the restraining straps. *Oh my God, the heat!*

"Stop that! Don't you know art demands sacrifice?"

Under the dropcloth she had thrown over the craggy student before she applied the plaster, Jake writhed in a transport of pain and fear. Irritated, Ava lifted a log from the fireplace and slapped it across his arms so hard all his breath boiled out through the one clear nostril, making a small explosion in his head. "Now listen. I am not about to take this off before it's time just because you're a weakling, and you think you can't take the heat. So if you have to grab something, grab this. Five more minutes," she said, glancing at her watch. "Can you hold still for five minutes or am I going to have to give you a shot?"

Instead of going on with the traditional recital, Ava paced the studio, looking at her watch. Compared to the living subject in the chair the shrouded clay busts and full figures built on carefully constructed armatures were pleasingly silent. Instead of attending to Jake, she lifted the cloths off first one and then another, touching them as if communing with old friends.

Jake stopped thudding his heels against the foot rests and fell silent.

Then as her tiny wristwatch alarm sounded Ava stepped over to the chair and, putting her nails under the mask where it joined the jaw, she tugged.

There was a moment of complete silence as she tugged and the vacuum held.

She tugged again. It refused to lift.

She threw her whole weight back. "I said, com*e off!*"

Then with a terrible sucking sound, the plaster separated from his face.

Jake shrieked.

"Oh hush. Not bad," Ava said, studying the mask. She kept her back to him, holding the thing up to the light. "The hair gives it a certain verisimilitude."

Behind her, Jake was sobbing. The hands that had been so anxious to go wandering were completely neutralized; in his pain, the student had forgotten about anything he and his mentor might be going to do together once she had removed the mask. He had forgotten about everything except the sudden shock of hair yanked out in patches of scalp and in places skin torn off the bloody tallow that ran just below the surface of his face.

"Oh," Benton Benedict sobbed. He was alone in his studio, for now. Because Ava was otherwise occupied, he was alone to put his head in his arms and weep. "Oh," he cried, considering the implications. "Oh my poor darlings. Oh!"

Ten

You stupid dumbhead wuss, Edgar thought, waking up in his own room in spite the vows he made when he sneaked out of school and hitchhiked to Charleston yesterday, and in spite of what he told Peter: that he'd rather die than go back. Edgar the wuss. Didn't he sit in Ava's lap in the car all the way to Wayward last night, he snuggled in like a baby even though he was too big and his legs hung down.

Ava held him tight and laughed.

He could feel her power. Ava's energy drove the family. Last night she turned like a lighthouse and beamed all of it straight at him. It was like being wrapped in deep velvet, riding home through the night in Ava's arms. They sat in the back of the darkened car with Thorne up front behind the wheel, planted like a basalt obelisk, driving without moving a hair. Mommy was so sweet last night! Ava cuddled him just like a baby and he was glad. She never much liked the brothers, even Peter, Edgar knew. When he was two she buried her face in his fat baby neck, confiding, "I had them too young."

He ran away and vowed never to come back but riding along like that with Ava crooning with her chin resting in his hair, Edgar felt the love. He did! He quit struggling and lay back.

"My darling baby," she said into the soft darkness, and when he yelped, "Baby!" she ignored him and went on: "Just think. You're almost twelve." Her voice was, he didn't know, *thrilling*. When Ava talked to you like that, you did whatever she said. "Twelve."

The way she said it was creepy. "I don't know if I want to be twelve."

"Yes you do. We'll have a celebration! Everybody's coming," she said.

"I don't want everybody to come." It's what made him run away in the first place. The birthday. That she wouldn't tell him what she had planned. "I don't know if I want..."

"Sh-shh." Ava hugged and rocked him like a real mother. "It's extra special, because you were born on the anniversary. Think of it, Edgar. The anniversary!

It's going to be wonderful."

"If it's so wonderful...." he struggled to sit up. "Why won't you tell me what it is?"

"But sweetie." Ava rocked and purred, lulling him. "That would ruin the surprise."

Even with her arms around him, he was scared. "What if I don't want it?"

For once she didn't make him say: Ava. She trilled, "You're going to love it. Just you wait and see."

The family welcomed him home like the fatted calf. Dad was weird but Ava gave him one of those looks and he just got smaller and let it all happen in spite of the fact that it creeped him out. They had a great big dinner waiting for Edgar with a welcome-home cake, Essie's fried chicken, his favorite; big old Jake made the salad and Ava's students Bill and Nelly and burly Jacaranda had made a sweet potato casserole with marshmallows to go with. He liked Peter better, but his big brothers Dirk and Luke made a fuss. His taciturn old brothers patted his head like friendly uncles. "Home safe, I see," Dirk said, and Luke thumped him on the shoulder, growling, "Good man." For once Ava let all the students sit down at the table with them instead of treating them like slaves so it was like a party, and after dinner she made a little speech about reunions, and how this was only the beginning. She said everybody would be coming in to Wayward very soon to complete the group piece for the ceremony.

Ceremony. The word sat in Edgar's stomach like lead.

Even this morning, lying in bed with the sunlight crashing in on him, the thought of it turned him cold.

Even in broad daylight the empty house was creepy too.

Outside he heard a rumble—no, he felt the vibration of heavy equipment rolling out. Elsewhere on the grounds an empty semi would be pulling away from the foundry shed where Thorne alone did the unloading and nobody but his parents was allowed. All month there had been extra deliveries: bronze, plaster for the molds, firing materials, wax in such quantities that Ava had brought in a crew last fall to air condition the storage shed. The family was working on a huge special project that they wouldn't talk about even when he asked. Benedicts from all over the world were coming to put it together and when Edgar tried to find out what was going on, even Dirk and Luke, who were usually nice to him, growled that it was none of his business. Yet. And he should go away. Then if he complained they said wait until his birthday, he would be plenty glad he had.

It made him sick to his stomach. Either that or he'd OD'd on welcome-home cake. Sitting up made him scared. He wished Essie would come the way she did when he was sick; she always seemed to know.

"Essie?"

Nobody answered.

He lay there and thought. Then he tried, "Dad?"

By now his father was probably in his studio. On a good day Edgar would be out there with him, working on his statue of Fuzzy, but for what seemed like forever now, he hadn't been allowed.

Like a baby he said weakly, "Mom?"

It was so bright in the room and so quiet out that Edgar couldn't tell what time it was. Late, he thought, too late to go to school. Somebody had turned off his clock radio alarm and let him sleep, so fine. The trouble was, he was having a hard time waking altogether up. The usual things in the house that he usually told time by had gone by: breakfast cleanup, people tramping out to the studios. It was too late for Essie to be vacuuming, which she did like an exterminator beating the brush for rats, and, he supposed too early for people to be coming back up from their studios for lunch.

His belly hurt. Hopelessly, he called, "Is anybody home?"

He had the feeling he ought to be somewhere doing something, but he didn't know what.

"If you won't come in, I'm coming out to get you," he said. "Come on, guys, I'm warning you." He was having a hard time getting out of bed.

His mouth was still sticky from Essie's cake and there was a humongous piece of it on a plate next to the bed. He was wearing the present his father had made for him, Dad began it while he was teaching Edgar to model Fuzzy, his first major piece in clay, and he'd put the finished work on Edgar's wrist after dinner last night: "I was saving it for your birthday, but. Well." It was a circle of silver tigers running head to tail, head to tail, animal lines so fluid that there was no telling whether they were racing or trying to eat each other up...

"What was that!"

He thought he heard a noise from somewhere deep in the empty house. His voice quavered. "If you're out there, who's out there?

Paddling like a kindergartner at his first swimming lesson, Edgar managed to slip out of bed. He pulled his jeans on over his nightshirt and stood in the door to his room for a long time, listening. He was certain there was *something* stirring, but it wasn't in the hall and it wasn't in any of the bedrooms and it wasn't in the attic, either; he could tell. Cautiously, he started downstairs. "OK, I'm coming to get you," he said.

Coming into the dining room he jumped. Pale, marbled eyes seemed to follow him, moving under a fierce brow even as the set of the jaw signaled that the owner would brook no opposition.

"Yow!" It was only that portrait over the mantel. Even in a picture, his great-great-grandfather had tremendous power. It was like an extra person in the room. Carefully, he backed away. "Oh," he said. "It's you."

Usually Essie was in the kitchen, but there was nobody around. There was a pan of corn bread on the table and he cut himself a piece and slathered it with jam and took a big bite and started chewing before he realized he wasn't hungry. He was beyond lonely.

He felt strange being home—guilty? Whatever. Kind of soiled.

Creepy: what he thought he heard. It was not speech and it wasn't sound, at least no sound he could identify, but he could not shake the idea that he'd heard *something*. Nearby. "Essie, is that you?"

Nobody answered.

"Essie?" He drifted from ground floor kitchen to pantry and upstairs to the dining room to the living room to the sitting room to the library to the music room to the conservatory, looking for the source, and between spasms of holding his breath he called, "Essie?" There was nobody on the first floor.

There was nobody upstairs, either. "Anybody?"

Yet he could not shake the idea that there was something in the house.

He could feel it.

"Come *on*." Prowling, the boy fetched up as he always did at the locked door under the back stairs to the cellar. From the time he first tried it, it had been locked. Bolted from the inside, he thought, even as the outside cellar door under the oleanders was firmly bolted from the inside. When he was little and Peter was still in school, before Luke and Dirk got too old to talk to, they made up stories. Peter said there was a colony of gnomes living under the house, fanning out in tunnels that led all the way to Oz. Luke said the cellar was filled with family gold, but crusty Dirk said no no, the place was filled to the ceiling with the bones of Benedict slaves. Dirk and Luke were so much older than him and Peter that whatever they said, you had to believe. Either way it was awful and it seemed safer to believe Ava, who told them there was nothing down there but trash left over from the old days, it was only a filthy old basement just like any other, that was all.

Then what was that he heard below, or felt moving? Ava forbade them to go down. She said she didn't want her boys getting hurt on all that abandoned junk, they could get tetanus or worse; she said there was nothing down there but rats and scorpions, and if one of them bit you, it would make you very, very sick, but Edger knew Ava often said things you couldn't believe.

He was certain now that the sound, or *sense* of sound that filled his heads and weirded him out beyond weirding originated somewhere deep in the belly of the house. And that it was human.

Trembling, he pressed his mouth to the locked door. "Are you all right?"

He whispered, "I know you're in there, say something." His breath caught in his throat. "Oh, please."

Whatever it was, it stopped.

No matter how hard he pressed his ear to the door or how carefully he listened or for how long, he heard nothing.

Edgar lingered for as long as he could bear the silence and then he went outside, heading for the studios. If he didn't talk to somebody soon, he would just plain go up the wall and across the ceiling and when he came down he would be nuts. They'd find him in pieces, hanging from the chandelier.

Oh, don't mind him, that's just Edgar, he's the crazy one.

Outside, the rest of last night's ride home with Ava came back on him, unwanted. Before he settled in her arms, they fought. Ava shook him hard. "Shut up. Be quiet. Remember, it's your birthday."

Furious, Edgar said the unspeakable. "God, Mom, what are you going to cut off of me?"

His mother snarled, "Stop it! This is important."

He'd thought, but did not say, *That's what I'm afraid of.* "I don't care," he said mulishly.

Ava bared teeth strong enough to rip him apart. "You don't understand. Everybody's coming. And you are the center."

"But, Mom!"

"Just think, Eddy. A hundred years."

"But *Mom.*"

"Be quiet. Remember. You belong to a great tradition."

This is what Ava laid on all her sons: "You belong to a great tradition." Edgar had it by heart before he could talk.

Struggling, he sobbed, "That's all you care about!"

"I care about you," she said. "You are my baby."

And like *that,* he stopped fighting her because it was true. When he was still in his crib Ava used to come in and tell him bedtime stories, using him like a confessional. And so last night they slipped into the old pattern, gliding along through low fog like tangled cotton with Thorne at the wheel. Ava talked on while Edgar sat with his head on her shoulder, listening to the sound the words made deep in her chest. "When I married your father the whole Benedict family was going downhill, along with their work. The family's reputation was in shreds. Listen to me, Edgar, and listen hard. I and I alone brought the sculpture back from nowhere and put the Benedicts back on the map. Now the world knows we are great artists and so when I ask you to do something, you do it without question." She lifted her head with that proud, glad look, his mother Ava, gorgeous and terrible. "Me. Everything we have is thanks to me. Your father has a lot to be grateful for."

She looked so joyful that Edgar had to ask, "Then why is he always so sad?"

"I and I alone brought back the power." Then she went on in surprisingly sweet tones. "And, dear. You are next in line."

"But, Mom, why do I have to..."

Ava threw her cashmere shawl around him like a butterfly closing something precious in its wings and said in that powerful way she had, that brooked no protest, "Because you are the youngest and the best. Now stop asking questions."

Somebody has to, he thought angrily, but that was last night.

Disturbed, he tramped along, thinking. If he couldn't talk to somebody soon, he would freak out and die.

He was heading for the family studios. With this big anniversary coming, Ava drove Dad and the brothers and all her students around the clock. Since January she'd harangued them at dinner, roused them at dawn and ordered them into the studios. She had her students so intimidated they wouldn't talk to anybody even after work, so Edgar passed them by. With any luck, he could scare up a conversation with Dirk or Luke.

He banged on Dirk's locked door. When Ava started with the anniversary, Edgar's oldest brother got deep into some great big secret piece; there was no dealing with him. Dirk, who looked the most like Ava and spent his waking hours trying to please her, worked through the night. Dirk would be in there right now, working on his big new piece. He always smoothed the wax with his right hand, leaving a mark that transferred, whole, to all his bronzes. His touch was made distinctive by the loss of the little finger on his right hand. If you spoke to Dirk when he was in one of these work fits, it was an intrusion. If you even tried, Hello, he whirled and stalked away. Right now, he refused to answer.

But Edgar was so lonely that he cried, "Come on, Dirk. I know you're in there. For Pete's sake, talk to me?"

If Dirk was inside working, he was so deep into it that he didn't even yell *Go away*. "All right for you," Edgar grumbled.

Next he went to Luke's studio and banged and banged. When he refused to take Go Away for an answer, his next oldest brother came limping to the door—something about a toe that had never quite healed, Edgar didn't know but it was weird. Behind him Edgar saw a lifesized figure in wax taking shape over the armature Luke had built for it—the figure looked like, what, a mermaid. Beautiful.

Resting his weight on his good foot, Luke leaned out. "Beat it, I'm working."

"Hey," Edgar said, "Can I come in?"

"Sorry, bro, I have to do this."

"I won't bother you."

His brother's face widened in a grin. "Not today, kid. I'm on deadline."

Edgar was trying to tell Luke he was scared lonesome, but all he could manage was, "I'm bored."

Luke leaned farther out, holding the door so he couldn't see in. "I told you, not today."

Edgar whined, "I thought you were glad I came home."

Luke reached out to tousle his hair. "I am glad, buddy. I'm glad as hell."

Edgar dodged under his arm. "Then let me in."

Luke's face went red underneath the beard. "I can't, I have a sitter," he said.

And emerging from the bathroom was a woman draped in a towel—not the first girlfriend his brother brought in after his wife got lost or whatever; Edgar thought he knew her—one of the daughters of the Cambodian family that moved into town last year. Shrinking, she avoided his eyes; there was clay streaking her arms, so—what?

Luke gave him a push and right before he closed the door he growled, "Don't tell Ava."

"All right for you, if that's all you care about," Edgar said angrily. "And all right for her too, OK?"

He slouched through the trees to Ava's studio even though he already knew she would not be charming and cuddly the way she was last night. She was only nice when she wanted something. If he knocked she'd shriek at him for interrupting. Nobody crossed Ava. Everybody knew she was the power here. When she turned against you all the sweetness inside her went out like a light. "All right for you too," he whispered to Ava's shuttered studio.

He went on through the woods to his father's place.

The Benedicts all worked in neat little cottages under the stretch of liveoaks between the kitchen wing and the foundry, while their students were clustered in unfinished shacks buried deeper in the woods: Jake and Bill, Petra and Nelly and Jacaranda, and up until he ran away or got lost or whatever, that nice guy Jimmy Daley, who had been Edgar's favorite. He used to tell Edgar stories and carry him around on his back. The student apprentices were Ava's idea. She and Dad had taken in students like laundry for years. In addition to bringing a dowry of $30,000 each, which would buy you a lot of bronze, they did chores. In exchange they got to study portrait sculpture with the renowned Benedicts. Students were a little like furniture, or heavy moving equipment—when Ava let them in the house they didn't talk much, just stood around in corners, filling up the rooms.

The rest of the time, they did her bidding. It was funny; they were all huge. Men and women, they were uniformly tall and heavyset, strong from hacking away at marble or moving stone. This was their big chance to learn how to work in bronze—the lost wax process, the books said, not too many people in the world knew how to do that, and do it right, and the acknowledged masters were the Benedicts. So what if the students spent half their time moving waxes onto the ramp outside the foundry and rolling bronzes away because Ava said they weren't ready to learn the fine points of casting yet? She said it was enough for them to work with latex and plaster molds and when she was good and ready she would let them pour bronze miniatures in the makeshift casting studio she had made for them in an abandoned shack. Her big, klunky student Jake was still working in clay even though the other three had graduated to wax. It was weird. They worked and worked, but they didn't seem to learn much. So far even the ones working in wax hadn't had miniature number one cast in spite of all Ava's promises.

In one awful fight Dad accused Ava of choosing students not for their talent or promise but for muscle. She gave him a look that would strip paint and said, "We don't need muscle here, Benton, we have Thorne."

Eavesdropping, Edgar thought: Right. If Ava's students were huge, Thorne was beyond humongous. Even now that he was almost twelve Edgar avoided big, silent old Thorne, who had been on the place ever since Ava married Dad. At any minute Thorne could fall on you like a giant redwood and smash you flat.

He hurried the last few yards to Benton Benedict's studio. For the master of the place, he'd ended up in the least attractive spot, but Edgar liked it because it was nice and far from the house. When he wasn't in school, he was supposed to be Dad's student apprentice. Last month he built an armature for a bear cub out of this and that—wood, wire, twigs. He and Dad were about to make the coating so he could begin with the wax. Edgar spent so long on the sketches that it took life and so he named it. Fuzzy. His hands were hungry for the work—anything to pull him out of the *weird*.

"Dad?" Edgar tapped. "Dad, can I come in and work?"

He heard muttering inside. He knocked again and Dad came. "Oh, honey, not until after your birthday, remember?"

Edgar scowled. "I thought you were *glad* I came home."

Dad did not say yes, he was. Instead his eyes got all watery and strange.

"Oh honey, it's just—we have all this work to do."

"But I wanted..." Edgar began, but he could not go on. He was so embarrassed; his chin started quivering—he was practically crying, so accidentally he told the truth. "I am just so *lonesome,*" he said.

A still voice quieted both of them. "Mr. Benedict, let the child in."

And Benton did. In the corner of the studio, covered with muslin, stood a lifesized figure that had sprung up in the weeks since Ava banned Edgar from the family studios. This must be Dad's contribution to the big ceremonial piece. The deadline was soon but the big figure was shrouded today. Instead he was working on a portrait bust—beautiful, even in the wax. On a stool next to it Essie sat, magnificent in a gold robe Benton had thrown across her breasts and tossed over her shoulders in an elegant drape.

When Edgar saw her, all his loneliness summed itself up and came out in a little bleat. "Essie! Where have you been?"

It was like talking to a stranger. To his surprise she didn't grin or hold out her arms; instead, Essie, *his Essie* shook her head and put her hand to her mouth with a stern, shushing look.

"What's the..."

Essie spoke out of a thundercloud. "Be quiet, child. We're doing something important here.

"But what?"

"Shh, son. The forces are converging. Good," she said so imperiously that it scared him. "And bad."

For the first time ever his dad looked frightened too. "Esther!"

"Essie?"

"That's all, child. Be easy. I just wanted you to know that."

Frightened, Benton said, "Esther!"

The woman Edgar had thought of as his second mother drew herself up. "It's his right, Benton." Not Mr. Benton or Mr. Benedict, just... *Benton*. "It's his right to know."

His father was pleading. "Essie, don't!"

Imperious Esther wheeled like an Amazon hurling a thunderbolt. "Don't you don't me, Benton Benedict."

Rushed, trembling, his father turned Edgar around and put him on the path back to the house. "I love you, Edgar, but you can't stay here."

"He can stay if he wants to," Essie said.

And now to Edgar's astonishment it was his father who turned into somebody else. He drew himself up with such power and authority that he looked like Great-great Grandfather's portrait—no, like that great big monstrous figure of God in the back garden.

"No," Benton said. "We have too much to do. Go now," he said, in the voice of God. "And don't tell anybody where you've been."

"...And that is as much as we know about the remarkable event that inspired the famous sculptor and founder of a dynasty of great sculptors, the renowned Beauchamp Benedict."

To the guide's distress, someone in the little group of sheep following her through the gallery in the small town nearest Wayward laughed an insider's laugh.

"Although many artists today work from clay positive to mold negative to the wax that informs the final mold, the best sculptors, like the Benedicts, prefer to model directly in wax. Unlike some, who build a form and then apply a thin layer of wax to make the final surface, the Benedicts build completely in wax shaped over an armature. In the casting process described on the labels placed in every display case, the wax is destroyed and the armature burns away, which means there are no multiples of Benedict bronzes. Each of these extraordinary works of art is unique."

A man said in a deep, firm voice, "Unique."

Unnerved by the interruption, the dumpy tour guide in the cardigan and the flowered dress scanned the faces of the group but did not see the speaker. As she led the little clump of tourists in their T-shirts in primary colors and their flowered jams and matching eyeshades along to the next part of the exhibition, a tall, saturnine figure separated itself from the group and slouched back to one of the cases where he stood, staring into the diorama that contained Beauchamp's maquette of *God and His Creation,* all that was left of the famous missing piece. While tourists straggled forward in sneakers and sandals, trailing puffy Mylar balloons with *Wayland Tours* stenciled on them in pink, the dark stranger stared intently into the miniature face of the miniature figure of God. It bore his great-grandfather's features.

It was as though some exchange took place between them.

"Yes." The deep whisper reverberated, circling in the marble dome.

Trailing candy wrappers, the little group of tourists eddied around the guide, who stirred uneasily and looked up, as if she could locate the speaker up there inside the dome. After an anxious little pause, she cleared her throat and continued.

"...The Benedict bronzes, of which this museum contains many fine examples, are what they are precisely because they are done directly from the wax. Difficult as it is to work in, demanding as it does an air-cooled environment, wax enables the finest workmanship and the most detailed likeness available, as in Beauchamp Benedict's inimitable *Aphrodite,* for which the infamous Evelyn Nesbit modeled shortly before her untimely death at the hands of Harry K. Thaw." The guide hesitated for a moment, distracted by an untoward snicker. "Unfortunately the actual details of the casting process, which distinguishes the family work from the work of all others the world over, is the Benedict secret which we are not at liberty to divulge."

That snicker. "Indeed."

The guide jumped. "Oh, sir..."

The saturnine figure looked up from the piece he had been regarding. Not a tourist. A tourist in no respect.

At his glare, the plump little docent said uncertainly, "If you'll just come along..."

Berton Benedict considered for a moment and then nodded. In two steps he had rejoined the group where the Chippewa woman with black glossy braids stood, a splendid figure, ideal for the project. For months he'd been looking for a model for the special project, but nobody in Paris seemed right. He was glad he'd waited to reach the States before advertising and interviewing models. He'd seen dozens by the time she walked into his hotel room. His ideal model, just when he was about to giveup. Beautiful. Perfect. She came into his life like a gift.

As the docent went on with her little tour Berton took his new model's hand, bending slightly to murmur, "Yes, Atawan. This is what we have in store."

Frowning—idiot guide, didn't she recognize the distinctive Benedict profile?—the docent went on with her memorized spiel. "And so the exhibits provided here give you only a rudimentary idea of what goes on in the lost wax process of pouring bronzes. To put it simply, the mold is made around the wax and then the bronze is poured, displacing the wax to make the finished sculpture, but the more complicated the piece, the more complex the process, as you might guess. As you can see the larger pieces must be done *in situ*, in a specially created firing pit. Ordinarily the mold is baked dry of wax before the bronze is poured—as you can see here there is an intricate arrangement of sluices and vents, but we have no idea what the ancients did or how they managed to create their brilliant effects."

Berton said in a low voice, "Come with me, Atawan. This is nothing compared to what you're about to see."

She turned glittering brown eyes on him.

"You will be perfect for us."

Statuesque in the soft leather dress, she had beautiful long bones and a profile sharper than the blade of a tomahawk. Beads and brilliant feathers decorated her black hair.

"This concludes our tour of..."

"Perfect," Berton said.

Scowling, the docent said, louder, "*This concludes our tour* of the Wayland Museum, home of some of the best of the Benedict bronzes, which also houses this teaching exhibition of their methodology. Although the family is reclusive and works under conditions of strict security for the protection of both the artists' privacy and that of their models and patrons, they have kindly underwritten this gallery for the sake of the many admirers of their work."

Berton couldn't suppress a snort.

"Although the family fortunes fell during the Great Depression and then mysteriously recovered in the early 1980s, the Benedicts have always expressed gratitude and concern for the admirers of their work."

Why did this make Berton laugh?

Glaring, the docent went on. "It is said that a great infusion of energy came to the family upon the marriage of the current head of the family, Benton Benedict to another sculptor, the famous Ava Pertreille, who signs her work with the simple double B that marks the work of all the Benedicts."

"*Infusion!*" Berton muttered, "That bitch."

"In any event the Benedicts began a great renaissance in the 1980s, achieving a productivity and prosperity that continues to this day." Seeing the end of her memorized talk in sight, the guide raced for the barn, concluding, "If you wish to see more, there are currently two shows of Benedict bronzes touring the United States, the portrait bronzes currently at the Museum of Fine Arts in Boston and the World War One groupings at the Eamon Carter Museum in Fort Worth, Texas. Thank you very much."

The little clump of tourists disbanded, some drifting into the museum gift shop while the others headed outside, straggling down on Bay Street to look for souvenirs.

In the hush of the main hall, where lines converged in the center of a circle of green marble, Berton Benedict looked at his grandfather's *Aphrodite* and then turned to Atawan. "I wanted you to see this. Understand what you are becoming a part of. History. Come." He pulled on her hand. "It's almost time for us to go on out to Wayward."

The guide's sweet voice puffed up behind them, quavering and ineffectual. "Oh sir..."

"Wayward," he said, louder.

"I'm afraid nobody is allowed to go to Wayward." Before the little woman could catch up. Berton wheeled and, like twin falcons, he and Atawan escaped.

His words trailed behind them like a banner. "To Wayward, where everything will converge."

In the doorway Benton turned and in the harsh glare of reflected sunlight the guide caught his face—the profile—and fell back as Berton led his model out into the afternoon. The last thing he said left her trembling.

"It's time for us to begin."

Eleven

Saturday afternoon; it's that time again. This is precisely what Father Jerome thinks, sighing: it's that time again and he has to do this. He hears reluctant footsteps coming down the church aisle, the moment of hesitation as the new arrival decides between the curtain and the door.

With a dusty sigh his single penitent slides into the dark side of the confessional, where he can try to name his sins without having to look his confessor in the face. They both know who each other are, but Jerome's penitent needs to pretend he is anonymous. When he entered the priesthood he was ready for everything except the unremitting hardship of hearing others' confessions. Idealistic Jerome had more or less expected he'd be easing worries and sharing pain. The surprise, then, was the fear people brought into the box with them, and the fact that instead of the sunny little room he had prepared for them they always chose the box, embarrassed and mumbling so he couldn't exactly hear, refusing to look him in the face. On Sundays they pretend they're somebody else. He can hardly stand the idea that something he does makes so many people feel bad. Most of his parishioners can't stand it either, so they don't come to confession any more—*Is it something I said?*

Except for this weekly visitor, who kneels in the dark and sighs and sighs.

Every Saturday Father Jerome keeps the bamboo shade raised in the sunny reconciliation room, in hopes. *If we could just sit down face to face and talk like reasonable men.*

He always chooses the box. The penitent kneels and the red light over the box window blinks.

Jerome lowers the shade and slides back the screen that gives on the confessional.

"Bless me Father, for I have sinned."

Although he's pulled down the bamboo shade to darken his side, Jerome has kept the little window open to the soft air of autumn; he can hear the cries of children at play and the vroom of drag racers down at the Pic Quik parking lot. On the other side of the screen the airless, curtained coffin is filling up with the fumes of distress, a combination of the penitent's bath soap and fresh aftershave and his specific smell, compounded by sighs and threatened tears.

Nobody says anything. After a while Father Jerome, who is not yet thirty, says, "What is it, my son?"

"Oh, Father, I have sinned." At the gentle prodding, his penitent, who's twice his age, begins in a strangled whisper. "Is it possible to commit a sin by letting something happen?"

"If you have the power to prevent it, yes."

Benton Benedict groans. "What if you don't know for sure what's going on?"

Father Jerome considers it: vincible versus invincible ignorance. "It depends on whether you can find out."

"Oh bless me, Father, I don't *know.*" After another miserable pause Benton says, "Am I responsible for what another person does?"

They both know who he is talking about, but Father Jerome can't figure out how to put the question without blowing Benton's cover and sending him running. It is a given of these confessions that they are new to each other each time Benton Benedict comes in. He could be any old penitent, walked in off the street, right? Wrong. These aborted confessions have been escalating. Without ever getting down to details, Benton has made it clear whatever's going on in his life out at Wayward is geometrically worse every time he comes in. He may want to pretend he's starting in with a clean slate, but Jerome can't. He has his responsibilities. "It depends on the person, my son,"

"She's, oh Lord, she's my. Ah. I can't tell you."

Why can't the man just come out and say he's talking about his wife? "And it depends on your relationship to her."

"I don't know about that either." Benton collects everything that's piling up inside, collects his grief and tries to hand it off to the priest. "I thought I knew how I felt about her, but I'll never really know."

If Jerome says the wrong thing now, his penitent will bolt before he gets to the point. In all the Saturdays he's been coming here, Benton has never said right out what he thinks he's done, so Jerome can absolve him. Much less urge him to do something about it. Help him sort out specific steps. All he does is kneel there suffering mutely while Jerome tries to find the right combination, talking until he hears the tumblers click. He waits for Benton to go on and when he doesn't, the young priest tries, "Son, if you want me to help you, you're going to have to tell me what's bothering you."

Which Benton both does and does not. "I am the lord thy God and thou shalt not have false gods before thee."

They are slipping into an old pattern. *If I let it play,* Jerome thinks, *maybe this time, he'll actually come out with it.* "If you won't tell me, I can't absolve you."

"Isn't it enough that I feel terrible?"

Here we go again. "Not quite."

"Oh Father," Benton begins, with great grief, "The talent." Remembering he's supposed to be anonymous, he starts over. "I mean, Father, that I and my brothers and my children were all born with, this, ah—talent?"

Jerome murmurs, "With talent comes responsibility."

"I may be a slave to the talent. The family talent," he says.

The priest's heart sinks. They are off on the same roundabout. "As long as you're not a slave to something else."

"That too."

"If you have something that needs forgiving, for God's sake, confess!"

"I can't."

"Otherwise I can't do anything for you," Jerome says.

There is another of those intolerable silences in which the priest wills the sculptor to say something, *anything* they can take as a starting point. Instead Benton's voice spirals into nothing. "I don't know what to do, I don't know what to *do.*"

Oh please don't cry. Jerome does his best to sound assured. "Try to do what God wants."

Benton makes a strangling sound. "I don't know what God wants."

"God wants you to use your talents to the greater glory of God," Jerome says softly. How many times have they been through this? "I would give a fortune to have your way with bronze."

He mumbles, "Wax."

Because Jerome can't quite hear, he soldiers on. "We're all supposed to do the best we can with what we have been given."

"But what if it—ah—pulls me in the wrong direction?"

"Then you're in trouble," Jerome says.

Benton says thickly, "It's more complicated than that. I wish I didn't have any goddamn talent—excuse me, Father. Any talent at all. I wish I had been born a ditch digger, or a brain surgeon, or a..."

If he says priest I'm going to bop him. In spite of himself, Jerome is irritated. If the old man would only come out and say what he *means* here. Instead he tries to wrestle the conversation into a corner where he gets Jerome to say, one more time, "God gave you talent because he wants you to use it. Now try and go in peace, OK?" and Benton cries, "I can't go in peace because it's...

because it's..." and Jerome says one more wrong thing and one more time his would-be penitent lurches up unabsolved and flees the confessional. "Just do your best and hope for the best, my son," Jerome says and can't stop himself from going on, logically. "You were given your talents for a reason."

Benton says delicately, "Not everybody agrees what that reason is. Oh Father," he says, "This is very difficult. Everything I did before she came, everything my father and his before him did—it was all for the greater glory of—well, at least I think it was, and listen, she's helping us further it."

He gulps. "She is! She says she's taking us back to Beauchamp's way. I mean, to my great grandfather's way. You didn't hear me say any names, did you, Father?"

"Let's just say I don't remember you saying any names."

"The thing is. The terrible thing is..."

"Yes, my son?"

"Nobody knows the truth about my great grandfather, not really."

There is another of those silences, in which Jerome thinks, *I can't come out and ask him if he actually thinks his great grandfather sold his soul to the devil. I can't even tell him that's not the kind of deal people can make. I can't even ask him what he thinks the deal was.*

Benton's voice drops into it like a block of granite, as if from a great height. "Nobody."

God and His Creation, Jerome thinks but cannot say. The man who made that beautiful piece must have loved God. He must have. And the rest of them! Look at *Susannah and the Elders,* all those sculptural groups in front of churches. The Benedict family has taken serving God to the point of obsession. All those lugubrious bronze Virgins with their faces drawn in grief. *Maybe there really is something strange that we don't know about*, he thinks, and then thinks, *Don't be ridiculous.* The best thing he can say right now is, "Whoever your great grandfather was, he's long dead now."

Benton says hollowly, "But she says she knows his way."

"But she is not one of you..." Cut yourself off, Jerome. Don't say it. Benedicts.

"She is and she isn't," Benton says.

Withdrawn and frustrating and inarticulate as he is, the man is so clearly in pain that Jerome has to find some way to help him help himself. The priest says firmly, "What happens to you in this generation is not decided by your ancestors."

That's what you think.

Wait. Something... What's the matter?

Creepy as he feels, Jerome goes on. "What's past is past."

What is there? Is somebody else in the church?

The past is never past.

What? When he goes on it is with less confidence. *But we have to offer ideal ways for people to attempt*, he tells himself. Now, try. "...And it isn't up to her, either. It's up to you."

The air is disturbed, as if by soundless laughter.

Benton sounds alarmed. "You mean it's my responsibility?"

Jerome tries to calm him. "Son. What you do is your responsibility."

Canny Benton slides: "Then I'm not responsible if what happens is caused by someone else."

Jerome throws the ball right back in his lap. "That depends on what it is and whether you can stop it and what you do about it." Then he thinks, wait a minute, if I let this string out I'm as much a party to this thing as he is. "Listen," he says, "Whatever this is that's eating you, I think you'd better tell me about it, and if you can't, you had definitely better take hold and stop it yourself."

It's as if he's hit the man with a club. Benton says in a low voice, "Oh my God, I can't." Then the reluctant penitent goes on hurriedly; there is in fact a figure looming in the main door of the church. "Oh my God I have to go but oh my God oh listen to me, Father not one word about any of this. You're sworn, remember," His voice teeters into hysteria. "Remember," he cries, loud enough to be heard in the vestibule. "The seal of the confessional."

Frustrated, Jerome forgets himself and barks, "How can I break it when you haven't told me anything?"

Benton says urgently, "Oh, it's you!"

"What?"

But he doesn't answer. Instead there's the sound of Benton being yanked out of the confessional, shouting as he goes. "Promise, Father, not a word to anyone about this!"

Alarmed, Jerome cries, "Hey, are you all right?"

"Not a word to anybody. Don't! Oh please stop it. Stop!" There is the sound of Benton being dragged away, calling. "Promise, Father, please!" His cry trails after him like a tattered scarf.

Jerome finds himself wrestling with the doorknob to the Reconciliation room; something heavy has been pushed in front of it. "Asshole, I'm already sworn."

By the time he frees himself and runs out to the street there's nothing there except an abandoned pickup truck with the Benedict seal on the door. Way down at the corner, the gawky, harassed, earnest young priest can see the Benedict limousine and even though all the glass in the back is tinted for privacy he thinks he can see the eminent sculptor battering the back windshield like a frantic goldfish with his hands like stars and his open mouth pressed against the glass.

It was night on the causeway. The black water was still and the only light showing was from the house at their backs where Edgar sat in front of a late-night TV monster movie with Esther and in the master suite upstairs, a troubled Benton Benedict sketched falling angels in the margins of his Bible and prayed for sleep.

Outside, the pair struggled down the path that led along the water from the foundry, one huge shape pushing the object on the dolly, while the slender, graceful one guided the wheels, keeping the heavily shrouded object centered so it wouldn't heel over and tip the dolly. In spite of their efforts to keep it steady and be quiet, a wheel hit a rock with a clank.

Although he could not possibly have heard it from his bedroom, Benton Benedict started so abruptly that the back line of the falling angel he was drawing slipped off the page. To his astonishment the pencil point broke off in his thigh.

In the dark water just off the causeway, something heard the two of them coming with their burden, and stirred.

In the TV room Edgar said, "So, don't you think the monster looks like Thorne?"

Esther didn't answer. She just gave him a hug.

"Well, don't you?"

"Oh child, child."

He shrugged her off. "Thorne doesn't like you."

"Honey, that Thorne, the only thing he cares about, he just cares about one person."

Because it was just the two of them in front of the TV tonight, he said, "I don't like the way he looks at me."

"He doesn't see you for nothing."

"Well I'm afraid of him."

"You don't have to be afraid," Esther said, hugging him in spite of his struggles. "I'll take care of you."

Even though it was dark and nobody much came down here to the point behind the house at night, Ava had swaddled the object as if wrapping a corpse for disposal: no need to tie lead sinkers to this blighted, ruined sculpture of hers: the model's fault. Damn Jimmy Daley for this. His broken likeness would slip into the water and go down like a stone.

In the master bedroom, rueful Benton Benedict pulled back the perforated nightshirt and looked at the lead from the broken pencil. It made a dark place just underneath the skin of his thigh.

Ava's voice came from some dark place within her. "I hate losing this."

"You've lost better."

"I hate losing time. It was supposed to be done by now. Would have been, if that damn fool hadn't..."

"Not your fault the kid bolted."

"We're on deadline," Ava said. "It's putting us behind. The others will be here soon."

Outside and alone like this they were in no way master and servant. Thorne said, "What's one angel, more or less?"

"This one was supposed to go at the pinnacle. He was such a pretty boy."

"Don't blame yourself."

"It's ruined. It doesn't matter who I blame."

"Then let's just dump the thing and start over."

But she couldn't quite let it go. "It was supposed to crown the piece."

"You'll do somebody better."

"You mean: Some. Thing." Pointing to the water, she repeated significantly. "Thing."

"Thing," he said. "Don't worry. You'll find somebody."

"Who, for God's sake? Dirk or Luke?" Her voice licked the air like an anxious flame. "I suppose you think I can start with Esther. Nobody touches Esther and you know it."

"Not my fault she has your number," Thorne said.

"I need a model," she said crossly. "If I don't have it ready by the time they get here, Benta or one of the others is going to come in here and cap the climax. Damn that fool Jimmy. Damn him for..."

"Quiet. Hush. Shut up, Ava, let's just do this. Do you know what your problem is?" When Thorne was alone with her like this his words exploded in strings. He was sick of talking in monosyllables. "Impatience."

"I need..."

He cut her off. "Patience!"

"Somebody beautiful," Ava said as they reached the causeway and began maneuvering the dolly out past the fringe of sawgrass to the deep place. "I've got to find a new model fast. Damn you," she said to the dark water.

A circular ripple disturbed the surface. Something out there.

Thorne said, "What's that?"

"Never mind," Ava said. "You don't need to know."

In the house rueful Benton squeezed the place on his thigh. The lead came out but the place stayed blue.

Downstairs Edgar wriggled out of Esther's grasp. "Honey, don't you want to see how they chase the monster with the torches?"

"Listen, Essie," he said, "Something's out there. Do you hear it?"

For a second she lifted her head and in the next second she lunged for the child and pulled him back to the safety and comfort of the sofa. "No, child, I don't hear anything. Shh. Shh. Sit down and be quiet. Let's us see how this movie comes out."

Outside something in the black water cried out. The woman guiding the heavy load on the dolly lifted her head and stopped in midstride.

"What is it? Do you want to dump it here?"

Instead of helping Thorne with the load she braked abruptly. "Stop!"

"For God's sake, Ava, what are you doing?"

"Not God's sake. Ever." she said sharply. "Mine."

"Then what."

"Just wait."

In the shallow water a pale face glimmered, opening like the dark center of a flower. It either was or was not still human; it either did or did not speak.

Thorne turned with surprising speed. "What's that?"

"Nobody. It's nothing." Working intently, Ava pushed and tugged, maneuvering the dolly to the edge. "Are you going to just stand there or are you going to help?"

Trapped in the quicksand, caught and dragged down but not dragged down far enough. Still alive.

Hearing, Ava made a quick calculation and changed the angle of the object she was preparing to dump. "Come on, Thorne, I only want to do this once."

With its mouth glued wide with mud and tears and mucous, it sobbed.

Thorne pretended not to hear. "I don't know why I've stayed with you this long."

Thock. She nailed him. "Oh yes you do. Now, *move.*"

Below, something living moved. It was blanched and bloated from days in the water; marshaling its last shred of strength for this final effort, it tried to speak. *Oh—*

"Goddammit, Thorne!"

Oh please.

"Just shut up."

"I wasn't..."

"Thorne. Push!"

But there was something down there. Something was... "Ava, I think I...."

"Shut up, it's nothing. Now push."

It may or may not have had a voice left; what came out sounded not like human speech or anything else it may have intended: *Help.*

Above, Ava said, "Now," even as impassive Thorne turned, crying, "Wait!"

And the desperate thing in the water might have gotten precisely what it courted as Ava and troubled Thorne toppled the ruined bronze angel in its likeness into the exact spot where the white face opened like a dying flower. Flawed cast and shamed model were joined in the quicksand in an amazing confluence, dying creature and lifeless matrix joined forever, fixed for centuries in the mud, the one weighing the other down on and on in perpetuity while their maker made guttural sounds that the panting Thorne would not make them out, although *she* knew. "Take that, Daley," Ava said, grinning at the splash.

In the house Edgar jumped to his feet and spun like a little pinwheel, crying, "What was that?"

Essie pulled his head into her belly and crooned soothingly, "Shh. shh. Nothing. It's nothing, son." It was a good thing he could not see her face. "There there," she said, hugging and rocking, humming and gentling the boy until he stilled and she could take him upstairs and put him to bed where she left Edgar finally. Shaking her head, the tough, intelligent, handsome Esther went back downstairs to her quarters, muttering a prayer for the sake of the poor worried child and his father, for her own sake and for the sake of everybody in the house and all the souls on the Benedict place at Wayward, both living and dead, both present and absent, along with the poor soul released by death out there in the mud off the causeway, Esther Manifort muttering all the way through the pantry and the kitchen to her own room off the kitchen wing, so preoccupied by the shape and magnitude of her prayer that she would not hear the thud of the little boy's feet hitting the floor in the bedroom above or the rattle of branches as he went out the bedroom window via the white wisteria that wound down off the porch roof, she was too deep in prayer to know what the child was doing, which may have been just as well.

Twelve

"You never explained why you left Wayward," Jude said. "Why was it so important for you to get away?" Yesterday Peter showed her Charleston, finishing at a crafts center where his friend Elaine looked at her jewelry and offered her a corner of the studio—if she stayed. This was not yet certain. She thought she was in love with Peter; they'd been together for two days and yet she had no idea what drove him or, more important, what troubled him.

Peter said only, "Coffee?"

"That isn't an answer."

He set it down in front of her with a beautiful smile. "There's stuff I don't like to talk about, you know?"

"I don't, really. If you hate your family, why can't you tell me about it?"

"I don't hate them, I just can't *be* them. I had to get out from under..." He broke off. "It's Ava. What Ava wants, Ava gets," he said bitterly. "And it's not necessarily good."

He looked so miserable that Jude rushed in foolishly. "All mothers are like that, right? Especially about what they want for their sons." The hell of it was that as she spoke she was replaying certain bad scenes with Phil Forrest's mother, who let Jude know she wasn't good enough for him.

Peter was up and pacing. He made a sharp turn. "Don't think you understand this, because you don't."

"I'm trying!"

He groaned. "You can't."

"Well you're not exactly helping!"

"Come on, Jude. Let's just be us. Forget the Benedicts."

This was so weird and evasive that she was tempted to back out now, before she got hurt, but this was Peter; if he loved her back, she had to try. "Peter. If we're ever going to be anything together, we have to tell each other everything."

Without even noticing what he was doing he pushed his hair back as if to let her see him better. "I know."

In this light she could see the jawline, the brow. His profile was as clean and bold as one of the family sculptures, but where even the best bronzes were still and cold, Peter blazed with life. "Please. If there are bad things in your life, say so!"

The word exploded. "OK."

It was a minute before he could go on. "So what it is, is. About Ava. She's. Ah." He paced while he talked, looking everywhere but at Jude.

"You've probably figured out that Ava's in charge out there. She came in as one of my grandfather's students and before she was done she married my dad. She claims she put life back into the family business, but with Ava, you never know, you know?"

"That sounds like a good thing, not a bad one," Jude said.

At the far end of the studio Peter stopped pacing and made a full turn. "You know how some things are more trouble than they're worth? This is one. You get what you need, sure, but you pay a terrible price."

His look of pain was so profound that she said, "If it's this hard for you, Peter, you don't have to tell me any more."

"You asked me to tell you, so you might as well know. Everything comes at a price. Now Ava has upped the ante."

"I don't know what that means."

He looked at her for a long moment. "That's the trouble. I don't either, not really."

This is worse than I thought. "Oh, Peter!"

"Don't worry about me. It's the rest of them." He quit pacing and came back to the table. "OK. So. She runs my father and she runs my older brothers and up until I made the break, she was running me. And Dad lets her, partly because she's hell on wheels and partly because he couldn't get dressed in the morning without her to tell him which shirt. Also, in the long run he owes her. His Aunt Benta and his brothers were doing OK in Europe but at Wayward, things were not so good. If you want to know the truth Dad was nothing when she came, and now..." He paused. "All this, about the Benedicts?"

"You mean the mystique."

He nodded. "They started out be famous but by the time Ava came in, the family was on the skids. Nobody wanted sculpture that looked like life, then Ava took hold and somehow it got better than life. No I can't explain so please don't ask. Anyway, now... Well, you know about now. We're famous again."

"And you don't want it."

"I don't want any part of it." It took him too long to find the next words. "Ava looked into the process and everything changed. Then she kicked, pushed, lied and cheated to get us back into the marketplace. She drives the whole operation. She got photos out to clients and slides to galleries and organized the show at the Mellon in the Eighties. It kicked off the new wave, and if everybody at Wayward goes through hell to keep her happy, fine. Give her trouble and she cuts you down, like, *Where would you be without me?*"

"And you don't want any part of it."

"I don't want to be that person."

When his pause stretched into deep silence she said, "You don't want to explain, do you?"

"Not really. No. Agh." He collected himself. "OK. To do work that good, you have to be willing to do certain things. She knew I'd rather paint, but Ava..."

Jude counted to thirty before he resumed.

"Ava is something else."

She shuddered. Some Weird Element: *what if he's in love with his mother*?

But that was not love in Peter's eyes. It was a strange mixture of loathing and admiration. "She engine that drives the family."

He could have been talking about a diamond drill.

"Now she wants something more from us. All of us. Something..." He couldn't seem to complete the thought or if he could, refused to put words to it. "I couldn't do it, OK? I couldn't *be that.* "

"Be what?"

God he looked agonized. "Whatever she wants."

"Oh, Peter."

"Legendary! I had to get away. It's..."

She said in a low voice, "Is it something terrible?"

He turned away so quickly that his face blurred. "I can't tell you."

Oh Peter, what are you afraid of? She covered her mouth to keep the words from coming out.

"I have to save myself. I'm not going to fall into it." His voice hardened. "The talent is a trap. So is the Benedict legend."

"I'm sorry it's so hard."

"It isn't hard. It's what I do." Peter stood with his canvases around him like allies. Gallant and foolish, he looked ready to do battle with the Benedicts: whatever they had done to become what they were. "I design for a living—posters, ad layouts, magazine spreads; listen. It supports the paintings."

"I wish."

"There's nothing you can do, so don't. And don't worry about Eds, he's OK. He's Ava's favorite, the only one she ever really cared about, so he's safe for now. And when he stops being OK he'll tell me. One squeak and I go back to Wayward and get him, we have a pact. But first I have to save my own life." Back at the table now, he pulled her to her feet. "I haven't explained anything, have I?"

Surprised by tears, Jude shook her head.

"Let me show you something." He turned, rummaging. "Maybe it will help explain."

Parting the canvases, he pulled out one canvas that looked nothing like the others. It was a painting of a grotto, all purples and greens and umbers, and at the center of all those shadows gleamed an exquisitely complicated mass that looked like disturbingly like Beauchamp Benedict's masterpiece, *God and His Creation*, but instead of rising in the fresh, sunlit Benedict garden, where Jude had seen the original, this monumental piece glowed like a jewel in a darkly complicated setting—rock formations, stalagmites, stalactites, this brilliant piece lodged deep in the center of the earth. Bright as it was, it was densely shadowed, and in the background shadows Jude thought she saw writhing shapes she could not define, and there was something so disturbing about these figures in the context of the central grouping that she fell back.

"Peter. God."

"It came in a dream."

"It's beautiful."

"You see?"

She couldn't find anything to say.

"There really is something different about us."

Overturned, she said in a low voice, "Oh, my God."

Peter's head snapped forward with a little click. *Exactly.* "My point."

Jude said, gently, "Maybe you'd better put it away."

He slid it back into place and covered it with a gaudy, joyful landscape. "I can't be like the Benedicts."

"Even though the Benedicts are..."

"Famous. Believe me, it's a curse." He stepped away from the paintings and turned back into the man she'd come all this way to be with—no weird elements, just a handsome, nice guy with an easy grace and a grin that made her grin too as he finished, "Now could we talk about something else?"

"Where do you want to start?" Her last words were muffled by his hug.

"Everywhere," he said finally because they had to stop hugging sometime but they stayed close as they began to talk.

Which they did, through the afternoon and into the evening, when they walked out in the soft twilight and bought steamed crabs and French fries and took them down on the seawall and sat and ate looking out over the water and talking about everything in the world, or everything except the

Benedicts. Away from the studio where the dark painting lurked behind all the other bright canvases Peter had made in an attempt to change or elude history; away from Gara's pretty, haunted apartment, they were just two nice people beginning to fall in love. When the last light faded from the sky over the harbor they moved closer. They sat shoulder to shoulder and in the logical extension of all their hopes, turned and kissed.

Hand in hand, with arms twined wrist to elbow, she and Peter went back to Mrs. Poulnot's house, sneaking in through the garden and creeping upstairs under cover of the racket from Violet's HDTV, Judith Atkins and Peter Benedict giggling, close and about to get closer, drifting through the studio and into the bedroom where they sank down so naturally that they could have been lovers for life, the naturally reserved Jude surprised by the joy Peter awoke in her and ready, in spite of what her head told her, to forget caution, forget waiting, forget she had ever been hurt. She would have, too, but two things happened at once:

The phone rang.

And just as they approached the moment, Peter went back inside himself to think.

Then he drew away suddenly and sat up on the edge of the bed with his head clamped between his fists. "Oh, God, I can't."

"Peter!"

Damn phone.

"I didn't want it to be this way."

Jude's breath jittered in her throat and it came out in an unexpected, horrifying cliché. "Don't worry, it happens to everybody sometimes..." Aghast at what she'd just said, she gulped.

He whirled, grinning through tears. "Oh, not that. Believe me, no problem with that, I just. Oh listen, Jude, I do think I really love you, and I do want this. I even thought we could be together right now and it would be OK. I just. I mean I can't start anything new until this is settled."

She was ready to weep from embarrassment. "What? What is?"

"It." He stood, somehow reinforced. "Settled. With her."

At this point they both became aware of the phone, which had been ringing underneath their conversation for so long that the answering machine clicked on. Peter's short message was followed by heavy, panicky breathing. It was like a little whirlwind in the phone and then, coming into the room at such volume that it threatened to be followed by the owner, they heard Edgar's voice: "Oh Peter, oh shit, oh please pick up." He was sobbing. They heard another voice approaching and Edgar's anguished yip. Then whoever interrupted slammed the phone back on the hook.

Peter turned to her: *You see?* "Even if I didn't have to go there, now I have to."

"After everything you said."

"Because of everything."

What did he look like standing there, Robin Hood or Lancelot, preparing to ride out? Jude blurted, "I'm coming with you."

"You shouldn't have to..."

"Please. Let's do this together."

He hesitated.

"We have to, if..." She fell silent. Let him figure it out.

There was a little snap as if of all the parts of a delicate mechanism clicking into place: *Right.* Peter spoke heavily, testing her. "It's a lot to ask."

"I don't care."

"Ava can be hell."

"I'll handle it."

Soberly, he marched her through the stages. "She already knows about you, Jude. She doesn't want you there."

This did not surprise her. "What about you, Peter? Do you want me there?"

"Oh, Jude. You know what I want." He took her hands. "Oh look, it's going to be hard."

"I don't care." Jude was relieved, excited. "Let's go."

Thirteen

I don't know if I can do this, Jude thought, going into Wayward with Peter Benedict. They were walking into a confrontation with Ava. Her standoff with Phil's mother left her frail in that department, but Edgar needed them.

Ava herself came to the door. She didn't seem particularly surprised. She said so smoothly that Jude could hear Peter's teeth crash, "And here you are, just in time for the celebration."

Peter protested, "I didn't come for the..."

Ava overrode him, saying briskly, "You'll need to work fast if you expect to be part of the piece."

"I don't want to be..."

"Enough!" He could have been an annoying student—no better, no more. It was as if nothing that mattered had ever passed between these two. This is how Ava dismissed him. "Hurry. You're wasting mytime!"

She might as well have smacked him in the face.

Next she turned to Jude, asking, as if she didn't already know, "And who are you?"

"Judith Atkins. I'm a—friend of Peter's?"

Anybody could see that Ava hated her on sight. It was obvious in the way she swooped down on Jude, all overblown sweetness and theatrical gush. "Well isn't this nice. Look, Benton," she said to Peter's father, who bobbed behind her like an anxious ghost, "look, it's Peter's model."

"I'm not..." *Anybody's model.*

"Mother, she isn't..."

"Of course she is." Pulling Jude into the front hall, Ava curved those sculptor's hands around her head like the wings of a bird and would not let go. "Look at this girl's head." She turned Jude's head like clay on a wheel. "And what a beautiful profile!"

"I'm not a girl."

"I can see you and I are going to be good friends." Ava could have been an aging star playing Lady of the Manor in her white canvas shift. Benton Benedict stood in her shadow, waiting. Jude tried to resist but Ava tightened her grip, turning her head once more. A sculptor's tool sat behind one ear like a pencil; she was so close that Jude's eyes crossed. "Such good friends."

Jude glanced at Peter, perhaps wondering whether he saw what she saw, but his eyes were glazed, fixed on some remote object. It was as if he'd forgotten who she was. Something visible happened to Peter the minute the front door closed behind them. He hung in air, suspended between rebellion and imminent return to helpless childhood.

Ava prodded, "Aren't we, Peter? Going to be great friends?"

"Whatever you say." This was not a speech you could read in any particular way. Peter had done what she expected; he'd filled the air.

Jude reached for Peter's hand and was grateful when his fingers curled around hers because there was nothing to be read in his expression, either.

Maybe Ava really was the Medusa. She could turn anybody to stone.

Ava was the vital presence here. She kept her coppery hair pulled back in a Psyche knot, and in the canvas shift she wore, she could have been a piece of work herself—a regal figure straight off the Parthenon—except that all the angles of her body tilted slightly, as if she'd been cast leaning forward, perpetually rushing toward something they couldn't see.

Peter whispered, "Are you all right?"

At the moment, Jude wasn't sure. The front hall was too dark, with shadows grounded in the heavy mahogany paneling and shadows collecting in the corners of the ceiling and at the base of the sinuously carved black newel post. The carved post was so big that when she backed into it, Jude turned to apologize. Instead she faced a crudely carved tangle of bodies straining up around a central figure, which raised an electrified torch. "What?"

"The freeing of the slaves," Peter muttered, "Essie's great-grandfather carved that."

Feeling crowded, Jude whirled to look up the stairs. "Who's that up there?" Those looked like people poised on the landings and lingering in the long hall behind the Benedicts. Straining into the shadows, Jude saw that they were dusty bronzes, standing around like people in a waiting room. It was so dark! There was the dull *whump* of the front door behind them—somebody new letting himself in—but she couldn't focus. The vine pattern in the hall carpet flowed like a black river, pulling her deeper into the house, and the velvety green palms crawling up the flocked wallpaper threatened to overwhelm her. Trotting down the hall toward them, Edgar was a jerky little silhouette.

There were so many things present here that in the dimness it was hard to sort out the living from the bronze. Peter's father stepped into the light, a handsome husk of a man, shaky and stooped beyond his years—he looked so *old.* He and Peter hugged in silence. When he greeted Jude, his hands shook. A fiercely modeled black woman in a maid's uniform stood behind Benton with all her teeth showing; her grin of welcome was more like a glare.

The heavy mahogany door slammed shut.

Somebody new came into the hall.

Startled, Jude turned. At first blush the tall man in the hall looked like a cast for a model of Peter's dad when he was young. The woman with him could have been one of Beauchamp Benedict's bronzes modeled on the great American past. She folded her arms across her breast like Katherine Tekawitha or Pocahontas—perfect. Too perfect; it was weird.

The newcomer spoke. "Benton?"

Benton's response was hushed. "Berty!"

Peter's fingers gripped Jude's so tight that she yipped, "Who?"

"My uncle Bert, he left after Ava started..." His shudder ran through both of them. "Doing what she was doing. Watch out!"

Just then Ava turned away from them. It was like a light bulb blowing out. Peter's grip relaxed. Jude discovered that she was dizzy from holding her breath.

"Peter! Jude!" Edgar hurtled into them and all Jude's breath came out in a little *wow.*

Ava was saying, "Well, Berton. It's about time you got here. And your model. Perfect. Come here."

"Oh yes," the newcomer said coldly. Putting the Cherokee woman behind him, he explained to her, "This is my brother Benton's wife."

"Ava," she reminded him. "We're all friends here, Berton."

He was icy. "After everything."

Ava chose to ignore the implications. "Berty. Dearest. After all this time. And what have you brought with you?"

Edgar whispered, "Hey Peter, hey Jude."

But they were fixed on Berton, who gave Ava a long, cold look. "This is Atawan."

Intent on her new model, Ava advanced; she made the same sculptor's measurement on the angry Cherokee as she had on Judith, sizing her up with cupped hands. "Wonderful."

"My model. Not yours." Angry, Berton wrenched Ava's hands away.

At the same time, Benton Benedict emerged with his arms spread wide. "Bert!"

Now that she saw the two brothers together, Jude realized that Bert was in fact the older one, but he was—what? Weathering it better than Benton

Benedict. He seemed taller. Undiminished. Whole.

In the heartbeat before the brothers hugged, Jude understood what Ava did to people. *That's why Peter has to get away from here.*

Berton stepped back and took his brother's hands. "My God, Benty. What's happened to you?"

Everything boiled into Benton Benedict's face then. He was too full of things he had to tell his long-lost brother to manage even one. "Berty. Oh, Berty," he said. "If only you'd stayed."

At Jude's elbow, Edgar simmered. Little pleas kept coming to the surface and popping like bubbles. She grabbed his hand and his fingers nipped like a crab. "Oh, kid," she murmured, still fixed on the aging brothers' reunion. "Oh, kid."

Benton's whole life shone in his face but all he could say was, "Bert. Oh, Berty, it's been so long."

Then Ava moved in on Berton, saying brusquely, "Of course you'll want to get to work as soon as possible." When her brother-in-law whirled in protest, she took his wrist and went on smoothly, drawing him along. "You'll want to pick out your studio before the others get here, no? First come, first served, I say. Benton will come with you, so you two can catch up while you're working. Time is short."

She managed to scoop up the two men and she pulled Atawan into her force field, saying, smoothly, "That's it. Come on, this way, Bert, you and your amazing model. We all have a lot to do."

All efficiency, Ava had them clumped and moving out. "Come on, we're on deadline, all of us. Everybody's working around the clock. We have to get this piece ready in time for the anniversary."

Next to Jude, Peter froze.

Jude murmured, "The anniversary?"

"Centennial," Peter murmured distractedly, "Great-great Grandfather's piece."

God and His Creation, she thought. "That big thing in the garden?"

"That and Ed's birthday," he remembered. "Oh God, it's Edgar's birthday too."

What was the matter with Peter, anyway? Why couldn't they just take Edgar and go?

"If you like, I can give you the studio nearest the foundry," Ava said. " But you always take what you want anyway, don't you, Bert?"

She pushed the brothers and the statuesque woman in buckskin down the hall like a strong tide, sweeping them through double doors. The mahogany doors slid shut. Exhausted and oddly drained, Jude turned to Peter, but before she could frame the first question Edgar said, "Quick, while she isn't looking. Come on, man, we have to get away."

Then somebody said, "Hurry, son. He's right."

Peter gasped like a dreamer jolted into consciousness. "Esther, I forgot you were here."

"She had you, son. She almost got you back."

He recovered himself slowly, like a stranger returning from a country where everybody spoke a different language. "Shh, Eds. It's OK. It's going to be OK." He was looking over the child's head at the handsome black woman who advanced with a grace that beggared the crisp maid's uniform; she had the bearing of a deposed queen, coming into her own. "Oh, Essie. What are we going to do?"

"Well Peter. Oh, son." They hugged. She was so powerful and immediate that Jude stepped back and let them play directly to each other. Essie said, "I'm so glad."

Peter shook his head. "Essie, I don't know what to..."

"I have the child all ready to go," Esther said firmly. "You stay here and I'll get his things."

"I can't go," Peter said. "Not yet."

She was like a thunderstorm about to break. "I think you'd better make it soon."

"Things are bad." Peter shook his head in pain and confusion. "I can't go until..."

"Son."

"Uncle Bert's here. The others are coming. Great Aunt Benta and Uncle Bernie and Uncle Bruce. The cousins, Beau and Will."

"Beaufort?" Esther grimaced. "You might as well know, Beau's dead."

"God!"

"Poor boy killed himself in Venice. See what I mean?"

"See?" Peter said: QED "That's the whole thing."

Esther finished, "He'd do anything to keep from coming back."

"But what can I do? I can't just walk out on it, I have responsiblities. I have to try to... I don't know what I have to do"

"Son, you promised to save this child."

By this time Edgar was dangling from his arm, wheedling. "Peter, you promised."

"Saving him may not be enough."

Essie wasn't so much ordering him as warning, "Stay and you may not make it."

"Pe-terrr you promised."

"I did promise," Peter said, but he was looking down the long hall to the double doors Ava had pulled shut. "But now..."

"Son, I brought you up," Esther said urgently, "and I know when it's time to let you go. Take this child and leave while you still can, and hurry. It's only going to get worse."

"That's what I'm afraid of," Peter said. He turned an agonized face to Jude. "That's what I'm afraid of, Jude. See?"

"Oh Peter, I am so sorry."

The black woman spoke like a mother explaining to her best-loved child, "Honey, I'll do what I can to help your daddy, but please."

Edgar yanked on his hand. "Pe-terrr..."

Then Peter Benedict turned to his kid brother and his tone tore Jude in two. "We're going, Eds. We are, I promise, but first I have to... I just." He was tortured by something she couldn't even guess at. "We can't go yet."

Edgar howled, "What do you want to do, wait until something awful happens?"

And Peter said—like—*that,* "Something awful is already happening."

"You want to let her boil us up into some statue or what?"

Jude gasped. "Peter, my *God.*"

Peter only said, "Keep it down, Eddy, OK?"

"*I will not keep it down*. You want her to fire us in the sand pit or sink us in the swamp or what?"

"Peter?"

Esther fixed him with her eyes. "Son?"

When Peter spoke again it was to all three of them, saying, out of something Jude could not comprehend, "I can't. I can't go yet. Not until it's settled."

"Until what's settled?"

"I can't say. I just have to do this, OK?" He paused. "Es?"

Judith was helpless here. If she had her way she'd grab both of them, Peter and the kid; she'd take Essie too, no matter what she thought her duties were. She would use all her strength to move them along the hall and out the front door of Wayward into the fresh air; she'd push all three of them down the driveway and into the car, Peter bound and gagged if that's what it took to get him away from here, but in the split second that she was considering all this, something strange happened.

In the charged silence that fell after Peter spoke, he and Esther had, mysteriously, completed the thought. Jude looked from one to the other and found them changed.

Peter said, "You understand, then. Right, Esther?"

Esther nodded. "Yes. All right then. Very well."

An unwritten transaction had taken place.

Whatever it was, it was major. It was agreed. Everything had changed. Even Edgar was quiet now. As if he understood.

Esther's voice rushed out to him. "Oh, son. Son."

Peter relaxed. He didn't have to explain any more.. When he spoke again his smile blazed. "Oh, thank you, Esther," he said.

"Well if that's a sample of your jewelry, it's very nice," Ava said in tones so condescending that it was clear she despised Jude's best and most beautiful gold fretwork hair ornament. Jude put it on for dinner tonight because it was beautiful and the weakest part of her wanted Ava to admire her work. She had dressed for dinner too, apparently the wrong thing as Ava came to the table straight from the studio, in a clean version of the canvas shift. "Pretty," Ava said dismissively. "Superficial. Nice."

"I see."

The smile made Ava's teeth glint. She could have been a tigress, protecting her den. "But nobody makes a life on jewelry. It's lovely, but don't you think it's a little cheap?"

"Mother!"

"Hush Peter, Judith knows I just want better for her. How much could that possibly fetch?" Ava was all steel and velvet, circling. "I mean, when I do portrait bronzes, I get thirty thousand per piece. Benton gets fifty, that's what I've done for the Benedict name. Even Dirk and Luke get twenty now, and they're still apprentices. So will Peter, now that he's come to his senses."

Next to Jude, Peter stiffened, growling, "No I won't."

Ava's eyes glowed yellow. "And your work, Judith? How much is it worth?"

In fact, Jude made her living temp typing and filling in at the boutique but until now it had never occurred to her to be ashamed. "Not much."

"Then, it's just a hobby with you." Then Ava said so smugly that it turned Jude's knuckles white, "Real artists support themselves on their art."

At the sideboard, Esther put the silver cover back on the chafing dish with a clank.

Remembering Peter's paintings, Jude snapped back. "Not necessarily!"

"Otherwise, they're nothing," Ava said. The contempt smacked Jude like an unsheathed claw. "There's no place in the real world for dabblers."

"Don't pretend you know me," Jude said.

Here they were at the long table in the elegantly faded dining room at Wayward, surrounded by silver-covered dishes and eating off the ancestral china with heavily ornamented dinner forks while Esther served and in the kitchen the students clanked back and forth with platters of fried chicken and spring asparagus. They were sitting down together for the first time, the Benedict family, with Benton's long-lost brother from Paris and a beautiful native American, along with the more or less prodigal Peter, who had come home with a new woman friend. In the candlelight the room was lovely, every surface gleaming and the atmosphere civilized, Benedicts around the table with glow warming their bent heads, and yet Ava Benedict was intent on stalking Jude; she wanted to hunt down, slay and skin the outsider and serve her for dessert.

"Trash," Ava said. "Pretty trash, but it's just trash."

Jude started to rise.

Ava purred, "There's no place here for mediocrity."

Underneath the table, Peter's hand closed on Jude's arm, holding her in place. "Ava, that's enough."

Her glare was like a lighthouse beam, raking from Jude to her son. "Why risk your heritage for a dabbler? You're a Benedict!"

Whap. Jude touched her face. Had Ava drawn blood?

"Mother!"

Even Benton protested. "Ava."

"You must understand... what did you say your name was?"

"Jude."

"Judith. We're artists." God, Ava had yellow eyes. "We can't tolerate anything second rate."

"Wait a minute."

"It might rub off."

"Mother!" Next to Jude, Peter was struggling with imperatives: what he most needed to accomplish here. He'd come to a decision that allowed him to protest but not to get up and go, and it was this that kept his fingers closed on Jude's arm so she could not leave without tearing away from her sleeve.

"Shh, Peter. I just want something better for her." Ava's smile was so sweet that it made Jude's teeth hurt. "Understand, sweetie, cheap work cheapens the artist's eye and we certainly don't want..."

Now Benton's tall, saturnine brother Berton closed his fingers on Ava's arm. Watching the current pass between them, Ava's uneasy smile, Jude understood that Berton and his brother's wife shared a past that she could not afford to let him resurrect. His bark broke the sequence. "Enough!"

As abruptly as she had begun, Ava abandoned her prey; Jude could almost see her back off, lashing her tail. It was as if Jude had ceased to exist. "Well, Dirk, tell us about your trip to the workshop at Ossabaw. Do they know anything we don't know?" In the shadows at the far end of the table Peter's craggy, silent big brother stirred as if struggling hard to escape the prison of his own reflections, but before Dirk could speak Ava passed on to the next thing, saying brightly, "Essie, I think we're finished here. You can have the students clear the table now." In a cozy tone meant to suggest she and the black woman were the best of friends she went on, even though Esther turned grimly, with no intention of answering. "What do tonight's cooks have for us for dessert?"

It was interesting. Jude saw now that with all her talk about high art, Ava had been intent on staking out her territory, positioning her victim. Benton might be the nominal head of this generation of Benedicts, but Ava was in charge. If she wanted to search and destroy, nobody at this table could prevent her. Perhaps from habit, probably for their own protection, the resident Benedicts sat quietly and let her lead.

Jude had the idea that when there were no outsiders present, there was no conversation at all.

While Benton slumped, his brother Berton and the statuesque Atawan sat clothed in dignity. At the far end of the table Luke and Dirk slouched in the shadows with their sleeves rolled and plaster of paris and clay under their nails. Except for little set speeches delivered on cue when Peter introduced them, they did not speak. Whatever kept them at Wayward kept them quiet. Luke was light-boned and graceful, with pale blond hair pulled back in a ponytail, where Dirk's thick curly hair marched down his forehead in a V that almost met his heavy brows and his head sank into the rest of him. It was clear to Jude that Dirk had been angry for so long that he no longer bothered to show it. They looked, what. Beaten down.

("Your brothers," Jude whispered. Bending to pick up her napkin, she asked, "what happened to them?"

"Ava," Peter murmured. "They loved women who couldn't take the heat."

Jude murmured back, "That's terrible.")

Ava spoke as if she had heard, "Art has its imperatives."

Given enough time she could probably ruin Peter too. Just wear him down, like a piece of stone that's been worked to death. S.W.E. Ava was definitely the weird element here. Anger flared like a candle at the touch of a match. Jude fumed. *I've been pushed around for the last time.* Taking a deep breath, she went forth to join battle with Ava Benedict. "Art," Judith said with force. "There are more important things in life than art." *Take that.* Heads turned.

Ava slapped the table. "Name one."

Jude was right on top of her. And *that.* She closed the trap: *snap.* "Life."

But the moment was diffused by a stir in the doorway; students in coveralls shambling into the room with extra plates and silverware, putting the coffee tray on the sideboard under Esther's supervision, moving chairs around on Ava's command. "Yes, Petra, there. You have all worked well today. Now join us for dessert." Ava's people, Jude supposed, two men and two women; she recognized shaggy Jake, the would-be guard who'd tried to chase her off the place. The four stood back so Essie could put a platter on the table. For dessert someone had made what looked like a replica of the main house, frosted in detail, right down to the color of the floors on the sprawling verandas and whatever Jude had hoped to accomplish by standing up to Ava was as good as lost.

When Ava spoke again it was as if nothing had happened between them. "Oh look. The cake. Nelly and Petra have outdone themselves. Sit down, children," she said and like huge, shy second-graders, the student sculptors took their places, thrilled to be included at Ava's table.

"Life is more important," Jude repeated.

But Ava let it go by, saying, "This is in honor of your return to Wayward, my dear Bert."

"You had no idea when I was coming, Ava dear."

Then as they were getting up from the table at the end of dinner, when Jude thought her tiny moment of defiance had been completely wasted, Ava Benedict, good lord, Peter's *mother* drifted past her on the way out of the dining room and in such a low voice that Jude wondered later whether anything had actually passed between them, delivered the last words of the exchange in tones that would wake her in the night, sweating and shivering, for years afterward: "Life. Life is nothing," Ava said.

"You begin to see how heavy it is," Peter said. "The history."

"But you don't have to..."

His voice shook with grief. "It's my family."

They were sitting glumly at the end of little dock just off the causeway, looking out over water so dark and still that a person could almost walk out across the surface and make it to the other side. She wished they could go now. "If you don't want to leave, I'd better call a cab." She pulled out her cell, looking for a signal, but Peter shook his head. "Don't ask why, Wayward's in one of those still, dead pockets. You'll never get a signal here."

She shook the phone, gave up on it, snapped it shut. "Peter, if you can't leave yet, let me take Edgar."

"Not yet," he said carefully. "If you love me, you'll stay here with me."

"I don't know, Peter."

"Whether you love me?"

Apprehension rocked her. "Why you have to stay."

"I just have to," he said simply. "There's something I have to do." Then he said something that lifted her heart. "I can't do it alone, I was hoping you..."

There was a rowboat tied underneath the pier, bumping against the pilings. Jude wondered whether the waving skirt of marsh grass surrounding them was easy to navigate or whether anybody rowing out at low tide would end up mired. She wished they could grab Edgar and shove off in the little boat but looking at the beckoning arms and broken wingtips of the Benedicts' drowned sculptures flanking the causeway, she understood that a force even bigger than Peter's mother held him here. There was something tremendous at work here—a power she could not begin to comprehend. If she wanted Peter Benedict, if she wanted them to go away together and go freely, she had to help him see this through.

Everything in her went soft. She whispered, "Of course."

"OK!" At last he could begin. "Ah. It started with my great-great-grandfather."

"*God and His Creation.*" Behind them, the raised hand of the central figure glittered above the oleanders: God's fist raised to cast lightning. "It's so beautiful."

"No. It's terrible," Peter said unexpectedly. "Essie told me he said in his diaries that it ruined his life."

"Diaries?"

"Gone in the fire."

"What fire?"

"His studio. Story is he set fire to his studio. So. Ah... Maybe he was trying to make up for it." Peter said.

"Make up for what?"

It was not a question he chose to hear. Instead he went on. "He worked like hell to turn himself into a sculptor, starved to buy tools. Until he went to Europe, he was self-taught. He made things out of dead trees, tried to model Georgia clay. He didn't know what he was doing, only that he had to do it," Peter said. "Until."

(Beauchamp Benedict, in his only interview: "I was alone in the woods and something smoked me. It struck like a thunderbolt." *Smoked me.* Bent over one of Phil's art history books, Jude tested the phrase, circled it in search of an opening she could look into and see what had gone on.) "What?"

"Something happened."

"What, Peter? What happened?" He was so disturbed by this, so confused and disrupted that she pressed. "Tell me what!"

Instead, he went on. "Beauchamp was stuck at Wayward because he was born too late, you know? End of the century. "His father didn't like keeping slaves, but he kept them, so maybe it was some kind of judgment of him," Peter said. "Was he good to them? No telling. Esther knows. God, Jude, do you think we're responsible for our past?"

"I think we're responsible for each other," she said.

"I don't know who to blame." History weighed so heavily on Peter that he found it hard to speak. "Agh. OK. Beauchamp was born broke and his folks died the same year. All he had left was an overseer and a banker in town. Essie's great-grandmother brought him up along with her son Stone, black, white, it was all the same to the two boys, boon friends. When Beauchamp was old enough he fired the overseer and he and Stone took over the place, two young guys running Wayward, Beechy Benedict and Stone Manifort. Planted just enough rice to get by, you know? But once you've done it, it's done until you harvest, it left them with nothing but time. So they sat around at night and made wood carvings, could have been something Earl thought up, like, his grandfather brought a piece from Africa?"

"Tribal princes," Jude said. Looking at Esther, she thought this was natural; the rest was probably ordained, already given and received; it was like remembering a dream.

"You saw the newel post. That was Earl's."

"But the bronzes."

"Once Earl found a wife he didn't need to fill his nights making statues, but Beauchamp was different. He couldn't stop." Peter's voice caught fire. "He had to make them more and more lifelike. The clay wasn't enough, he wanted them to look better than real. He almost killed himself trying to breathe life into them. They had to be eternal. Like bronze. So he sold off some land and booked passage on a steamer to Europe to learn how. He left Stone in charge. By the time he got back Stone had three kids and the place was running fine, they were happy but Beauchamp was driven, so my great-great grandfather just, they called it, *repaired* to his studio to work.

"I think he was lonely," Peter said.

"Then one day he went out into the woods and, I don't know, something happened. Something big. It smoked him."

Alerted, Jude murmured, "Explain smoked."

"I can't. Something happened and his work got very, very good." Words defied him. He shook his head and tried again. "Something happened and it came alive."

"*God and His Creation,*" Jude said.

Peter shook his head. "That was the last. Once he hit on the secret, he had a long career. The first pieces were.... Overnight his work went from ordinary to magnificent. They said nobody had cast full figures that way since the Greeks."

"Lost wax."

"Right," he said moodily. "Lost wax."

"Other people do it."

"But it's not the same. They use positives and negatives, complicated molds with bolts and vents, but for Beechy, it was very simple." The weight of the past rolled up behind Peter, pushing him to an unwanted conclusion. "Oh, Jude, I think he did some awful things."

"Peter!"

"He did some awful things and *God and His Creation* was the last. The culmination. Then, God! He kidnapped it and brought it here."

She said in a low voice, "Was it that hard to find?"

"In those days, yes. He. Ah. OK, it was hidden in the marsh until Ava came and married Father and made him dig it up. She. Ah. I don't know. Now it's out there in the circle. Jude, my mother has spent her life here unraveling old Beechy's secret, but so far she's only found parts. I'm just afraid..."

"What, Peter? What are you afraid of?"

Grief wrenched the words out of him. "That's what I have to find out."

"What is she doing that's so terrible?"

He shook his head, grieving. "She wants us to get it all back."

"You have brothers. Let them do it."

"It's not as simple as you think."

Jude cried. "I don't know what I think,"

He took her hands and turned her so that they were facing. He said, "They never found Beechy's body, you know?"

"The books all say he died."

"Something else happened," Peter said.

"What?"

"I don't know! They buried a bronze likeness instead. He just. I don't know. By that time old Bernard was all grown up and running things. So, Beechy?" Troubled, Peter corrected himself. "Beauchamp?" He did not go on. Instead he stared out over the water and while he brooded, Jude found her eyes drawn once again to the little cluster of drowned sculpture with its broken wingtips and beckoning hands; was the Benedict secret buried there, with the drowned figures? Was the solution buried with them? Brooding, Peter took a long time, trying to decide which thread to pull to untangle the snarl of myth and memory. At last he said, "What really happened was, he disappeared."

At which point Jude, who had been doing well so far, tough Jude Atkins began to crumble, saying, "Oh God, Peter, this is so creepy."

"This is really bad, isn't it?"

"Oh Peter, please let's get out of here."

"I can't," he said. "Maybe. Tell you what. I can't go yet, but you could. And sure. Take Edgar. Here are my keys." He stood abruptly, and his tone was bright and joyful. "And you'll wait for me, in Charleston? This is great."

Minutes later they came barreling out of the shadow of the darkened house at Wayward, tugging sleepy Edgar along. They crossed the dark driveway at a dead run, heading for Peter's car. They were at the bottom of the drive when something as tall and big around as a tree separated itself from the stand of liveoaks. He was less like person than a black hole in the darkness, the void into which all life disappears. He was enormous, terrible.

"Going somewhere?"

Peter groaned: "*Thorne.*"

Fourteen

Thorne was huge. Sitting here in the thin light from a crystal bedside lamp in a stranger's bedroom, Jude tried to assimilate what just happened. All she came away with was the sheer weight of Ava's personal assistant, his tremendous size. It was too dark out there in the driveway for her to make out his face. No. Thorne's face itself was too dark: coarse hair and thick beard, heavy brows obscuring expression. He moved Jude and Peter and Edgar along the drive in a profound silence. It was like going along in front of a rolling boulder. Peter vibrated like a struck tuning fork but did not argue. With a weary look, he went along. Even Edgar knew better than to protest. They moved into the house in front of Thorne like kids running ahead of a thunderstorm.

Now she was here. Somebody had taken her things from Peter's room and left them in this small back bedroom. It was probably once a maid's room, tucked at the head of the kitchen stairs like an afterthought. Maybe she should have resisted, told Thorne she wasn't one of Ava's students, to be pushed around because Ava ordered it. She could have dodged under his heavy arms and struck out for town on foot, or sneaked back downstairs and phoned for a taxi, but it was late, she was spent. Wayward had used her up. Jude had hit that metabolic low point that has nothing to do with the hour of the day, really, or the presence or absence of light, but is, rather, a condition of life. Like her cell phone, Jude was useless.

It's too dark.

She tried to tell herself everything would look better by daylight, but now? Everything was just. Too much.

It's too dark.

For Judith Atkins, tonight at least, it was too late to do anything.

She lay down without changing and crashed into sleep.

Things did look better in the morning, but only because it was light. By daylight, the house looked less threatening. Everything was on the same grand scale but sunlight made the house at Wayward looked shabby, as if the proprietors had lacked the energy to undo the work of time. There was the room she was staying in, for instance—chipped woodwork, faded, peeling paint slapped on over flowered wallpaper, which bled through; damp breezes lifting tired lace curtains over a window that gave onto the water—garish new chintz bedspread, ancient rag rug that had been scrubbed to death. The flowers in the hall paper had faded to brown. Waiting outside Peter's room, she realized that everything the Benedicts had chosen to express themselves spoke of privilege—and neglect. There were cobwebs in the chandelier and cobwebs festooning the sconces. The mossy carpeting was worn to the threads in places and the bronzes clustered in corners like apologetic houseguests had a neglected look, as if they'd been set down some fifty years before and were seldom dusted and never moved. It was as though all the owners' energies had been directed elsewhere for so long that the house was withering, like an unwatered plant.

"Peter?"

She knocked again. She wanted Peter to come out and tell her none of this mattered. She wanted him to come out and be glad to see her, OK? But there was no answer and when she tried the knob the door was locked. Peter was gone. She was alone here in the Benedict citadel, and she would have to go down to that elegant dining room and face Ava without him to back him up.

By daylight, the house was nothing like she thought. Wayward was in an advanced state of decay, but the hall carpet was a once-magnificent Persian runner; that was a Mary Cassatt hanging in the alcove on the second-floor landing and the paintings lining the hall were oil sketches by painters whose names Jude recognized: the tiny Childe Hassam just outside her bedroom, a little Eakins, a Turner sketch.

The paintings, the crystal, the gilded mirror above the inlaid wooden escritoire in the alcove all suggested that the Benedicts had both money and position for so long that they could afford not to care what other people thought. What was it Peter had called them that first night? *Decayed aristocracy.* Even though he hated it, he'd said with a certain measure of pride, "The only thing that matters to them is the work."

And what matters to you?

Oh, Peter.

Shaken, she retreated to her room. She needed to put on bright colors this morning, to make herself strong. *I'm OK,* she thought, pulling out a red scarf. *I'm doing all right.* Then she saw the framed snapshot of Peter with Gara. Was it here last night? There was Peter hugging the laughing black-haired girl who looked like a glamorous Snow White. Whoever emptied the drawers and changed the bed last night overlooked it. Or put it here, Jude thought, like a warning sign. It read: PRIVATE PROPERTY KEEP OFF; Musing, she picked it up, looking into the face of a pretty girl who looked back at her, smiling as if innocent of her future.

"Gara," she murmured. "Oh shit."

Something shook her, and Jude could not have said whether it was fear or something else, some *other* stirring in the belly of the house.

"I probably knew," she said to the snapshot of Gara Sullivan. "This had to be your room."

When she put it down her hand lingered, as if she honestly thought she could read the unwritten. "But why did you leave it, and when? And where did you go?"

When she thought about it, she didn't have to ask.

"Ava. You had to get away from that bitch."

She steeled herself. Go on. Go down and face her. Get it over with.

It was easier than she thought. By the time she came into the sunshot dining room Ava was gone. Everybody was gone except for Edgar, who twisted his fork in the middle of a pile of ruined pancakes, and Petra, the plump, pretty student who lurked, waiting for Edgar to finish so she could wash his plate. The French doors were open and beyond the water sparkled. The air off the marsh was damp but sweet and from the direction of the foundry she could hear a dull, regular sound, a muffled thump—Thorne at work, she supposed, but doing what?

Edgar slouched over his pancakes and wouldn't look at her.

She wanted to hug the boy and apologize for them getting caught last night. She wanted to make him tell her what awful thing made him phone Peter that day, desperate to escape this place. She had to know what Edgar was afraid of, what he knew that she didn't know. She wanted to huddle with him, planning what to do next. But Petra was dusting aggressively, apparently intent on hearing everything they said. Spying, Jude supposed. Like Thorne, Ava's students did Ava's work. Lifting a limp piece of toast from the rack on the sideboard, she sat down, gnawing indifferently. When Edgar didn't look up and wouldn't talk to her, she tried, "Hey, Eds."

Attacking with the handbrush and dustpan, Petra knelt, energetically sweeping under her feet.

Jude tried to sound offhand. "So, where's Peter?" Interesting. In the past three days she and Peter had become so close that she knew when she was going to find him in a room and when she was not. She already knew he wasn't in the house.

Petra got up from her knees suddenly, jarring the table with her head.

"Eds?"

Edgar wouldn't answer.

"Look, I'm sorry I crapped out last night."

Petra cleared her throat and the boy cut his eyes in Petra's direction, warning: *Shut up.*

"So," Jude said, too loud. "D'you think it's going to rain?"

Crosseyed with concentration, Edgar shoved so much food into his mouth that he couldn't possibly talk.

Then Petra said unexpectedly, "If you're looking for Peter, forget it. They're all out in the studios. Nobody comes back until dinnertime."

"Fine, I'll just."

"Nobody bothers them in the studios." Petra's face shone with the passion of the convert. "The first law is, Nothing interrupts the work. Now if you're finished, I'll just."

"Right," Jude said, getting up.

Petra added, "I'm in a hurry to get to the studio."

Chewing her dry toast, Jude left the dining room and, trying to look aimless, wandered out of the house. She sauntered into the bushes that flanked the house and once she had cleared the garden where just anybody could see her, she darted for the woods. She had to go carefully because the studios were all alike, rustic cabins with windows covered with parchment that let in light but guaranteed privacy. Peter was in one of them. Now she had to figure out which one. Then she could kite in a note or scratch at the door to let him know she was waiting; he would come out and then they could...

Preoccupied, she went along with her head down until she bumped into someone hurrying the other way. "Oh!"

"Oh!" Ava scowled at the interruption.

"I'm sorry, Ava, I..."

The eyes Ava turned on her were so cold that Jude's throat closed. Ava said sternly, "Who are you?"

Jude coughed up the words. "It's me, Ava. Peter's friend."

"Do I know you?" It was as if yesterday had never been. "What are you doing here?"

What was the matter with the woman, didn't she remember? Hadn't they been introduced, hadn't they sat through that awful dinner last night? "I overslept. Since you're all working, I thought I'd... explore?"

She might as well have been talking to a bronze. Ava did not remember. She said coldly, "Whoever you are, we don't allow tourists on the grounds."

Or was it that she chose not to remember? Jude said, louder, "Mrs. Benedict, I'm looking for Peter."

"What do you want with Peter?" Nothing broke the surface of that blank, insulting stare.

Well for one, I'd like to get him out of here. "We have to talk."

"You want to talk to Peter." Ava could have been examining a specimen. "Who did you say you were?"

"Judith. Judith Atkins." The devil took her and she said, "Peter and I are engaged."

And the part of Ava Benedict that stood back, judging, suddenly returned. "Wait a minute, Ms..." Ava's eyes narrowed and her tone changed. "Hold still." The bitch. She took Jude's chin in her hand. and without asking permission, pulled out a ruler and sighted along it.

Pulling away, Jude said, "It's Jude. My name is Jude."

But Ava was fixed on the work at hand. "Oh, right," she said so absently that there was no way of telling whether she actually remembered. "Peter's friend."

Yes, bitch. If she and Peter really did marry, Jude thought, they'd better move somewhere far, far away. "Peter's friend."

"Listen, whoever you are." Ava's tone swept everything else before it. The fingers she closed on Jude's arm were alarmingly strong. With the force of a woman who moves heavy objects every day of her life, Ava hurried her along the path and into one of the studios. "I need that profile. Come along."

Which was how against her will Jude found herself arranged on a stool in Ava's studio, draped in silk and placed just *so* while Peter's fierce mother turned her head with strong fingers. She would mold and carve until Jude saw her own face taking shape in the wax. If she submitted, it was for a number of reasons, not the least of which was the hope that this would soften Ava, so whether or not she gave them her blessing, she'd let them go.

At the very least, next time she'll remember who I am.

"You don't just marry a man," Jude's mom had said in the wake of her breakup with Phil. "You marry his mother too."

Parched on the stool, following Ava's orders, she tried to imagine what that would be like.

"Ordinarily I move from life mask to maquette," Ava said. "But we're running short of time. Beautiful brow!"

So her misgivings were complicated by Ava's flattery. One of the famous Benedicts wanted to replicate *her face.* Imagine. Jude Atkins, a good enough jeweler but nothing extraordinary in the looks department, immortalized in bronze. "I'm not exactly Psyche."

"I've already done my Psyche," Ava said without missing a beat.

It was like talking to a machine.

If Ava saw her at all, it was as an object, which Jude supposed was better than being invisible. Until now, that was what she was. "Turn," Ava said. "That way." She could have been placing a jug in a still life. "You have an interesting face."

Beginning with wax formed over an armature, Ava worked with mesmerizing speed and skill. Jude had to hold still; she was not to get down without permission and after a certain point she could only look at the parts of the room she could see without moving her head. Here in her studio, the autocratic Ava moved with such authority that Jude comprehended her power. For practical purposes she was Ava's Benedict's prisoner, Jude Atkins, who woke up this morning thinking of nothing but escape. If the family history kept generations of Benedicts here, if Ava saw to it, it was in the service of their art.

Tacked to the planks in front of Jude were passionate, hasty sketches—plans for parts of a tremendous, complex shape suggested in a snarl of squiggles on a scrap of notepad page. On the floor along the wall sat a series of negative faces, plaster casts of figures whose expressions ranged from peaceful to desperate. The shaggy one reminded her of that guy Jake, who had confronted her the first day and who for whatever reasons had stayed in the kitchen last night when the other students came in for dessert. There were silks and chiffons and a collection of hats and cloaks hanging on hooks in Ava's studio and in a corner, a lifesized figure covered with a dropcloth. There were more figures at her back, Jude knew, but if she twisted or moved her head even slightly in an attempt to see, Ava snarled and wrenched her back into position.

And the sculptor: it was amazing. Measuring, shaping, studying, paring, smoothing, reconsidering, forcing her medium with her thumbs, Ava Benedict moved from wax to life and back so surely that Jude began to think it was her own face Ava was contouring with such speed. Hands and sculptors' tools flashed until Jude lost focus and her concentration; her vision blurred. As hunger and fatigue hit, she felt not so much diminished as altered by what was happening here. She had the idea that at the end of a very long time she would step down and look into a mirror and see Ava's likeness instead of her own.

She had no idea how much time passed before the studio door opened behind them and Ava whirled like a tigress surprised over a fresh kill. Her voice was low, savage. "What are you doing here?"

Jude couldn't see the speaker, but she recognized the voice.

Benton cried, "My God, Ava, what are you doing?"

"I had to replace Jimmy Daley."

"But the girl. Peter's girl."

Troubled, Jude stirred. It was like coming back to life. In another minute she would collect the will to break free of Ava and under cover of the beginning quarrel escape, at least for the time being. But for the moment she sat quietly, still in the grips of process. She was locked in the spot where she knew now that the missing Gara Sullivan had sat: Judith Atkins, no great beauty but with a very interesting face, Ava said, listening as Benton Benedict's voice came up from great depths. As if dredging them up from the tomb, Peter's father dropped three words into the charged silence, in his despair both sounding the alarm and freeing Jude:

"How could you?"

"The work," Ava said as Jude slipped out the door and hit the path running. "I do what I have to do."

Fifteen

Boy, the last thing Edgar wanted was to be all by himself today, but it was half past lunchtime and he was stuck in his room with all his plastic models, from the X-guys to antiques from *Star Wars,* alone. Everybody he cared about was off somewhere.

Even Peter's new girlfriend was gone. She was off in Ava's studio; from the porch he saw Ava stop Peter's girl cold in the front yard, like, his mom kept Jude from coming back into the house. She and Jude exchanged words that Edgar couldn't hear. Then Ava dragged her back to the studio. His mother always gets what she wants, and it pisses Edgar off. When he went to tell Peter, he couldn't find him. Peter wasn't anywhere. Edgar supposed that in spite of fighting the mother tooth and claw, Peter was right back in his studio that Ava fixed up for him, locked into the place that he left home to escape, just like Luke was in his studio and Dirk was in his studio, which meant Ava was going to win the game with Peter just like she'd won everything else, she wins every time. If she could get back Peter and make him do her bidding, then there was no escape. She would get Edgar too, which sucked.

She'd get him if he couldn't think of something fast.

How? I'm only a kid.

Last week Ava set the trap by starting this stupid model of Edgar's head. ("Come on, sweetie, you're going to be part of a truly historic piece," goddammit, she *twinkled* at him, the bitch mother of all time, going: "and if the Teddy you're making with Daddy is any good I promise, we'll incorporate it somewhere around the base of the anniversary piece.")

It isn't a Teddy, Mother. It's a Kodiak bear.

Cows thought if you took their snapshot you stole their soul, Peter said, and Edgar thought maybe he was right. There was the problem of the toenail parings for one thing, that Ava insisted on collecting. There were the snippets of Edgar's hair that she picked up off the floor at the barbershop and there was his absolutely favorite *Star Trek* Klingon, all these pieces of Edgar that somehow got wired into the *thing* Ava made to put her wax on, what did she call it, the armature. Well, he would armature her. "There are only about eight people in the world who know how to work directly from the wax," she said at his last sitting. God he hated the sittings, that's one of the reasons he ran away. She said, "And seven of them are in your family." Like, he was supposed to be proud. "And the armature," she said, "is everything. Sit up straight, sweetie. You have a nice big head, just like all the biggest stars."

Don't fucking condescend to me.

"Smile, baby. Aren't you glad?" She was smarmy-nice enough, but when Ava looked at Edgar that way it was like what she really wanted was to peel off all his hair and skin and mold his wax likeness on his naked skull.

"Benedicts put themselves into their work," Dad told him one happy day last winter when they were just playing together, Edgar modeling Fuzzy on the floor of his dad's studio while the old man worked. It was the last sweet time Edgar could remember. The anniversary plans were already rolling but he could care less. Then Daddy said, "And you're coming up on a very big birthday."

"My birthday." Right in front of his very eyes, everything changed. He heard himself squeak, "Don't hurt me!"

His father turned, surprised. "Why Eds, what do you mean?"

edger was surprised too. He would give anything if he and his dad just lived in a tract house and Dad went to the bank in the mornings, like normal sixth-graders' fathers did. Edgar touched his father's maimed ear. His voice cracked. "What are you going to cut off of me?"

"Oh, honey, honey," Benton said, hugging him hard. "Remember, you're a Benedict."

A Benedict. It was beginning to be awful. He howled, "I don't care!"

His father sighed. "Son, you might as well know, we Benedicts pay a price for being special. Understand, there is a thin line between art and life."

Well if you say so, Dad. If it's so great, why are there tears falling out of your eyes? Edgar mumbled, "Not it."

"And for your next birthday, Mommy..." Benton nudged him with a desperate, bright grin. He wasn't really smiling but he tried to sound glad. "Mommy is going to model your head."

Thud. It had begun.

Edgar's belly cramped. "None of the other kids have to."

"That's what makes you special," Daddy said.

"I don't want to. You can't make me."

Then Daddy hugged Edgar so hard that he squeaked. "Shh shh, honey. Daddy isn't going to let anybody hurt you," but Edgar could feel him trembling. Even his voice trembled. "And when you get bigger, you can have your own studio."

"I don't want a studio. Leave me alone!"

Benton just went on hugging and rocking, rocking and hugging while tears ran down his face, "Shhshh, honey, shhshh."

Edgar took on so that Ava had to set him up in the parlor window for his portrait bust instead of the studio. She turned him this way and that like a rock so she could get the best take on his head. He wanted to go downstairs now and smash the thing but Ava had drawn the velvet curtains to keep the sun off the wax and the lump that looked like him was shrouded in plastic and covered with a cloth for protection, whether its or his, Edgar could not say. To tell the truth, he was scared of it. He might pull off the cloth and find out she had done something awful to the face, and the secret, scary part of Edgar that divined the truth suspected that one day soon he'd catch his reflection in the parlor mirror and discover that she had done the same awful thing to him. Still, if something weird was going to happen to you, better here in the house, with people around. In the studios, you were dead meat.

When you met the Benedicts in their studios, you were already on the losing side. Once they got out there and got involved in what they were making, they lost track. When his family went to work every one of them went inside what they were doing, and if you happened to blunder in on one of them working, they glared like you were a lump of dirt or a cockroach that had gotten in the way.

It was safer here. Edgar liked sitting up here in his room, gluing together these dumb plastic models of monsters and rockets and racing cars. The thing was, you could, like, open them up and see what they were made of? Like, what they were formed on. These models were open secrets, unlike the things his family made. They were light and colorful, like life, instead of being heavy, like bronze. He'd rather glue plastic than work in clay because.

Because.

Something. He was not sure. The bronzes made him scared; the waxes made him scared. Even modeling the bear made him scared.

Ava scared him. "Understand the honor, baby, unless one of your brothers brings home a decent wife, you're the last Benedict there'll ever be." So. Like it or not, he was Guest of Honor at this great big mystery anniversary for *God and His Creation*, that made Essie so anxious and Daddy so sad. He didn't even know what he was supposed to *do*. All Ava said was, Important something-something, what was it, *renewal of the vows*.

"Shh-shh," Essie said when she found him crying the night before he ran away. "I won't let anything bad happen to you."

But there was this big *event* coming. What if he messed up in front of all the relatives? Or worse? Plus. Listen! Last week Edgar started hearing noises. There's something in the cellar.

He heard it down there. If he pressed his ear to the door real close he could swear he heard somebody calling his name, *Eddd-garrrr...* although he couldn't be sure of that part because they—*They???*

They. It.

Whatever it was, it was coming from too deep. Filtering up from the undercroft, the sound came through so many layers of the land below Wayward that at this distance, *Edgar* and *Help* kind of sounded the same.

Damn Peter, he thought, off doing Ava's work like a good boy, he just plain knuckled last night at the first sight of Thorne. Yeah, Thorne was huge and menacing, but why didn't Peter bop him or shoot him or something, so they could run off? If Wayward really is a trap, Peter will never get out if he won't fight, and if strong, grown-up Peter can't get out, how can Edgar expect to escape? If Edgar couldn't run away and make it stick, if the three of them don't get out of here before the ceremony...

The possibilities creeped him out.

Dude, pull yourself together.

Edgar took a deep breath. "OK."

Something in the cellar. He'll start with that. Gotta find out what's in the cellar.

He gulped. *Just not yet.*

Jude would help, he thought, but he saw Ava drag Jude back to her studio. She would be getting her head done by Ava like Edgar was getting his head done and Gara was supposed to have gotten her head done, except at the last minute Ava got all interested in doing a full figure of Gara Sullivan and would have, too, if Gara hadn't run off in the night. Edgar never much liked Gara—too pretty-sweet for his taste, but he could certainly see her wanting out of this creepy place.

Extremely creepy, with the noises in the cellar louder every night to say nothing of all the pounding and thumping over at the foundry. Plus Ava's students keep hulking around doing her bidding like bit players in a creepshow: "Yes, Ma-stah." Ava, she takes their money and promises to turn them into great sculptors and they sell everything and come here. She tells them all that they have talent just to get them to do things for her, but that's bullshit. It's a different story when they aren't in the house bringing her nightly absinthe and cream or doing chores like good campers, like at the end of the month they're going to get a gold star. Can't they see Ava thinks they're lower than shit? She uses them like farm machinery, and they love her for it, and that's creepy too.

And now the relatives have started turning up, beginning with Uncle Berton Benedict blowing in from Paris last night with that Pocohontas lady to model for him. There are Benedicts coming in from London and Tokyo any minute now. Worse yet, all the Benedict men look alike: Dad and this brother Berton. His own half-brothers, Dirk and Luke and even Pete, they all have the same profile, like something you'd get off a dime. Dumb Eds is stuck with it too, locked in behind the family face.

Family talent, family legacy, family myth, Edgar grew up on it, had it piped in through the baby monitor, fed to him at meals, tucked into every bedtime story Ava ever told, on top of which Ava just added the last weight, the ball-buster for the ultimate bench press: *family responsibility.*

Well, he would responsibility her.

At least Essie was on his side. Trouble was, Esther was off in Daddy's studio getting herself modeled too. Bad idea, Edgar thought, it put her out of reach. Rotten luck. He could sure use her around now. He would really like to talk to Essie for true, because there was bad stuff going on. Nothing you could tell the cops about, OK, because after all a Benedict is a Benedict, even Edgar, but there was stuff happening that, well he couldn't exactly put his finger on it, except it was bad and he just, like, *knew.*

That he couldn't deal with alone. The cellar was big and dark and had at least three subcellars that he knew of, but the door under the back stairs was locked and Edgar couldn't pry it open; he'd tried. The one time he, like, went for it with a chisel, Thorne popped up like the Terminator, WHAM, and he backed off fast. Nobody messed with Thorne. If the students did everything Ava said, Thorne did things even before she said anything. He was humongous, with eyes like twin searchlights, big old Thorne who was always *there* and never sat down for a meal with them, not in all these years. It was weird.

It was also depressing. Enough to make you go out and jump off the end of the dock. Wuooww. Like probably happened to poor Jimmy Daley, that Edgar was kind of friends with? Like, what if that's what happened to Gara? What if Edgar was, like, cursed, and bad things happened to everyone he ever cared about?

Why were his plastic models rattling? Right. He was shivering like a puppy caught in the cold-house where Ava stored the waxes until they were ready to slather on the slurry and pour the bronze.

Ghah!

Edgar fled his bedroom like a freed gerbil and hurtled down the pantry stairs, roaring through the dining room and out the French doors. He was about to slide down the balcony railing when he saw something stirring out there, beyond the raised fist of Great Grandfather's *God the Father*. It stopped him stopped cold.

There was something moving on the water, just off the point. A power-boat cut the water like a shark's fin; somebody killed the motor so it would glide in silently. As Edgar watched, the tall figure in the stern poled in to the end of the dock and a slim figure in black rose like a Ninja avenger and stepped onto the dock.

It was astounding.

Even more surprising was the fact that nobody came running out to intercept this person. Probably because Ava had made it clear they were working on deadline, there was nobody left to patrol. The students were all klutzing around in their studios and the family were all in theirs, making these effigies, and Thorne... You never knew about Thorne, but the noises in the foundry continued, which meant he was probably socked in there doing whatever Thorne did, so to all intents and purposes little old Eds here, Edgar Benedict alone saw the arrival and it was up to Eds to sound the alarm.

In hell.

If this worked out right, Edgar could run down and tell the newcomers his story and they would take him away in their boat.

Grabbing the rail, he flew, or slid—hit one step, skipped three, hit another and in the next bound landed on the gravel running, crunching through the oleanders. He reached the dock just as the boat sped away and the new arrival stepped onto the property at Wayward with a forceful stride that surprised Edgar, because it turned out to be a woman and the white hair and the gangs of wrinkles made it clear that she was really, really old.

"Please," he began, before they were really close enough to speak. "I need your help."

The elegant stranger pointed, hissing urgently. "Quiet."

He stopped. It was embarrassing. Edgar and his big mouth, right in the middle of some kind of surprise operation.

He looked. "Oh shit." The eagle beak, the strong jaw, the eyes: who else? "Another Benedict."

Her grip was even stronger than Essie's. "Quiet, Edgar."

"How did you..."

"Be still. Nobody knows I'm here." As she spoke, those arresting blue eyes skimmed the terrain—studios, outbuildings, looking beyond to the overgrown spot on the far side of the student shacks, where the old-fashioned cold-house still stood, hidden by undergrowth. She considered for only a moment and then struck off for the cold-house, pushing Edgar along ahead of her.

"Wait a minute," he muttered, digging in his heels. He had the crazy idea that sooner or later somebody would stuff him in the cold-house along with the waxes, they'd come in and slap slurry all over him and when it hardened they'd lug him over to the foundry and instead of pouring and displacing one of the waxes, they'd pour molten bronze right in on top of him. "Help?"

"Shh! I'm not going to hurt you, son."

"I'm not your son!" To his surprise, when they reached the cold-house, the strong old woman strode on by, propelling him deeper into the woods. "Where are you taking me?"

"I know a place."

"How?" Oh, right. She grew up here. She was one of *them*. What he couldn't figure out was whether this woman was a good Benedict or a bad one. Early in life Edgar had perceived that there were two kinds of people, good and bad, and the hell of it was trying to know which were which, or how to tell, or what to do about it once you found out.

They were almost at the far edge of the property when to his astonishment the old woman parted a stand of bushes to reveal a desiccated shack. She started pulling vines away from the door. "Old slave quarters," she murmured. "Thought they might still be here." She let go of Edgar long enough to get the door open and then stood back like a proud householder ushering him in. "This is as good a place as any," she said.

"Place for what?" Edgar hung back. It was dark in there. Now that they were clear of the house and the studios, he dared to raise his voice. "I *said,* place for what?"

Ava would have punished him for insubordination or acted hurt and not answered, but this old lady who both looked like his father and didn't look like his father just regarded him with cool blue eyes and said, "Place for me and Wataru to wait it out. Understand, I am expected, but only you know I'm here."

Her eyes were so level and clear that he felt unaccountably secure with her. Instead of challenging, Edgar whispered, "What are you going to do?"

Only when the old woman sighed did he understand what a long trip it had been for her and how tired she must be. She collected herself and answered. "Whatever's necessary." Then she held out her hand to him like a four-square straight arrow scoutmaster waiting for him to shake. When he did not, she took Edgar by the shoulders and drew him closer so they could look into each other's eyes, equals, no, *confreres,* more or less man to man.

"Go now. Don't tell anybody I've arrived. If they ask about me, you don't know. Got it?"

"I don't even know who you are."

She seemed amused. "You're Benton's son."

"Benton and Ava's son," he said dutifully, although he was less than happy about belonging to his mother right now."

"Right. Ava's son. Not one of poor Elaine's."

"You knew my..." Daddy was married before Ava, and he and that woman had Dirk and Luke, but she was dead and there was no noun for that. "I don't know what she is. Was."

"Elaine. I did. But now..." She grimaced. "Never mind. You look just like your father when he was a little boy."

"He was never little," Edgar said sadly. "He's always been old."

"It's that damn woman," she said under her breath.

Resentful as he was, this made him defensive. "Wait a minute. I don't even know who you are or what you're doing here."

"I'm here for the reunion. I came all the way from Japan." She smiled, waiting for this to catch fire. When he did not respond she said, "Didn't your mother put up that screen I sent you, or show you any of my cards?"

"I never saw any cards."

"Edgar Benedict, do you know who I am?"

"No Ma'am."

"Of course," she said. "That damn woman has rewritten our history. Probably erased me right out of it, like she erased poor Elaine. Listen to me, Edgar Beauchamp Benedict." She waited until she had his full attention. The smile she gave him trembled with sweetness. "I am your great aunt Benta and I've come to end this thing."

It was strange. He thought he heard a door opening somewhere in his life. He was excited without knowing why. "End what?"

"Things you ought to be afraid of," she said.

He still was not certain what she meant. "You mean, like..." How could he say *my mother?* Edgar was ashamed to be afraid of her and from the bottom of his heart he was ashamed to let anybody know. He couldn't complete the sentence. "Like what?"

Benta looked at him wisely. "I think you know."

That smile; he liked her. He said tentatively, "You mean I might not have to have my birthday?"

"There's no way out of birthdays," Benta said, looking so deep into him that Edgar squirmed. "It's all in how you handle them."

He was too scared to make her explain and too polite to tell her to stop. He said uncomfortably, "Can I go now?"

"Not yet. Soon. In a minute." She was rummaging in the pockets of her black trousers. "I have something for you."

"Huh?"

"Say Yes, Aunt Benta," she said, smiling. "Just to put us on the right footing."

"Yes, Aunt Benta." How nice to see her smile!

"Better," she said. She hesitated at the edge of a sigh. "Remember, I'm old." Benta found what she was looking for. She pulled it out of her pocket. "Hold out your hand."

When he did, she dropped the object into it. It was hard, cold. The edges were sharp. He was afraid to look. "What's this?'

"Take it and get going before anybody finds out you're here," she said brusquely, dismissing him.

"But."

"You know what it is."

"Wait a minute, how..."

"And don't tell anybody you saw me or the boat or Wataru. It's all right," she said.

He opened his hand and looked down. It really was all right. She had given him the key to the basement. Gasping, he ran.

"Hurry," she said in a chilling whisper that carried. "You know what to do."

Sixteen

"Oh Berty." Benton surprised his brother Berton with a preemptive hug. "I'm so glad you came."

Leaving their studios as if at a prearranged signal, the long-separated brothers had paced different quadrants of the grounds, pretending they'd been brought outside by artistic problems that could only be solved on the hoof. Now they emerged from the woods so nearly at the same time that it might have been prearranged, Benton pretending not to notice Berton, Berton playing oblivious until they collided in the weedy circle in front of the main house at Wayward: *Oh, it's you. Imagine that.*

"You understand why I had to come," Berton said.

Benton was dimly aware of the rattle of an engine approaching; a rickety car had barged through the main gate; it was rattling along the road into Wayward—could be anybody, one of Ava's deliveries, maybe. If the driver didn't interrupt Benton and his brother, Ava would send one of her students to break up the conversation, Benton knew. She didn't let him have friends. He and Berty didn't have long. Benton was like a speed-reader, trying to make out the text written on his brother's face. "You came for Ava," he said, testing. "For the anniversary."

"No." Berton corrected him so firmly that Benton grinned. "For all our sakes." After all these years of separation his brother regarded him with an expression Benton remembered from childhood: the wise, loving look born of the kind of experience that knows what is to come. "This." He gestured angrily. "It can't go on this way."

Benton's voice shook. "What are we going to do?"

His big brother exploded. "It has to change! God, Ben. How did we let it come to this?"

This was the question Benton asked himself every time he went into the studio or passed the foundry, where Ava and Thorne worked alone. "We all made a deal," he said quietly. "Don't blame yourself, Bert. You weren't even here. You left for Europe when it first came up."

"But I profited. God, I profited," Berty said. "I'm as much a party to it as you."

"You were thousands of miles away."

"It's my fault." Berton looked up at the house, at whatever he saw behind the gracious facade. He said out of great grief, "I never should have left you to handle this."

"Don't. You weren't here. You're not involved."

"We are all implicated," Berton said. With his maimed index finger, he brushed his brother's damaged ear. "We all did this."

Benton's breath shuddered. "But that's the only thing you did. Whereas I..."

"It was talismanic, Ben. The parts stand for the whole."

"You can't even begin to see the whole." Benton raised his voice to compete with the clatter of the approaching vehicle. If he was aware of Edgar bobbing on the veranda, desperate to talk to him, he was too distraught to see. He said gravely, "You... Did not... Assent to the rest."

"The scraps we all gave stood for the rest—whatever it is." Tall and strong as Berton was, his voice was as light as a boy's. Benton could barely hear him. The car clanked into the circle in front of the house, dragging its muffler. Bert said, "And we all prospered. We did."

"I'm afraid we did. Oh, Bert. If everybody had stayed... Maybe we could have stopped her."

"Nobody wanted to stop her," Berton said quietly. "Poor Benty, you had to carry it all. You suffered the most, but that doesn't make you most responsible."

"But I *am*. I married her." He whispered, horrified, "I let her proceed."

"No. Understand, Benton. Present or absent, we let her do it. All of us." The car sounds stopped. "Whatever she does. What is it exactly, anyway?"

"I can't tell you." Benton covered his face with his hands.

"Don't know or don't want to?"

"Both."

On the long porch, Edgar advanced and at the sight of something Benton had dimly noted but had not yet taken in, retreated. Where did he go? What did he see?

"Listen." In the silence Berton's Benedict's next words stood one at a time, solid as a row of monuments. "It was worth it."

Benton nodded sadly. "It made us famous."

"We're in every major gallery in the world."

"In cathedrals," Benton said, without telling his brother that he was, in exchange for certain reassurances, crafting a St. Jude for Father Jerome's rickety little wooden church in town. ("I can't promise you salvation, nobody can," the priest told him, "but I will do my best to see that you don't have to die without a priest.") He said tentatively, "So some good has come out of it."

"Listen. The work was brilliant." Remorse was at war with pride in Berton's face.

For a second, pride overcame Benton's regrets. "It still is. So I guess we have to thank Ava for that. But this new piece..."

Berton drew himself up. "When she asked us to come she got more than she bargained for."

"...It's gone too far. Berty, I don't know what to do."

Behind them, a car door opened and shut with a tinny crash.

Berton began, "No. *We* don't know what to do. But we do know this. We have to do it now."

They should have gone on but there was no continuing. The old woman who had struggled out of the car crunched toward them through the grass. Broad as she was, she stood tall in spite of her age and her enormous weight. She was like a barrel in a flowered skirt but the set of the shoulders, the massive biceps made it clear that much of her bulk was muscle. She could have been anywhere north of sixty and south of eighty. Surrounded as it was by pinky-white hair scragged back into a disorderly knot, her face was smooth as a Buddha's. She rolled along in sloppy, overrun shoes, rasping, "All right, where is she?"

Berton said in cold tones, "And who are you?"

But Benton could have been his antebellum great-great grandfather, welcoming a newcomer to the plantation; he did everything but bow. "How do you do."

She snorted. "I've been better."

"Ma'am?"

"I come to get the bitch." The woman was angry, no, furious. "Where the fuck are you hiding her?"

"I beg your pardon?"

"My daughter, the ungrateful bitch."

"Your daughter? Your daughter's here?" Benton whirled in distress. "Who is your daughter?"

"You know damn well who she is. Lording it up down here while I boil up hog scraps to get enough fat to make my biscuits and pour on the broth and call it a meal."

"I'm sorry, but I..."

She flashed broken, stained teeth. "I don't know who's been working on her, but the checks have stopped."

"Oh dear!"

Berton stepped forward to join ranks with his brother, "Ma*dame*, is there something we can do?"

"Just lead me to her. It's time for an accounting."

"I'm sorry, I don't know who..."

"The fuck you don't. I know you're hiding her," the old woman said angrily. "You been hiding her for years. So step aside." Her voice ratcheted up a notch and then another, penetrating the house and all the studios and outbuildings. "Come on, Hank Etta, sing out. Your Momma's come to get you." The big woman wheeled, collaring both brothers. "You guys ain't did her in, is you?"

Berton said automatically, "Why, no. Of course not."

Benton's response was more complex. His hand flew to his mouth. He looked around wildly. "Oh God, I hope not."

"Then where the fuck is she?"

His gaze shifted here, there, as if he could locate the missing Hank Etta in one of the outbuildings or in the muddy waters off the point. "Is she... ah... one of Ava's students?"

"Hank Etta don't study shit, OK? She fucking runs the show!" The intruder let go of their shirtfronts and turned her full attention to the embattled Benton. "Are you the responsible party here?"

The brothers spoke as one:

"Yes I am."

"We are all responsible."

Then Benton began carefully, "Madam. Whoever you are..."

"I'm her goddam Momma, asshole. Now I don't know if it's you that took my money I'm supposed to get or that goddam husband of hers, but—"

"...whoever she is. Ah." Shaking off his brother, Benton put the words down between them, setting them out one by one. "What makes you think something has happened to her?"

"I already told you, the goddamn checks is stopped."

Turning away from them, she bellowed, outraged. "Hank Etta. Goddammit where are you? Hank Etta Hutson, if you can hear me, you come the fuck out and show yourself." Shouting, she commanded the driveway with her feet spread wide, challenging her daughter to come.

Nothing happened. Nobody came.

She let all her breath out: *Pah.* "See, that proves it. If she was OK she would have come running."

"Maybe it would help if you described her..."

"If she wasn't dead, she'd be out here hugging me hello. I'm her Momma after all."

"...Whoever she is," Benton finished.

"You wanna know what she looks like? I'll tell you what she looks like. She looks like me." Because the three of them were more or less marooned out here in front of Wayward and the Benedicts weren't budging, she fell back for a second, thinking, and then patted all her pockets until she came up with a snapshot. "OK, OK," she said, thrusting it into Benton's face. "Here's her picture. She looks like this. Or used to. This here's my Hank Etta's high school graduation picture. Are you going to take it or what?"

Benton went white.

"Benty, what is it?"

Ashen, he showed his brother. "Look."

"Imagine. Imagine that. Just imagine!" Berton began to laugh.

The big woman brightened. "You've seen her?"

Berton was laughing so hard he couldn't speak. Red faced and tearful, he nodded.

Benton said brokenly. "I live with her."

"So OK, she ain't dead or anything, she's fine."

Suppressing his laughter, Berton managed to answer. "Madam, your daughter is better than fine."

"Well then where the fuck is my money? And where the fuck is she? After everything I done for her. The checks done quit coming, see?"

She was not aware of what this did to her audience, of Benton's distress or the series of expressions playing across Berton's face as he said, "So much for your very great lady, baby brother. So much for the elegant Ava Pertreille."

"I had to butcher the cow to get money to come here."

"So this changes things, doesn't it, Ben."

"You know how it is when you get down to the nub," she said.

"Doesn't it?" A new sound distracted Bert momentarily; a slick little rented car, rolling in through the avenue of trees.

"I come all this way and now I want results." She bellowed at the woods, "Hank Etta, honey, Momma's here."

In spite of which, Berton pressed. "Doesn't it? Ben?"

As the new car stopped, the fat woman barked, "You know she's in here. Just show me where."

Benton was too upset to speak. He pointed to Ava's studio.

"Fine," she said. "That's fine." Now that she'd located her prey, the old lady was content to stand out here in the driveway for as long as they were content to let her. "OK, then. I want that daughter of mine out here in five minutes, unless that goddamn husband of hers has drug her off somewhere."

"I'm the husband," Benton said. Behind him, two new arrivals spilled out of the car but he was too distraught to see.

"Oh sure you are. And I'm the Queen of France. Now listen, I don't know who you are or what your game is, but I want to see them, my Hank Etta and that big old worthless husband of hers."

Benton drew himself up to speak. Shaking his head, Bert put two fingers on his lips.

"Great big quiet-ass hulky-bones, I never did know what to make of him." The fat woman turned at the crunching sound of somebody big approaching, coming out of the woods by Ava's studio and heading their way. "Oh shit, look. There he is."

The brothers swiveled to look. It was Thorne.

In a split second the fat woman went from angry to downhome expansive. "Well Thorny," she said as Thorne emerged from the bushes and bore down on them, expressionless as ever but with his huge body angled forward in haste. "Thorny Hutson, it's a treat to see you. Now what you done with my sweet Hank Etta, and why the fuck did the money stop?"

What Thorne said to his mother-in-law—his *mother-in-law!*—was lost to the Benedict brothers because they were embraced, no, surrounded, by their British brother and his beautiful mistress. Troubled Benton and delighted Berton turned to see Bernard approaching with his arms out, crying, "Bernard, Bernie, what kept you?"

"Benty, Bert, you rank, ugly bastards," said Bernard, who had the same Benedict face. Pulling Keesha into the little circle they made, Bernard—Bernard Benedict junior until their father succumbed to certain poison in his systems and died—tried to hug both his brothers at once.

When the brothers turned back to the problem at hand it had evaporated. The old lady was gone. Thorne was leading her down the path—not toward Ava's studio, as expected, but away, to the foundry. They thought they heard him saying, "Come with me, Mom Lassiter. There's something I have to explain."

You know what to do. That was easy for her to say, this strange Great Aunt Benta that came all the way from Tokyo, but Edgar didn't have a clue, and if he wanted Daddy to help him, well, tough rocks. When he saw Daddy was too wrapped up even to see him, he went inside to think. What with everything, he was beyond scared. Edgar was strung so tight that you could have snared birds with him. Still he had the key to the cellar, and with Daddy and all them focused on the front of the house, all these strange people boiling in, he could unlock door and suss out the secrets under the house and nobody would know.

Sounds were coming up from the cellar for sure. They were getting louder now. Edgar used to think he'd do anything to get into the cellar and see what was going on, but now that he actually had the key, he was scared shit of going down.

The racket made him wonder if the thing or things knew he was coming. The *presence* roiling the guts of the house seemed to be hissing, whether in one voice or many, he did not know. He heard breath rasping, unless whoever or whatever lurked down there was whispering over and over in a wild, incessant plea. Edgar used to think it was crying, *H-e-e-l-p.* Today was different. Something was calling his name.

Edgar. Ed-gaaar.

"Leave me alone!"

Edgar.

"Oh shit. Oh, shit!" He didn't know what to do.

Aunt Benta handed over the key like a gift. Or an obligation: *You know what to do.*

Who did she think he was, really? How was he supposed to know?

Dammit to hell, Aunt Benta, you think I'm so smart. Well, he wasn't, he was only smart for his age, which was eleven and 99 100ths. Oh God, he would do anything to keep his birthday from coming up. No. He would do anything to make it go away.

Even go into the cellar?

Ed-gaaar.

Shut up! He fled. He went skidding into the empty kitchen, bleating in a voice so thin that it was embarrassing, "Essie?"

She wasn't there. Nobody was. So much for that, he thought, and was about to turn and escape the house when he heard it again. Insistent. Clear. It came from behind the locked door, where one voice seemed to separate itself from the unidentifiable murmur of many, calling, *Down here.*

The terrifying sound had not changed, but something was at work on Edgar—curiosity so strong that he writhed, inadvertently grabbing his crotch. He was riveted, eaten up by curiosity compounded by guilt and intensified by... what was it, fear? He didn't know. What he did know was that standing here with his ear pressed to the locked door was beginning to be scarier than turning the key and going down.

Ed-gaaar...

"Shut up."

Ed-gaaaaaaaaar...

"Oh, *please* shut up!"

Eddd....

It sounded just exactly like his dad. He would do anything to make it stop.

Even go down. But he was having trouble getting started. Like, taking out the key. When he put his hand in his pocket it bit him like a baby alligator. "Soon," he muttered. "Not yet, but soon." He went to the pantry for the battery-powered lantern. When he turned it on he thought he was ready to try the key, but he wasn't, not really. Then he went into the kitchen and got the butcher knife and stuck it in his belt, but that didn't seem to be quite enough. Next he went back up to his room for his plastic hard hat and loaded his pockets with the hammer from his tool set and a couple of sculptors' knives and tried again. And when he couldn't get up the nerve this time he went back into the kitchen and stuffed his pockets with brownies that Essie had left cooling on the stove for him. "Essie," he said in that lame, thin voice, scared that she'd come along and stop him—no, scared that she wouldn't. "Es?" Listen, at least he could get her to go down cellar with him. But she wasn't anywhere.

Then accidentally he put the key into the lock and turned. There was a click as it disengaged. It left him breathless and jittering with excitement. *This is it.* After all the time he spent listening at the crack and trying to find his way in, the cellar was his. All at once there was no sound, at least none that he could identify. There was only a tremendous hush.

Now the racket was inside Edgar's head, like a hundred car alarms going off at once and thousand fingernails scraping across the blackboard of his brain.

Oh shit, he thought. Freddy Kroeger could be down here, curled up in the furnace, or a zillion of his ancestors' dead slaves turned into zombies, or white alligators big as submarines, or... He gulped. Something worse. His breath caught in a sob. *What have I done?*

With nothing to hold it shut, the door fell wide. Edgar had to think fast, hurling himself onto the knob and pushing it shut. *What if there really is something awful down there, and I've let it out?*

In spite of his weight against it the door opened a crack. A black, fetid vapor escaped, curling into the room. Something must have died down there, a possum or a coon, he thought, but what could get in from outside? Edgar had been around and around the foundation, trying to see. He hadn't found so much as a chink. He opened the door a crack wider. Frightened, he teetered on the sill. The stairs went down into deep places he couldn't see.

Shadows rose like fog. He wanted to run to bed and pull the covers up over his head.

He couldn't go down.

Then he did.

It was that sudden.

A light went on in the depths. As it did, somebody spoke. The voice was paper-thin, but distinct. It could have been his dad speaking, or somebody very like his dad, courtly, patient. "Thank heaven you've come."

Rocked by a little miracle of recognition, Edgar pulled the door shut behind him and started down.

From below came a sigh of relief.

What had seemed cavernous, terrifying, was suddenly manageable. The wooden staircase did not go straight to the bottom. Instead it gave onto a wide landing just a few feet below. Edgar thought he saw another staircase heading off at a right angle to another level much farther down. Right now, he didn't have to deal with it. Instead he aimed for the landing. If anything bad happened, in two minutes, tops, he could be back upstairs, safe in the house. The muttering or hissing that he had heard for so long and was afraid of came from much lower down. On a marshy coast where half the shoreline seemed to be floating, Wayward was built on bedrock. The cellar must have been carved or blasted out by Edgar's ancestors, with every crack caulked and staircases shored up by four-by-fours. Whether they kept slaves down here, or used the place as a stop on the underground railroad, somebody had made sure that unless the masters of the house wanted it, nobody could get into the deep cellars of Wayward and nobody could get out.

Creeping down one step at a time, Edgar approached the light. It came from an opening carved into the wall on the landing. At the bottom, he saw the opening gave onto a little cave. The mouth was covered by an iron grate.

The person who spoke his father's voice said, "It's all right, son."

Clinging to the wall, he hesitated. "Dad?"

"Don't be scared, son. It's only me."

"Dad?" Then he saw. All his breath left him. "Oh, wow!"

It was like seeing a bear in its habitat at the zoo.

The grate covered a Spartan bedroom—cot, iron table straight out of an old jail movies on late night TV, washstand and single light bulb dangling from a cord. Everything including the occupant was at least a hundred years old. The light glinted off the spokes of a stainless steel wheelchair. Unlike everything else here, it was motorized. Anachronistic. New. As Edgar hit the landing, backing into the rail to keep from coming too close to the inhabitant, the creature in the chair pushed a button and whirred forward until the front wheels bumped the bars. The chair rolled along under a stainless steel tree.

It supported a battery of bags and pouches whose contents traveled down a series of tubes, through needles and into the raddled body of the passenger. At the bottom of the tree, two steel arms supported murky-looking bottles that held whatever gross matter and fluids came out of... Edgar thought it was an ancient, ancient lady. Sitting in the chair, wrapped in laprobes and trembling with the cold in spite of shawls and a wool cap, she blinked at Edgar with odd, colorless eyes. "It's about time," she said in a version of his father's voice that had grown faint and crumpled with age, "I've been waiting for you."

"Ma'am?"

"Ma'am?" the old relic barked angrily, "Ma'am? I don't see any ladies here. Now, come here. I've been waiting for you!"

Edgar grunted. Surprise. It wasn't a lady, it was an ancient guy, glaring out of a yellowed, shrunken version of his own dad's face. "The hell you have," Edgar said bravely. "You don't even know who I am."

"I know a lot more than you think."

Cranky, Edgar thought. Just like an old lady. Extreme age had wiped out the difference. It was awful. "Who are you?"

"That's not important," he said. "Wait a minute, yes it is."

"What do you want?"

"Son, you have to hurry."

Edgar shivered. "I'm not your son."

"Oooooh, yes you are." The captive glanced anxiously, up the stairs, then down, as if expecting something to cut this interview short. "When you get to be as old as I am, people mush together, the living, the dead. To tell you the truth, son, I don't care who you are or what happens to you, as long as you get me out of here."

"Out of this cage?"

He was too old to move much but his gesture was much bigger than his cell. "For a start."

"The lock. The bars. I can't." Edgar took in the size and apparent weight of the chair, the grate, the padlock and the stairs. "Even if I wanted to."

"It's only a cage," the old man said, looking down at the trembling arms and legs concealed masses of covers.

"This place?"

"No. The body. This."

"Wait," Edgar said. "You want me to *kill* you?"

And the ancient person with his father's face spat, "Whatever it takes."

Edgar would never remember exactly what they said to each other next. At first he thought he was having some kind of vision. Shadows bubbled up over the edge of the landing, puddling around his ankles, his knees, swaddling his throat; he didn't remember closing his eyes, but squiggly lights went racing across them, closed or not. From below, the stir, whether of bodies or of voices, intensified until it filled his head, crowding out thought. Edgar found himself swaying, ineluctably drawn to the next stairway, the one that went down. And down. He drifted to the top step and, clinging to the rail, leaned out to see. Looked down. Gasped.

The old man's bark brought him back. "Don't go down there!"

And the tension snapped. Edgar folded up like an old deck chair. He said, "I have to sit down," but he was thinking: *I almost jumped.*

"You damn well better sit." The old man said, "That's good. Now slide over here on the floor, closer to the bars. I have to talk to you and I don't want to yell."

Still shaken, giddy and sick to his stomach, Edgar looked at him cautiously. "This is close enough."

"No. Closer." His voice changed. "I'm not going to touch you, son. I'm too damn old to hurt anyone."

He wanted to, didn't want to.

"Come on, son." The old man was at the end of his strength. His voice trembled with exhaustion. "Closer. Don't make me waste my breath."

Edgar obeyed. He was close enough to see that the old man with his dad's voice and a desiccated version of his father's face was regarding him with his father's eyes, so filmed by age that they were without color. He noted wildly that a single white hair sprouted from the old man's chin. The teeth were worn to stubs but the mouth was set in the same line as his father's. Stricken, Edgar murmured, "You're one of us, aren't you?"

The rusty noise that tore out of the old man could have been a death rattle; Edgar had to look carefully to see that he was laughing. "That's one way of putting it. I'm one of you, all right." His head lifted. "In a certain sense you might even call me the first."

"Wait a minute. Grandfather Benedict is dead."

"And I'm not."

"So you're not my grandfather." The next thing he said came out in a long, reverent sigh. "But you're so *old.*"

"Exactly. Now do you know me?" The old man blinked expectantly.

"Not really," Edgar said.

"Do I have to carve it in stone for you? My name is Beauchamp Benedict. The first. If I have this right, I am your great-great grandfather. Now lean in close, because I'm only going to say this once."

Seventeen

Jude never expected to spend all day in the studio. When Ava caught her outside and brought her back, she never intended to stay, but this was not a woman you said no to. Five minutes and she'd split. Five minutes, she told herself. Then you will excuse yourself and go. She let the sculptor make herbal tea for her and drank two cups just to be polite. She sat down for a minute, just to be polite. She assumed the position on Ava's stool, but just for a minute, just to be polite. Then everything blurred. For reasons she won't be able to remember or understand, hours passed. When Ava stopped working a minute ago, Jude found herself still sitting here.

A disturbance outside caught Ava's attention. Angry, she slapped down her tools. "Hold the position," she said, adjusting Jude's head until she had it *just so*. "I'll be right back." Then she stalked out.

This was Jude's chance to slip down off the stool and quit the studio, but whatever scene Ava was playing with the intruder outside unfolded at the bottom of the steps that led down from the only door. The only window was set in the same wall; she'd never get past Ava. Nobody on the place at Wayward crossed the woman. Nobody.

On another day she might have armed herself with a sculptor's tool—anything—and fought her way out, but something in the herbal tea Ava plied her with put Jude in a zone where nothing mattered, really. Nothing at all. Odd shapes standing under shrouds in the corner of the studio? What the hell. Fact that she hadn't seen Peter at all today? No problem. Everything's OK, she told herself, perhaps because the buzz this stuff Ava brewed created was tremendous. Everything in her relaxed; her thoughts slowed down; she was beautifully fluid, floating along far above everyday concerns. Peter? See him soon of course, because in this zone adverse outcomes were out of the question. Mmmm, sure, just as soon as we're done here, she thought happily, and little Edgar, who was so agitated last night? You know how kids are, impressionable, cute little guy, she thought, wonder where he is. When

Ava's done I'll go in the house and sit down and play video games with him, wonder what he's doing now, with his dad and big brothers occupied and Ava out front arguing and me relaxing here... Oh, somewhere, she thought fuzzily; he'll be fine, that nice Esther is taking care of him.

Outside, voices rose—Ava's and one of those deep country voices that defies gender, incohate but sliding from one point to another on a crazy seesaw of entreaties and reproaches, veering between amiable drawl and angry rumble—fight, Jude mused, yawning.

Still, it was boring sitting here on the stool where Ava had positioned her; Jude wasn't stiff, exactly, just less in control of her limbs; her hands in her lap were all flopsy and her heels kept slipping off the rung of the stool and it came to her in a dream that it might be good to step down just long enough to stretch... favor to Ava, she told herself, giggling, *fava to Ava*—stamp around on the floor a little, to make sure your feet aren't asleep like the rest of you, tea made you so lazy, laze daze...

Could not figure out how she ended up on her knees when all she wanted to do was wake up her feet, get the blood moving and settle back on the stool, Ava could come back in that door at any minute, she realized with an inadvertent giggle. The last thing she wanted, now that Ava had honored her by beginning a portrait sculpture (They cost thirty thousand! If you had to pay...) was to have Ava find out that she'd broken the pose. The woman had a temper, it would be goodbye posterity, Jude would be her ex-model, wait, since when did it matter to Jude what the bitch thought of her? Something in the tea... if she cared what Ava thought it must be something in the tea...

All this simmered while Jude knelt, tracing lazy circles in a puddle that she found here in the—was it sawdust? No. A film of some dark fluid that had dried under the wax shavings. Interested, the way small children are interested in phenomena they find but can't identify, she made herself stand and tottered around looking for... what? She couldn't remember. Then she did. Looking for water, she thought, a rag maybe, Ava will be so happy if I clean up this ugly smear. Something spilled and dried up all the way down there on the floor... Staggering—hey, nothing to worry about—she found the pot of Ava's special tea and emptied it on the puddle that had dried on this particular segment of Ava's studio floor and then, because she knew how angry Ava would be if anything went to waste, she took rusty water out of a coffee can and refilled the pot and dropped to her knees again, scrubba scrubba with her skirt until the patch began to come clean. Then, addled by Ava's potion, she doubled over stupidly with her nose brushing the floor, staring at the spot she'd failed to clean, trying to identify what lay underneath. The tea had melted the curls of wax so if she wanted to see, she had to scrape with her fingernails. Time blurred and she scraped away, and, sophisticated twenty-first century person that she was—smart, in spite of the drugs—Jude murmured drunkenly, "I've heard of glass ceilings, but I've never seen a glass floor." Then, leaning closer, she thought she saw... at this point Jude was too far gone now to know what she saw... a desiccated face, she thought, looking back at her, great black cavity in the middle—the mouth gawping, flames in two pits that were its eyes crackling in a naked skull; crazy with uncertainty, she shuddered and clawed until, like an answer marker in a Magic 8 Ball, the face vanished in the murk below, leaving her reeling from the drugs and blinking with uncertainty because in her current state there was no knowing whether that was a real face she had really seen or only the aftermath of a bizarre dream. When she looked up, it was business as usual in Ava's studio: sunlight warming the ceiling, angry voices outside. What were they...

If Ava finds me like this, she'll be mad.

Outside the voices went on. Curiosity brought Jude to her feet, unless it was obedience, unless it was fear that if she looked again she really would see some horror glaring back at her out of the darkness below.

I should go, she thought, insofar as she was still thinking, but the tea Ava had given her was intense and pernicious and she could not... Sighing, she got back on the stool. Part of her wanted to lay her head on the windowsill and sleep, but what would Ava do if she came back and found out her model had gone to sleep on the job? Worse, that she had changed position. Instead she fixed on the unfolding scene between Ava and the intruder, passive, recording without responding, entranced.

Eighteen

It was scary and exciting, crouching here on the landing while this ancient, ancient person pinned him with those beady eyes, rattling on like this was his first chance ever to yack up his story. Edgar should be going; he should be scrambling upstairs this very minute. He should slam the door on all this and lock it up tight before anybody found out, but he couldn't tear himself away. He ought to turn his back and walk away before Ava or somebody came up to the house and discovered him doing... what was he doing, that was so terribly wrong? He didn't know, but it made him feel guilty. The living mummy had him now. Caught him with a story and held him tight. Edgar couldn't leave until he knew how it came out. The boy was in the wrong place doing something terribly wrong and he knew it, but how could he leave before he found out what happened next? Enthralled, Edgar crouched, deep in the old man's history. It wasn't his own history, not a bit of it, but in some odd way that he couldn't figure out, Edgar knew it pertained directly to him.

"Heh," the old man said. "You may wonder how I'm still alive. A hundred-plus, I know it's disgusting. Bald. No teeth. Any fool can see I'm too old to be around, and God knows I would be the first one to admit it, but here I am."

Edgar gulped. "Amazing."

"It isn't amazing, it's a curse. Look at these feeding tubes! The drains. The bags for piss and the bags for shit. The bitch is keeping me alive."

The sigh that rattled out of him was tremendous. "Cursed for being an artist. Like your father and his father and his father. Do you know how fucking old I am?"

"I'm sorry."

"Maybe you'd better just go."

"No sir. I don't want to. I mean, I can't."

He snorted. "Of course not. You're a Benedict, and the Benedicts are cursed. You'd better get out before the curse grabs you! Art, it's a wonder, it's a horror, I grubbed mud out of the marsh to make figures, and what I did was companion, mistress, all. You do not need a lover when you have art. The art is everything. Stone Manifort and I passed sweet winter nights working in front of the fire, ironic that his children's children's children are stuck here, taking care of me. That winter we worked along, inspired! You can see Stone's best piece in the front hallway—the newel post he carved the winter before I left, it came to life, but mine—the minute it was finished and I stepped back to admire, I saw it was only clay. Sculpture is like sex, you have no idea what it feels like until you've done it, and once you do, you have to keep doing it over and over again. *Another*. The pieces cry, *Better*. Make your best and it goads you, *More*."

He was silent for so long that Edgar wondered if he had died.

Then he coughed and went on harshly, "I sold off fifty acres and went to Europe to learn to work in bronze. You know the lost wax process; all the Benedicts use it now, but with me, it was all new. I thought all I had to do was find perfection in the wax and cast it in bronze, and I'd have it. I could smile and quit trying. Walk away.

"Listen, sonny. Art is like a fire, it consumes. By the time I came home Stone was married and they had two children. I withdrew to the woods. Stone and Belinda they took care of me. Every day I would stumble out of my studio to find food baskets they left. Another man would have died of sexual frustration, but I had the work!"

They'd been sitting here for so long that Edgar's feet were asleep. Never mind. Above him, the great house was still.

"The work. I made models from life and models from death masks and I thought I saw life shimmering but they cooled as soon as I stepped back. The life went out. I worked for five years and not one piece I did was fit to cast. I was only Beauchamp, and they..."

Long sigh. "They were only wax."

"Then, my God, one night I fell into a fever and in the lost, mad moment between life and death I stormed out into the woods, shouting, roaring, "God, or whoever, I don't care who you are as long as you help me!" Something huge answered: *Put yourself into the work.*

"First I mixed blood and spit into the wax, but it wanted more.

"You've seen your brothers, you've seen your father; it's not that hard to lop off a great toe or the tip of a finger, form it in there as part of the armature that supports the wax. When the molten bronze fills the mold and the wax boils away, the life goes into the bronze. I gave my ear, and you? Due to the course of events—blame your rebellious brother, who refused—a major sacrifice is in order, nothing disfiguring, child, but grave."

Edgar scrambled backward. "No way!"

"Stop. Wait! *I said, hold still.* I'm not going to let them hurt you. Be quiet and hear me out.

"I lost the ear to my *Aphrodite,* and she was the first piece good enough to cast. Listen, child, it was little enough price to pay. When I stepped back to look at *Aphrodite*—she lived!

"And oh my God I could already hear the insidious prompting. *That's good enough. For now.* I fell down in a delirium, and when I woke up it was as if none of this had happened. I was hungry all over again.

"And this is what drove me: the lust, the dirty voice asking: *What's next.*

"From then on, understand, the work did well enough. A planter from Louisiana came with his beautiful daughter and paid a fortune for my *Aphrodite.* Commissions came. Museums came and all the money did was feed the flames.

"It wanted more. *More.* I gave it more and as I did so I could hear the clamor: *More is never enough.*

"The next two years were torture. The pieces were getting better and better but this—vision!—shimmered just out of reach.

"And there was more. I fell in love—the beautiful daughter of the man who bought my *Aphrodite,* my Helene. I had to model her, and as I molded her beautiful head, I began to envision, no, lust for *God and His Creation.* My ultimate piece.

"What did the force want from me? I gave a little toe and the tip of a finger—see? But it wasn't enough. Then, what? I guessed it might be like the dead man in the bell. Son, it is said that in the forging, all great church bells are formed around the dead man, the enabling corpse trapped in the bronze at the neck."

Edgar heard him gasping for the breath to continue. It was terrible.

"If you must know, I even tried it—first a corpse robbed from a grave, but the bronze was just as dead. In desperation I tried a living animal and then a dying man I abducted from the hospital in town. I told myself he might not mind departing a day early, but he screamed all the same. Even before I cracked the mold, I knew. The dead man was only a dead man and the work was just bronze."

The old man was sobbing now. Deep, disturbing sobs.

"Understand that I was driven by the vision. *God and His Creation.* Sketches could never catch... the piece evolved in my mind, quivering, begging me to give it life. The pressure drove me screaming into the woods. I ran praying, no, shouting: 'I'll do anything to make this live. *Anything.* In the name of God, just tell me what.'"

Agonized, he choked it out. "I do not think it was God who answered."

He said, "One minute I was whirling under the sky, desperate, and the next, I was like a vampire staked at the crossroads, flat on my back. I knew!"

He said, "Then I came to myself and found somebody leaning over me: face like an angel, 'Are you all right?' It was Theron Poulnot, who had come over the causeway and onto the property without a thought for what might happen next. 'I—yes. I think so,' I said, and let him help me up. Then I let him help me inside the studio. And then I said, 'You have a remarkable profile, whoever you are. I'd like to make a model of your face.'"

He said, "Understand, that's how we start. That's how every one of us will start. With the compliant model. You know the rest. No, you're too young. But she'll tell you. Your mother, the bitch."

With a sob, he said, "Theron Poulnot became the first figure in *God and His Creation*. I needed more. I gave it my Helene."

The old man was weeping freely now. Riveted, Edgar was dimly aware of a stir in the staircase, whether from above or below, he did not know; he was fixed in place by terror and curiosity until some external force broke the spell and he was released.

"My beautiful Helene. Of course I put myself at the apex—to look at me now you wouldn't recognize it, but that's me. But I was not like them. I was the artist. I could step into place and then step down, while the rest..." His sigh echoed in the sub-basement... or was that the sound of a hundred other sighs?

"Once it was done I felt guilty, guilty and soiled. I didn't release it at once, I kept it on a pallet here. I even vowed never to do it again. I built the family chapel to make up for it. I peopled my chapel with figures of saints and angels, good work, none of it built on blood, and all the time I knew the evil work was better; please pray for my soul."

After a moment, he lifted his head. "Listen. *God and His Creation* lived. Like nothing else, it *lived.* It sat in the foundry shimmering, begging to be seen. Hah. In my folly, I thought that now that I had given it life, I could put it away and rest. I married sweet Marie Beaulieu, we had a daughter and a handsome son; Stone and Belinda said, 'Now *that's* the way a man's supposed to live.' Stone guessed how much the work made me suffer. He offered to dismantle my studio, but no. I still had the hunger and I made piece after piece and tried to bring it to life without the terrible sacrifice. By that time my work was known and commissions came in. I did them well enough, but the wax said: *we are only wax*, and my bronzes? They reproached me: *we are only bronze.* I knew my best work was hidden and my greatest work as yet undone. It shimmered in the vestibule of the uncreated. Luring, seducing me. The art called me. Its voices were many and loud, urgent, prurient. The hunger drove me, calling: *More.*" He groaned.

"God forgive me, I heard. And I gave it more.

"And I was recognized.

"And I made the next piece.

"And the next.

"And... Oh, I repeat myself. But I've been alone with this for *so very long.* And all the time my poor dear Marie, so lovely and so pure; I never told her the truth.

"And all the time *God and His Creation* sat on its pallet in the foundry, waiting to go forth and it lived. All those voices, calling! *Let us out!*

"I did what I had to, both to justify and atone. I sent it to Washington to grace the National Cathedral."

The groan that came out of him this time reverberated like the groan from a hundred throats.

"Then my children—my *very own children* found out and betrayed me. They put me here.

"Of course they were sculptors. My daughter gave the finger, my son the tip of the thumb. It was the day *God and His Creation* rolled out into the sunlight, bound for the nation's capitol. They saw it and they were astounded. Envious. Remember, art burns from the inside out, like lust, and they were artists. My children begged me for that last secret. 'Oh Father,' they said, 'We want to be everything you are.' I loved them. What could I do?

"I tested them. I asked the question. 'Everything?'

"They said, 'Everything. We are willing to do everything.'"

It was dark down here, it was scary down here, Edgar had been here much too long but he was caught in the recital like a fish in a net. "Um, secret?"

"I asked my children, 'Even things you would never do?'

"And they were hungry, *hungry*. They said, 'Whatever it takes.'

"So I initiated them. The work knows no limits. My children did. You have probably already guessed what happened. I had begun my masterpiece. *The Third Circle of Hell.* They stopped me before I could complete the piece. If you go to the subcellar you will see. They took a crew and removed *God and His Creation* from the cathedral before it could be installed; they took it away by night and brought it here. Then my sanctimonious son said, 'Father, it's too beautiful to destroy, but I want it here as sign and symbol of the end. Now you have to take this cross and swear that this really is the end,'" the old man finished with a bitter laugh.

"Don't they know there is no end?"

Mesmerized, Edgar murmured, "And now you're here. How do you..."

"Oh, that. My children were idealists, not sadists. Stone and Stone's descendants took care of me.

"My children gave way to their children, and then theirs. The family fortunes went downhill. Still artists, still working, but forgotten. *Serves them right,* I thought. But I was here."

"But you're so old, and you're still *alive*!"

"Awful, isn't it? It's my punishment." The old man's head sank into his chest. With a tremendous effort, he lifted it and went on. "Then she came."

"Who?" *Gotta go,* Edgar thought, because he knew. He didn't want to hear, he had to hear.

"Ava, the bitch. She moved in on the family and consumed it like a flame. After she married my grandson she scoured the house down to the foundations, searching for the secret," he said and Edgar's heart sank. "She dug me out. She wasn't even surprised. 'Old man. I knew you were here *somewhere.*' She rubbed up against the bars like a leopardess yearning for a mate. 'Why are you in this cell?' She used her body to make me tell. She would not free me but she would not leave me alone, either. Until I had revealed the truth."

He was weeping again. "God help me, I thought she would let me out. I taught her how. You know the rest."

Something upstairs. Edgar heard something upstairs. His voice quavered with anxiety. "Not really."

"Think! The first thing she did was close the chapel. She took all the statues and plunged them in the waters off the point; so much for atonement."

Something upstairs; he ought to leave, he couldn't leave.

"And now..."

Upstairs, run upstairs.

"Oh dear God, footsteps. Up there. Child, get under my lap-robe, you have to hurry! He can't find you here."

"Who?" Which was more horrible, the menace he couldn't see or the old skeleton drooling in his mechanical chair? "Who?"

"Never mind who. Hurry! Oh hell, if you're that afraid of me, just go. But first. Take this warning, and take it well. When she models you, the woman is doing two things. Son, listen! She is preparing the enclosure. It is both the matrix and the trap."

Oh, man, Edgar thought, frantic. *Oooh maaan!*

"Up the stairs now, they're only as far as the parlor. Hurry. Faster! Oh dear God please hurry and whatever you do, lock the lock!"

Nineteen

Shadows inside the abandoned Benedict chapel are so deep that the young priest is afraid to enter. Crepe myrtle and kudzu are thickly twined around the little structure; vines seize his shoulders as he bends to look inside. If this really is the Benedict family chapel, it's been a long time since there was anything sacramental here. For Jerome, every church is populated by the spirit of God, but there is nothing sacred in this place. No spirit at all.

Is anybody here? It's so dark in the little chapel that he will have a hard time making out the figure of the one who summoned him—that hasty, whispered phone call, abruptly cut off. Who's hiding in here, waiting? Is it his usual penitent, or somebody new? What if there's nobody here at all? Jerome half-expects to go back to his boat and see it drifting in mid-channel with the anchor rope cut, and in the deeply suspicious part of himself that he tries to suppress, he wonders if some sinister, unknown Benedict is lying in ambush, waiting to do him in.

Still, he has his responsibilities.

After all, he is a priest.

But he doesn't want to go in. Getting here was hard enough for Father Jerome, paddling along the shoreline in a small boat according to instructions, wading in through the mud in his clericals, with sawgrass clinging to his legs and slashing his hands until the blood runs. It's even harder to shrug off the vines and poke his head inside the low Gothic arch. "Are you in here?"

Nobody answers.

He didn't come all this way for nothing, he tells himself. So he does the last hard thing. Crossing himself like a diver about to plunge, Father Jerome ducks inside.

A low whisper greets him. "What kept you?"

Who is it? "It took a while to find a boat."

"I had to lie to get time off from the studio. I had to tell them I was modeling a self-portrait. I've been waiting all day."

"Why couldn't I come by motorboat?"

"Too much noise."

"Why couldn't I just bring the car?"

"You never would have made it. They're watching the roads."

"Who are *they?*"

The exasperated rasp surprises Jerome. "Do you think I'd need you if I knew?"

In this small space the whisper sounds familiar but not familiar. Assuming it must be Benton Benedict who's summoned him, Jerome whispers, "Son, do you want to make your confession?"

"Who, me?" Astounded by the suggestion, Peter speaks in normal tones. "Why no, I don't think so. No."

"Peter! Why didn't you say it was you?"

"It's hard to explain."

"For Pete's sake." Jerome reproaches him, not priest to parishioner, but one kid to another, for lord's sake they used to *play* together. "We could have had dinner, knocked back a few at The Red Dog."

"No we couldn't," Peter says in strangled tones.

Now that his eyes have accommodated, Jerome sees his old friend is perched on the little dais where the altar would have been when there was still an altar. From the looks of things, that was quite a while ago. Somebody has stripped the little chapel to the ribs: altar, hangings, *prie dieux*; everything is gone, even the figure on the crucifix, and the cross remains only because it's a structural part of the north wall. It is like visiting the tomb of somebody dear; the absence is palpable. Jerome sits down next to him. "What happened to this place?"

Peter shrugs. "I don't know. Until last night, I didn't even know it was here. Essie told me."

"What else did Essie tell you? What's going on?"

"No idea. That's the trouble." Peter sets down the next words like markers in a game. "I thought you could tell me."

"How am I supposed to know?"

Troubled by the events of the past few days, Peter barks, "Come off it, Jerry. You know more than I do."

It's dark in here, his trousers are wet to the knees, there's mud squelching in his shoes. Jerome doesn't know whether he's been called here as friend or priest, and because he's uncomfortable with the idea that it's the latter, he snaps back. "I haven't been out here since we went crabbing in fifth grade and your mother ran me off. Now do you want me to perform an exorcism or a deconsecration or what?"

"It's not an exorcism situation," Peter says. "I don't know what it is." Then he hits Jerome with another of those significant pauses. "But you do."

"How the hell am I supposed to know?"

"You've been hearing his confessions," Peter says quietly.

The information thuds home. "Oh my God."

There is a long silence in which the young priest reflects that around his friend Peter, he can be an ordinary person, while Peter's father, who is forty years older, kneels in the confessional like a guilty child, murmuring, "Bless me Father, for I have sinned." And every time he sighs and makes the sign of the cross over Benton's bowed head, Jerome can feel the full weight of responsibility descend. *I don't even know if I like carrying souls.*

Peter says, "Help me, Jerry. OK?"

The responsibility. Jerome is afraid of what is to follow. He says in a low voice, "What do you want?"

"I have to know what he's doing," Peter says.

"Well you can't. Ever. Seal of the confessional, OK? It's one of the great prohibitions."

"I don't care what it is."

"If you were a Catholic, you'd understand."

"Ava wouldn't have it," Peter says. He has no way of knowing that Benton secretly defied Ava and dashed water on the heads of Peter and Eds, one of the few things their father has confided to the priest. Although Ava doesn't know it, Peter's and his brother's names are in the baptismal registry in the little church in town, along with Dirk's and Luke's: something Benton blurted in one of his abortive confessions, aborted because he always flees the possibility of absolution.

The young priest sighs. "I know."

"No false gods."

"No God at all. She's an atheist."

Peter corrects him. "Anti-theist. So you'd better tell me what you know."

"I still can't tell you, Peter. If you were a Catholic you'd understand."

"It wouldn't make any difference," Peter growls. "I'd still try to choke it out of you."

Jerome is only half kidding when he says, "It's a sacrilege to hit a priest."

"It's a matter of life or death, OK?"

"So's this. What you tell me in confession, I die before I reveal."

"That might be how it ends up," Peter says darkly.

"Not if I can help it," Jerome says. "I can't tell you what I can't tell you, OK?" He does not have the heart to admit that the old man is always so upset and distracted in these confessions that there isn't much to tell. Benton sighs and murmurs and conjectures; sometimes he weeps, that's all. "But I'll do anything else you want, OK? You're still my best friend."

"Jerry, for God's sake."

"That's part of it. I'll do anything else you want. Just tell me what to do."

"How can I tell you when I don't know what's wrong?" In a voice charged with urgency, Peter rushes on. "Something big is going down here, all the relatives have come back to Wayward and my kid brother is getting his head modeled, and, shit. I'm in love with this girl and Ava is modeling her, which ought to be fine except she modeled Gara and then something happened to her. Jerry, I'm scared."

"What do you want me to do? Call the cops, help you lock your mother up?"

"Nobody gets near her."

Jerome, who took karate long before he entered the seminary and has kept it up ever since says, "Not even a harmless priest?"

"You haven't seen Thorne."

The priest remembers the shadow in the church door—the man who has aborted all Benton's confessions *just by being there*. "Maybe I have."

"So look," Peter says. "There is some kind of deep dark family secret, hell, you probably already know it, like probably my dad told you, he probably told you a lot of stuff that could help me—oh shit, Jerry, come on, this is *me!*"

It is clear that there's more going on at Wayward than Jerome can infer from any of Benton's confessions. In an alternate universe, he and Peter could sift through Benton's words looking for clues so they could make a plan. Jerome's silence is harder for him than it is for Peter, but there's no explaining this to him. Instead he says painfully, "You want me to die for you, no problem. You want me to go up there and shake the truth out of your mother, I'll try, but this other thing, OK, I can't. The..."

"Seal of the confessional. Yeah, right," Peter says bitterly.

"I'm sorry."

Peter chokes. "It's about the art. Whatever Ava's doing, it's about this *thing* she's designed. We're supposed to be making the ultimate piece. It's about the family heritage."

Jerome thinks it will not be giving anything away to say, "Or the family curse."

"Whatever. I don't know. Jerry, when I was twelve she cut my finger off!"

"What..."

"The woman is a tigress, going for the gut. She wants more than you can give. 'The work,' she said when she did it, but something inside me said, *no.* And now Eds is turning twelve..." Shaking, he goes on. "And all the time Dirk and Luke did everything she said, while Ava told me behind their backs that their work was shit. She said I was the deserving one, like the family secret was some kind of prize that I alone was worthy of; that is, until that day when you and I got caught and she ran you out of here..."

"All I wanted to do was play in the basement."

"I'm sorry about what she did to you."

"I knew you are." The ribs healed nicely but Jerome's left wrist has a permanent crook where the arm meets the hand.

"When I saw how Ava hurt you, something in me froze. No way in hell was I going to be her creature. I threw my clay and tools in the swamp and melted down all the wax and poured it out into the sand." Peter sighs. "So they yanked me out of Beaufort High and sent me to boarding school up North."

"I thought they didn't want you hanging out with me. Gullah kid, from town."

"No. I was wasting her time. Nobody stops Ava. She decides to take a hostage. She goes and has another baby, wham, nine months flat after they ship me off. She shows her new baby Edgar to me and says, 'Look, Peter. He will be everything you aren't,' which translated means, Ava will do whatever Ava has to, to get what Ava wants. To her very own son. To anybody who gets in her way."

Jerome won't be giving anything away if he tells Peter, "She's not like us."

"That's why I'm so scared."

As Peter speaks Jerome is rummaging: is there anything he can do or say to prevent whatever horror is coming?

"Interesting how you spend your life running away from something and end up back in the middle. They sent me to art school, but I fought. Instead of sculpting, I paint. You can't hide things inside a canvas; what you see is all there is."

"What do you mean?"

"The sculptures. Inside. It's all wrong. Shit, Jerry, I'd rather die than do that. And now here I am."

The priest is distracted by a slight vibration in the floor—something big approaching through the woods; the intruder walks silently but his footsteps shake the earth.

"Before Ava came to Wayward the family business was in the toilet. Now everybody wants their stuff. Ava came and something changed." Peter's voice rattles with regret. "And I still don't know how, at least not for sure. Do you know my mother's left nipple is missing?"

Jerome is listening but not listening; there is somebody outside. *Watch out.*

"Cut off. Whap." Peter is fixed on his recital. "I thought I could just say so what and walk away from it, but now."

Or some huge thing. *Watch out.*

"There's Eds. Ava is making this great big *thing* out of Edgar's twelfth birthday and I can't let it happen. I have to stop it. It's why I had to come back."

Alarmed by something sensed rather than observed, Jerome begins a silent prayer: *Kyrie eleison.*

"What she can't get out of us one way, through me, she's going to take out of Edgar, and in spades." Peter pauses. "She's going to—I don't know! I have to get into the foundry!"

Jerome listens to the silence. *Christe eleison.*

There is only silence.

"I thought I didn't care what happened to me, but. I'm in love."

Kyrie...

Peter goes on. "I thought I could end it on my own, but now..."

Jerome says in a low voice, "What do you want me to do?"

"Tell everybody, I guess. Bring help. Go back to town and come back with the police."

Eleison. "God bless you."

Peter's voice is thick with emotion. "God bless us both."

Kyrie adinos.

As the priest ducks through the little opening and plunges back into the woods Peter's voice follows. "Hurry. Take care."

Christe ex adinos. Out in the open, Father Jerome begins running hard, so fixed on his mission that he will not heed the figure in the underbrush ahead of him, thick as a tree and so still that he takes it for a tree until in the next second it moves. The fleeing priest is yanked out of his tracks, seized and overpowered so quickly that the unspoken prayer finishes itself in the dark place where the soul goes when the body loses consciousness.

Twenty

Summoned by Thorne, who faded into the woods as soon he brought the news, Ava had left her work, left that girl perched on the stool looking perfect... and for this! Furious, she hissed, "What are you doing here?"

The woman she hated most rumbled, "What the fuck do you think?"

In seconds the little patch of dirt outside Ava's studio became an arena. Broken light filtered in through the trees, fragmenting on the heads of the combatants. They faced off like players in a Greek tragedy or a gladiator and some great brute locked in a contest that could end only in hell. One was tall and regal while the other slouched with her head down and her shoulders bunched like some coarse beast. Gross in flowered hopsacking that fit less like a dress than a slipcover, she shuffled on fat feet barely contained by slashed basketball shoes.

To Jude, drowsing on her stool by the studio window, they would look like creatures from alien civilizations accidentally marooned on the same planet.

Ava kept her voice low so the girl in her studio—her model for today—would stay posed on her stool with the velours draped low on those beautiful shoulders, unaware of the confrontation outside. "You bitch, why couldn't you stay home and wait?"

"You bitch, I been waiting in Oak Hollow forty years!"

"Emma, I promised to send for you."

"Don't you Emma me, girl."

"You promised to leave me alone."

"You promised to keep the money coming too. Now, cough up!"

Something in Ava snapped and she cried, "I cain't!"

"But yer gonna," the old lady said, "elst I'll whup you!"

"I caint. I coultn't let loose of it cause we're gettin' ready," Ava whined in the identical white-trash twang. "We're fixing to do somethin' a lot more important than you,"

"Hell with that," Emma spat. "You owe me money!"

Ava bared her teeth, snarling like a gutter rat. "I don't owe you fifty cent!"

Alert, Jude would have been shocked by what the fight had made of haughty Ava Benedict, but the tea had pulled her out of herself and left her floating somewhere else. From the stool where she had retreated, the scene outside the studio looked like a movie unfolding in a different world. She could not know that different as they looked, these two sprang from the same place in the earth.

"You trashy bitch," Emma growled, "living high off the hog while your momma starves."

"You're not my momma, you greedy sow!"

"I was so hungry I hadda chew rags..."

"Like I care, you chunka fatback!" At the sound of her own voice, Ava broke off. Angry that she'd slipped, she slapped her hand over her mouth. Then she lifted her head in the old imperious way. "Now, listen, woman, and listen carefully. I am an artist. We are all artists here, and we are on the verge of something great."

"...hadda boil up my shoes to eat." Emma's eyes were small and canny, like a hog's eyes. "Great what?"

"That's none of your business. Now, go."

"*You* are my business, miz *ar-teest*!" Emma raised fat arms. "Now come to momma, Hank Etta."

Ava flinched as if she had been struck. "Don't call me that!"

"I'm your mother and I can call you anything I fucking want." She was getting louder. "Miss Hank Etta from Oak Hollow."

"Don't... you... ever... call me that!"

"Hank Etta, Hank Etta, Hank Etta Lassiter," the old woman added, escalating. "Or should I say Hank Etta Lassiter *Hutson,*" Emma said, driving in the stake.

It was at this exact moment that, disturbed by the rising voices, Jude slipped down off her stool and drifted to the door. She opened it and stood blinking, still drugged and only dimly aware.

When she spoke again, Ava's voice was dangerous and carefully constructed, like steel under velvet. "How much do I have to pay you to go away?"

"There ain't enough money in the world, Hank Etta." The old lady gestured toward the house, the gardens, the outbuildings. "Not after I seen all this."

"Come on. Five hundred? Will a thousand make you go away?"

"Shit, baby, I'm not going nowhere. You in this big house and me in this croker sack, livin in my car." Great wobbling bags of pale flesh strained the sleeves of her terrible dress as she advanced with her arms outstretched. "Imagine, us back together, after all these years. Come give your old momma a hug."

"Get back!" Ava used her forearm like a blade. She could have been fighting off a monster or defending herself from a grizzly. "I'm not your baby."

"Hell no, course you're not, you're all growed and got your own children." Emma was getting louder and louder. "But we're still family, Hank Etta."

"You were never my momma. Not really."

The old woman said, with malice, "OK for you, Hank Etta Lassiter, how come you're looking at me out of them same piss-green eyes? Hank Etta Lassiter *Hut*—"

"Don't! They'll hear you."

"Say please."

Ava hissed savagely, "Please stop."

Now that she had her victim nailed, Emma pounded in the stake. "You mean, Please stop, *Momma*."

And in that split second Ava slipped back into the diction of Oak Hollow. "Momma," Ava groaned.

This is how Jude happened to hear this last exchange without knowing what it meant. She saw Emma's premature grin of triumph, just as Ava looked over her mother's head for the help she had summoned—how? As if on cue, two of Ava's students—heavyset, powerful Jake and sturdy Petra—trotted out of the woods, bearing down on Emma from behind. The daughter's head dipped in acknowledgement, but she went on talking to her mother as though they were still alone. "Can't I ever get away from you?"

"Now why would you want to get away from your momma, Hankie Etta?"

Ava's tone changed. With calculated warmth she said, "Oh, Momma." She almost smiled.

This use of her name so disarmed the old woman that she actually smiled when Ava advanced and gripped her fat shoulders. "I knowed you cared for me."

"Whatever," Ava said coldly, moving her along.

Touched, Mrs. Lassister had no way of knowing her daughter was positioning her for the next move in the game. "You'll always be my Henrietta," the fat woman said. "We two are bonded by blood."

She should have been warned by Ava's voice, which slid without missing a beat from simulated warmth to her usual tone of command. "Not in this life, Emma Ray," Ava said with force, "Not ever, you cow!"

"*Momma*. You call your Momma by her right name, you hear?"

With a sudden shove, Ava toppled her. Squealing, Emma staggered and fell backward into Jake and Petra's rigid arms. She spat and struggled. "Let go. Listen, you, I... Hey, what are you doing? Let go a me!"

Shivering in the doorway, Jude blinked. She could not parse what was going on.

"Thank you, Jake. Petra." Ava might have been directing the disposal of a piece of furniture. "Put her where she'll be safe."

Emma wriggled, protesting. "Wait just a darn minute."

The students said, "Yes, Ava."

Jude shook her head but could not clear it. Not even fresh air helped. She didn't know what was going on, but she didn't like it. A face in the floor, she didn't know if she'd seen that face in the floor, but Petra's stiff nod of acquiescence and the new light in Jake's eyes were all too real. She said, through what seemed to be a mouthful of wool, "Ava, I should go."

Ava was dispatching her students. "You know what to do."

Propelling their captive, they wheeled in tandem. "Yes Ava."

"Thank you for your interest in the Benedicts." Ava said icily as they dragged her mother away.

Struggling, Emma squalled, "Wait!"

Ava wheeled on Jude. "I thought I told you to keep the position!"

"I did, but you were gone for so long... I just."

"Come, then," Ava said, drawing her back into the studio, "sit down. This piece is going to be beautiful."

"I wish..."

"Perfect," she crooned seductively. "Come on."

"I wish I knew."

Ava put her on the stool, turning her head with firm hands. "Look, dear. That profile!"

"I don't know." Jude was upset by what she'd just seen, what she thought she'd seen before—below! She was addled by the tea and at the same time drawn by the artist—*she called me dear*, because sitting in this studio under the eyes of her adversary, watching her own likeness emerge from the wax, she felt as though she'd fallen under the hands of a superior lover, whose touch would leave her elevated and forever changed. "I don't know!"

"Beautiful," Ava said, absorbed. Her hands flew over Jude's face, from her face to the wax, from the wax to her face. "Yes, like that. Now, shh. That's it, that's it. Perfect. We have to hurry," Ava said, making love to her, to the work, "it's going to be a wonderful likeness. To the life."

Whether or not she wanted to, Jude held the pose; she wanted to fight the drink Ava had given her, she wanted to give in to it. She wanted to be beautiful... no, she wanted Ava to make her beautiful for Peter, but at what cost? She didn't know. She felt languid and anxious and troubled by the voluptuous warmth that drew her into it—just being here. Part of her struggled to the surface. "But that woman. What were we..."

"That was nothing. We don't have much time. Now, hold still."

"Your mother," Jude said uneasily. "Was she your mother?"

"No."

"You called her Momma."

"You heard." Something in Ava clicked. Her breath came out in a sharp, "OK."

"That poor woman. And they were dragging her away."

"You want to hear about it? Fine. You will hear about it." Ava said in a firm voice that brooked no argument, "but only if you do as I tell you, and hold still."

Twenty-one

"I already told you," Benton Benedict said. "I don't know exactly." They had come into the house for a family council and his brothers were interrogating him like KGB operatives grilling a subject. *They didn't come home to help me,* Benton thought sadly. *They don't care about me. They just came to find out what Ava knows.*

Severe, angular Berton reproached him. "Apotheosis of the family secret. Key to our success and you don't even know what it is?

"I never have. I only know it's terribly wrong."

"If it's so bloody wrong, how come we're all making a bloody fortune?" Rotund Bernard raised a maimed hand. "How come it made our work so good?"

"Put ourselves into the work," Berton said. "As ordered. And look how far we've come!"

Benton shook his head. "The fingers. The ears. They're the least part of it. The rest... it's wrong!"

"Wrong to be famous and prosperous?"

Perhaps because he'd lived so long in France, Berton's question was subtler. "What do you mean by wrong?"

"Evil," Benton said.

They were working him like a pair of hounds. Berton asked, "What do you mean, evil?"

"Sinful!" Shamed, Benton spread his hands. "I don't know."

This brought Bernard out—jolly Bernard, reddened by nights in British pubs. "What do you mean, you don't know? Your wife is doing something sinful and you don't what she's doing?"

"I mean I don't know exactly," Benton said uncomfortably. "It's a secret process."

"Explain *process.*"

He choked. "I can't." The early evening shadows in the drawing room seemed to advance another foot with every word his brothers said. Benton and his brothers, whom he loved so much and missed so terribly all these years, were closeted in the drawing room—his own drawing room in the house he had kept up all these years at Wayward, Wayward, which they had escaped as boys, leaving him to carry on and in the long run, pay the price. Benton's own drawing room, and they were treating him like the bad steward, called to an accounting. He said, "Whatever it is... we all profit."

Harshly, Berton put the question that troubled them all. "At what cost?"

Now they had put it to him, and he had to admit he did not exactly know the specifics of the price fate had set.

That they all profited from.

"Ava found out what to do and how to do it," he said wearily. "She told me not to worry my head. Then she told me it was none of my business. Then she told me if I kept prying, something terrible would happen to my boys. Martha's children, Dirk and Luke. Our boys Peter and Edgar, even though they are hers as well as mine."

The brothers sat with their heads bent over the little round card table, sketching with their fingernails in the green felt. Glad as they were to be reunited, the three kept their shoulders high and their backs rigid, braced against the enemy that strikes from behind.

Bernard said, "You let her go ahead with the, I dunno, *process,* without knowing what it was?"

"After the first bit, yes. The blood sacrifice was nothing. Until you tried to figure out what the next step might be." Pain turned his face grey. "*I was afraid to ask.*"

Berton said, "You mean all these years with her and you still don't know?"

"Ava and I..." Benton sighed and could not stop sighing. "We're not that close."

"You didn't ask?"

"After a while I stopped asking." He put his hands to his mouth to stop the sighs from escaping and spoke through laced fingers. "There are some things you don't want to know."

Bernard bored in, trying to X-ray his soul. "Then you don't even know how these armatures are made."

"Afraid not."

At which point his brother Bert—*his own brother* attacked. "You keep the machinery going, and you don't know how it works?"

"It seemed better not to," Benton said, ashamed.

Berton's saturnine face grew even darker. "And now you want us to help you dismantle it."

"Before anything worse happens."

"And you don't even know what it is."

"There are things I've been afraid to look into." Benton paused heavily, thinking, *This will convince them.* "Like the cellar," he finished at great expense to himself.

He thought this detail would galvanize his brothers. He could not do this alone; he couldn't even do it with Essie's help, but he believed he could do it now that he was surrounded and reinforced by the other two—Benedicts all. Now that he had them here. Together they could force their way into the cellar and end this for good and all.

But his brothers' response was troublesome.

Bert asked deliberately, "What makes you so sure this is wrong?"

To Benton's surprise, Bernard put a hand on their gaunt Parisian brother's arm. "Business is good right now, Ben. Let's don't rock the boat."

If only Aunt Benta would get here. She'd know what to do. Looking at his brothers, one stout, one spare, both intent on the same thing, Benton said heavily, "I mean it's got to stop."

"We're here to stop Ava, right enough," Bert said, surprising him, "but that doesn't necessarily mean we want to give up the process."

Benton groaned. "You don't know what goes into the process." *Aunt Benta would know what to do.*

"After all, we're all doing rather well," Bernard said. "Don't want to boot the golden calf off the place, now, do we?"

Or Grandfather. He'd know. "The secret," Benton said. If only he could explain! "Ava got onto it right after we were married—she wouldn't tell me how."

Berton was on his feet, pacing the room like a Giacometti, an elongated version of real life. "Old Beauchamp's secret. Our great grandfather's legacy."

"That Grandfather saw fit to bury." Benton was in extreme distress now. "It would help if we knew what it was."

Bernard laughed. "If only we had Grandfather here we could ask."

"And he'd tell us. Then we'd know what to do." Berton said sourly, "but Grandfather is dead."

"They're all dead."

"Don't be so sure." Trembling, Benton considered his brothers; perhaps without knowing it he had moved them to the position he wanted them in. He cleared his throat. "I think it's in the cellar," he said.

"What?"

"Everything."

Just when he thought he had them, a reedy voice in the doorway broke the thread. "Dad."

By this time Benton was too distracted to respond.

Both brothers had turned on him, asking, "What is?"

"The secret," he said. "But it's locked. If you would just help me break in...."

"Dad."

Berton swept past the distressed child in the doorway without seeing. "Why can't we just ask Ava for the key?"

"Makes sense to me, Bert." Bernard said.

"Daaad!"

"You don't understand." Distraught, Benton was both aware of Edgar hovering and not aware of him. "I think we are all in..."

"No reason at all," Berton said. "Let's put it to Ava when she comes back to the house."

"...terrible danger," Benton finished anyway.

At which point Edgar seized his father's elbow and jerked hard, almost unseating him, "I said, *DAD*!"

And stretched beyond his tolerance, embarrassed by his own powerlessness and hurt by his brothers' indifference, Benton turned on the child, shouting with such force that it drove Edgar out of the room, "I'M BUSY NOW EDGAR, GO AWAY AND DON'T BOTHER ME."

Twenty-two

Odd, how you can think you have seen something terrible and heard even more and still be sitting here smiling. Jude wrote it off as a dream. Drugs, she told herself without wondering why she had been drugged or why, in fact, she had submitted. Positioned on Ava's stool just *so,* bending under the sculptor's hand as it moved back and forth between model and emerging likeness, Jude was dreamy, as pliant as wax. Seduced by her own image. The wax was beautiful and the feeling that warmed her as she saw her face emerge was so intensely sensual that she could no more end this than she could have stopped in the middle of an act of love.

"Sorry for the interruption." Ava's tone was light-years removed from anybody named Hank Etta and from anyplace like Oak Hollow. This was Ava Benedict, the tiger. Regal. Sure. "We'll do as much as we can before dinner. Tonight I'll need you again."

"I don't know if I can..." Jude hadn't seen Peter at all today. Doors slamming and crunching footsteps suggested new arrivals; there were things she should do and things she should be afraid of, but since late morning—that tea—she had lost touch.

"But you will," Ava said, "because you're essential to this piece."

"Oh. Oh!" She was caught up in the age-old seduction of the artist's model, the rush that comes with knowing you've inspired a work of art. You may die but this. This will last.

Ava tilted Jude's head. "There. You're perfect. You are going to make my masterpiece. *The Marriage of the Worlds.*"

Was this what Peter meant when he said Ava could get anybody to do anything? She repeated it like a spell. "*The Marriage of the Worlds.*"

"The biggest thing the Benedicts ever wrought. My best, all their best, joined in a single, monumental piece..."

"With me in it."

"Yes. We finish tonight. And tomorrow, everything will converge."

"What will?"

With a gesture, Ava swept the mouth off the wax image. "You'll see soon enough. It will be magnificent. Some of the elements just arrived, the rest are already in place, except for this. And tomorrow at sunrise?" The pause was more loaded than even Ava knew. Startled, she drew herself up. "The rest."

"How..."

"Hold still!" Ava made a fresh cut in the wax that pleased her. "Better. It's lucky I found you."

Jude saw herself dropping the velours and grabbing her clothes, but her body stayed where it was. "I feel so dopey."

"Have some more tea. It helps my models to relax."

What had happened to her in the hours since she woke up late and stumbled down here after breakfast? What happened to the day? "No thanks."

"Take it," Ava said, pouring from the pot—what was in it now—water Jude had poured out of a coffee can, but Ava didn't know that.

Still groggy but aware, Jude drank dutifully. She managed without making a face.

Smiling, Ava tipped her head with strong fingers. "There. Perfect. Excellent. I'm so glad we're going to be friends."

Friends. The woman had the touch of a surgeon—or a lover. Could Ava really mold people according to her plans? *Wait,* Jude's inner sentry said. *Get out.* But the rest of her responded dreamily, *Not yet. Not now, when we're so close.* Close to what? She could not have said, exactly, except in relation to the unmistakable image of Jude Atkins emerging from the wax. Just now she needed this more than she wanted to escape. Her likeness in bronze, crowning some huge new piece. *I'll be in all the books. Take that, Phil Forrest. Art historian. I'll be one of those dreams you can only read about.* Her reverie hit a bump and stopped short. *That Peter hates.*

"I'll make you famous," Ava hummed, rubbing her thumb along the wax jawline. Jude stopped trying to move. Ava looked into her pupils with a little nod. "I suppose you think it's funny, that fat hick claiming to be my mother."

Jude closed her eyes so Ava could not see into her. "Mmmm."

"Don't you," Ava said experimentally. The murmur satisfied her. "Well, she is."

"Oh!" Jude knew there was something wrong, but it was like hearing of a distant train wreck; she was far from the twisted wreckage; the cries for help were audible now, but still remote.

"You came along at the right time," Ava said. She touched Jude's upper lip with something that smelled of cloves and peace came into her head in a rush. "It's Peter. I need your help."

Peter. Is there something you're forgetting, Jude?

"I'm afraid of what he's going to do."

Jude tried to raise her hand, but couldn't. Yet.

"Now that we're so close. I can't let him rush in here and destroy it. Everything I've worked for. Everything we've made." She whirled on Jude and her eyes flamed red. "But you can help."

Jude made herself nod complaisantly.

Ava finished, "Now that you're part of it."

Unnerved, Jude sat quietly, still and vigilant. *Listen. Find out what she wants.*

"I gave Peter the world but he threw it away. Same with the others. The mighty Benedicts." Satisfied that her captive audience was listening, too fuddled to remember and too nearly paralyzed to act, Ava went on. "Great reputation, and they let it go to crap."

In a heartbeat, the elegance melted away. Ava transformed. She wasn't Ava any more, she was that sexy little tramp from Oak Hollow. "They don't have no idea what it's like to go hungry. Do you know what it's like?"

Jude didn't speak. Maybe she couldn't; she wasn't sure. She knew enough to hold back when, testing, Ava smacked her face.

"I thought not. Well, I can tell you a thing or two. I came up in Oak Hollow, wide place in the mud. If you never saw us, you haven't seen poor. Momma had us down on the corner in front of the Gold Eagle with our clothes in shreds, singing for small change, we got home late and she beat us for never bringing home anything decent. Well, I'll decent her, she fucking couldn't cross her goddam legs, she spent half her life nursing and the other half pregnant. She and Pop took on like warthogs behind the sheet and I had to sleep with the brothers, and the stuff that happened, you don't want to know. Momma, she didn't care what they done to me, she just kept humping and every year another baby popped out. Then she would go, 'Hank Etta, you mind the baby, you stupid bitch,' and the only toys we had was dolls I carved for us.

"Ugly, she wanted me ugly so Pop wouldn't get into me. I don't see why she thought he wanted me over her when they were all the time humping and them babies kept popping out. She dressed me in crap hand-me-downs and I looked awful. I washed in the pump but I smelled so bad at school that kids made fun of me.

"You think I didn't hate my life? You think I didn't hate them kids? You don't think I wanted to get out and get even? Well, one day there was this fire at the school, and I won't tell you who was hurt or why or who done it but I will tell you that if you make a person mad enough, they'll move hell to get back at you."

She had forgotten the work; she'd forgotten Jude; she'd forgotten everything but her story.

"And all the time somebody was watching me."

Jude's eyes narrowed, but Ava didn't see.

"Watching, but who knew? In junior high I did certain things for Mr. Fremont and he bought me a dress; he said it would bring out my natural coloring, so I thought I was doing one thing but it turned out I was doing more than one. He was the art teacher, he had this plastic clay, so while I was looking over my shoulder with one eye to see was he hot that day, with the other I was making these models of the brothers and squashing them up one by one by one, and the more I worked the more the models got to look like the people and I swear that every time something bad happened to my models, something bad happened to them.

"It wasn't like, you know, voodoo. Instead they got it in 'Nam, them five fuckers my big brothers got drafted and they got themselves into bad shit in Nam and they died, but by that time I was far away from Oak Hollow. See, Mr. Fremont was giving me money for sex and more money to shut up and I married Thorne when I was sixteen just to get away."

Rapt, Jude listened. Only when Ava put her thumbs on her eyelids to lift them did she become aware that the woman thought she was in a trance.

It was at this point, with her model apparently frozen, that Ava said, "The first time I seen him, I was running away from the brothers in the woods and he cut them off with a look so fierce that every last one of them turned tail and run. Then he turned me around—I was thirteen—and he said, 'Girl, when you get big enough, I am going to marry you.' So I had that to remember, and I did. Then he stared deep into me and said, 'I would do anything to make you happy,' and he has."

Jude knew better than to ask.

"I used the money to go to art school. And Thorne? He will do anything for me. Anything. He talked my way into the Benedict studios and he convinced old Bernard that I was going to be famous. He even made Benton, that's your boyfriend Peter's father, say OK sure, Dad. Take her on. He lugged clay and stoked fires in the foundry, just to be near me. I was the first student here. Old Bernard, he was very grand. Always wore a white suit to dinner, good teacher, but he was very grand and that woman, Martha, Benty's first wife, she thought she was pretty grand. Sneered at my accent and my country clothes, she treated me like shit. Well, I showed her. Nobody looks down on me! It takes you a while to get out of Oak Hollow and even longer to wash the mud out, and Benton's first wife Martha, *tres elegante.* I studied her like a book and when I knew it all I slammed her shut and put her down. And then..."

Ava broke off for so long that Jude was afraid. She was about to slip from the stool and try to make a run for it when Ava shook herself and continued.

"Then I learned the absolutely biggest thing. Old Bernard was hiding something. From me. From all the Benedicts. I tried to get it out of him but things happened and he died. Don't ask. Fucking Benedicts, so grand. Well I showed them." Wheeling, she began to pace the studio. Her heels rapped on the studio floor as she talked faster. "Have shown. Am showing. Will show."

Jude clenched her teeth. What would happen if she tried to get down now. Would she make it? Would her legs buckle?

Ava turned, saying grandly, "With this ceremony, I'll show them all. I'll show the fucking world."

Jude sent her mind scurrying after loose ends; it came back with a murmured question. "Thorne."

"Oh, Thorne. How could I marry Benton if I was married to Thorne? Did I tell you he would do anything for me? He will. Things happened. The wife died, don't ask. So much for fucking Martha. And I made Benton feel all better and then I got pregnant with Peter and Benton married me."

Ava had told Jude too much, much too much, but the story was going on its own power now.

"Remember, Thorne will do anything for me. And when we're finished here..."

Confession made Ava brazen. She stroked Jude's cheek and went on with the mysterious confidence of a woman who knows her source will never get a chance to repeat it. "When you know how to use your body, you get what you want. Old Bernard whined when Benty and I moved him out of his master suite, but by that time he was over. I will not tell you exactly how this happened, but Bernard died. And I thought. This is it. Now I have it all. But then..."

The pause told Jude that Ava was studying her subject. Was Jude too far out of it to hear? To know what was going on? Carefully, Jude let her mouth drop open. She let moisture drip.

Satisfied, Ava went on. "Did you ever notice how the minute you get what you always wanted it turns out to be not what you wanted after all?"

She sighed. "It was that way with the Benedicts. I looked at the books and we were borderline bankrupt. Their work had been going downhill for years. The sacred, holy Benedicts were on the skids. The new work was lame and they knew it and commissions... well, there weren't any commissions; the place was a shambles and all the time I thought I heard—I don't know, it wasn't voices, it was *something.* Something under the house."

Hang in, Jude thought. *Be still and wait.*

Ava said in a deep voice. "I went down."

Experimentally, Jude flexed her hands—stronger than she thought.

"HOLD STILL! Hold still while I'm modeling you! If it wasn't for me," Ava said, "the Benedicts would be in the toilet. All of them. See, it was me that found out what was missing, and me that turned it around."

Hidden by the velours, Jude bunched the muscles in her calves.

"You have to put yourself into your work," Ava said with a strange laugh.

Jude flexed again. One. Two. One. Two.

"You know the rest."

Again. One. Two. One. Two.

"If you don't, you will." The woman's face was so close that Jude could smell the *cassis* on her breath. She kept her eyes closed. Listen. Wait. Shut your eyes and wait. "And now your beloved Peter wants to wreck everything and push us all right back down in the mud. Everything the Benedicts have done. Everything the first Beauchamp Benedict did and everything I've done. So you see, I need you."

"For..."

"To keep Peter."

Breathe, Jude. Flex. One. Two.

"Until I really need you." She did not explain. "You're easier than the others. Prettier than I thought you would be, and soon..."

Jude was coming back to herself in stages. It was like slipping out of a stranglehold—no, like wading through quicksand to escape the marsh.

"First," Ava said, "I need you for this. You have to keep Peter here. Understand, whether or not you believe in destiny, this is Peter's destiny. He is the best! The others are just tools." She went on, silky and seductive. "So you understand how important you are. And when this is done I'll make sure you are remembered..."

Jude listened without moving. And in the next second Ava betrayed herself, lifting her subject's eyelids one more time, and in the moment before the hammering on her studio door began, saying so coldly that it brought Jude to her feet: "In bronze."

Twenty-three

Creepy, it was all God dog creepy, knowing his shriveled ancestor or whatever night monster that claimed it was his relative was down cellar with God knows what-all stirring in the undercroft several stories below the landing where it crouched in its rolling chair with all the tubes and drains..

When Edgar heard grownups talking it was a relief. He lit out for the dining room, thinking thank God, all he had to do was tell. Daddy would take care of it, and if he couldn't? At least Edgar wouldn't have to carry this all alone. Wrong! His dad was in so deep with the uncles that he blew off his very own son even though Edgar knew he was his father's favorite, at least until today. Daddy got all pissed at him, like life was serious and Edgar wasn't.

It was bad, not knowing where Essie was or what about Peter, with Daddy out of reach plus mad at him. He was worse than alone. Clocks ticked too loud. Shadows crawled. He freaked and ran outside even though it was late in the day, with supper not started and darkness sneaking in, and for no reason he could see, he began walking circles around the house.

It was dumb, what Edgar did next, unless it was very smart. He ducked in behind the shrubbery, skirting the house like he could peek in somewhere and spy on the ancient creature, even though every window in the foundation was sealed tight. Now that he knew there was something down there and he sort of knew what it was, he thought there might be a way to spy on the thing without it knowing. The problem, he realized, was that the ancestor or whatever it was wanted him to help it, aka kill it or some other damn thing as yet to be described, and the very idea scared him shit. If he could just watch it for a while, maybe he'd know what to do. If only he had Essie with him, or Peter—face it, he needed some grownup, any grownup willing to sit with him for a little while and study the poor old thing and tell him what it was and what to do.

The basement windows were pretty much battened down, he discovered, feeling scared and relieved, but in the kitchen foundation—just about where the basement stairs started down—a stone was loose. He levered it out and uncovered a chink in the stones underneath. No light came out, but when he put his eye to the hole he thought he saw a distant glow, constant, but faint. He ground his face into the stone, trying hard to see more, but the light was deceptive. It came from no recognizable source, not the swinging bulb on the first landing and not from the cell, but from somewhere deeper. There was no observing anybody in this light and there was no knowing what drove the old, old man or in fact, what was going on. It was only when he pulled away, squatting on his heels in confusion, that Edgar heard the voice—if it was a voice—carried on air so troubled that he had no idea where it was coming from: *It's tomorrow.*

Terrified, he scrabbled backward. "What's tomorrow?"

Tomorrow is your birthday, son.

"My God." He bolted, sobbing, "My God!"

He didn't stop running until he hit the end of the dock. Nice out here. Clear of the trees, out from under low branches with heavy beards of Spanish moss. Shut of the horrors inside and underneath the house. It would be nice out on the water right now, he thought, when you're out on the water in the Carolinas, even at night the skies are so clear that you can imagine it's still light.

Out here nobody can sneak up on you.

Nobody can grab you.

There's noplace to hide, so nobody can jump out at you.

He wanted to untie his rowboat and get in and start rowing and not come back until day after tomorrow, when his birthday is good and past, so, cool! Feeling better, Edgar untied the hawser and jumped into the boat.

"Ugh!" He landed on something soft.

Mud all over the thing, slurry, he thought, one of his brothers had thought to cast this wax and then thought better of it. Big, fat, misshapen, it had to be ugly as shit or it wouldn't be here, but why did his brothers get fixed to model it, and what was it doing in his boat? *Bad,* he thought. *This is bad.* He gave the thing a shove. It was too damn big to move, whatever it was, so damn his brothers for making something too ugly to cast and too big to move and damn them for ditching it in his boat. Then, being a Benedict, he began to wonder what exactly Dirk or Luke had made, that was so hideous, so he took his bailing can and sloshed some water on its head. When Dirk or Luke or whoever dumped this thing in the boat the slurry was probably still wet. Now it was beginning to harden so he sloshed it again and started wiping with his hands, thinking the wax was softer than usual, maybe that was why they'd dumped it, something wrong with the slurry, something wrong...

When his fingers slipped into a pink, wet opening and he felt the tongue and under the pressure of his fingers, the stirring of false teeth, he yanked his hand out of the mouth, gasping. Only terror kept him from ripping the Carolina sky from top to bottom with a scream.

Twenty-four

What just happened? Too much for Jude to assimilate. Breaking free of the drugs that had kept her here for much too long now, she was released from Ava's studio by a series of arrivals. Edgar was the first, shouting and hammering.

Behind him came Thorne.

When angry Ava threw open the studio door, Jude saw the big man looming behind Edgar, whose pounding had driven Ava to answer the door in the first place.

She tried to slam it on her boy before he could speak, but parts of Edgar were wedged in the opening—a shoulder, one arm, his anxious face. Ava snapped, "Not now, Eds, we're working."

He was wild, frantic, too crazy with fear to realize Ava was hurting him; he inserted the rest of himself, flailing and yelling, "THERE'S A DEAD BODY IN MY BOAT."

Behind him Thorne said, "No there isn't." In the next second Ava's huge, faithful dog's body had pushed the door wide, following Edgar into the room.

"Mom. Mooom!"

Ava hissed, "*Go away.*"

But Edgar stood firm.

Looking over his head at Ava, Thorne said, through tight lips, "Something's come up."

She was still trying to grapple Edgar outside and down the steps when Benton Benedict burst in, followed by two Benedict look-alikes—both brothers, Jude saw. Benton turned to them and said, too late, "Berton. Bernard. Let me do this."

Before Benton could stop him, tall, gaunt Berton grabbed Ava by the shoulders and turned her around so that they were facing. Grimly, he said, "All right. It's time for some truths."

"Berton and I need answers," Bernard said. "What's going on?"

"Berty, Ben, be gentle, that's my wife! Oh, please. I'm sure there's a simple explanation." Distraught, Benton tugged on his wife's hand, begging. "Tell them everything's as it should be, Ava. Now? Oh, Ava. Please!"

With Ava stormed by distractions, it was easy for Jude to slip down off the stool and quit the studio. Today was awful, she thought, now that she was free. It was frightening and exciting, being nailed in place by those sculptor's hands, stripped to the bone by those cold sculptor's eyes. How could she let... how could she possibly let? The rest of the sentence was too ugly and humiliating to form. At the time it had been strange and seductive, sitting for Ava, but everything was different now that she was free. She felt a little like a rape victim, still coming to terms with what had been done to her.

Jude had been sitting for so long that she felt strangely disembodied, cut loose from herself and adrift under the liveoaks and Australian pines. It was like being dumped into real life at the end of a dream she could not shake.

Fresh air helped, but not enough. What was she doing out here draped in gold velours, with gold Grecian sandals on her feet? What had Ava done to her hair? What was Ava doing anyway?

Oh, right. The masterpiece. *The Marriage of the Worlds.* In her own way, Jude would live forever. People a thousand years from now would look up at this great bronze sculpture and see her face.

She was still adrift outside Ava's studio when Edgar came hurtling out and brought her back to earth. "Jude," he howled, "what are you *doing*?"

The smack of flesh on flesh grounded her. "Oh, Eds! I don't know."

"And where's Peter?

Ashamed, she shook her head. "I don't know."

"I told Ava, but she wouldn't listen. I tried to tell her and she kicked me out. She wouldn't even..." The next sob strangled him. "And now I can't find Peter. Jude, Jude, there's a dead body in my boat and nobody cares! So where's Peter? I really, really need Peter."

Peter. Oh, this made Jude want to cry. She said in a small voice, "So do I."

"We've gotta find him. Something awful's going on."

He was crying. She touched his cheek. "What happened that's so awful, Eds?"

Thorne came thudding out of Ava's studio just then, barreling into Edgar before he could say. He took the boy's shoulders in huge hands. "I don't know what you thought you saw, Master Edgar, but I was just down there and there's nothing. The boat is empty."

"Yeah right it's empty." Edgar added in an undertone, "Now."

Ava's hulking factotum shook his head. "Master Edgar, you've been imagining things. If you want, I'll take you down to see."

"No thanks, Thorne."

"Son, you're being irrational. Come. Let's us go down there and see."

"No way! I have *things* to do." Edgar backed into Jude with a little thump. She locked her arms around him so they made a solid front, glaring until Thorne took the message and turned away. Inside the studio, Ava and the Benedict brothers talked on and on. Now that he had somebody on his side, Edgar said, "Right, Jude?"

"Right. We have things to do." Better. She was feeling stronger now, braced by the fresh air. "We have to find Peter."

"We can't. I looked everywhere." He grabbed her hand, digging in so deep that she yelped. "Plus. Jude. There's one more thing."

God, she thought. *No more.* "Don't tell me, OK?"

"Really," he said anyway. "It is *so weird.*"

Unsteady as she was, Jude was the grownup here. "Can't you just tell me, and then we'll go find Peter?"

"We have to do something about it! Come on. I have to show you. Oh, wow. Jude, I don't know what to do." His voice was high and wild. "I don't know what to do!"

"Can't Peter... Ow!"

"Oh, Peter. Peter doesn't care." Edgar could not let go. His nails dug in until the blood came. "He isn't anywhere!"

"Oh, Eds. What is it?"

"Please, Jude. We have to do something. You have to see! "

"What's so terrible?"

"You won't believe it unless I show you." Now that he had her on the path Edgar danced ahead, jittering. "I'm scared to go back down there alone, OK? Please!"

"OK," she said on an even note chosen to calm him down. "What do you want me to do?"

It was a simple question. Finding the answer was a struggle. Edgar's face clenched like a little fist. "What it is, is, we have to find out. There's. Ah. Something we have to do."

"Eds, make sense. What?"

"You've kind of gotta be there," Edgar said irritatingly, "but we can't just go down there. Not without knives and stuff."

"Knives!"

"A crowbar. Whatever," he said. "In case." His voice got so thick it almost choked him. "I was in the cellar," he confessed.

"The cellar." Without knowing whether or how she heard it, Jude felt the rush of air like the breath from a thousand throats. Last night, she could pass it off as a bad dream, but this was now.

"Well, partway down. Come on. You have to see it. It's." When she hesitated, he said hurriedly, "Oh we don't have to go the whole way down, I promise."

Jude shuddered. There could be insects down there, scorpions, snakes. Horror stirred in the darkness even here, outside the Benedict house. She was aware of a change in the air: something vast exhaling, the rustle of—what? Limbs stirring, or something worse? She felt the monstrous black breath of evil, and it made her afraid. "Maybe we should tell somebody."

With tears flying, Edgar lashed out. "Like who!"

And so Jude understood how alone they were. "What is it, Edgar? What are you so afraid of?"

"It's only to the first landing, OK? I promise, I'll take care of you. I've stashed Dirk's lantern, OK? And this..." He thumped his pocket. "Daddy's gun."

"What do you think's down there?"

"That's the trouble," Edgar said. "I don't know." He hesitated. "No, I know, but I don't *really* know. Not all of it. I don't know what I'm supposed to do. I was down there and I found him? I was talking to him." He hiccoughed like a rubber toy. "And..."

"Wait a minute. Talking to who?"

"That's the whole problem!" He groaned. "Then... somebody came and I had to go."

She reached for his hand. "Kid..."

"If you can't handle it, fuck you, OK?" The rest came out in a fluting little zigzag of uncertainty. "I'll just go alone."

Now it was Jude's turn to grab Edgar's hand and pull him along saying firmly, "Not on your life." Hurrying, she became aware of Ava's velours drape clutching her breasts, her belly, her thighs; it was soft and sensuous and it made her feel a little dirty, like Ava's touch. She had to get rid of it. She walked so fast that Edgar had to trot to keep up. Just inside the kitchen, she stopped.

"What are you *doing*?"

She pulled a gardener's smock off the hook. "I have to get out of this *thing*."

"No time. We have to hurry. Before Thorne comes back." Edgar whispered, "I'm scared of Thorne."

"I can't. Not yet." Jude clawed at the velours that caressed her ankles and trailed between her legs and without thinking, she shrugged it off without caring whether Edgar saw. Quickly, she slipped on the heavy canvas smock. And was no longer Ava's thing. "OK," she said, exhaling at last. "OK!"

"Hurry."

Rummaging in Essie's drawers, Jude dropped a knife and a cleaver into the deep pockets of the smock. She understood that she was arming herself against some danger she did not know and could not even anticipate. "Let's go."

Edgar headed for the basement door, wrenching the key in the lock with such confidence that Jude was as outraged as he was when it didn't open. "Son of a bitch!"

"What's the matter?"

"It opened before." He gave it a kick.

"Shh. We'll go in a window."

"Can't. I've been around a hundred times. It's all boarded up."

"Maybe you missed one." They left the kitchen and under cover of thickly planted azaleas and oleanders, began a desperate circuit of the house. There were indeed windows in little wells below ground level, and each of them was set into the foundation with cement, boarded, bolted and wired, with the early, rusting wire renewed by an iron grating corroded shut. Whichever Benedict had sealed the windows in the first place had done it decades ago, and with such care that it was apparent that he'd intended for them to stay closed to the end of the world. And somebody else had come along to reinforce. What was down there, that had upset Edgar so, Jude thought uneasily, and what were the Benedicts trying to hide? Whatever it was, it must be terrible. The windows were countersunk and double-sealed. Looking for one where the grating seemed loose or the frame looked flexible, Jude crept along behind the shield of the bushes more or less confidently at first, but she was running ahead of fear.

Frustrated, Edgar lowered himself into the well in front of the last window they found and began hacking at the frame with Jude's butcher knife.

"Come on, Eds," she said softly, "this isn't working."

"Son of a bitch, it has to." His breath came in angry sobs.

"Well it isn't." It was getting late; there was a chill in the soft air and stark pines and liveoaks seemed to be creeping toward them, preceded by their shadows. Pretty soon all the Benedicts would be coming up to the big house from their studios—Thorne from the foundry!—and she and Edgar would be discovered here, dirty and ineffectual. "Maybe we'd better quit for now."

"I'd rather die. Come on."

"Where are we going?"

"We'll hack our way inside."

Following him through the kitchen, she noted platters on the counter. Food laid out for a cold supper by a cook who had other things to do for the afternoon. "They'll be back soon, Eds. There isn't time."

"We have to try, OK?" He looked up at her out of a face pinched tight and aged by fear. "My birthday's tomorrow and I'm so scared!"

A whiff of Ava's fragrance curled around Jude and made her murmur, "*The Marriage of the Worlds.*"

The look Edgar gave her made her want to weep. "That's what I'm scared of."

And so at last Jude comprehended the stirring deep within the house. "Oooh, Eds," she whispered. "This is worse than I thought."

"I have to get in there," he said doggedly. "I'll beat the door down."

"They'll hear you." she said. "Maybe we can break the lock."

"It won't work. Nothing works." He looked up at her out of an old man's eyes. "It's almost my birthday."

"It's OK, Eds, it'll be OK." She would promise anything to make him feel better. "I won't let anything happen to you."

Scorn aged him another ten years. "Just like Peter, right?"

"Peter." Jude was too preoccupied to hear anything but her own hollow voice asking, "What are we going to do?"

"Oh Jude I am so scared."

There was a sound from below. Footsteps on the cellar stairs.

Jude's heart congealed. "Careful!" It was then that the door opened—from the inside—and a tall, very old but still beautiful woman emerged. Jude put the child behind her. "Who are you?"

"Hush," the old woman said. "Be quiet." With strong, powerful hands she turned Jude around and shoved her through the basement door into the dark. Then she extended her hand to Edgar, who gripped it like a toddler. Smiling, she set him on the landing next to Jude.

"What," Jude cried. "What!!!"

"It's OK," Edgar said, "that's my Aunt Benta. Aunt Benta, this is my friend Jude."

"Hurry, you two, hurry!"

"Aunt Benta, did you see him?"

The old woman's breath shuddered. "I saw him and I'm sorry."

"Isn't it *awful*?"

"Shh, dear. More awful than you know."

"Who's down there, Ms.—Benta?" *Oh God*, Jude thought. *There really is somebody down there*. Her voice got away from her. "Who?"

Benta said, "You'll see him soon enough..."

"Wait a minute," Edgar shrilled, "aren't you coming with us?"

"And you'll know him. I can't, Eds. I have things to do."

"You have to come with us!"

"No. Now hush, boy. Be quiet. Hurry."

"Wait," Jude said, even though she understood they were beyond waiting. "What do you want me to do?"

"Quickly." Just before she locked the door on them, the tough, handsome, venerable Benta Benedict made the sign of the cross on her great-nephew's forehead, saying, "Go down."

Twenty-Five

When he finally came to, Peter understood that one of Ava's devoted slaves had bushwhacked him as he came out of the family chapel. Ava's pawn for the day had blindsided him and knocked him out. Whoever it was dragged him to the foundry and lugged him inside. It must have been Jake, he thought, testing the strength of the clothesline looped around him like ropes around Gulliver. Only Jake the klutz would make such lousy knots. Ava told Jake he had talent when what she meant was, he could do the heavy lifting because he was almost as big as Thorne. She kept him around to do certain jobs. Unless, of course, Thorne clubbed him. Damn Thorne, with his rocky face ripped out of Mount Rushmore and those enormous hands. What did his mother do for these men, what did she tell him, that made them work so hard for her? What did she give, to make them do her bidding? He didn't want to know.

Once he could sit up without keeling over, it was easy to undo the knots. Peter had been knocked out, carried here and dumped like a sack of clay. At least they'd dumped him on a mattress. This must be where Thorne slept. His black hat hung from a peg and his foundry boots stood in a corner. Studying the objects with which huge, implacable Thorne surrounded himself, Peter found out more about Ava's silent assistant than he'd learned in years of trying and failing to talk to him. Thorne had quite simply been around for as long as he could remember, like a useful piece of furniture whose function was waiting to be revealed.

Thorne's possessions told the story. There was a bible stashed here in his corner, with paper so greased and worn by fingering that it flowed like silk when Peter riffled through the pages. On the side table were a crushed flower in a jar and a couple of botched ashtrays—like a child's first efforts in ceramics class; on the crude bookshelf were several empty sketch pads with spiral bindings clotted by shreds left by an owner who ripped out his drawings and destroyed them as fast as he made them. Surprisingly, the craggy, uncompromising Thorne also kept volumes of love poems by writers whose names

Peter did not know. Shelved next to the books was a collection of notebooks labeled *Verse.* The spirals were clotted with the remains of poems that had been begun and hastily ripped out. Poor son of a bitch. So big, so klunky and so much in love. Troubled, Peter pulled out one ruined notebook after another, riffling pages until he found one survivor, the poem Thorne had forgotten to destroy. It was a haiku. It was touching and terrible:

To see your face
I will forever keep silent
And must keep my place.

His next find drew a dozen fragments out of his subconscious and assembled them with a *click.* It was a black-and-white snapshot of Ava taken on some sunny day in her teens, tacked to the shelf that held the books of poetry. The deckled edges were blunted by much handling. Stretched on the sand like an old-fashioned bathing beauty, the girl who would become his mother, cradle of this generation of Benedicts, pushed one shoulder forward seductively and pouted at the man holding the camera.

"Oh Ava," he whispered. "You bitch."

Unfinished as it was, cut off at the waist by the bottom of the frame, the monolithic shadow cast on the sand by the photographer could not be mistaken.

"Thorne, you poor bastard." If big, sad Thorne stayed here all these years doing Ava's bidding because he was in love with her, if she'd switched him around like a trained grizzly and given him shit for thanks, who else did she have in thrall? How many other people was she keeping that he didn't know about? If she had that kind of power, could she trap him too? There was the possibility that now that she had him here, she could keep him here forever.

Until today Peter believed could outrun his mother, free himself, make his own place on the far side of the world—better: the dark side of the moon. He thought he could separate himself from Wayward, forget the foundry and whatever went on here, but that was before. Last night she brought him home against his will, but last night he thought that together, he and Jude would take Edgar and go. Questions, distractions, mysterious arrivals kept him here.

When he woke up today he thought he would find out what Ava was up to and bring it to a halt. He'd confront her, call the police, whatever it took. Even in the chapel with Jerry he was still confident, but now...

Everything was different and not different.

Disturbed, he lurched out of Thorne's cubby into the open space where the Benedicts' bronzes were cast. The foundry. *When you come into your own, you will see the foundry,* Ava had promised, in the days when she still thought she could bend Peter to her design for the family. She ruffled his hair, pursing her soft, red lips like a lover. *When you are truly one of us. Then you will see.*

Instead, he left home. This was the first look at the foundry.

The place was bigger than he thought, crowded with massed shrouded figures and, beyond, several fresh bronzes cooling in their casts. The enclosure was lighted by a strip of fluorescents hung from the rooftree. It was like being trapped inside a wax museum, surrounded by shrouded shapes that might at any minute shrug off their canvases and start to move, closing in on Peter. In the center of the great room was the sand pit where Ava and Thorne did the pouring and beside it the cauldron crouched on a banked furnace like a ready monster, waiting to disgorge its molten contents into the plaster mold below.

Beyond the furnace, beyond the individual pieces waiting under their canvas covers, tidy as veiled corpses, in the far corner of the foundry, where Thorne lined up pieces on the loading dock for shipping, a massive grouping stood poised as if waiting to spring to life and lunge through the sliding doors. Even shrouded as it was, the sculpture seemed to ripple under the canvas, every line in it straining forward. Its enormous veiled silhouette was irregular and disturbing; to Peter it looked as though the canvas covered dozens of massed bodies straining to be free, creating an outline that strained upward like a breaching whale. The thing stood on an outsized pallet on a railroad flatcar, locked in place on tracks that led outside. Ava's *Marriage of the Worlds.* It had to be.

Which is why we are all here.

She had told the interviewers from *Art Forum* and *Newsweek* this piece would be the Benedict family's collaborative masterpiece. Timed for the hundredth anniversary of the mysteriously missing *God and His Creation.* No, she would not divulge any more details until the unveiling. No, she would not let reporters into the foundry; why should she even consider it, when only certain family members and her foreman were allowed inside, and then only for the pouring?

Foreman. That would be Thorne.

The pouring. He noted that the cauldron was heated to a disturbing pink-gold, almost ready to pour. Ava would be coming back with her bond slaves, and soon. On the platform in the sand pit underneath the giant cauldron stood a plaster that Peter knew surrounded one of Ava's waxes, waiting to be cast. His eye told him this particular piece was probably designed to complete the huge grouping at the head of the launching ramp. The form was slighter in stature than some of the other plasters, suggesting that this was the figure of one of those small, strong, women with neat bodies, rather like—

"Jude!" Stunned, Peter reached out to touch it and discovered that he could not. His mind whirred, running in place. Next to this first plaster, lined up and waiting, was a plaster cast so small it could only be Edgar, the wax image of his baby brother encased in plaster, waiting to be displaced by molten bronze.

Muttering, he rapped the thing with his knuckles and then whirled at some imagined sound, decided it was only the crash of shadows colliding with his fears, and moved on to study the trail of discarded plasters that lay in the sand, molds for bronzes that had been cast and polished and set in place in the pedestal of the big piece. One, he thought, was a negative likeness of his brother Luke's long-departed wife, and another looked so much like his uncle Berton's Atawan that he had to wonder how it had been made so quickly. They didn't get here until last night. Then he understood that Ava hadn't bothered to wait for the others to make the waxes she expected to cast. She had used the life masks she ordered Berton and the others to make in their own studios and send on ahead so that—what had she told them? So that she could refer to them in making preliminary sketches. He could almost hear her: of course we want you to bring your models here so we can all be on the place, working on this great piece together.

As nearly as he could make out, the great piece was all but completed.

"You bitch. You got them here under false pretenses."

How else had she lied? He rushed on as though he had her here.

"You don't need models at all!"

Stricken, he faltered. "But if you didn't need them, why did you bring them here?"

Unnerved, he looked into another of the discarded casts—negative plasters of bronzes that had been poured and polished and locked into formation in *The Marriage of the Worlds.* He found himself looking into a noble Asian face that was clearly at odds with its body: Great Aunt Benta's model Wataru must have been cast from the life mask she had sent, because as far as he knew, Great Aunt Benta hadn't even gotten here from Yokohama. The head looked as though Ava had hastily grafted it onto a body with sloped shoulders and a funny, simian slouch that reminded Peter of Jimmy Daley.

"Pretty cheap, Ava."

Troubled, he touched the plaster negative with his foot, rolling it over in the sand until its blind face no longer reproached him.

He murmured, "You lied to the relatives, didn't you?"

He knew what Ava would say: *One of the first rules of art is expedience.*

"What else did you do?" Reading the plaster negatives, he saw that this was probably what she had done instead of casting Uncle Bernard's wax of his model Keesha, and good Lord, Ava's wax of her own craggy, obedient student Jake. It didn't make sense.

You think these things are done overnight?

"What are you up to, Ava?" he muttered, looking into the face of his newest discovery with a start. It was Luke's long-absent wife, in negative. "What are you doing here?"

He groaned. "What are you doing to them?"

She had bypassed the wax altogether and cast a dozen figures from life. Freed the models and poured bronze into the plasters.

"What are you doing and what do you want?"

Hurriedly, he pulled the shrouds off some of the single figures and saw in turn faces he recognized and faces he didn't recognize, all placed like sentinels drawing him along to the central piece, Ava's long-projected *Marriage of the Worlds.*

The piece drew him as had nothing else. He had to see it unveiled, but he had no idea how to get at the mechanism that raised the canvas shroud. Instead he lifted a corner of the tarpaulin here and a corner there, trying to get some sense of the elements: a leg in work boots and coveralls here, suggesting a figure not unlike one of Ava's changing cast of students, and there feet and legs rising to a trunk that looked like Esther's, and over here a long, graceful moccasined foot. Even at this remove the whole thing was powerful, sinuous, shimmering on the verge of life.

It was enormous. Sinister. Still.

It was only bronze.

It spoke to Peter, who might have gone around it several times, tugging at the tarpaulin, kicking the winch until it yielded, raising the tarp to reveal the huge, unfinished work. He would have seen *The Marriage of the Worlds* unveiled, if he hadn't tripped and almost fallen on a felled image, bound up in its tarp. He was aware as he righted himself that there were people heading this way in some numbers, he heard them coming along through the woods without worrying about who knew; the woods were filled with twigs cracking and the overlapping murmur of voices as they crunched toward the foundry. He had to hide himself or find a way out of this place before they came in and caught him here. If nothing else he had to make a *plan,* but something about the sculpture lying in the sand—an angle or attitude that was alarmingly familiar—drew him, and before he did anything else he had to bend and tug at the canvas that hid it. He bent over, mesmerized. He could not have said what compelled him to uncover it. He just had to pull off the canvas. He had to look into its face.

"Gara!"

The likeness was one of Ava's best. Peter remembered the perfection of the wax—how well it was shaped, so graceful and beautiful, so faithful to the model that in his grief he'd wanted to destroy it after Gara ran away. It should have been one of his mother's best pieces, but something happened in the pouring and there were imperceptible bubbles marring the otherwise perfect face and for this reason Gara's likeness lay here in the sand pit, discarded.

Flawed or not, the thing was vivid, beautiful, gleaming with life—a classic Benedict bronze of the finest quality—it had that *glow* the best of the Benedicts' work had—this great beauty thrown away because of a casting accident. Still it was Gara's likeness, so filled with life that Peter couldn't bring himself to cover her face again. Rushed as he was, with unseen others converging on the foundry, he couldn't turn away.

"Oh, Gara." Crouching, he looked into her blind eyes. "I thought I could stand off from this—I thought I had, but there is no way in hell to say that you're not part of..." His breath shuddered and as keys rattled in the door at the far end of the foundry he managed to complete it—whatever you're part of."

Transfixed, he bent his head and shoulders as if settling his own responsibilities around him like a leaden cloak.

"Oh, Gara." Everything piled up in him—love, fear, grief—and he leaned forward to kiss its cheek. As he did so, something uncanny happened a long way off, in the bowels of the house.

And the light in the bronze face went out. The spirit had fled it.

Twenty-six

As Peter Benedict struggled to consciousness on a lumpy pallet in a strange place he was only beginning to recognize as belonging to Thorne, the door to the basement swung closed behind Jude.

She stood poised at the top of the cellar stairs with Edgar gripping her arm. The staircase yawned below like a dark throat. There could be ghosts down there. Hidden enemies. Feral cats. Every crawling thing that fed in the coastal waterway could be hidden in the lower depths waiting, crouched and ready to spring. What if the staircase ended in muddy quicksand? For Edgar's sake, she made her voice firm and strong. "OK, Eds. The light."

He raised the lantern and switched it on.

She gasped. "OK," she said firmly and could not move.

Edgar squeaked, "OK."

Outside the closed door, footsteps sounded in the kitchen. People coming. Coming for her? Jude whispered, "Shit!"

And so they plunged.

Unlike most buildings in tidal country, the foundation at Wayward was set on bedrock. It looked as though an early Benedict had built his house over a cavernous hole in the rock. Stone blocks covered with tabby made up the foundation, but the cellars were descending caverns. In the little light available, the cavity could have been any size and any depth. Jude had to assume the outlines conformed to the outlines of the house, but the place was so big that it swallowed the light and there was no telling how far down it went. Who knew how many levels the stairs led to, once you left the first landing. To her surprise, the air was fresh. It smelled strongly of marsh and salt water. And it was still. If Jude heard something in the night—that rush of air being expelled in a tremendous groan—she heard nothing now, beyond footsteps overhead as assorted Benedicts came into the kitchen from the studios, and below her, Edgar's feet pattering down the stairs.

"Come on," he hissed from the first landing. "He's here."

On the landing, Jude stopped cold. To her left, the stairs led down, into yawning darkness. Did she hear something calling, or did she only imagine it? She turned, thinking to go on down.

"Don't!" Alarmed, Edgar jerked her back. "Over here!"

"But Eds, I thought I heard..." Poised to go further down, pulling against Edgar's dead weight, she heard the air below come alive in a long breath that was both a sigh and not a sigh.

"This way. Really." He tugged her back onto the landing. "He's in here."

With a little shudder of relief, she turned and for the first time saw why he had brought her here.

There was a small barred cave here on the first landing. Unless it was a cell. Edgar was saying, to the person inside, "I bet you thought I'd never come back."

The voice that came out to meet him was dry and faint, half whisper, half moan. "It's about time."

Jude blinked. Edgar was at the door of—my God, what was this place? The boy cleared his throat like a dancing school partner and presented her. "So. Ah. I don't know what to call you."

The shrouded skeleton propped in the wheelchair stirred within its blankets and said faintly, "Beauchamp will do."

"This is my friend, Jude Atkins?"

Now the wispy figure in the chair lifted its huge head like the master of the house. "Beauchamp Benedict."

"Beauchamp?" Jude snapped forward, staring. Leached of flesh, barely covered with the electrified ghosts of hair, the head was unmistakable. *Beauchamp!*

The old, old man was studying her. The voice that was not quite a voice rasped, "Lovely, lovely." Then the living mummy raised its hand slightly in what might have been a wave.

Edgar said, "Jude, this is my great-great-grandfather."

"How..." She could not frame the real question. *How did you get here?* All she could manage was, "How *old* are you?"

Beauchamp said, "When I made *God and His Creation* I was forty years old."

It was like meeting a god. Jude murmured, "Your work—it's beautiful."

He groaned. "At some cost. Child, hold up the light."

Edgar did. Jude saw her profile cast on the back wall of the cell. The noise coming out of the old man was like newspapers crumpling in a giant fist. "Ava is a monster, but she has an eye."

And the noise was... Jude started. "You're... *laughing.*"

"Oh, young lady. Young lady. That profile! Good. Perfect. It's inevitable." His next words came out in a measured way, so nearly inaudible that, repelled though she was by the odd laughter and the fact that he was long past dead, she pressed close to the bars to hear. He whispered, "Oh—my—dear—you—really—*are* in danger."

"What?" Terrified, Jude reached for his hand. In the second before the chair rolled backward and the bleached wreckage of Beauchamp Benedict the first slipped from her grasp, his shriveled fingers tightened on her hand. "What did you say?"

"Come close. I'm only going to say this once."

Electrified, she did.

"You are in terrible danger." What the ancient sculptor said next did not make sense to Jude at first, but in the next terrifying second, it did.

"What," she cried. "What?"

"Two things." He gasped, struggling to form an explanation.

After too long, it came. "Your image is the matrix for the enclosure, and the positive from which the negative is cast, so that's one thing. And the other." He stopped so cold that she wondered if he had died.

Riveted, Jude waited for the rest. "What?"

He buried his face in both hands. "Oh my God, I am so sorry."

"The other!"

At last he looked up. "The other is yourself."

"What do you mean?"

He was... he was sobbing! "Believe me, I'm sorry!"

"Sorry!"

"Sorry I started this. I wish you could just kill me and that would make it stop."

"You're my great-great," Edgar said loyally, "I can't."

"You're going to have to do it in the end," Beauchamp said. "Besides." After a weighted pause, he finished. "It's what I want."

"But you're family." Edgar's turned away unexpectedly. He spun wildly, distracted by distant vibrations.

"You would be doing me a very great favor," Beauchamp said.

Jude reached out to the old wreck trapped in the wheelchair, murmuring, "But you're history!"

"And I started it. And I say when it stops." Old Beauchamp's next words flicked like a knife between Jude's ribs, rattling her heart. "And you and you alone can help."

"How?"

"Because you, my darlings, you have to stop Ava. You must not let her...

You must..." Shuddering, he broke off. The silence was sudden. Denser than night.

"What," Jude said in a low voice. "What do you want us to do?

The ancient mouth gaped. It gaped so wide that for a minute Jude thought he had died in mid-thought. She didn't want to look inside; she couldn't *not* look inside. The gums were green with age. There was something in there—in the mouth, inside his head, in the silence, that she had to pull out and identify—what? She heard herself pleading: "Oh, please don't die."

He may not have died, but he didn't move either. Jude could not hear his breath.

"Mr. Benedict, please tell me. I must... What!"

Now it came. "Be afraid."

Edgar whimpered, "Jude."

"Why? It's just..." Everything inside Jude was rushing in a different direction—toward this old man and what he had done—she could not comprehend it; away from him, toward Peter, no, toward Ava in spite of everything, because the most vulnerable, vainest part of Jude Atkins, who was nobody in particular but could be *somebody,* that part of Jude was still drawn to *The Marriage of the Worlds* and her place in it; whether it was Ava's drugs or something more she was still drawn, spinning into its center like a toy boat into a whirlpool.

"Jude," Edgar said urgently.

Unaccountably dizzy, lured by the fragrance of Ava's sweet tea, she swayed.

Edgar's voice yanked her into the present. "Jude! Upstairs."

With a start, she turned and saw him—brave, scared little Edgar Benedict, who *needed* her, hissing, "Hurry. It's him."

Moved, she promised, "Oh, Eds, I'll take care of you!"

"But first," Beauchamp Benedict said and could not finish.

"What do we have to do?"

With a great effort, old Beauchamp took in a shallow breath and spoke. The next words word struck her one by one, like a hammer on a block. "You. Have. To. Take it apart."

Edgar tugged. "Jude, upstairs! I hear them!"

"Take what apart?"

"The life inside the work. Oh dear God I hear him too. Hurry. Hide! Here he comes." Beauchamp was rushed now; desperate and hopeful, anxious and pressed as he was, he managed a formula that was both precise and terrifying. "You can't just kill me and expect it to be over, any more than you can just kill her and expect it to stop." He coughed, out of control. He spat and recovered. "You can't even do it by destroying the—armature—to *God and His Creation*."

Overhead, a key rattled in the lock.

"The armature!"

There was no time for Beauchamp to explain. His eyes were filmed with emotion, but he kept his voice steady. "The life. It must be disassembled as elegantly as it was put together."

"*Disassembled!*"

"Everything has to go at once."

"That beautiful piece?"

It cost him dearly to say what he said next. "No. The engine that drives it. Everything."

"I don't..."

"Hurry," Edgar said, but Jude was too engrossed in the puzzle to turn and follow. "He's coming!"

Desperate, Beauchamp cried, "Take us out. Out into the air!"

Upstairs, the door opened. Thorne's voice resounded in the stairwell. "Who's down there?"

"It's OK, Eds. I won't let them hurt us. Eds?" Jude turned away from the old sculptor to see Edgar standing at the lip of the black hole where the stairs made a right angle and continued down.

"Hurry." The child's voice dropped to a whisper. "He's here."

Thorne's voice was surprisingly gentle. "Who's down there with you? Who is it, old man?"

Beauchamp croaked, "Child. Not that way!"

"Don't make me come down there," Thorne said. "Answer me!"

Jude whispered, "What are we going to do?"

Poised on the top step, Edgar whispered, "Go down."

"No!" Beauchamp was begging. "In the name of heaven, no!"

"Who's there?"

Teetering, Edgar said, "Hurry. Come on."

"No!" the old man wailed. "It's too terrible. You can't!"

"We have to!"

"Not down there." Old Beauchamp's voice was fainter; at the end of his strength, he pleaded, "Not alone. You have to get help."

The child said bitterly, "There's nobody to help."

"Who is it?" Thorne's shadow loomed in the doorway above. He was taking his time here: odd. Why did he threaten from the top of the stairs instead of coming down?

Black vapor swirled out of the pit below. Julia did not so much hear as *feel* a dozen people groan: that rush of sound that had disrupted her night. "What are we going to do?"

Impatient, Thorne shouted, "I'm coming down." Would he hurt the old man? She didn't know.

The old man bleated, "Nooo."

Jude lingered, torn.

Savagely, the boy shoved the lantern into her belly, hissing, "Take this and go." Then in a little kid whine completely unlike any he'd used here with his great-great-grandfather, he yelled, "Hold your water, Thorne. I'm coming up."

Jude started upstairs after Edgar but he turned and gave her a shove, and before she could regain her balance, scrambled up and slammed the door, leaving her alone on the stairs while he faced Thorne. She thought to wrench it open and do whatever she had to so to protect him, but there was a click as Edgar shot the bolt, shouting, "Here I am, you fucking son of a bitch."

"Don't use that kind of language with me."

Frustrated, worried, she retreated to the landing while Thorne rumbled on, in an argument she could not hear. Then Edgar shrilled: "Nothing, OK? Just fucking nothing, all right?"

After that the boy's voice dropped and Thorne's voice dropped and she turned back to Beauchamp Benedict in his cell; the wheelchair had swiveled in the half-light. She spoke, but he did not answer. His back was to her she could not for the life of her tell whether he was still awake or whimpering out of a deep, helpless sleep. Caught here between two worlds, she had no choice but to go down.

She took the lantern on and moved out.

Oh, Edgar. Thorne would kill him if he knew what was going on. Thorne would kill her if he found her here. Or Ava would. She thought now that Ava would kill them both. Fresh air, she thought, it's coming from below, she told herself, there is another exit. Have to find it. Go down and find it, that's all I have to do. Find Peter, but first I'll look for the kid. Just turn up wherever they are sitting, pretend I was out for a stroll. And if she's laid one hand on that boy, I'll...

Rushing, she blundered through the archway at the bottom of the stairs, turning her face this way and then that, looking for the source of the fresh air. There must be another way out. Whether or not the house was filled with Benedicts, she had to find it. If she walked into a family grouping now, she would know at once whether they were with her or against her. If they were against her, she and Peter had to escape and come back with the police or, lord, the Marines,the national guard, anybody she could convince. They'd come on to the property at Wayward and dig if they had to, whatever it took to crack this place open and find—God, she didn't know.

There was something down here, that she did know. She and Peter and the police would find this—*thing*, whatever it was, that the old man had hinted at, what had he said, *the spirit of the piece,* and when they did they were going to have to, what was it the old man had said? "Disassemble it. As elegantly as it had been put together."

What did he mean?

Jude didn't know. What she did know was that she could not go on alone. But pressed as she was, frightened and disoriented, she made a false turn and it was thus that Jude Atkins found herself standing in a small grotto underneath what must have been the gracious Benedict music room, shivering.

A flash caught her attention: something glimmering in a niche in the grotto wall. She thought she caught something moving; she thought she heard something stir.

Then she saw it and did not know what she thought.

So it was here in the sub-basement of the great house at Wayward that Jude Atkins found not what she was looking for, exactly, but the details to identify and anchor her fears and change everything she did from that point on.

What she found standing in the niche was both gorgeous and terrifying—white, pale and purified, with the excess flesh flensed as though leached of imperfections from within, so that the flawless skin was taut and lay close to the bone; the figure stood with its eyes closed as if in a refreshing sleep but she was standing, erect and beautiful and perfectly preserved, not so much snared as supported, held upright inside an armature of silver wire—braces for the arms, which were extended toward the beholder as if begging, or offering—silver wire coiled around the legs, circling the loins, the belly, the breasts, a rope of braided silver wire contouring the silvery velours shift that clung to the body in a sensuous drape that made Jude shiver because it was so familiar, but this was not what shook her so profoundly that it almost overturned her. Rising above the beautifully modeled head she saw the astonishing glitter of metal and glass—IV bottles hanging from a stainless steel tree, and with a sick feeling she saw the equation completed below, drains carrying off the waste, all the basely functional parts of life drained away in the purification of art so savage that it stopped Julia's breath.

"My God!"

Riveted, she shone her light up, from the carefully placed feet to the cold, still face. Even in death Jude knew her, leached of color and superfluous flesh.

Raising her hand like a priest making a quick blessing, she murmured, "Gara Sullivan."

The eyes opened.

"Oh, God," Jude said. "Oh my God you poor thing." Frantic, she clawed at the network that snared Gara Sullivan in a frenzied attempt to help, and as she did so, could not figure out whether the bizarre framework of heavy silver wire was keeping the girl in, artfully imprisoned, or whether it was, rather, holding her up. Finding the wire soldered at crucial points, she knew she couldn't do much for Gara without tools—pliers, a bolt cutter, a hacksaw, when all she had was the cutlery she'd slipped into the pockets of the canvas gardener's smock. Her hands played over the framework as if she could bring Gara Sullivan back to herself by patting her and murmuring the right combination of things.

"It's OK," she said, "It's OK. I'm here."

The silence was so dense that she had to keep talking. "I've just got to figure out how to get you out of here."

The eyes were wide; Jude had no other sign that Gara might hear her, much less understand. She was all too strongly aware of the layered darkness surrounding them, with shifting boundaries held at bay by the light from her bobbing lantern, which she could not seem to hold still. She knew this dank cellar was by no means the bottom level. If there was a way down, she knew, it was also a way up for whatever lurked below. "I need to get us both out of here."

Gara was so still that Jude realized she was, essentially, alone here.

Still, talking helped: *We're in some kind of dim hell here, but at least there are two of us.* She said with a desperate optimism, "If I can get you loose, can you stand up by yourself?"

The lips were sealed as if by a transparent glaze and Jude had no way of being sure whether the captive beauty could hear her, much less understand.

"It's OK," Jude said shakily, "don't worry if you can't."

There was a slight change in the air; she had the idea there was movement elsewhere on this level, but so far as she could tell Gara Sullivan had not even drawn a breath.

"You *are* still in there, aren't you?"

She did not like the silence. Nor did she like the tingling at the base of her skull; she whipped her head around to see whether she'd been followed.

"Agh!" she barked like an animal giving a warning. Then she turned back to the prisoner in the niche. "Oh, Gara," she murmured. "Don't be scared, it's only me." It seemed important to keep them in some kind of human dimension, so she reached out to chafe Gara's hands. "Let's see if we can get some circulation going."

Then Gara twisted slightly on the wires supporting the outstretched arms and one of the hands fell limply. "Oh, I'm sorry," Jude said, hurriedly trying to put it back. It was not like touching anything human. As soon as she released the hand, it dropped, dangling. Gleaming though the figure was, apparently shimmering with life, Gara's skin was as cold as the grey velours that clung to her body, and the perfume that did not so much surround as emanate from what might still be Gara Sullivan was an unearthly mixture, redolent of incense and chemical preservatives, so that Jude had to wonder whether there was something else being piped into Gara's body along with nutrients. She studied the blue eyes, trying to read some expression. Softly, she said, "Are you all right?"

Gara Sullivan was beyond speech.

"Oh, please. I need to know what to do for you."

The beautiful caged girl was completely still.

"Come on, Gara, come on." Jude reached for the dangling hand. "I didn't come all this way to have you die on me."

Everything was still.

"I came to help you, OK?" Jude gripped the fingers and squeezed, hoping that if Gara couldn't hear her, she could at least feel her. "I'll do anything I can."

Gara did not move or speak.

"You were really in love with Peter, right?" Jude listened to the silence. She tried to tell herself she felt blood moving in the hand and she went on, spelling out something she was only now admitting. "Well, I love Peter too."

It was like talking to an effigy.

"Oh, Gara." Near tears, Jude whispered, "How did you get like this?"

She imagined she heard a tinkle as the IV swayed and two bottles collided, but Gara Sullivan, or that which had been Gara Sullivan, was completely still.

"Did they drug you? Should I pull out the IV?" She thought she saw the head move in a vestigial nod. Shuddering, she disconnected the tube that bled into Gara's arm. Then she waited for Gara to come to.

She thought Gara was waiting.

"Come on, Gara, come back, OK?"

The body in its framework gave a shudder.

"You have to wake up and tell me what to do." Jude blinked and discovered she was crying. "Don't worry, I'll stay with you."

But the tall, graceful figure was still.

Distressed by the silence, Jude stroked the cold hand, murmuring on and on. "Gara, what happened to you? Who did this to you, who put you down here? Please, oh God, Gara, who was it?" The next thought knifed in, going so deep that it threatened to unsex her. "Tell me it wasn't Peter. Please."

The hand in hers may or may not have twitched.

"Oh please," Jude murmured, pressing her lips to it. "Please come back, OK?"

When she looked up, weeping, thinking to find the hint of the answer in Gara's face, Jude saw the eyes were closed.

"Don't die, Gara. Don't die!"

But as she watched, everything changed. The glimmer went out. The suspended figure stayed as it was but it had stopped being a person, or anything that had ever been a person. Instead it was opaque, as though some inner light had been switched off.

Jude was sobbing with grief and doubt, when she became aware that something worse was happening.

Approaching footsteps sounded in one of the caverns.

Twenty-seven

In the gracious room far, far above the grotto where Jude stood, paralyzed, Ava's cold supper was being served to the few Benedicts present.

Moving around the dining table, Esther passed the platters of smoked turkey and asparagus vinaigrette to the few people actually sitting there and then put servings on the plates of the others, in the expectation that sooner or later they would arrive. Rigid with resentment, she fixed plates for her baby Edgar and the girl Jude Atkins, even though she had no idea where they were or whether they were expected, any more than she knew where Peter was. She was afraid for him, but she was afraid to ask.

In the kitchen before dinner, giving orders in that grand manner she loved to use with Esther, Ava had told her to put on extra place settings for Miss Benta and her model Wataru, who were overdue from Hokkaido, but not to set a place for Mr. Peter because he had been unavoidably detained.

Esther had said uneasily, "Detained because..."

Ava was too brusque. "Never mind."

Then hadn't Esther given the woman a thoughtful look, and hadn't she asked carefully, "And what about the other two guests?" She had even added, "Ma'am."

"There are no other guests," Ava said. She did not explain what had happened to Atawan and the black woman who was perhaps more to Bernard than a model; she just went on laying out the evening's orders as though they didn't exist.

"Mr. Bernard's Keesha," Esther said. She liked the Jamaican, and she hadn't seen her since she arrived, two of the students had just vanished her. "That Indian woman, Atawan."

Ava corrected her with a sharp look. "Native American. Parsley on the platter, I think, and you will do the serving. I need my students in the dining room, but naturally you will not set places for them."

Esther's tone would have leveled a weaker woman. "Yes Ma'am."

"I want everything to be perfect. This is a big night for us." Ava had chilled Esther to the core with: "The biggest."

She tried to buy time. "But Edgar's birthday isn't till tomorrow."

Ava corrected in that snide, superior way of hers. "*Mr.* Edgar. Now, are you going to serve dinner or do I call Thorne?"

"Whatever you say..." Esther's tone was neutral but she glowered: *You don't threaten me.* In the end she would rip this handsome, monstrous woman apart, bone from bone, nail from fingertip, classic face from that chiseled skull, but too many things were uncertain now, too many people she cared about were abroad in places she could not necessarily locate. Anger had to wait, so, smile. "...Ma'am."

"Good," Ava said. "Thorne has a lot to do right now."

Thorne. Big, sad man, didn't eat in the house with the rest of them, slept curled up like a dog on a mat in the foundry, but Esther saw how the big outsider with the great bull neck and broad shoulders followed Ava with his eyes. Esther didn't know whether Ava meant she would get Thorne to serve the table in her stead or summon him to punish her for causing trouble, but she did know that whatever Ava proposed, Thorne did. Right or wrong he would do it to the death, and he did everything she wanted.

They were at a point of convergence here.

Something big was going on out there in the dining room, and something even bigger was scheduled to unfold tonight—not yet, but in the deep, shadowy reaches, when the world wonders if the sun will ever come up again. Esther wasn't sure she could get out from under Ava's eye and elude Ava's watchful students long enough to get off the place, or if she could make it out and hitched a ride to town, whether she could put together enough of a story to bring help. At bottom, she had no idea what was about to happen here. All she knew was that for as long as dinner was actually going on, she and the people she cared about would be safe.

She took her sweet time arranging the platters.

Disturbed as she was by the missing pieces and all the people who had somehow drifted out of her ken and fearful for what might be coming, Esther stood tall. She had to be strong for Benton. Her Benton that she had loved since childhood was in trouble and so were his get and progeny. Her baby Edgar was in danger and her favorite boy Peter was off God knows where; he was too much in love to go off of his own free will and leave his nice new girlfriend behind, not after whatever happened to Gara Sullivan—and what that was, Esther could not know for certain. Here one night, gone the next.

Esther should have fled this place, gone to Morehouse after all, started her life, but even before Ava, the Benedict family lived under a cloud and generations of Maniforts took care of them. Love and duty kept Esther Manifort here. Even after her dear Benton married that pale, appropriate girl Martha from Petersburg, Esther loved him too much to leave. Somebody had to stay back and take care. Esther has spent her life her taking care. Then Martha died and Ava devoured him and she stayed, even though she could hardly bear it. Somebody had to take care, because from the beginning, the Maniforts were as loyal as they were brave.

Something had been settled in the minutes she spent in the kitchen, rinsing the consomme cups and preparing the platters.

As she came into the dining room Ava was saying to the others, "Then we're agreed."

The grouping around the table told Esther everything: Ava sat like a queen in the grandfather chair at the head, with Dirk and Luke at her right hand and her left: a solid front. The four students clumped next to the sideboard, close enough to do her bidding but fixed at a deferential distance, to make clear that they were by no means part of the family.

Ashen, Benton stood behind the chair at the far end, still trembling from whatever encounter had just played out.

Ava was saying, "After all, it's not going to hurt the child."

Pain made Benton grin like a gargoyle.

She went on, "Not in the long run."

Now Benton clenched his jaw until Esther thought she could hear the hinges crack, but it was clear he'd said all he was going to say. Esther had loved this man for too many years to believe that he would agree to anything evil or destructive, and even though he had modeled her in wax and the bronze was cooling in its cast tonight, destined for *The Marriage of the Worlds,* he would never do anything to hurt her.

"After all," Ava said.

Trembling, he clutched the back of his chair for support. Clearly Ava had pushed him too far. Whatever had just passed between them threatened to undo him.

Ava finished, "It's only symbolic."

"Nothing is only symbolic. The blood runs through everything." Shaking with the effort, he shouted: "I will not have it!"

Ava did not blink. It was as if he hadn't spoken.

"If you have to do this," Benton said at last, "don't use Edgar. Use me."

Esther's head lifted. Do what? She did not know. *Oh, Benty!*

Coldly, Ava assessed her husband of many years. She could have been studying a block of plaster. "Sorry. You won't do."

Esther bit the inside of her mouth to keep from shouting. Ava, with her

God damned exigencies.

"You gave, Benton, you gave because you had to. And you." She spoke to Berton as he slouched in, late to the feast. "You gave when your time came." She turned to ruddy Bernard. "And you gave."

Benton turned to his brothers. "Help me reason with her."

But Ava prodded them. "Right?"

At a time when her Mr. Benedict—Benton!—most needed their support, neither brother spoke. They hung in space as if waiting. What were they doing here at Wayward after all this time, Esther wondered. What were they about?

"Berty?" Benton's voice broke. "Bernard!"

The surprise, then, was the brothers. The way they stood apart. Neutral, watching Benton and Ava in their odd, unspoken life-or-death struggle. Any fool could see that something bad was coming down and yet neither of them moved to stop it. Why didn't they *do* something? Interrupt, or change the subject? Stop her?

Finally, Berton spoke. "We're here to protect the family interests," he said quietly. That was all.

"But you promised. You said..." Benton choked on the rest. With his hands spread wide, he appealed to the brothers. "I hoped for better from you."

"Promised what?" Ava's eyes raked them. "You promised what?"

There was an intolerable pause. Neither answered.

Ava probed. "Berton?"

"Nothing," Berton said.

"You said what?" Ava asked Bernard, but Bernard wouldn't look at her.

Benton pleaded, "In the name of God, say something!"

Alert, attentive, Ava studied them. She was waiting too.

After a long silence in which Esther clashed silver on the platter, delivering slices of ham on Beauchamp Benedict's gold-rimmed Haviland with angry little slaps, tall, gaunt Berton Benedict, who had come all this distance to complete the family masterpiece, said to his brother, "We owe it to Ava to see this through."

"After all," Bernard added gravely, "look at everything she's done for the family."

Ava snorted, "You mean after everything I've done for the family finances."

Berton grimaced. "That too."

She was laughing. "Come on, Benty, this won't hurt Eds, it'll be the making of him. Would I hurt my own flesh and blood? It's such a little thing."

"Oh, God." Benton staggered and almost fell. "Oh, God."

Esther passed close behind him; he sensed her presence and righted himself before they touched. She stood silently, close enough for him to feel her warmth. "Excuse me, Mr. Benton," she said, pretending they had accidentally collided.

"Yes, Esther," he said in a tone nobody else could parse.

And this proud African American, who could have gone to Morehouse or Harvard if she'd wanted to, fell into the remembered cadence of the black matriarch who makes clear her place in the household even as she defends it with the ritual pretense at service. "Now Mr. Benton, it's time to sit down. You all had better sit down and eat your food before it dries up on the plate."

All right, all right, let the truth free me; I'm so tired, it's been so long. I should have told them, it takes a listener to make the confession complete, you see, I am old and guilt makes you weak and that walking obelisk is stronger than I ever was. It is his job to keep me here, sometimes I think he was sent not by Ava but by the work, our beautiful, greedy sculpture bent on keeping the life within it so it can proliferate, a legion of Benedict masterpieces marching into infinity, while generations of tortured, gifted Benedicts take it on and on, into the future.

I told you that Galena and I were in love.

I did not tell you what happened to her after she stole into the studio and surprised me at my work. "I love you," she whispered, "but this has got to stop," all that and she didn't even know. She begged me to come away but the work was crying out to me, Not now, when we are so close. *I was young, I thought I could have it all, I said, "Oh my darling, let me model you." And all the time I was working I felt the forces within me stirring in my veins and in my loins, goading:* faster *and my hands were on my wife but my soul was in the work; then for the first time since I put my own flesh and blood into my Aphrodite, I heard the force that drove me saying:* Yes.

I wanted it not to happen, could hardly wait for it to happen, feared it, would have died to prevent it, no, I needed it no matter what. I held Galena in my arms and they grew strong as silver wire, binding her, and as she twisted within the framework my body made it came to me. The rest.

I saw the rest of it. I saw it whole, and it was tremendous.

I cried out. "No!"

You see, I thought I could save her from the work. Or for it.

Then I staggered out into the night and I made my prayer, if that's what it was: God forgive me for the answer, it smoked *me.*

But I still believed I could do this and still keep Galena safe.

Enter poor Theron Poulnot, who became the first figure I modeled in the new mode. You will see him holding the Tables of the Law, marching in the vanguard of the massed figures in my brilliant God and His Creation.

And Galena?

I have told you. No, I have warned you: The work takes what it wants. And what it whispered to me, while I was completing it? It stands for the fact that you love her the most. Do not even try to understand. I hope you never have to understand.

Oh my children, she is in the work.

She is the work.

And that bitch Ava got the secret out of me.

God, forgive me and help me end this, so I can die. If you can't forgive me, God, help me destroy the bitch.

"Your son," Benton said to Ava, weeping. They were alone in the pantry and in the stunned rapture of discovery that everyone had turned against him, Benton imagined that he could reason with this woman. "Your very own son. You won't do this to him, will you? Your flesh and blood..."

"Stop that. Let go. I do what I have to."

"Ours. He's only a little boy!"

"Exactly," she said. "And it's his birthday. Just let's do what it wants and then we can celebrate."

"Our son." He was at the end of his strength, too distressed to read the implications: *what it wants.* "Please don't hurt him."

"After that, I have a surprise. A wonderful surprise."

"How can you even think of hurting him?"

"Shut up, will you? It's just a little blood."

"Oh my God."

"It's only a little thing, Benty," Ava said in the seductive tones that so warmed him in the year Martha got sick and died. It disgusted him to think he'd been led all this great distance by his prick.

"It isn't the blood, it's what it stands for," he said, not certain exactly what this meant.

Now Ava turned a basilisk face to him. The eyes were yellow slits. Although he did not recognize the text, she could have been reciting. "It stands for the fact that we love him the most."

"I won't have him hurt."

"Don't worry, he'll be fine. He'll be one of us," she said.

Groaning, Benton seized his wife by the shoulders, both startled and repelled by the sensuous mouth she raised to his. Aflame with rage and shame, he shook her. "I—won't—have —it," he said grimly, baring his teeth and rattling Ava so her neck snapped at every word. "I—will—not—have—it."

She went limp with a luxurious grin and when he finished, vibrating with fury, Ava threw back her head so her thick, bright hair flew in a way he could not help remembering with a surge of lust, and laughed. "What makes you think you have any choice?"

"I'll kill you first."

"Do that," Ava said, smiling. "And they'll kill him. Count on it."

"I'll kill you now, Ava."

"Not if you want Edgar safe."

"I'll take him to Charleston." A sob rose up. "Baltimore."

"Too late for that," she said. "Thorne has him. If Thorne so much as *thinks* I'm in *any danger...*"

Tears slid over Benton's eyes like a scrim, obscuring vision. "You wouldn't."

"Only if I have to," she said.

"Oh, dear God."

"Stop that, Benty."

"God!"

"God can't help you. It's too late. This has gone too far." With practiced familiarity, she reached forward and with the tip of her little finger flicked the moisture from the corner of his eye. "There are too many of us." She took his hands. "I know you love Edgar, we all do. But we need him, too. Come. We are approaching the moment."

"He's only a child!"

The next thing his wife said rocked Benton Benedict backward in a series of freeze-frames that flattened him. She said in cold tones that there was no mistaking, "Exactly. It fits the pattern."

Staggered, he took this in gradually, in measurable stages. One. Two. Three. His voice dropped to a harsh whisper. "You really do know something I don't."

"Exactly. I know what to do." Thus Ava confirmed what Benton only now understood. "Did it. Because you were too weak."

"What have you done?"

"What I had to, Bent," she said so smoothly that he understood, and wished to God that death would take him. "Exactly what I had to."

"But my grandfather. His generation put it behind us!"

"And look what happened to the Benedicts then," Ava said. "How do you think I brought this family up from rags? How do you think I got you back on your feet?"

Anger shook him. "I wish to God you hadn't."

The snide, superior grin she turned on him then made him want to smack her. “You’d be in the poorhouse and you know it.”

“We had our lives.”

Her eyes flashed. “Now you have me.”

This broke him in two. “I know.”

“And if you do as I say you will continue to have Edgar.”

With firm hands, Ava turned Benton around and marched him back to join the others. “Come along, dearest. We are almost at the moment.”

Twenty-eight

Aching, struggling to his feet in darkness, Jerome thinks he knows where he is—in one of the cellars under Wayward. He should know. Ava kicked him off the place for trying to get in here when he was a kid.

The Benedicts ran a link in the underground railroad back in the day. They smuggled slaves out through the undercroft at Wayward, which is why the Maniforts are beholden. His great-greats told their descendants, and Mama told him.

"The Maniforts have a duty, as a result. The first Benedicts led slaves to freedom through that basement." Then she said, "Now it's up to us to free them," and could not tell him what it meant. "There's evil down there, honey. Some day they'll need you. When it's time, you'll know."

He tried to tell Peter. Something down there. Something they had to do. They were in fourth grade. Ava caught them poking at the locked door with a chisel. Oh, she was mad.

She called me a nasty little nigger boy, but I don't think that's what she was mad about.

That was the day she exiled him. Her handsome face clotted with rage. The things she said, and he was only ten! He is still a little afraid of her. That day he was surprised, humiliated, guilty, and all the time Mrs. Benedict was hammering on him, shouting, Jerome sobbed in despair, wailing, "I'm only trying to help!"

And what have I done for them, really? He thinks now: *All I do is hear her husband's confessions.* And wonders what he will be called upon to do today.

Is it still today? He doesn't know. Someone ambushed him outside the chapel, dragged him here. They hauled him into the bowels of the house through a hole in the ground, opening rusty doors that had been long buried and silted over by floods. It was like entering limbo. He heard air rushing out as the doors fell open, voices twining in a mad lalation, the cries of people with no tongues, without knowledge or memory of any language spoken.

Reflexively, he raised his hand to bless the suffering.

And, terrified, heard the susserus of a great *Amen*. Jerome was almost grateful for the next thing that happened: a wet crunch as somebody tired of his wild struggles and brought hammy fists down on the back of his head, bludgeoning him to oblivion.

He does not know whether he heard or only imagined a deep, low voice saying in flawless diction, "Sorry, Father. I'm only being cruel to be kind."

Time escaped him. Hours later, unseen persons raised him. He remembers stirring in the darkness, a wet cloth on his face. New hands dragged him out of the depths and dropped him here. He has no idea where he is under the house.

Groping along walls, the priest navigates in darkness, slouching from chamber to chamber. At last he sees light glowing on the cavern walls ahead. He thinks it's a mirage. "What? What!"

A woman warns, "Stop! Don't come any closer."

But the light draws him; it is like finding an oasis. "Please," he says softly, "who are you?"

"No further." Someone turns the light directly on him. "I have a knife."

Jerome has been in darkness for so long that his eyes dazzle. He could no more turn away from the light than stop breathing. "Don't be frightened. I'm a priest."

"Here?"

He doesn't answer right away. If his abductors didn't strip it off him in their struggles, she will see the Roman collar.

"Oh," the girl says, relieved. "You really are a priest."

"Jerome Manifort," he says, and as his eyes acclimate he fixes on a figure behind the girl. White and beautiful, it hangs in air, as though from a rack. What? He can't make it out. He keeps talking to reassure her. "How did you get down here?"

"Edgar brought me. How did you..."

"Peter's kid brother?" Jerome baptized the boy—tremulous dad, absent mother, proxy godparents—and hasn't seen him since.

"Oh." Her voice melted. "You know Peter."

"From the sandbox," he says distractedly. He is fixed on the object at her back. Bound in silver, it looks like the Virgin in some garish European roadside shrine. "What's that?"

"I think." Her voice breaks. Oh, God. It's." She chokes. "Somebody who used to know Peter."

The effigy slumps in its framework, beautiful, emaciated, dead. It is a woman.

He says softly, "How did she get here?"

"I don't know. I don't know anything. I was trying to ask her, and..." The girl's light jiggles; she is sobbing. "I was about to ask her, and then..."

"Shh," he says. "Be cool."

"She was OK just a minute ago."

Jerome looks at the beautiful thing that is no longer a person. "She was never OK."

"OK," the girl says shakily. "But she was breathing."

"She couldn't be."

"She asked me to pull out the tubes," she sobbed. "At least I think she did."

"This is..."

"I thought it would help her get down." Her voice broke. "But it didn't!"

There are no words for what this is. "Monstrous."

"First she was... Whatever. Then she wasn't."

"Let me see."

Trembling, she steps aside.

"Who did this to you?" he asks the dead woman softly.

"Do you, ah, know what to say for people like this?"

"We have a prayer," he says, touching the wires. "Can we get her down?"

"I don't think so. I tried."

"All right." Gently, Jerome sets the girl aside, and unselfconsciously puts together as many parts of the prayers for the dead as he can under the circumstances. With his thumb he will make the sign of the cross on the lips of the dead woman, and he will make the cross on her eyes and ears and, separating the wires with deep sadness, over her heart. Then he falls to his knees and continues. When he makes the final blessing there is a stir that makes him think that there are other spirits here, that they have heard and are responding. He finishes to a hush so profound that he wonders who or what exactly has been put to rest here. Only when he rises does the room seem to breathe again.

Then he turns to the girl, who sits with her back against the archway and her knees drawn up. "Do you know where we are?"

"More or less." She gulps. "What are you *doing* down here?"

Sadly, he says, "I was supposed to help Peter."

"Is he OK?"

"I don't know. Big help I was. He sent me for the police," he says and is surprised to hear her make a little grunt that falls somewhere between surprise and gratification. "Now look. Somebody clubbed me. I don't even know what time it is."

"Late."

"Or what day."

"What happened to Peter?"

"He was counting on me." Jerome means: *I was counting on me.*

"What did they do to him?"

"I don't know."

The girl says, "Oh, God." It isn't a prayer.

"This isn't about God. It's something different." The implications are dreadful. Grieving, Jerome shakes his head. "I should have been here to stop it."

"There's something terribly the matter here."

The burden of heritage descends on him. *All these years, when I stayed away. How much of this is my fault for leaving?* "I know."

"Father, we have to get away."

Thinking it through, Jerome approaches a conclusion that was ordained before he was old enough to know the mandate or what would be expected of him. "That's not all we have to do."

"Peter. We have to save Peter."

"And Edgar." Stormed by understanding, Jerome says, "We have to save them all."

Unexpectedly, the girl raises the lantern. "You look awful."

Jerome touches his face and for the first time is aware of blood drying and disfiguring bruises. "Outward and physical signs of..."

"What?"

"You don't want to know. *All those confessions,* he thinks, swallowing guilt. *Why didn't I act on what the old man told me? Poor bastard, he didn't ask for it, but he did. God forgive me for what I have left undone.* "Something I should have been doing."

"You didn't do this," she says. "I don't know what did."

Pull yourself together, Jerome. "Tell me how you got here."

"I came down with Edgar. He found the old man."

Jerome feels each hair on his head standing separate. He is very close to something he perceives but does not yet recognize. "The old man?"

"Really old."

"What old man?"

"Older than dirt. You're going to think I'm crazy, but..."

"No," he says. Jerome still does not know what's coming but the responsibility staggers him. *Kyrie eleison.* All those confessions, the family stories mesh all at once and he says without understanding, exactly, what he knows or how he knows it, "I already know."

She breaks off. "About the old man?

The old man. What Jerome had passed off as legend turns out to be another stepping stone toward destiny. "God help me, yes."

"What are we going to do?"

Christe eleison. Too moved to speak, he spreads his hands.

"Are you all right?'

"Not really. I don't know." Tries to pray: *Not my will but thine.* "I think so." Now it is Jerome leaning on the girl instead of the other way around. When he can, he asks, "What are we going to do?"

Now it is the girl—no, young woman—who is supporting Jerome. She is stronger than he thought. She rights him and lets go. She will have no way of knowing that he is trying to find the right prayer. "We could ask the old man."

Jerome tries his legs and finds out that he too, is stronger than he thought. His voice is soft; he could be talking to a lover but it is not necessarily the girl he is addressing. "Yes. I think we'd better."

They're coming. Electrified, Peter made a flat dive into the dirt and rolled. He went to ground under the railroad flatcar designed for Ava's prodigious sculpture.

The foundry was lighted only by the rosy glow of the cauldron, radiant with molten bronze. Then the doors fell wide. Fluorescent strip lights went on. From where he was hiding, Peter saw only the legs and feet of the people coming in. Oiled by wine, they chattered like actors in a crowd scene in a midsummer masque. The tone was almost festive, but Peter knew better. Ava could at any minute fly into one of her profound rages.

The day he left Wayward, she let fly with a bronze maquette that left a scar on his temple. "Go ahead," she screamed. "Leave!" Standing there with the blood running down, he heard her last blessing—or curse. The words rolled in one at a time, like stones sealing a crypt. "You will share in the sin and never see any of the glory."

He was too angry to ask what she meant. Ava, who wiped the bronze and folded his blood into her stained handkerchief.

It replayed in his head. *You will share in the sin.* Under cover of the shuffle and chatter of arrivals, Peter Benedict said grimly, "No. I'm here to end it."

What appalled him now was the number of people his mother had brought with her. He identified them by their shoes and by their voices: Ava and Thorne and Ava's students, he thought; the size fourteen motorcycle boots belonged to Grant, who never spoke; next came Jake and Nelly and Petra, shuffling in Birkenstocks and heavy coveralls. When Ava cried, "Are you with me?" he heard his uncles, Berton and Bernard muttering—assent, he supposed.

Where was Benton?

Father. Peter allowed himself to hope. *Maybe he's gone for the police.* Unless he is locked up somewhere, used and then burnt by Ava and rocking with shame. Poor bastard, he must have lived with this—*whatever it is*—this family curse, or dark secret, all his life.

If Benton knew, why in God's name didn't he make it stop? He must have known what Ava was doing. He saw her riding herd on Luke and Dirk, could he not stop her? Sure he grieved when she drove Peter away, but he didn't stop that, either. What else did he fail to stop? He must have seen his wife seducing students, seducing Thorne, seducing whoever she took her pleasure with. Did he know what vile pact Ava sealed to make the family prosper? He had to know, Peter thought. So did the uncles. They knew and they let her. Because they were afraid? Or because they were greedy?

All these years, he thought unhappily. *You knew and you let it happen.* Then shame rolled in. *And I ran away instead of fighting.*

His head came up so abruptly that it hit the axle. Blood sang in his ears and his face burned. *But I'm here now.*

So everybody was accounted for except for his brothers, Dirk and Luke. He couldn't guess where they were or know whether they'd help if he made a break for it, or lunge and grab him. There was no getting out now, no bringing help. There was only Ava.

"So you understand the dynamic," Ava told Benton's brothers. "Everything will be realized here. My students will help us, and I can already guarantee their silence. We need to get the piece ready for unveiling."

She went on, "The, ah—*other component*—is in the boathouse. I left Luke and Dirk in charge. When we open the doors here, they'll bring it out. The press preview is Thursday, and Friday our piece goes to the Metropolitan. The first Benedict sculptural grouping since *God and His Creation.*"

Berton said, "And you say it will be even better."

"Trust me. It will be magnificent. We can take what old Beauchamp did and stand it on its head. *Then* we'll see who is the genius here," she said in a voice so ugly that Peter's belly crawled. "You've seen the sketches. We'll pour these last two pieces and put them in place for the final phase and the unveiling. But there is one more thing we have to do. Together."

Bernard said, "The offering."

"Edgar's initiation."

Peter thought he heard a stifled cry.

"Yes, but that's not enough," Ava said. "Not this time. The Benedicts have done well, but to keep it going, we have to give something back." After a terrible pause, she continued. "Put more of ourselves into it."

Bernard rasped, "The blood."

Berton said grimly. "The blood."

"Yes," Ava said. "To create life."

And for the first time Benton Benedict spoke. He shouted, "No."

Peter's heart jumped. *Father.* He was here after all.

But Ava went on as if he didn't exist and if he did, he was nothing to her. "To seal it." Her voice was like molten bronze, pouring into the cast to displace the wax, congealing in all the crevices. In hiding, Peter shuddered. "Let's just say we're renewing the family's lease on life."

Bernard said, "Or the family's—pact?"

"Call it what you want."

Berton said, "Blood pact."

"This part of it," Ava said.

Lying in the sand under the flatcar, Peter bit his knuckles until blood came.

Ava went on, "Thorne will do the casting. He has been with me ever since I learned the real truth." After a significant pause she said, "Beauchamp's secret."

Berton growled, "That you won't tell us."

"Not yet," Ava said.

"You know, we *can* force you," he threatened.

"No you can't." Ava was pacing now; Peter watched her strong feet in the Grecian sandals going back and forth, back and forth, faster and faster. "And you can't bring this thing to fruition without me. Understood?"

"The secret."

"The secret. Every one of you knows some part of it, but you wouldn't be here if you knew it all."

Someone said in a low voice, "No, you wouldn't be here."

If Ava heard she made no sign. "Understood?"

There was a pause.

The brothers said, "Understood."

"Fine. Let's do this." She added, "With Thorne's help, of course."

Thorne's deep voice filled the space. "Of course."

There was a moment of silence. Peter heard ominous muttering. Then Berton said, "Benton is not pleased."

"What Benton thinks is not important. I only need his model."

"And you have her?"

Essie!

"I have her," Ava said. "And the wax Benton made..."

"That's mine!"

"Not any more, Benty. It belongs to the ages now." She went on smoothly, "We took it out of your studio last night. And the rest... The rest will be taken care of."

Bernard said briskly, "So all we have to do is finish assembling?"

Ava laughed. "After the offering. And then..."

"Then?"

What she said next was both terrifying and thrilling. "It will take life."

A low moan came from some unidentifiable source.

She said, "Understand, we are upon the anniversary. Naturally I'm extremely happy to have all the senior members of the family present."

Peter heard Father say, "Except Great Aunt Benta."

"The hell with Benta!"

He said, "Nobody acts without Benta."

"That's all you know," Ava snapped. "In the spirit of the pact, we have everything we need."

"You have no idea what we need," someone muttered, but again, Ava was too driven to hear anything that didn't please her.

"Tomorrow's the anniversary. And we are going to mark it with a piece greater than *God and His Creation*. It's almost complete," Ava said. "I've already cast Benta's Asian from the life mask she sent. There's only one loose end that I can see and I'll have Grant wrap that one up." Answering an unspoken question she said, "And the Indian figure and the other African figure are of course cast from your waxes. Thorne saw to it all this afternoon. So we are almost ready. Agreed?"

After a long silence in which, apparently, she counted to twenty, Ava said in measured tones, "And you assent to the method."

Peter's uncles chorused, "If you say so."

"And your models' places in it."

This came out in a long sigh. "If you say so."

"Then we are agreed to all of it."

"If you say so."

"And Edgar's place in it."

Benton groaned aloud.

"To guarantee the future," she said.

Like good students, they chorused, "To guarantee the future."

"And to bring our first major piece to the world, whatever the cost."

"Whatever the cost!" they cried.

"Thorne, the bronze?"

"Almost ready to pour."

"And Dirk and Luke are ready in the boathouse?"

Thorne said, "Everything's there except the prototype for the wax you made today. Athena, to crown the piece."

Someone said, "The girl."

Flattened in the dirt between the tracks, Peter bit his hand to keep from shouting. *God.*

"Grant," she said, "go find the girl. I think you know where to look," she said. "And we need Peter. Thorne, go untie Peter and bring him. It's time he saw what makes the Benedicts great."

God!

"Now," she said, "it is time to do it."

The stairs leading up were dark and treacherous. Below them, black vapor curled up from the subcellar, beckoning, alive with sound. When Jude reached the upper landing she was surprised. The old man's cell door lay open. The lights were on. The ancient Benedict was awake. As she crossed the landing, the huge, blanched head snapped up. The old man watched, avid and preternaturally alert. Somebody had replaced his rack of IV bottles with plastic packets hung from the back of the chair. It was as if he'd been retrofitted and made ready to roll. Words drifted out like bits of ash.

"Where've you been?"

Jude said to the priest, "This is what I wanted to tell you about, I don't know why I couldn't."

A long shudder shook Jerome and made him stagger. "I see."

"Are you all right, Father?"

He was rapt, listening for something she could not hear. "I knew."

Jude became aware that she was pressed to the bars of the old man's cell, not straining to get inside but, rather, straining to escape whatever stirred below. It took her a minute to understand that it was the lure of the cavernous darkness at the bottom of the stairs.

Ole Beauchamp broke the silence; extreme age and impatience made him querulous. "Are you going to come in here or not?"

Jerome hung back, asking, "What do you want, old man?"

"Hurry up!"

The priest said to no one, "What does he really want?"

"We have to get him up those stairs." Jude couldn't quite make herself go inside the cell. Wary, she asked, "Who got you ready?"

"Somebody, I don't know. Some Jap came out of nowhere and did all this. He left without explaining. Now come on in."

Jude started into the cell but Jerome raised a hand. *Wait.*

"I can't do this without you, Father."

"Father!" The old man's voice shattered into a thousand shards. He turned beady, bird eyes on her. "He's a priest?"

Jude nodded.

There was a disturbance in the blankets that swaddled the ruined body of the sculptor. After much too long a withered hand emerged. "Father?"

Jerome said, "Yes."

The hand twitched in a desperate attempt at the sign of the cross. "Bless me Father..."

With a nod, Jerome entered the cell.

"Hurry up, Father," the old man gasped. "It's time."

The priest raised his hand to make the sign of the cross.

Beauchamp shook his head violently. "No no, not that, not yet! Not until it's done!"

Advancing, Jude said, "Until what's done?"

He had to choke out the next words. "We have to end this."

Jerome spoke out of what might have been a trance. "End what?"

Beauchamp's laughter was as abrupt as it was alarming. "I think you already know," he said to the priest, and Jerome lurched as if he'd been shot. "Come here. Lean close. I have to tell you."

Carefully, they moved closer.

"You have to help me stop this," old Beauchamp wheezed.

In strange ways, looking into his face was a little like looking into Gara's before the light went out behind it. Both teetered on death's doorsill. Old and ugly as he was, with his face leached of flesh, devoid of color in some of the same ways as Gara's, Beauchamp Benedict was still clinging to his soul. Jude said, "What do you want us to do?"

"You alone can stop this, you two. The instrument of God and the instrument of love. Don't blush, girl, I know who you are. But children, be careful." His breath came and went in agonizing gasps.

Jude took hold of the chair. It was so loaded with equipment that it was hard to move. "First we have to get you out."

"No. You can't end this by breaking me out of here." The old man went on in a desperate whisper. "You can't end it by killing me."

Jude tugged and pushed but she couldn't budge the heavy thing. "Father, help me. We have to go!"

Jerome's voice cut through the dimness. "Wait!"

Now that he had them, the old man was fixed on finishing what he had to say. He beckoned them closer, whispering, "It will only end when you destroy it."

"Destroy what?"

Jude struggled with the wheelchair; it was an intransigent deadweight. "Please help me with this thing. Let's get him out and then we can go find Peter. Please!"

Jerome shook his head. "I have to let him finish."

"Thank you." The old man's words fell like leaves, one at a time. "Children. Father. I'm afraid you're going to have to do what you most fear."

"Oh, please, Father. I can't do this alone." Jude was crazy to get out of here, to get outside, to put this burden down and do whatever it took to find Peter and leave this terrible place. "If we don't get him out we'll never find Peter. Hurry!"

"Not until we know what we have to do."

The priest's sweet gravity was maddening. Couldn't he see that it was Peter who mattered here, and Peter was in terrible danger?

Jude said through clenched teeth, "And Edgar. We have to help them all!"

"Not yet," the old man cried. "Not until you understand!" When he spoke again it was after an unendurable pause. The effort left him breathless. He could have been wrestling bronzes out of a sand pit and setting them down in front of them. "Understand."

"What," Jude cried. "For God's sake, what?"

"I am part of what's going on here."

The priest's head went up. Mysteriously, his eyes glowed.

Old Beauchamp nodded and went on. "But I am something more. I am part of the process."

"Yes." Jerome was in the grip of something Jude could not see.

"It must be disassembled as elegantly as it was put together. It must be done."

"Yes," Jerome said, mesmerized.

"But not yet." To Jude's horror, Beauchamp Benedict the first hooked fingers like talons around her wrist and pulled her close so she would hear it too. His jaws yawned like the subcellar. "And not here."

"Don't, please! Let go!"

"What," Jerome asked. "Where?"

The old man's breath came out in such a long, slow hiss that for a second, Jude thought it was his last. It was a long time before the words came. "Down there."

Twenty-nine

In the end it was the priest who got the old man down the flight of stairs into the subcellar, laying him on the pallet in his cell with his IV pouches on his belly so Jerome could take the chair down first. He worked with such gravity that it was clear to Jude that he had more on his mind than logistics.

He turned to Jude. "You stay here with him."

"I will."

She had no idea they would be waiting for so long.

On the bed old Beauchamp wheezed, "What's keeping him?"

The possibilities were too many and too dreadful to talk about. Jude gulped. "I don't know."

There was an intense silence as seconds extended into minutes. Jude was afraid to look over the rail to see if Jerome was still visible or whether something in the darkness had swallowed him. Even though the priest was better than six feet tall, and she'd armed him with a knife and a lantern, she was afraid for him. She waited with the old man, who was exhausted by the move from chair to bed. She thought she ought to be praying, but nobody had ever taught her how, and even if she knew the right forms, she wasn't certain of the mailing address. *Oh please,* she thought. *Oh, please.*

Finally she heard his footsteps on the stairs. At least she hoped it was him.

After too long Jerome surfaced again, rubbing cobwebs out of his hair.

"What!" she cried. "What's down there?"

He didn't exactly answer. "It's very black."

"Like, too dark to go? We could always just..." *Not have to do this,* she thought. "Take him outside."

"No!" The old man was quick. "To do what's needed, we have to go down. Let's go. We need to do this so I can die and have it over with."

Jerome faltered. "Is that all you want from me?"

"To finish it."

"I can't kill you. I'm a priest."

The old man said craftily, "But you can say last rites."

"Over you?"

"Over whoever needs it," Beauchamp said and wouldn't look at him. "Now pick me up."

Shaken, Jerome said, "If you know what's expected of me, just tell me."

"You spend your life working for a God you can't even see and you question me?"

"I can't help you if I don't know."

"You'll know when we get there." Beauchamp was staring at the priest with an intent, bright look, like a bird waiting to be fed. "Don't be afraid, Father. It's all right."

"Mr. Benedict, I don't even know where we're going."

"You don't have to. I know. Now, move!"

"Yes, Mr. Benedict." Carefully, Jerome put the fragile body of the once-great sculptor over his shoulder and started for the stairs, carrying him so carefully that he glided along almost without moving, afraid the ancient bones would shatter on contact, like porcelain.

It took everything Jude had—all those formless prayers, or were they incantations, to get moving. Putting off the moment, she scoured the cell and came up with another flashlight and a battery-powered high-intensity light, which she put in the pockets of the canvas smock.

Jerome called from below. "Are you coming?"

"Yes." She headed for the stairs while the little prayer, or mantra, formed itself inside her, playing on a loop; she murmured nonstop, not even aware that she had found a designation for the force she was begging to help her: *Oh please. Oh God. Oh, please.*

Don't look. Ignore the dank smell coming up from a deep, fathomless crypt that had never known daylight.

She hoped.

Ignore things that moved or didn't move or pretended not to move and keep going. Just keep going, Jude.

It helped to understand that for the moment, at least, the things that breathed or moved or somehow made their presence felt below—whatever lived in the chasm underneath the house was completely still. Her feet echoed on the wooden steps: *clop clop clop.* A thousand fears ran ahead of her.

Jude didn't know what she expected to find at the bottom of the stairs—zombies waiting or mutant insects or animals bleached white by aeons of darkness or simply a hundred dead souls massed to receive her, crying, *Sister.*

Then her feet hit the dry bottom. She hadn't died. She'd made it down. She'd made it and everything was OK. So far, and if indeed there was something else down here, keeping its distance, she was too giddy with relief to know.

Jerome had the old man back in his chair. He was untangling the snarl of IV leads, hooking the bags to the rack.

Jude said into the hush, "Where is this?"

The old man answered, "At the beginning."

They stood at the beginning of a long passageway shored up by brick, with the ceiling supported by square brick pillars.

Jerome touched the brick. "This is where the slaves came to hide?"

"This is where my father hid them until the boats came," Beauchamp said. "They helped him build this place because they knew he loved them, and I think they loved him. When it was safe he led them down to the water by the back way."

The priest nodded. "Right. The back way."

Jude's voice lifted. "Then there's a back way." It was dark down here in the belly of Wayward, it was cold and the cellar was deep; all her life she'd been claustrophobic. Now she could feel the whole great weight of Wayward pressing down on her.

"Did you think I was leading you into a trap?"

Instead of answering, Jude pressed him. "So there's another way out."

"In the end, yes."

"And you'll show us?"

"When it's time." Beauchamp turned to Jerome. "The slaves couldn't leave right away, it was never safe. So while they waited here, they helped with the work. Making this place."

"Paying their debt."

"If you want to call it that."

The priest said heavily, "You'd think all that would be done with by now."

"The war?"

"Indebtedness."

The old man made a noise that could have been a laugh. "I'm here to tell you, no debt ever stays paid."

Jerome sighed. "I know."

"None of the slaves knew why Father wanted to go so deep into the undercroft, but I suppose whatever prompts the greatest acts compelled him." The next sound that came out of the old man could have been a sigh. "He thought he was doing one thing when he was actually doing another."

"What was he doing?"

"Preparing this," Beauchamp said. "For me."

Jude whispered, "Where are we?"

"Close to the heart of the work." Old Benedict paused to make clear the significance.

"The work..."

When she thought he would never speak again, he finished, "That we are going to disassemble now."

"Just the three of us?"

He said brightly, "It only takes one." *Surprise.*

"One!"

Jerome seemed to relax slightly, as if the cable stretching him taut had been cut. "Then all we have to do is help. And you're going to tell us what to do."

Jude said at the same time, "And you're going to help us get out?"

"One way or another, yes." Now that they were in the subcellar, old Beauchamp's voice was stronger. He directed them with confidence. "Up ahead, there's a turning. Go right and then go left. Child," he said with sudden solicitude, "are you a strong child?"

Jerome said, "I think so."

"Not you, son," he said. "I mean Father. I know you will be as strong as you have to be. After all, you're a Manifort."

Jerome seemed taller. "Yes."

"I mean the girl. Miss, are you strong enough to do this?"

Oh please, oh God, oh please.

"If you aren't strong enough, you'd better turn back now." The chair creaked as the old man leaned forward, waiting.

Was he holding out both hands in entreaty? Threatening with raised fists? Jude didn't know. At the moment she didn't see him. She had her eyes screwed shut. She was turned in on herself in a silent moment of what she later decided must have been prayer. Bright spots and shooting stars and flecks like newborn fireworks raced across the backs of her closed lids and were displaced suddenly by a fugitive vision: her wonderful Peter whipping his head around so fast that she couldn't even make out his expression. *Peter.* Rocked by love, she understood. *I'd do anything for him.*

Now it was Jerome's turn to ask Jude, "Are you all right?"

Her voice fluttered with uncertainty. "Of course I am."

Beauchamp asked, "Are you strong enough to come with us?"

When Jude spoke again it was with such force that it startled them. "Yes! It's OK." She was surprised by a laugh. "I'm fine."

Too hearty. Excited. Unaware that this was by no means all she would have to do. Or that they were not alone down here.

The old man said, "Very well."

He tapped Jerome's arm and the priest hooked the lantern on the arm of the wheelchair and pushed on into the dark.

Jude followed.

Now that they had begun, she found that she was all right going along in the dark behind Jerome and their ancient guide, even though the way was long and their destination unspecified.

In spite of the fact that Wayward was almost surrounded by water, the subcellar was dry as old velvet. Jude thought she felt a current of cold air brush her face; she had the idea that they had passed from manmade spaces into some kind of natural cave, that they were entering vaults and caverns extending under the house—who knew how far?

She thought she heard a new sound: remote, furtive. Footsteps? Then she saw the chair bumping over rocks, and put it to that.

Guided by Beauchamp, Jerome rolled the wheelchair into a new corridor. At the far end, they made a sharp turn. The next corridor was lined with enclosed spaces at regular intervals, niches set in the walls like so many box stalls. Beauchamp said, "This is where the slaves slept while they were waiting for the boat. It's a good idea to keep your lights trained on the floor here, so we don't lose our way." With sudden urgency, the old man added, "I don't want you getting distracted."

He reckoned without the generations of women born long after he should have died, women brought up to question instructions instead of following blindly.

Jude flicked her light from side to side in the vaulted corridor, thinking, *Pandora and Lot's wife, right*?

She was both prepared and not prepared for what she saw. In a way, she was not surprised because she had, after all, seen Gara Sullivan in her niche, still living and carefully arranged by artful hands, set on a base and connected to life support and then forgotten. Jude Atkins came back down here and went deeper knowing they would find much, much worse, and what disturbed her now were the differences between Gara and what she saw here. Unlike Gara, these figures had been moved into the grotto and arranged in their niches before the IV was invented and the blood transfusion even imagined. Something else kept them preserved in moments of beauty and passion, and whether it was the spirit of the work or the will of this fragile, passionate old man who wanted so much to die, she could not have said. What she did know was that the secret to the Benedict success stood here, figure upon figure both alive and not alive, once-human forms forever fixed between life and death in this corridor far, far beneath the great house at Wayward.

"So this is it," she murmured.

And without turning as Jerome sped him along, the old man said, "No. This is only partly it."

Arrested by what she saw, Jude lingered, and if there was indeed something moving in the shadows behind or beyond her, or something or someone lurking at the periphery, she was too caught up in the horror to know.

These things were not living. Unless they were. Not knowing would haunt her long after this was finished.

Each figure stood in a glistening metal frame that was also a structural element, silver wires adjusting the body in an attitude she recognized from photos of famous Benedict sculpture. Each was sealed in a glass case that spared Jude from knowing whether they had begun to decay—whether the remains of the sculptor's dream were putrefying, and had begun to smell. From here, they looked perfect. This poor girl behind glass could have been Beauchamp Benedict's famous *Aphrodite,* forever fixed in supplication, but this was no bronze figure. The Aphrodite in the glass case was instead the real body of a real woman about Jude's age. "Oh," she murmured, raising her hand to touch the brittle surface. "Oh!"

Here was his famous *The Runner,* and in the next cubicle like a saint in a grotto stood Beauchamp's most famous figure of all, *Mary Magdalene.* These were not the bronzes but, rather, the prototypes that had sat for the waxes, and even now, a hundred years later, they looked the same. The figures were not dead, exactly, but they weren't alive, either. Shuddering, Jude stopped in front of each and turned the beam of her light up, to catch the face. In each case the eyes were open, with huge pupils set in irises clear as glass, but if the soul was still present, it did not show itself.

Dear God.

Transfixed, she didn't hear herself say, "Dear God."

She thought she heard a sigh.

While behind her the shadows coalesced and seemed to get denser. Something moving. Something was moving. Something was moving back there. A stone chinked on glass and she whirled.

Turning, Jude was distracted by an object too ghastly to look on: half body, half skeleton, with its base obscured by a puddle of decomposing flesh at the bottom of its glass case, still carefully sealed against time and damage from the atmosphere.

If the old man knew she had seen, he gave no sign. He said, to the priest, "There were a few mistakes."

Then they turned another corner and he snorted.

Beauchamp Benedict's reproach rattled the air. "So this is what Ava's been up to. Pathetic," he said. "Clumsy."

Hung on their racks, limed and varnished and shot full of preservatives, were the figures in Ava's abortive attempt at a monumental sculptural grouping. The clustered corpses Jude saw fixed in position on a flatcar—a discus thrower here, there a naked nymph—were only corpses.

Beauchamp snorted. "Failures."

Looking into one face, Jerome said in a low voice, "My God."

"Bloody failures."

Gravely, the priest made the sign of the cross over the fresh corpses in the grim arrangment. Then he dropped to his knees in grief and made as if to begin the last rites.

"Not yet!" The old man's harsh voice halted him. "Bless me Father," Beauchamp said. "Now you know why I have to end this. Stop that. Get up and get moving, we're almost there."

"But this is so awful."

"Get up, Father. Promise me."

Still on one knee, Jerome lifted his head. "Sir?"

"When it's over?" Puzzled, Jude thought, or thought she heard or felt rising from somewhere deep the words: *Then it will be over.* And could not be sure.

Old Beauchamp's voice shook with grief. "When it's done, then you must come back and do the others."

Still half kneeling, troubled and deeply reflective, Jerome said gravely, "If that's what's wanted."

"That's only part of what's wanted." With surprising energy, the old man slapped the side of his chair the way he used to speed his horse. "Now come on. Hurry. We're almost there."

The two could have been acting parts in some arcane drama that Jude didn't know and couldn't imagine; they proceeded as if beginning an old, old ritual. Crossing himself, the priest stood. "Yes, Mr. Benedict."

And they approached the last chamber.

Hurrying to catch up, Jude would not see the drama unfolding in silence in the corridor behind her. Remarkably silent in spite of his size, Ava's swift, heavily muscled student Grant surged around the last corner on cat feet, advancing with his nylon net raised, swinging in an arc intended to snare Jude and pull her out of the configuration before Jerome or the old man guessed that she was missing.

Thirty

The massive bronze grouping on the platform above Peter's head creaked and shuddered as Ava's students added new pieces, slipping the fresh bronzes into place so neatly that the base must have been slotted to accept them.

Jude, Ava was going after Jude. Or Grant was, on Ava's orders. Stony, musclebound Grant grunted and went out to get his Judith, who happened in accidentally because they were falling in love. Ava had earmarked *his girl* for some part in this anniversary piece she was planning. *Marriage of the Worlds.* There would be a ceremony before the unveiling. Shit, he didn't even know what it would be, except that as she had done when Peter was twelve, Ava would lop some small piece off of Edgar or take some blood from him, all to serve the family legend. She entrapped, she snared, she hurt people Peter cared about and all the time he was stuck here in the dirt under the flatcar, trying to figure out how to get out past the grim, massed Benedicts—past Thorne!—and how in God's name he could stop this even if he did.

At Ava's command, Grant left to fetch Jude. Peter heard him lurching along in those size fourteens like the Iron Giant with a hardon while he lay face down in the dirt floor of the foundry—not trapped exactly, but immobilized, clinging to one of the rails on which the great flatcar rested.

When all the time Jude... He didn't know where Jude was, or what was happening to her. He couldn't blow his cover here and there was no way he could send help because in this hellish place where his mother was in charge, he had no allies—not his father and certainly not his uncles. Jude! He couldn't even warn her.

Another heavy thump. The flatcar rocked with the added weight.

"There," Ava said.

There was a whoosh as the heavy canvas tarp slipped back into place, settling around her monumental bronze like a giant skirt. Trapped as he was, Peter waited, safe enough for the time being. Under the pressure of Ava's orders to do this, move that, they'd gotten too busy to send anybody to Thorne's quarters to fetch him. As far as Ava knew, he was still out cold on Thorne's smelly bed. As far as Peter knew, they had no idea he'd escaped.

He could hear her out there, haranguing. He thought he heard his father, begging her to stop and listen to reason.

Peter already knew nothing would budge her.

What he could not know was that as preparations continued, Ava did in fact go looking for him. He couldn't know that she'd come back empty, her face turned to onyx. Without saying a word, with only an imperious sweep of the arm, she ordered the others to search. He had no way of knowing that while the Benedict brothers worked on the big piece, the search went on. Then a big hand closed on his ankle and the force of the jerk broke his hold on the rail. Before he could think of a next step he was dragged out into the sand. Ava's student Jake bent over him, so flushed with anger that Peter rolled over and snapped into a knot to protect himself because he knew before Jake did that he was going to kick him.

Jake only kicked once.

Peter waited, but nothing happened.

"Get up," Jake said.

A lot had changed since Peter first rolled into the sand under the flatcar. The Benedict uncles, Berton and Bernard, were massed with his father at the base of the stone furnace that supported the giant cauldron on its swivel. The vessel was operated by levers that moved easily; even a kid Edgar's age could control it. Once molten bronze had been poured into the first plaster mold in the sand pit below, they swiveled it so a stream of liquefied bronze cascaded into the next. Ava stood near the base, looking into sand pit below, where the molds of her last two figures waited, ready for the pouring. When they cooled she would complete the assembly on the flatcar.

Oh, stop! Peter thought as Jake forced him along, *Whatever you're doing.* Trapped, he knew he had to forestall the last movement in this weird and dangerous progress. Kicking, biting, he struggled to free himself. He wanted to barrel into Ava and knock her off her feet. He wanted to hit her, hurt her, reason with her, do anything to stop this, but the more he struggled, the tighter Jake held him. Ava's apprentice wrenched him off his feet and tightened one steely arm around his neck.In the second before Jake closed his forearm on Peter's windpipe he shouted, "*Mother.*"

She did not turn.

"Mother, look at me!"

He might as well have been shouting at one of old Beauchamp's statues. She saw him, but she didn't. Or she saw him and she didn't care.

"Think what you're *doing*!"

Her indifference was devastating.

There would be no reproaches and no entreaties here; Ava would not demand an explanation. She would not have him killed, at least not now. She didn't give a shit. Peter was nothing to her now. After all, he had rejected her master plan. As far as Ava was concerned, Peter was over. To her, he was less than an object, dumb as a discarded plaster negative waiting to be disposed of.

The rock floor they had been walking on had been rising gradually ever since they left the hall of abandoned models. It was as though they were coming out of the belly of the house. In the corridor ahead, Father Jerome had parked the wheelchair. He was hurling himself at the great wooden door to the last chamber, the one Beauchamp had been guiding them to all this time. It sagged with age, digging into the floor as he pushed. Heavy, inert, the door didn't yield.

"Jude, come help."

From a distance—how had she gotten so far behind?—Jude called out but the sound was cut off before it reached Jerome. "Coming!"

As the priest squinted into the corridor he had just escaped—*did I hear something?*—Ava's apprentice closed on Jude Atkins from behind with one arm raised, twirling the net Ava had given him, along with instructions he had taken hours ago but kept to his heart until he was needed. Ava's huge, earnest, unstoppable student Grant came here with instructions: how to enter the underground labyrinth and how to immobilize the girl without doing any visible damage, because the girl's place in this—the piece itself—depended on her presence: Ava needed her alert and aware, untouched, because the capstone of *The Marriage of the Worlds* must be perfect. Unblemished.

Now, he thought as his arm went up, swinging the net. Then he gasped as iron hands seized the arm and wrenched with such force that it parted from its socket; Grant would have shrieked but by that time a wire tightened around his throat, severing the larynx and the neck, the spinal cord, cutting between body and soul before the sound could leave his body. All this happened in a silence so profound that Jude, who had joined the assault on the doors to the last chamber would not be aware of the action or what came after.

"Done, my dear."

In the shadows, Benta Benedict murmured, "Yes, Wataru. Thank you."

Ahead, old Beauchamp's head lifted. What had he heard? What did he think he heard? "What," he cried as the door yielded and Father Jerome pushed him through. "Who's there?"

And behind him the lean and graceful, powerful Benta said—to her grandfather? To Wataru? "Our part is done. You can go now."

Even before they wrenched the door open, Jude heard the rustle inside, as if of many waking souls, and when Jerome gave it a final shove and it did swing wide she was less surprised and frightened than reduced to speechless admiration.

This last vision stood on its own with no glass protecting it from time and decay because miraculously, none was needed. Beauchamp Benedict's masterpiece lay open to the air.

The massive grouping stood in the middle of the room on a rolling platform that could have been an antiquated flatcar; rusty track stretched into the dimness beyond it and if she'd been in control of her body, Jude might have thought to run away and follow the tracks outside to safety, but she found she could not move. Instead, like Jerome, she was ensnared. She stood, enthralled by the simple presence of the huge object in front of her.

Riveted, she stared.

It should have been ghastly. Instead, it was familiar.

"Oh," she murmured. "Oh!" *God and His Creation.* Jude had read about the historic bronze, she had seen reproductions and studied photographs when she was a little girl sitting on her father's lap and found dozens waiting for her in books, looking out at her like old friends. She had come to Wayward at last and seen the sculpture up close, and she had studied it so carefully that she knew it by heart. The outlines, execution, everything was as much a part of her memory as her mother's face. This was Beauchamp Benedict's magnificent *God and His Creation,* that was mysteriously removed from its site in front of the National Cathedral, the glorious merging of massed forms that she saw standing in the circle behind the main house here at Wayward.

No. That she saw here.

It was the same.

No, it was not here, and this was not the same.

It was like and unlike, volatile and confusing.

The discovery shook her to the soul.

This was different.

Like the bronze in the circle behind the house, Beauchamp Benedict's masterpiece rose from a triangular pedestal, so that the lines of the sculpture thrust forward even as everything in the design rose up around the heroic central figure. Here in the awesome hush of the subcellar under Wayward, art and life were inextricably mingled. Here were the living models for *God and His Creation,* perpetually locked in the attitudes of the bronze, and metal and flesh should have been separated by age and time, but instead they were bonded here, preserved, together forever. The armature was so beautifully wrought that there was no way to distinguish the prototypes from supporting framework, except that in this amalgam of metal and flesh, the flesh still breathed. The thing was made up of bodies. Living bodies. Ghastly as it was, it glowed with strange beauty. Every line in it rushed forward, and up; there was a beautiful, armed woman in the vanguard with wings on her heels and wings on a circlet around her head; two archangels followed at her right hand and her left, rushing as if to catch up with her, and behind them half a dozen others surged, completing the group, hurling themselves on and upward with the four evangelists on their shoulders, while around the base lions and dolphins leapt over waves, leaving a foamy wake. Elevated by the others, the four evangelists raised their arms to support the giant conch from which the central figure burst with shoulders thrust back as if to crack his chest and his hands spread to give light to the heavens, the figure of God.

Beauchamp Benedict's masterpiece.

The mystery was that the figure of God had no head.

In the next second Jude was thunderstruck. She thought she understood why.

From some deep place within him, Beauchamp Benedict rumbled, "Yes."

There was a soft little noise, like the cry of a dying kitten. One of the figures may have spoken.

"Darlings," The old man murmured. "Just as I left you." He could have been speaking to a favorite child.

The figure of the nymph in the lead may have shivered, straining against the framework.

When Jude looked closer she thought she saw dried blood under the silver circlet. She cried, "Who are you?"

Did it move? The whole creation seemed to change slightly, as if under the pressure of movement from within.

"Oh my God." Distressed, Jerome rushed forward.

The old man barked, "Stop that!"

The priest was tugging at the wires, trying to dislodge them. "I have to help them!"

"Not like that," Beauchamp thundered.

"But she's alive!"

"They're all alive, Father," the old man said. "One way and another. They live through the work..."

Trapped down here in the undercroft, unchanging.

"And in the work."

Jude tried not to look, could not keep from looking; the mystery then, was not how the sculptor had kept them this way for so long, but that they were the same as when he left them. Looking closer, she thought she dried tears on the face of this one, and on that one, matter—tears, froth, some bodily essence—caked at the corners of the mouth. "Are they..."

Beauchamp finished wearily. "And the work lives through them. Now it's going to have to live without us."

Trembling, the priest drew himself up. "Then I have to..."

The old man groaned, "It's too late."

Jerome's hands played on the framework. "I have to bless them."

"No. They're all gone, Father."

"But I can see them! Oh, these poor people!" Jerome tugged the framework, trying to free them. He paced the length of the piece, from glorious figurehead to the foam at the stern. "They deserve a Christian burial."

"Yes, but not yet!" Trapped in the chair for years, Beauchamp Benedict half-rose on ancient legs, teetering as he cried, "Not yet. You can't let them down yet."

And like a psychic receiving secret messages from the next world, the priest said as if from memory, "Not until it is accomplished." And stood back from the piece. And fell to his knees and began to pray.

"Yes. Not until it is accomplished." Exhausted, the ancient sculptor collapsed in the chair. His voice was thin with fatigue. "I didn't think it would take us so long to get here."

Jude murmured, "What do you mean?"

The old man asked, "What time is it?"

"I don't have a watch. It's late, I think."

"How late?"

"I don't know."

At the end of his strength now, Beauchamp was shriveled and gravely diminished. Where his models seemed unchanged by the decades, he was fragile and insubstantial as so much dried, empty skin. Even his voice tore into pieces that floated away almost before they could hear. "We have to do this before sunrise. Father."

Jerome was beyond urgency now. He bowed his head, so tightly knotted into his own skein of reverie that Jude couldn't reach him. She made as if to touch his arm.

"No." The old man stopped her. "In his own time."

They waited for Jerome to come back.

While the priest meditated, they sat. Now that they were almost at the moment, autocratic, driven Beauchamp Benedict went back inside himself to wait. Suspended between now and the next thing, they waited while Jerome meditated and Jude looked into her hands and wondered if she would ever make it out into the daylight. Then, when she was ready to weep from sheer helplessness, the priest returned to himself with an audible *snap*. He stood. "OK."

The old man said, "Then, you're ready."

Jerome nodded. His whole body shook. "I think so. What do you want me to do?"

This is how the old man surprised them. He said, "Move this thing outside so it can die."

One of them—priest? Woman? Sculptor?—cried, "All these souls!"

The words echoed in the chamber, whirring and rustling as they spread as if on the breath of a hundred captive spirits, held for decades and aching to be released. *All these souls.*

Old Beauchamp's head dropped and his frail body rattled with guilt so fierce that his feet clattered on the chair's steel footrest. When he could, he cleared his throat and went on. "One of the rules of art is to protect your work before you take care of your family. I have arranged this. The doors open onto the ramp. I'll show you how to attach the pulley."

Thirty-one

Slashing and battering in a desperate attempt to free himself, gnawing and kicking, Peter found himself being dragged to the edge of the sand pit where the others stood at Ava's back, waiting for the pouring.

Above, the cauldron glowed orange, swelling in the heat waves like a raging troglodyte. The heat was almost intolerable. Thorne stood at the ready, masked and wearing asbestos gloves. The two molds which Peter took to contain wax likenesses of Jude and Edgar waited in the pit below. The shapes were like mummy cases that take on the character of the occupants, and Peter's heart ripped in two because he had no way of knowing whether there were waxes encased in the plaster as before, or whether Ava had the living models trapped inside them.

No, he told himself. *That isn't Jude. Grant went to find her.*

"Turn Peter so he can see," Ava said to Jake. "He has to see..."

"Yes, Ava."

Everything in Peter surged to the surface in a rush of hatred. "No!"

"...And be part of it."

Jake slapped his fat hand over Peter's mouth but the words boiled up. *I will never.*

Someone cried, "Never."

Father?

"For you are part of it." Ava turned on Peter with a cold, proud smile. "We are all part of it."

A voice he hardly recognized said, "Ava, he's your son."

Peter made a strangled sound. *Father.*

And his father whirled on him with an expression that flooded Peter's mouth with unexpected tears. Changed by the events of the last few hours, Benton was burned out by grief. His hair was not so much white as devoid of color. "Ava, our sons. Peter. Edgar."

Ava didn't hear.

"Our boys!"

Her eyes skimmed Peter's face so swiftly that he knew she had forgotten him. "I do what I do, Benton. And you will help me."

"I'd rather die."

"That's fine." Behold Ava, deep in this act of creation, or destruction. In the fluorescent glare her face was less than human. Cold and metallic, like a mask of silver. She was like an engine grinding to create the future. Rapidly she turned from one to another of those present—Benton's brothers, her broken husband, Jake, Nelly, Petra, loyal Thorne, numbering each one, ticking off the tasks each would do here. Step by step, she was preparing for the unveiling.

Even though he remained physically present, Benton withdrew, turning white as whatever spirit he had left went somewhere deep inside him. He was so still that it frightened Peter, while Ava was in constant motion. She strode from one point to the next, jumping into the sand pit to check the plaster casts containing the waxes, going from one student to another to make certain they were all at their stations and understood what they had to do.

Petra stood at the pulley that would raise the canvas from *The Marriage of the Worlds* and Nelly and some student whose name he'd never learned waited with winches to lift the casts of the last two figures, still in the plaster molds, and swing them into place as soon as the pouring was completed.

"These last two can cool in place in the grouping," Ava said. "I made allowances for it in the construction. Now let's open this place up so we can get started."

At her signal Bernard Benedict went to the end of the foundry and threw his weight against a lever. With a rumble, the giant rolling doors slid wide, revealing the ramp that led to the water. As if by preset signal, the fluorescent strips that lighted the place went out, so that water and sky sprang into the opening like a picture coming to life on a television screen, a striking celebration of dawn. A flight of birds lifted.

Peter was surprised at how beautiful it was. The shifting surface of the water glittered and here and there, dark shapes protruded—hands and wingtips of ruined bronzes. The marsh grass made a black outline against the sky above the waterline, which beginning sunlight was turning a pale grey.

Bernard moved back into the group stiffly, like a lead soldier being marched by a huge, willful child.

"Berton, I want you to check the boathouse. Be sure Dirk and Luke are ready."

As his gaunt expatriate brother moved out, Benton Benedict groaned. Berton was gone for several minutes. After a time the people in the foundry heard a double *thud* as the doors to the boathouse opened. Next the sweet morning air was disturbed by sounds that could have been moans or cries for help; *Jude!* Peter thought, gnashing at Jake's forearm in a desperate attempt to get away. That could be Jude calling and there was nothing he could do to help her. The big student hung on as though he didn't even feel Peter's teeth.

He had thought he and Jude would walk into Wayward and thwart Ava and make their escape. Instead he was trapped in a pattern of his mother's making: Peter Benedict, who had let this thing go on for so long that there was no stopping it.

Deep in the undercroft, Jerome threw his entire weight against the cables attached to the flatcar that held the living prototypes for *God and His Creation*. One man should not have been able to do this, but after the first jolt of flesh against wood and steel, the great platform began to move. It was as though the souls of the undead joined the priest in the effort to dislodge the flatcar and keep it moving. Going along the last corridor in the dark, Jude walked behind the rolling platform, pushing the old man in his wheelchair. The creator rode along in the wake of his massive, swaying heap of beautifully arranged bodies like a figure in a nightmare that is destined to repeat itself into eternity. Terrified, Jude was caught somewhere between prayer and cursing. The platform was moving, but so slowly that she wanted to let the old man's wheelchair go and get behind it and push.

She wanted to ask questions, was afraid to ask, wanted to get rid of the old man, was terrified of losing him. It was clear that ancient as he was, kept alive by a series of tubes and drains, debilitated by the weight of too many decades on the earth and further weakened by his captivity underneath it, fragile and nearly helpless, Beauchamp Benedict did indeed have power over what was going on at Wayward.

God, she thought, looking at the top of Benedict's shiny head with its few wisps of white hair bobbing, *What if he dies before we get there?* Age had withered him so his features collapsed in a thousand wrinkles; she thought she heard his breathing falter. Ahead she heard Jerome's sharp, painful breaths as he struggled to keep the assemblage moving. *What if we don't make it?*

The old man made a sound.

"Did you say something?"

He repeated that noise—sob, sneeze, whatever it was.

The chair was so heavy and the way so hard that she said, "We're never going to get there."

Then he touched her. His arm snaked up and the scaly, saurian claw circled her wrist and she jumped. The old man drew her close, so he could wheeze into her ear. For a mad second she thought he was laughing. "Don't worry, it's all downhill from the..." He broke off, gasping.

"Are you all right?"

"...Threshold," he finished. Or was he choking?

"Oh, please! Please hang on."

She wasn't sure he was still breathing.

"Don't die!"

The ancient head turned. The eyes Beauchamp Benedict turned on her had lost all color, but there was something in the face—an amalgam of guilt and foreknowledge that was unexpectedly touching. Beauchamp struggled to get the next words out and in so doing, summed it all up—his duty and the dilemma.

"I can't."

And Jude responded out of a feeling she could locate but did not immediately recognize, "Damn right you can't, OK?" Tears sprang. *My God, do I love this poor old man?*

"Yet."

She went on reassuringly, "Don't worry, I won't let you!" If she thought she was making him feel better, she was mistaken. The rack of his shoulders vibrated like a coat hanger in the wind and she understood that he was sobbing.

Jerome said, "We're here."

The rolling platform rumbled to the crest a stop.

"Now," the old man said.

"Sir?"

"Put me out front," old Beauchamp said, and Jude pushed him past the whole of *God and His Creation* to join Father Jerome. He had paused with his left hand on the wheel that operated the pulley, and with his right, was making the Sign of the Cross.

As it turned out, someone had already undone the locks. The double doors fell open.

The sky hit Jude in the face. They were on the threshold, teetering between dark and light, underground and the surface of the earth, captivity and freedom. This must be what the slaves had seen, emerging from the bowels of Wayward to board the boat to freedom.

There was a little silence in which the old man sat with his face working, regarding the dawn, while Jude looked to Father Jerome. Bruised as he was, with clothes disheveled and his face dirty, the priest had put on dignity along with the purple stole he pulled from his pocket and put around his neck. He had taken it out as if this were any ordinary Saturday and he was preparing for confessions. Jerome stood in front of Beauchamp Benedict, offering, "Do you want me to hear you?"

"Too late for that," the old man said.

They became aware of the outline of a huge, dark shape standing between them and the water, waiting to be rolled into position. At first it looked like a massive sculptural grouping, but in the deceptive grey light that slides in to mark the time between the end of night and the beginning of day in the Carolinas, it was hard to read anything correctly. It could have been a sculpture silhouetted—the lines were beautiful! Then they blurred. Jude thought she saw some portion of the monumental shape moving.

"God."

"God!" Beauchamp Benedict put his hands on the arms of the chair in a futile effort to stand. "Is that what I think it is?"

"Don't get up," Jerome said.

Shrugging off the priest's hands, the old man groaned. "This thing has gone even farther than I expected."

"Stop, don't. You're hurting yourself!"

"Never mind, I have to do this." Agitated, old Benedict pulled the IV needles out of his hands, tearing the skin like paper. Oddly, no blood sprang. Freed from the last of his life supports, driven by the burst of energy that is born of last chances and in its own turn spawns maximum efforts, Beauchamp Benedict, founder of the dynasty of brilliant, doomed sculptors, gathered himself for the impossible. He made a final spring that threatened to turn into a collapse and within seconds, was standing. He launched himself at the priest, who caught him; it was like supporting a phantom.

Jude cried, "Be careful!"

"Now," Beauchamp said.

"What?" Supporting him, Jerome said wildly, "What is my part in this?"

Old Beauchamp pointed to the top. Then he croaked, "Put me up there."

Before Jude could parse it, Jerome had answered. "I can't!"

But the old man and the priest were bonded in need, prepared to do whatever came next. Beauchamp ordered, "Now. Into the arms of God. Do it."

"But it will kill you!"

"Yes. Put me up there. Now, Father. Please!"

Jerome looked at Jude over the old man's head, putting the question. Pain played across his face while Jude considered it. She nodded. And the priest nodded. "Yes, Mr. Benedict."

The ancient body was light but unwieldy and the priest hesitated at the base of the prodigious monument and considered. "I don't know exactly how to do this."

"I'll go up first," Jude said. "You can hand him up to me."

"You can't, they're..."

The old man supplied the last word. "Dead. Just, not yet."

She wanted not to know this. "You need help."

He could have been a courtly planter, graciously refusing. "Not from you, my dear."

"It's OK," Jude said, and did not know whether she was afraid of damaging the structure or afraid of being damaged by the things imprisoned within the framework. "At least I think it is."

"I'm sorry, but you can't do this."

Then a new voice froze them where they stood. "No, child. It's not yours to do."

Holding the old man like an outsized baby, Father Jerome turned. "Esther!"

Still clad in the velours draperies she put on for her sitting, Esther Manifort stood in the pale dawn like a figure in Beauchamp's gallery of the undead, with every line in her body set in an attitude of determination. "We know what we have to do," Essie said. "We Maniforts."

Jerome's voice lifted. "Yes."

She advanced on the priest, bending to study the fretwork of bones and living flesh he carried. Esther looked into the eyes of the ancient sculptor for just long enough to let him know that she knew him, and that she knew what they were about there. "Son," she said to the priest, "you've grown. Your mama must be proud."

"Your family." Jerome lifted his head with a proud smile. "My family."

"All."

Without knowing, Jude understood that they had completed some mysterious transaction.

So it was Esther who put both palms on the edge of the rolling platform at chest height and boosted herself up.

Jude rushed forward. "Let me help."

Agile, beautiful and ageless, Esther was also swift. By the time Jude's fingers closed on air she was already standing on the platform, looking down. She was magnificent. "No, child. This is for us to do."

So together, Esther and the young priest gentled the old man onto the edge of the platform and from there up the stages of the construction until Beauchamp Benedict did in fact lie in the arms of his God at the apex of the grouping he had named *God and His Creation*. Unlike the rest of the figures in the construction, this central figure was bronze, and, until it was bizarrely completed by the old man, headless.

Now that Beauchamp Benedict was in place at last, his throat opened in a sound that was neither sigh nor groan: “Aaaaaaaaa.”

And the descendants of slaves freed by the Benedicts gave the platform a push that tipped it over the threshold and sent it rolling slowly over long-buried tracks. Plowing along, it pushed a fresh path for itself as metal connected with freshly uncovered metal.

Thirty-two

When Berton Benedict, recently of Paris and beloved of the native American woman Atawan, returned to the foundry, he seemed shaken by what he had learned. Tall, elegantly lean, he seemed to grow another foot taller, as if the knowledge had somehow completed him. He said only, "It's all in order."

Ava laughed. "And you understand."

"I see what you're up to." Berton looked from Ava to his brother. He spoke to her over Benton's head. "He doesn't know, does he?"

"He doesn't need to know," Ava said.

"Why wouldn't your sons let me into the boathouse?"

"You don't need to know," Ava said. "But you can guess, can't you?"

Berton shuddered, "It's monstrous."

"It's necessary."

"For the work," he said.

"And the work will live forever." Ava could have been going down a checklist. "The figures are all in place?"

"All but one or two," Berton said. "Or so they told me."

"Oh, that girl." She ticked Jude off on her finger: just another item, like a dash of salt in a recipe. "We can always put her in place later."

Peter grunted. *Wait a minute!*

Ava looked right past him. "We have to do this before sunrise."

"You mean *you* have to do this," Berton said.

"Aren't you with me?" She nailed the gaunt sculptor with a glare. "Are you?"

Bernard moved in to join forces with his brother. "What makes you so sure it will work?"

"It worked for the first Beauchamp Benedict, the whole world knows it did. It will work for us." Triumphant, Ava finished. "And the whole world will know us."

"Even with the missing figures?"

"We'll get them," Ava said. "We'll get them all, sooner or later."

Berton was studying her with an expression that baffled Peter. "And you'll take care of them?"

"Whatever it takes," Ava said. "Now are we all here?"

"Wait!" Galvanized, poor, troubled Benton Benedict yanked his wife around to face him. "Wait a minute, Ava." He gripped so tightly that she winced. "What figures?"

She said coldly, "The prototypes. Let go."

"*Prototypes.*"

Ava looked at her husband with great scorn. "Did you think the work made itself?"

"Ava!" He shook her until her teeth clashed.

"Did you think you and I made it?"

Benton could not stop shaking her.

"And made it live like that?" Now Ava threw her full weight against him, bearing down with her eyes blazing and her jaws wide, like the doors to a furnace. "Did you? The blood sacrifice was only the beginning. Now it wants more."

"More!"

"Idiot," she said with terrifying scorn. "What did you think we were doing?"

Broken, Benton sobbed aloud, "I don't know what I thought we were doing!"

Ava was ablaze, incandescing as if she could flow into his consciousness and scorch his brain. She was standing too close to Benton to see what the knowledge did to him and too angry to care. "We didn't make our success," she raged, "and you know it. We made a deal. Now let go of me, you stupid bastard."

And Benton let go of her so suddenly that she almost fell. What was he thinking, Peter wondered. He wanted to rush at his father and rattle him until the truth fell out, raging: *What were you thinking?*

"That's better. Now are we all ready?" Standing back, smoothing her canvas shift where Benton had crushed it, Ava could have been a ship captain, taking the con. "Now, Jake. Bring Edgar."

The big student let go and walked away. Freed, Peter calculated the odds. The students. Thorne. The uncles, whose faces were ciphers. Jake. Who could he count on? For the first time, he and his broken, desperate father locked eyes. Peter dipped his head, putting the question. *Not yet,* Benton told him without speaking. *Not yet.*

The next things happened so fast that only years later would Peter and Jude be able to put the puzzle together.

Jake returned, carrying a bundle. With a chilling smile at her husband, Ava whipped off the tarp to reveal the unconscious Edgar. Drugged, Peter supposed, surprised by fresh knowledge. *Just like all the others.* He thought of Jude and his belly trembled. First, there was Edgar. The boy stirred at the smell of fresh air and the pressure of unfamiliar hands. Loosening the rope that had been tripled around the child, Jake took a cup of wine from Ava and passed it under Edgar's nose even as his mother—his *mother*—ran a wet cloth across his face. "Wake up, son. It's time."

Blinking, Edgar coughed and sat up.

Peter strained, willing the boy to look at him. *Eds. Over here.*

Edgar shook his head, blinking and confused.

The silence held them all in place.

"What the fuck?" Edgar said in a thin voice.

"Language, sweetheart," Ava purred. Now she closed in, muttering into Edgar's ear, so low that nobody could hear, and now she led him to the pedestal that held the cauldron. Then, gripping the child's shoulders with both hands, she said in a low voice, "Now, Benton." And pushed him at his father so hard that he staggered and almost toppled before his father reached out.

Lifting his head, Benton Benedict raked his wife with a lighthouse gaze so intense that there was no seeing what was going on behind his eyes.

She said, "The child."

He took the child.

"And this." Ava produced a sculptor's tool.

He took the tool.

"Now this," she said, giving him a silver cup. Peter recognized it as the chalice from the defunct family chapel.

He took the cup.

"You know what you have to do," she said.

Resting his chin in the little boy's rough hair, Benton locked his arms around Edgar and stared at her over the child's head. He stood without speaking.

"Only a little blood," Ava said, and she could have been talking about an alloy. "To mix with the last of the bronze before pouring." Her voice deepened. "A little flesh. Understand, it is essential."

So that at the moment when Ava makes clear that she is willing to sacrifice her child to bring her work to life, the huge flatcar on the threshold at the mouth of the tunnel underneath the house tips and hangs for an instant. Then, in a spray of sand as metal connects with track, it begins its progress. It rumbles downhill toward the water on rails that will bring it to a halt in the open space just outside the foundry. There it will stand poised, this bizarre amalgam of man and prototypes, monument and maker thundering into the family's field of vision with the inevitability of the heartbeat just before the last. Here comes the maker and destroyer—Beauchamp Benedict, ancient but still living, caught in destiny like a prehistoric insect in amber, rolling toward freedom in the lifted bronze arms of a God of his own design and his own making. Here is Beauchamp Benedict, approaching the instant of recognition of his sins and, in an act of brilliant, crashingly appropriate atonement, ending them.

Inside the foundry the assembled Benedicts do not hear, exactly, but shift in their tracks and wonder why they are so uneasy.

Fixed on the molten cauldron and the pouring of the last two bronzes, they both do and do not know what is approaching.

Holding Edgar like a new Abraham pretending to sacrifice Isaac, Benton Benedict feels the rumble, however. The implications reverberate in his bones and inside his skull, where he is making a decision. The pressure of Benton's hands lets Edgar know that his father will die before he'll hurt him.

At the same time, Bernard and Berton Benedict are moving forward, their faces fixed and impossible to decipher.

Enthralled, dutiful, drawn into the impending ceremony, the students wait dumbly in their places. In the shadow of the pedestal with the cauldron, Peter stands forgotten.

At the edge of the sand pit Ava shifts impatiently, glaring at her husband. "Do it," she says louder, in case he is too stupid to understand.

And standing by the cauldron, Thorne waits, sweating.

Each person present knows in a unique way what share each holds in this extraordinary effort, and each will comprehend it completely, falling back as the attempt of the dynasty to perpetuate itself is recognized and destroyed here. Words will elude the Benedicts. Nothing they can find to say will serve them.

And all the time, Beauchamp Benedict's huge, terrifying prototype with its creator caught in the arms of the central figure of *God and His Creation* approaches, the destruction of the past rolling down on the aspirations of the present.

Dirk and Luke Benedict will be the first to see it coming. The distant thunder of iron wheels makes them wild with expectation. What is it that disturbs the dawn on this great morning? What's happening here? What's gone wrong, and who will be blamed for it? Standing at their stations next to the platform Ava ordered them to roll out of the boathouse at dawn, her

Death Star of sculpture with its grim passengers, the brothers will cry out in recognition.

It's Beauchamp's God!

Oh, God, they will think. *Has it come to judge us?*

Here is Beauchamp Benedict's *God and His Creation,* emerging in the pale gleam of the Carolina morning.

It is dazzling.

Fixed on their own platform, trapped and watching, pieces of the construction Ava ordered for her would-be masterpiece cry out. Here the living and the dead are held in place like so many logs, in a simulaecrum of Ava's long-planned monument, *The Marriage of the Worlds.* Parts of the piece are still quite fresh—Atawan and Keesha and several others strain against the metal that binds them, struggling and groaning.

In the hours he and his brother spent in the boathouse, waiting to bring forth this construction and roll it out to the waterfront for the quickening, Luke Benedict has reconciled himself to the presence of his beloved in this assemblage—it is almost like having her back—but seeing all thus, Dirk weeps for all the women he slept with and brought to Wayward in his time because he sees them now, ensnared in the grand plan for Ava's *Marriage of the Worlds.* Some of the fresh figures, like his uncles' models, Keesha and Atawan, and a few whose names the brothers do not know, are half awake and straining against the web of wire and metal strips Ava and Thorne used to make the assembly. Others—the failures of Ava's understanding of the process—are dead, gutted, perhaps, with the vital cavities stuffed full of spices and the veins infused with preservatives, although in some cases the preservation process is imperfect and shards of bone shine through melted flesh.

In its own way, Ava's piece, in concept at least, is beautiful and terrible—a mass of representatives of all colors and races twined around a central stem like the figures in a fruit bowl—but where every line in Beauchamp Benedict's sculptural grouping rushes forward and up, straining toward heaven, this piece is heavy and earthbound. It is clear that when Ava's bronze is unveiled it will be like the model, slightly clumsy, too crudely executed to soar. In fact, there are gaping absences in the device, empty frames where figures are missing. Wataru. Esther. Jude Atkins. What? What else is missing?

As Beauchamp and his glorious vision gather speed and rumble past them, Dirk and Luke will fall away from Ava's hateful, dead failure and spread their hands wide and cry out, begging for forgiveness. Thunderstruck, they will forget whatever orders Ava gave them on maintaining the drugs pumped into the IVs, and the struggling victims caught in her design will regain consciousness and join the struggle, shouting for someone to help them.

As Esther and Father Jerome come abreast of Ava's piece, the components come back into themselves like returning souls and start screaming.

"Oh, please!" Keesha cries from the scaffold.

Atawan does not speak, but her eyes are blacker than as rips in the fabric of the universe.

"Aunt Essie." The priest takes Esther's arm, expecting her to stop and help him free them.

"Not now." Esther pushes on. "Not yet. Be quiet, child. We have this to do."

"Mr. Benedict?" Jerome looks up at the patriarch, but old Beauchamp is caught in a transport so profound that he cannot speak, much less divine what is happening here.

Running along beside Beauchamp and his creation, Jude will see living and dead bodies trapped in the new assemblage which she knows is Ava's work. This botched, hideously beautiful but doomed effort could only be Ava's. In the bitch sculptor's base creation, everyone—the living, the dead and the figures whose souls are in transition—every figure is draped in a grey velours shift like the one she tore off today in the Benedict kitchen.

Jude throws back her head, screaming to the skies.

Both Esther and the black priest turn to quiet her. At their backs, Jude sees the water. There is a small boat putting out, carrying two figures in black. The slighter of the two stands suddenly, ripping off a hood, or knitted cap. Daylight catches her fall of white hair. It is Benta Benedict, departing. If the Benedicts in the foundry cannot speak now, at the moment of completion, the Benedict in the boat can.

Their great aunt Benta's arm completes an arc—a wave. Her voice is faint, but it carries over the water. "Goodbye, Grandfather. God bless you."

Does old Beauchamp hear, and does he tremble?

"The family did this," Benta cries to them all, departing. "The family let it go on. And the family will undo it."

Inside the foundry, Benton gives Edgar a quick hug and a rough shove. He pushes with such force that the boy rolls to the back of the platform, where he will be safe. At the same time, Peter hurtles into Thorne. This is so unexpected that in spite of Thorne's size, Ava's hulking husband, lover, her Fated doomed partner falls back a step, off balance. Before he can regain his footing, he loses his hold on the lever that tips the cauldron. Half toppled, he throws up his hands like a drowning man and falls backward off the platform and into the dirt below.

As he does so, Berton and Bernard put strong hands on Benton, not to stop him, as Peter feared. They are supporting him!

Now Berton speaks for both of them. "Did you think we'd let you go through this alone?"

"My friends." Benton shouts for joy. "My brothers."

If Thorne does not rush to regain his feet and resume his position it is for a complex of reasons ranging from love to jealous fury. His reasons are so strong and so many that none of the others will know for certain; they can only guess.

This sequence of astonishing rejections unfolds so fast that Ava will not have time to prepare herself for what happens next. Her child Edgar—her *little boy*—comes rocketing out of nowhere and shoves her into the sand pit...

As Peter Benedict and his heartbroken father join hands on the red-hot, searing handle of the cauldron. Even though it singes through the skin and burns their palms to the bones they tip it, sending the molten bronze cascading over the figure of their lover, mother, destroyer.

Her hands fly up, but she doesn't scream.

Outside, the platform bearing *God and His Creation* gathers momentum, escaping its guardians. It rolls past the foundry and moves faster, faster over the sandy tracks that have been in the ground since the beginning, laid as though for preceisly this operation, and plunges through the marsh grass at the water's edge. In seconds flatcar, formation, models, all sink to the muddy bottom of the inland waterway. The weight of the thing—figures, bronze, supporting metal, platform, old man—is so great that it seems to accumulate, driving the prototype of Beauchamp Benedict's masterpiece deep into the quicksand. *God and His Creation* descends into the mire and keeps descending. As it does so, a deep, wild communal sigh fills the air, as if of many souls escaping.

Soon there is only the bronze cornucopia showing above the surface; then there are only the raised arms of the headless figure of God, with fierce old Beauchamp between them, lifting his own arms, straining as though he can use this vehicle to raise him close enough to touch the floor of heaven. His great head is the last thing showing above the surface of the water. In seconds Beauchamp Benedict—art, artist, artifice, all—sink beneath the surface. If at the end the old man cries out, it is not in fear, but in triumph.

Almost at the same time another sound fills the foundry. It is so deep, piercing and distinctive that at first nobody, not even those present, who have worked in bronze all their lives, will know it. Underneath its tarpaulin the bronze of Ava's ambitious, doomed *The Marriage of the Worlds* cracks in two and topples, ricocheting off the edges of the platform and thudding into the sand in jagged pieces.

One half fills the space between the platform and the casting pit, where Ava's outline hisses and glows as metal meets and hardens on living flesh; the roughly poured bronze shimmers pink and then begins to cool, with the color going right out of her. The other half of the cloven *Marriage of the Worlds* crashes through the outer wall of the foundry, letting in daylight.

Supporting Benton, Peter sees the out-of-doors: daylight, and framed in the light, the three people he loves most. They stand in the fresh opening like newly minted mortals at the dawn of creation. Jude. His Jude! His Jude is there—Peter's heart lifts; she's all right!—and behind her is his best friend Jerry Manifort, correction, Father Manifort, who looks like an archangel walking out of the fiery furnace, triumphant. In another minute the priest will separate himself from the others and sink to his knees in the mud at the verge of the water. Next to him, not looking into the foundry but away from it, toward the house, is Essie.

Fixed on Jude, who stands staring after the vanished flatcar: *she's all right!* Peter is only partially aware of the moment at which his father sees Esther and steps away from him, electrified. Father and son are too charged with elation to notice that their burned hands are seared and shredding.

"Essie," Benton calls. "Esther!"

But Esther is looking at the house. She raises her hand, as if for silence.

She is listening.

Father and son stop where they are and they too listen.

There is one more thing waiting to happen.

There is a shudder in the air, as if of seismic plates shifting in a huge psychic accident. Something tremendous has departed. The air is clear. There is nothing left now but silence.

Esther nods. "It's all done," she says.

Done. Peter hardly recognizes the feeling: after all these years of guilt and worry, he is released, liberated and joyful. After all these years of temporizing, it's done. He has come back and met the family destiny and together with the others, he has vanquished it. Now he is free to go. Peter scrubs his fists down his face like a man reborn. He is only dimly aware that there's something the matter with his hands.

He calls, "Jude?" Startled, she looks up and sees him.

"Peter!"

They start running. They meet at the broken foundry wall. Jude steps inside. Without exchanging a word, they both know that whatever comes next, they will do together.

Outside, Esther waits. She does not come in and she doesn't move away, either. She is watching the owner of Wayward.

And standing next to the sand pit where his wife smolders, Benton Benedict changes. The years he aged in these last hours slip away, along with the years he lived in Ava's shadow.

Without glancing at the rapidly cooling lump of bronze that had been his wife, he moves outside to join Esther. Ashamed to have been Ava's slaves, ashamed to have been here and do this, the students drift away. Under orders from their uncles, Dirk and Luke work at the scaffolding of Ava's prototype,